BF4ever

GEORGE P. MATHEOS

ISBN 978-1-957582-18-4 (paperback)
ISBN 978-1-957582-19-1 (eBook)

Printed in the United States of America

Also by George P Matheos:

Mirages of the Rub al-Khali
The Man Who Killed Osama
Pure Magic

To my wife
Victoria Ashly Craig

*What is a friend but
a single soul
dwelling in two bodies*

-Aristotle

The Four Best Friends

Four teenage girls, Sharon, Robin, Kitty, Myrna, all gorgeous blondes, best friends forever since the sixth grade, walk together, two by two, as usual, one April morning, on their way to their loving Magnolia High School in Sherman Oaks, California.

Sharon is the prettiest of the friends, and all the boys in her class, want to fuck her. She glows with teenage sensuality, a quality which incites people to want to take her in their arms and make her their own. Young as she is, she knows she's beautiful, and every time she looks in her full length mirror, she loves herself, though sometimes she wishes she weren't so beautiful. Aware that pretty girls are often taken advantage by bad people, she is already scared to death of what the future might hold for her. But for now, her fear centers mostly around Hank Merker, star quarterback of Magnolia High, who, she's well aware, is determined to fuck her while they're still in high school. Trapped by the multi-media gossip of her school's culture, she feels trapped by star Hank's macho reputation.

Robin is the daughter of the CEO of Pioneer Bank of Southern California which may account for her refined demeanor. Her features are classically symmetrical making her seductively beautiful with an aura of brilliance. Her blue eyes sparkle, and combined with her beauty and intelligence, she can be very compassionate to the world around her. She is *formidable*, but her considerable lovely qualities, to her dismay, can make her appear aloof. She wants to be popular, but the boys maintain their distance, fearful she might devour them. She has a smart smile and a discerning eyes that make it difficult for the boys to pin her down. Above all, she is secretly in love with and dreams of Hank Merker, her best friend Sharon's boyfriend. Every time Hank says "Hello" to Robin, her flawless beauty blushes with intelligent embarrassment.

With a lovely face and an articulate presentation, which makes use of extensive vocabulary, Kitty is sassy bright and always flirtatious. The only dyed blonde of the lot, she is of slight build, but graced with a fine ass and finer breasts, for a teen. Boys love Kitty because her petite appearance doesn't threaten their still-developing egos. When she was much younger, her mother had impressed on Kitty that to say "no" to a boy, when asked for a dance, for example, was to be impolite: "So, always be polite and say "yes" to all boys who ask you to dance with them," she had often reminded Kitty. Since then, Kitty has always been polite, especially to the big boys on the varsity squads whom she loved the most because of the easy way they lifted her up high, their arms around her fine ass. But of all the boys that she would want to lift her off the ground, Hank Merker was the one whom Kitty loved and dreamed about. Sometimes she wished Sharon wasn't around. It had been obvious to Kitty that Hank was simply not interesting in her.

Myrna 'worked' as a librarian's assistant, picking up attendance slips, in the school's library. During study periods, boys loved to go to the library instead of study hall to get a glimpse of Myrna. She has a gorgeous Dutch milk-white complexion that blushes pink when Hank and his boys come to the library. Her loveliest attribute, by far, is her delicately well-rounded ass, easy to the eye beneath her expensive clothes. She is hugely intelligent with an understated shrewdness that points to a successful life. Nobody looking at Myrna's beautiful face would ever think of her as dumb. She's very popular with all of the good-looking boys in school who love to kiss and fondle her and she loves to be kissed and fondled, but only by those she allows, least she be thought as too easy. She has no doubts about her sexuality, and no doubts that she could get Hank any time she wanted.

With the exception of Sharon who comes from a Catholic middle class background, the other three friends are filthy rich, thanks to their hard working Protestant parents who have, more often than not, inherited much of their wealth. With clear certainty, sooner or later, the four best friends, and not only, will give themselves to Hank Merker because he is the star quarterback of Magnolia High.

*

"What say yee, friends, who's walking commando today," asked Kitty, loudly?

The girls were well-groomed and stylishly elegant, as always, and the boys did gallantly follow behind them, in close proximity to their fantasies, but not too close, least they be destroyed by the girls' fearfully tight filling asses. During these early morning teenage rituals of 'look but don't touch' coyness, played out every school day, the girls pretended indifference to the penetrating stares from awkward boys ogling and charging behind them, their eyes gleefully glued to the best friends' well-rounded always teasing buttocks. It was a typical school boys' harmless amorous response to a bewitching young girls' teen hormonal display of adolescent awakening most natural.

"Are they still behind us?" asked Sharon.

"What do you mean behind us? You thinking sodomy, Sharon?' loudly giggled Kitty, and the others pretended embarrassment.

"Not so loud, Kitty!" hushed Myrna.

"They're just idiotic little boys," said Robin always disgusted with the same stalking shit from stupid boys just barely out of middle school. "Jesus, they're just too stupid! What do they expect us to do? Drop our panties?"

"Well, yeah, if you're wearing any," said Kitty.

"As usual. I'm sure you're not, Kitty," said Robin in fake disapproval.

"Go ahead, Sharon. It's Hank and his boys, and you know he's got the hots for you," said Myrna, and she discretely gave a little gentle shove to Sharon.

"Leave me alone. What am I supposed to do? Skip class and make out with Merker all day long? You guys are all crazy," said Sharon.

"I wish I had the star quarterback of Magnolia Hi sniffing my panties," said Kitty.

"Except you're not wearing any," said Myrna.

"Sharon, he's right behind you; right behind your derriere," continued Kitty.

"Sharon likes Hank! Let's tell him right now Kitty," said Myrna.

"Don't you dare say anything … please, please, please," whispered Sharon staring straight ahead wishing that there be no misunderstandings from the crowd behind her.

They all giggled at Sharon's still juvenile reactions, but not too loudly, being aware that the boys were closing in on them. Not one of the best friends had the balls to turn around and say something to the boys behind them; not even a small smile.

So they continued the ritual of denial, of not wanting any boy sniffing behind them least they be thought as easy; not even Hank, the most famous hunk school varsity, first string, quarterback, dreamboat of all the girls of Magnolia High.

"Let's face it girls: one can never say enough about our Hank," said Kitty. "He is a gorgeous Hunk … Hank the Hunk."

"Shame on you, Kitty," said Robin, who couldn't have cared less about high school nonsense like hung quarterbacks. "All you can think about is Hank the Hunk."

"So do you, so do you all," said Kitty.

"You're wolfing again, Kitty," said Myrna.

"Listen to prissy, prissy, Missy Myrna, the Beloved," Kitty laughed out loud.

"Please let's stop and let them pass us up," said Sharon who was trying to somehow hide her fabulous ass from what she thought was probably the laser gawking of the boys even though she wasn't commando.

Why can't they stare at the others, she thought?

"Tight ass Sharon," said Kitty.

"You talking to me?" said Robin.

They slowed down to make way for the boys to pass them up, but the idiot boys halted short of the opening, and instead crossed to the other side of the street, their pretended game of indifference still on, though one of the boys was heard to say, "Go ahead, Hank, say something to her."

Most famous athletes, regardless of origin, are naturally attracted to blonde girls even though some might be dyed blondes. The boys would have loved to say something smart to the four beautiful girls of Magnolia High but they were still just too inexperienced.

"Stupid fucking idiots," murmured Myrna to no one in particular.

"What do you expect? They're still babies," laughed Robin to Sharon's relief.

They walked the sun-speckled sidewalks to their school. The walk, the sidewalks, the trees lining the streets, they're all the same walks to school that are part of everyone's memories of walking to school. Nothing, in all people's memories, about walking to school, has ever changed. It's one of those lovely rituals that remain immortal. Who is not envious of the young walking to school? All love the memory of these morning walks.

Except Sharon.

Not only during these walks to school, but also in the school itself, classrooms included, in the middle of a lesson, Sharon always had the feeling of being watched, of being suffocated by the fantasy stares floating throughout the room, all around her; and weirdly worse, that everybody was telepathically touching her, all the time, in and out of the classroom. It was during these psychical pre-occupations that she often wished she weren't so beautiful; that maybe then people would stop staring at her. And in the unpleasantness of her mental distress, her fantasies would carry her out of the classroom and far away from school where she could be alone, away from the babbling crowds of her mind. Alone and away, where she could be beautiful without feeling freakish and bothered.

She wondered whether her beautiful friends felt as she did. She wasn't at all sure what it meant to be beautiful, and whether she really wanted to be beautiful, but she loved the attention, in spite of the stress her good looks brought her. She prayed that it wasn't simply something just physical, that there would be some spirituality to this cursed beauty that she had never asked for. She knew that physical beauty was all too temporary. Confused, she felt alone, though she knew that everybody wanted was pawing her.

The thing Sharon didn't know about blonde girls, as the friends now walked to school, is that they all have good looking blonde mothers who pathologically praise their little blonde girls to appreciate their Hollywood and God-given infantile glamour, and later adult sultriness. The constant praise is intended to keep the fantasy, the myth, the tradition alive: the belief that all blondes are naturally beautiful; even buck-toothed blondes are beautiful. The illusion is joyfully taught and is handed down from mother to daughter: all blonde little girls are beautiful by virtue of their blond hair and blue eyes and, in time, they'll be able to get any boy they want. Pretty much all societies are in tune to the blond myth. Every girl wants to be a blonde; the world is full of dark-eyed blondes.

"You know, people, there are more serious issues plaguing today's world than your constant babble about boys," said Robin breaking into Sharon's daydreaming as they got closer to the school.

"Like what?" said Myrna who also was game to serious discussion. There was a certain amount of stiffness between Myrna and Robin.

"Well, racism, for one. After more than two hundred years American society is still as racist and segregated as ever…"

"I agree," said Sharon wishing to run away from the silent secret of her marvellous ass.

"Even after all the effort by people like Martin Luther King Jr. and President Kennedy to push for equality and integration, especially in schools …" somebody continued; everybody knew the story of inequality and injustice.

"There's only one way to achieve integration," said wide-eyed Myrna, "and that's to marry them; and you know it."

Audacious as the thought might have been, there was a certain amount of truth to the potential of integrated marriages as a solution to many of America's social ills. Though obvious to most American high school kids, hardly anyone in the broader blond American society talked about integrated marriages, with the possible exception of prime time TV who always reported fake news anyway. Still, the subject, fortunately, one way or another, is continuously being covered in American high schools' history classes, and although pathetically repulsive to the privileged socio-economic white conscious mind, pretty much everyone, especially blonde high school girls, agrees that something has to be done to erase segregation from the face of the nation, and the most obvious course of action is to "marry them".

In the case of our four best friends forever, when the topic had come up, what had made the class discussion believable was that the teacher was a young handsome African-American male. Marrying them, then, was another bull's eye disturbing shocker from Myrna who had a way of directing conversations, like segregation, to the painful truth of a difficult subject deserving a lot more looking into. Most of the time, Myrna couldn't have cared less about 'the truth' though one of beloved Myrna's qualities was that she always had easy answers to complicated issues wherein all could be resolved with more investigation and research.

"These are serious problems requiring a lot of study and research. There are no easy solutions to these things," was the way the young good looking African-American teacher had put it to the class and all the girls' in the class agreed with his summation. More research was required, and then marry them.

"You know what you get when you mate a black person with a white person?" blithely asked Kitty as they walked beneath the rich flowering white magnolias.

They knew it would be politically incorrect, but everybody acquiesced to Kitty's everyday bottom of the barrel a-political humour.

"What?"

"You get an African-American," said Kitty and everyone scoffed pain.

"Kitty, you're a Nazi," said Robin.

"Anyway, it hasn't been two hundred years," said Sharon.

Back on their route's magnolias, and tall date palms, and beyond the indecent stares of bad boys, and even while preoccupied in serious conversation, the girls never strayed far from their true calling, instinctively tossing their long, fine, golden hair playfully around their lovely necks and shoulders. Over and over, in synchronized fashion, again and again, like a mating dance in flight, they sensed the joy that was in their hearts. If only they knew the effect they were having upon those trees, what wondrous thoughts would fill their minds.

"I wish I weren't so old," said Sharon looking pensively beyond the pregnant jacarandas and lustful magnolias with their huge creamy white flowers.

"You're not old, Sharon, none of us is old. We're only fifteen; wait till you're eighteen, or even twenty; then you can say you're old," Kitty wanted to make up for her earlier indelicate humor; she was doing her usual best to recover.

"Or imagine getting to eighty! What a pain in the ass that would be! Eighty, right behind you, Sharon," and with that, Robin cupped a feel of Sharon's well rounded ass.

"Cut it out, Robin! What are you? Gay?"

"No but you are."

An elderly gentleman who had been taking his early morning constitutional walk caught up with the girls and had heard their conversation regarding age. He quickly passed them up, smiling to himself, but saying nothing to them. The girls didn't even see him; he registered transparent empty, which is often the case with young girls encountering older gentlemen.

They think they're invincible, he thought. They think the whole universe revolves around them; that this ephemeral moment will never end.

Only yesterday he too was like them.

He envied them and suddenly wished to do them harm. He was jealous of their strength. He had so little time left and they had a lifetime before them.

Damn time, he thought trembling to keep his feet steady on the sidewalk.

"Hi Sharon," a male voice had caught up with the best friends.

"Hi," said a subdued Sharon.

For the life of her she had no idea who this boy was.

He was in her English class.

He shyly moved on, hugely embarrassed at the cold response from Sharon.

"All right, Sharon!" said sarcastic Kitty. "Got yourself a bite there."

Chapter One

It was in Sharon's character to believe in lovely daydreams carefully preserved in the archives of her mind. Lovely, lovely thoughts which, repeated over time, become true.

*

He gently lobbed the dark purple grape carefully targeting her adolescent cleavage well defined between her growing breasts impatiently showing off through her barely sleeveless tank top. She recalled the shiny grape, a vivid image permanently stored with love in her mind, the scene unfolding longingly before her persistent blue eyes, as she lay on her bed, grown up now, affectionately daydreaming of that tender day of her young girl's years. Her mind froze the scene in mnemonic space giving time for her eyes to reload the beautiful face with the sweet demeanour and aggressive coyness of the sixth grade boy, on that field trip bus, on that spring day of the many years before. As if it were yesterday, she remembered that he had missed his aim on his first try and she thought she was to blame. He playfully smiled his determination to reach her through her youthful breasts which she innocently, slightly, exposed, for the attention they deserved, beneath her white shirt. Shyly she blushed, and on his next toss, she immodestly moved her chest ever so imperceptibly forward, and up, and caught the grape between her small breasts, as he had wanted her to do. From a distance she sensed his impatience to touch her, and felt his fixed charge as something new, full of uninhibited energy that affected a strong sexual response in her. She was embarrassed because she didn't know whether to remove the grape now firmly settled between her stirring breasts and training bra, or just hold it in secret excitement where it had lodged. She took deep and hard breaths and put her hands between her knees. In silence she felt the uncomfortable self-consciousness of her pounding heart that was so grownup personal. Motionless she sat on that bus, facing the ruddy-faced boy and felt the warmth of the newly discovered excitement as she, for the first time, experienced the strange feeling of someone taking her breath away. She was in love, and full of excitement she felt her breasts agitating hot against the coolness of the firm grape nestled in her young girl's chest. Strangely, she felt aroused all over her young body.

He smiled hard, as if he knew how she felt, and she smiled back.

Bemused by the coyness of her first boy sexual excitement, daringly she looked hard at the triumphant smile of the determined boy, and she felt pleasure. From a distance, his eyes penetrated deep into hers; he knew what he was doing, and she smiled back her pleasure.

*

In the privacy of her early morning awakening moments, she opened her eyes, but the sweetness of the long ago memory stayed intact in her mind, as if present time had merged with that magic instance of the past into one perpetually paused-forever frame. In the pleasing reflections that often accompany waking up, a gripping nostalgia had melded the time of her first love with the present satin sheets sensations of her bed. Her long legs and now adult breasts intertwined with that long ago memory, and it felt good. And for Sharon, that union would remain intact for all time. As it was then, so it would forever be in her busy mind, wherein she would still be the blossoming young girl in love forever. And like most girls' recollections of first love, still lovely sweet was the youthful eagerness of that day when she first felt the weird and wonderful thrill of romance in the flirtatious eroticism of being alone with a boy; the utterly beautiful sensation of a boy wanting her, and she him. Fondly, she recalled that later on that school field day-trip, as the rest of the group was meandering through the San Diego Zoo, for one brief moment, he held her by her hips, looked into her young girl's, crystal clear blue eyes, kissed her lips ever so gently, and dared to touch her baby breasts. With a softly echoed sadness, she would patiently dwell again and again on that memory that she never wished to forget.

Like the wholesomeness of a country love song that never leaves one's mind, such innocent love, so long ago, so very young, so very brief, Sharon never again encountered. During days when disappointment or sadness invaded her heart, she always found comfort in the recollection of the warm tender feelings in that long ago but still most powerful memory of her twelfth year. So enchanting had been the affection of that first love, on that spring day, on that field trip, that it forever imprinted on her soul an adolescent girl's first erotic smile that always wonderfully unfolded on her rose painted lips that were a gift from heaven.

*

The sensation of the grape between her breasts forever clung to her mind. Whenever a boy danced with her, she would think of grapes. The size of the grapes became a kind of measuring stick of how much she liked a particular boy: the bigger, firmer the grape, the more she liked the boy holding her in his arms. During school dances, when she danced a slow dance with a boy she liked, her mind filled with sensational purple grapes. She knew the purple grape sensation was the real thing because some boys made her a lot sexier, while those whom she wasn't interested registered sour. When she first met Hank and he smile-spoke to her, she sensed a few grapes bumping on her ass, but, strangely, nothing, even when he first kissed her; and likewise nothing on all subsequent making out sessions. She attributed her grape-less reaction to star quarterback Hank to his guttural utterances as his preferred method of intercourse. After all, it would have been unnatural to be a star quarterback on the high school varsity team and be cleverly articulate at the same time. So, it was mostly raisings when Hank held her hand.

She rolled on her back on her fluffy expensive, king size bed and playfully touched her breasts, exquisitely mature now. She was proud of her firm pointing breasts, difficult to hide under any modesty, the envy of all women, and accessible only to her husband. They were luxuriant beauties, splendid to the eye and touch. Aroused by annoying stares wherever she went, she had finally accepted her fate that her gorgeous breasts would be a permanent target, invariably full of the lusting attraction.

She gently pushed them up and sensed her nipples harden red, at all times obedient and receptive to her devotion.

She thought of grapes and her nipples hardened.

Surely they are jewels of love, gifts from the gods, much more than the simple pairing of DNA, she sighed at the satisfaction, as she gently caressed them, lying naked on her immense purple satin sheets that stretched across her royal bed. Strange that she loved her breasts so much. But then, if the world loved them, why shouldn't she? Definitely some sort of psychosexual hang-up; she didn't care.

Carefully she touched her upright nipples, and made them red and hard and wicked as any woman could wish. Uplifting, she shyly blushed, which was rather silly because she was alone in her own bedroom at that moment. And as she sighed and moaned her secret pleasures, she sought the fresh-faced image of that handsome boy of long ago, even though she was hardly a flawless adolescent girl now days.

Well into her narcissistic moment of breath-taking recollection of adolescent sensuality, she now felt like a well-brushed Siamese and had an urge to naughtily lick herself but didn't know where. She rolled on her bed and let the satin caress her naked body, the smoothness of the sheets making her purr as hungrily as any wanton pussy cat. She had long ago understood perfectly well why men found her erotically appealing but equally forbidding, and there was thrill in her morning affections. For who would dare offend an angel? In and on Sharon, the Good Lord had sketched and chiselled flawless curves and soft lines blending all around her adorable body celestial lights of pure whites and pinks in mysterious tones of perfection and love which transcended all incarnations of genetic material. She was gorgeous all over her perfectly sculptured, graceful body.

She sought happiness and thought pleasure was the means to it so she put her hands beneath her breasts again and gently pushed them up, teasing them as she often did during these moments of lingering loveliness. She looked in her full length mirror at the other end of her flowered luxuriously furnished master bedroom suite; she felt so very fine, stroking, and stretching her long legs way down, lying down, and touchy-feely here and there, tactfully she smiled her way to another lovely climax.

She really had nothing else to do, and so, she rolled over, and once again over, on her king size bed, and smiled a half-awakened smile as if the world around her were a perpetual May full of the impetuous little sins she always loved to act out. For many years now, she rarely got out of bed before her morning reassurance ritual. She loved to leisurely hold back the time by running her hands all over her still firm body, feeling her stimulating sensuality, all over, every morning, and long after her husband had left the house to play out his manly role of husband provider, which, she had to admit, he was pretty good at.

Loving husband Hank Merker was not a bad guy, and he did the best he could to make her happy, and she really didn't have any right to complain about him, though she now found merciless comfort in doing so. At the very minimum her feelings about her husband had become very ambivalent and she blamed him for all her unhappiness but especially for marrying her too soon. It was true, he had been her high school sweetheart, of sorts, the meaning of the word implying more of syrupy candy than of love. They had been going steady during their last two years in high school, a period that included a lot of tedious sex for her. She never really understood the significance of the ritual of being exclusively with only one person in a kind of forced coupling called 'going steady'. Looking back on it, going steady was like out of the Middle Ages, like arranged, forced marriages; for why else would you go steady?

Well there was the sex part, she thought. It would have been highly amoral to be fucking if you weren't going steady.

Not every couple that went steady in high school wound up married, but Sharon and Hank were not your typical couple. He was the star quarterback, and she was the prettiest girl in school, and the gossip had it that they were made for each other, and the whole school expected them to be together forever. It was a twisted fate that, in agreement with the expectations of their friends, mindlessly led to their mind-numbing marriage all too soon after high school graduation. Throughout their affairs and marriage, Sharon had searched for some understanding of what was pushing them to wherever they were heading, but Hank's presence made it difficult for her to divine. In her mind, he held no surprises.

After their quick marriage, and without ever a hint of complaint, Hank daily did his thing and brought home the bacon in large enough quantities that would have satisfied most wives but not Sharon who had come to desire more than just bacon. And the more he realized that what he was bringing home was unsatisfactory and insufficient for his wife, the greater his efforts to bring home more stuff, though he had no clue what to bring because she never made specific requests, as wives are prone to do. The more he tried to make her happy the less she was impressed. It was a stupid, dull, monotonous life they had unpeeled for themselves. Lord forgive her, for many years Sharon had cared little about her husband, and even less for her husband's successes in the marketplace. He wanted to spoil her with his kindness, but she wanted to be spoiled by … she didn't know what … and was responding in nasty fits purposely denying his kindness. In more and more mindless little fights with her husband, she bickered and continuously complained for what she called, out of nowhere, the lack of "culture and adventure" not being there, in the emptiness that was their bacon bloated lives.

"I'm losing it, Hank. I'm losing you. There has to be more than this," she would nastily complain in the middle of their fucking.

"What do you want from me?" poor Hank would huff and puff away.

"I don't know, Hank; I just don't know," Sharon would malevolently continue to interrupt their coitus. "All I know is that there has to be more than this."

"Ugh, baby, it doesn't get better than this," he would flatter the fucking drama which was still full of exciting pleasure, as he lay on top of Sharon.

"I love you Hank," she would try to recall purple grapes, not sure of what she meant.

"I love you too, babe," he would comfort as he walked away to shower.

It was a life of habitual mumblings since neither of them had anything significant to ever say to each other. She casually trotted a continuous chatter of juvenile remarks as unattended complaints; they were mindless airs of disordered demands soliciting for more and more of ridiculous nothings from him. At first he had tried to understand her, but her blurred post-adolescent fumbling became formless sounds to his ears and eventually brought poor Hank to his emotional knees. He thought the deficiency was in him, that he lacked the refinement that her baby-soft ass demanded, confusing him further and making her wants, and needs, and wishes indistinguishable. It was all too much, endless, and he tired of her always complaining for no apparent reason, and he eventually gave up listening to her, her voice having lost all its intonation on its way to his ears. Though he never stopped thinking of her as the beautiful woman that she had always been, he had become most irritable of his wife's bothersome pretensions of always pressing to appear more important than their current status warranted. Neither of them had come close to a college degree but that didn't prevent Sharon from posturing that she was special, that she was intellectually grander than he or his friends. Her vague inaudible mumbles of dissatisfaction, often delivered without opening her mouth very much, finally convinced Hank to keep away from Sharon and her bullshit sense of self-importance. He gave her everything that he earned, as he had always done in the hope of not losing her, but she had remained numb unappreciative of his generosity. She had become a "dumb broad", he would confess to his close ex-high school buddies. Every day of the week, he would wake up and leave home early and come home late dreading even those few hours at night that he might have to spend with his beautiful but otherwise miserable wife.

"She's full of shit," he would comfort himself on his way to bring home the bacon.

Somewhere in shocking quick time, years before, their high school sweetheart souls detached, went their separate ways, and left the married couple speechless. It was a pattern familiar to Sharon, for her parents had also bound themselves speechless in an oppressive life. Hank's decline and fall from Sharon's grace, and hers from his, now unconcealed, had been insidiously sneaky in its progression across their cold marbled-covered kitchen floor soon after their childless marriage turned into a miserable cohabitation of meaningless familiarity, assuredly leading their tense way of life to certain collapse. The fast expiration of their union picked up speed and became relentless towards its crash, and all the time frothing frustrating emotions from a crippled past. As awkwardly as their high school marriage had merged from opposite directions, so, likewise, it was now deflating in every direction. During these depressing, grey days, and weeks, and months, and early years, Hank's only loving attachment to Sharon remained his immature high school sexual fantasy of being married to the prettiest girl in class, for Sharon had remained as beautiful as ever. Depressingly, like her mother's delayed realization of her pathetic marriage to husband Anton, for Sharon too, the recognition slowly surfaced with certainty that she was in a bad marriage; that she really never liked let alone loved Hank; that she really hated her husband for all the humiliating real or imagined physical or emotional abuse he had forced on her, and for taking advantage of her teenage innocence, he the abusive high school star hero, she just a naïve girl trying to fit into the mores of American high school hero worship; and her unforgiving soul would load up with hatred.

In retrospect, the whole Sharon loves Hank, Hank loves Sharon eulogy, chanted even by her best friends, a monotone predictor, had been dead from the start, and she now felt trapped. Hank was a loser, not a hero, and she wished it weren't so, but these things happen.

*

She tried, but constant belittlement of their intentions would impeded their attempts at understanding. The ambiguous romance that was the energy of their high school days slowly deflated into a patronizing reality full of scorn for each other. She thought she had the brains and he thought she was a cretin. He had been brought up to think, that, if you had a good arm to throw a spiral fifty yards, brains were not necessary to a winning life. From a young girl, she had no huge expectations. Searching for excuses to argue, intellectual disparities, even when not real, were as good as any argument to invade their retreating marriage; and whenever the heart-breaking reality of their predicament set in, dark thoughts further confused their personalities. There was little doubt in her mind that she came from superior cultured stock, as opposed to Hank's uncouth parentage that valued only football aimed through automobile tires; there was little doubt in his mind that his wife was out of touch with reality.

Sadly, the youthful fondness for each other's teenage fumbling sex that had betrayed them to think of their teenage lust as true love would not ever repeat, Sharon and Hank had come to realize. Though Sharon remained the sex kitten that she had been for Hank, he for her had become a huge hangover which she was unable to shake off. Day by day, Hank precariously dangled in a marriage more and more tenuous as he sank from star-athlete lover, to anonymous hot dog kiosk vendor, and then, somehow rebounding, to a major bigtime restaurant entrepreneur. Sharon was mutely indifferent to his successes, and he didn't quite know why or how, but he was very excited to be making all that money selling roast beef and mash potatoes. Every time he bought a greasy spoon place that his accountant recommended, it made a lot of money for him, until he moved into the major leagues buying multi-million dollar restaurants with real chefs. Hank was pleased to count his money and just watch football on TV with his loyal high school buddies. Everything was going well for the ex-quarterback, except for his marriage to his onetime high school sweetheart.

"You still fucking that coloured waitress, Hank?" she would indifferently ask.

"Ugh, she's just a fuck, Sharon. It's pretty boring between lunch and dinner time, at the restaurant. Can I get something for you?"

"My God, she's the ugliest thing I've ever seen Hank. Do you fuck her in your cruddy little office or quick bang her in the dining room?" she would laugh.

"You're nuts, Sharon, and it's getting worse."

He really could not understand what Sharon wanted from him. He would have given anything to have relived those simple high school days with young Sharon again. But then, not as sad or as ungrateful as it might have appeared, after almost eighteen years of marriage, he sensed he didn't exist for her.

Going back with Hank was no longer anywhere in Sharon's mind. Unlike the boy on the bus, Hank simply wasn't there.

Chapter Two

She woke up without opening her eyes fearing where she might be. Even with her eyes closed she knew she wasn't alone in another series of strangers' beds. She didn't want to do it, but it was difficult to deny the beautiful memories of her Ethiopia lover. You tell yourself, this is the last time, but it never is, she half-awake sensed his dead weight arms around her, as she had the night before, dancing salsa with one more slick stranger in the scum sullied disco, one of several where she would voluptuously dance the nights away. Disoriented from the night's drinking, she was devoid of meaningful sensation, and in her still half asleep state, as she lay in the sunken bed, she remembered bending and rubbing her silken tight ass against her newly selected dance partner, and she could still feel all his hardness. He was just one of many dance partners that night, and other previous similar nights. She didn't care who they were as long as they were young and muscular, and always black, remnants of Ethiopia. She was the white queen, pure gold, among the mostly Jamaican-Americans who did resemble Ethiopians. Sometimes she went to these clubs with her husband David who would stand by the bar and watch his wife pick them off one by one all the time rating their serpentine manhood. None of the men she asked to dance with would deny her.

Her father's not so subtle insistence that she marry a white boy made Robin not want to, though eventually she conformed to her father's wish by marrying lilywhite-boy David Calder. Ever since middle school when she first became aware of social issues confronting America, she too conveniently adopted the soundness of the solution, the way to resolving the racial quagmire of prejudice and integration was to "marry them", as she especially was fond of reminding daddy. But, lucidly, when the time came, she married David Calder, of Northern European extraction, who was far removed from any racial dilemmas.

"You marry a black guy and I'll bring no more chickens home for you to eat," was the way Pioneer Bank CEO rich Daddy Robert Sargent had honestly put it to his daughter.

Robin recognized Daddy's comments as racist, but who wasn't now days. More than the political incorrectness of his words, her concern focused on the not so subtle insistence, bordering on incest, of Daddy's resolve to choose the husband who was to fuck her.

"Do you think she's screwing black guys," Mr. Sargent would ask his mild-mannered wife Helen during Robin's high school days.

"Where would she find them," would be Helen's reply.

Unexpected events, especially the peculiar way she wound up being married to a man she didn't love, a fate destined by her Daddy's manipulated demands for a white boy husband, made it psychologically forbidding for her to have any correspondence between what she might have instinctively desired and what she settled for. Like all the nice girls who live in the sanity of always being protected from harm, she too secretly wanted to partake of a lewdness and of indiscretions, and yes, of sins that would put some fun in an otherwise Godly American way of life. Two years in Ethiopia as a Peace Corps Volunteer had awakened the dark side of her modest appropriateness; suddenly, she became aware of all her primitive Africa instincts with all their immortal pleasures shattering the unconscious repressions of her simple American educated mind which surfaced as a wild jungle of lovely sensations. The rebelliousness that smacked of naughtiness that she happily discovered in Ethiopia, far, far away from Daddy, taught Robin that there was no such thing as ugliness in the briefness of life, and that anything goes. She thought herself lucky to have understood the beauty of defiance at an early age.

"When you're near me all darkness disappears and I can see so much clearer," when depressed, her mind romantically would recall her Ethiopian lover, defying the repressed stubborn thorn that would prick her Daddy wounded heart.

Taferra was dead now, so what more could she have done at her age but to live the pleasures of her uninhibited youth? She would smile with disdain at her easy life of booze and infinite shopping malls, all made possible by Daddy's money. She had dropped out of the pure white clouds of the Addis Ababa high plateau into his African arms, expecting nothing more than the brief romance of sensual abandonment to be felt more intimately, more physically than any fantasy on banker's row. Alone, now, back in the good old USA, she searched for that magical instant that she knew would never unfold again, for Taferra was dead.

"She likes to rub the salsa in the nude," David had once greeted one of Robin's young acquiescent studs recently arrived from Kingston. He had dared to ask Robin for a dance and though David pretended he didn't mind, he understood that she was back in Addis.

"Your genius is definitely dancing your ass off on the voodoo floor, my dear," he would bitterly try to embarrass her. His words fell on empty pities.

He would contemptuously laugh pretending he didn't care which one of the undulating shimmy boys she would later fuck that night. After her raids away from home in search for sex in the hot and furious African primal dances, David had given up on her and her insensate lies that had deadened his feelings for her; he couldn't have cared less about whom she fucked. Bitterly he hated her for the way she dumped endless humiliation on him, and she hated him because he was the wrong man for her. They had nothing more than vitriolic sympathies for each other and their touch was always frigid.

Oh Lord, let the night last one more minute, don't let me wake up like this, Robin ached the pain of loneliness, hoping the morning's light would bring a different day. Let me stay one more moment in his arms, and with that memory, she turned toward the body next to her, and almost shrieked in horror.

God in Heaven, what an atrocious thing it was. Eyes wide open now, Robin saw a big black guy with a short kinky black-grey beard in deep sleep, stretched out next to her lovely flesh, likewise nude. He was completely naked and stunk of redolent puke. With eyes in shocked delirium from too much vodka, Robin tried to imagine Taferra but she couldn't.

"Shit, shit, shit," she said and ran out of the room.

*

She thought that her downfall began when she was caught shoplifting inexpensive underwear in Macy's department store on Fashion Island in Newport Beach. Caught red-handed, pink panties in her Dior bag, her face got red and she was glad that the ladies intimates were in the basement where few men shopped. Displaying vivacious liveliness, she cleverly outwitted the sixties year old lingerie manager with an endless rationalization of lies, and an arrogance born of wealth powered by a large number of displayed credit cards. But the shame of being caught in an act of bass-class petty crime felt heavy on her mind and she could never unload it.

"I don't know what came over me to steal cheap underwear," she later told Myrna of the embarrassing story at Macy's, and Myrna laughed, knowing that Robin was not a petty thief.

They were having coffee, sitting in a small and cosy booth, just the two of them, in one of those obscure, unpretentious little strip mall coffee shops that still served their coffee in porcelain cups and saucers that pleasure the intimacy of endless friendships. In a Southern California sunny mid-morning, quiet in the wide open spaces well defined by wealth, two childhood friends, to the exclusion of no one, met for a cup of coffee, and to speak and add more words to the million tales already said between them. In the subtle tradition of life, it's the unending stream of words between two people that makes for lasting friendship. Just a cup of java to unload and kill some time.

"Maybe it was because David and I were having our usual marital fights at the time. For sure it was not because of lack of money. I always had tons of money because Daddy was there for me, and I was married to a white guy, to Daddy's thrill, so I don't know what came over me. We were stupidly trying to make it on our own. We fucking challenged ourselves to make it on our own and pretended that money was scarce, even though Daddy was ever present, there a millionaire, and I definitely could've afforded underwear," a blush of modesty surfaced on her cheeks.

"Were you commando that day?" asked Myrna.

"I don't remember," said a pissed Robin.

"I mean it could've been that you were cold and you wanted to cover your ass and not because you didn't have any money …"

"Myrna, you're beginning to piss me off. It's times like these I wish I smoked."

"What the hell were you doing at Macy's, anyway?"

"Well, you don't shoplift at Niemen Marcus," said Robin.

"Why not?" said Myrna.

"Nobody shoplifts at Niemen Marcus," asserted Robin.

Myrna reached across the booth table and took Robin's hand which felt cold.

"Did you ever go commando when you were in Ethiopia?" said Myrna.

There was a long thoughtful delay while Robin considered her response.

"I did it a few times when I first got there and it felt great to go primitive. But then I found out that most poor Ethiopian women, of all ages, but mostly older women, maybe grandmas, but who could tell, were going commando all the time, so it was no big deal."

"It must've been messy when they were having their periods," said Myrna and they both let out a hearty laugh.

"It was mostly older women who went commando, Myrna."

"Come to think of it: that's why cities are built next to rivers or by the sea," said Myrna.

It wasn't funny, and betrayal rushed into Robin's eyes. She loved Ethiopia and the Ethiopians, and that was a terrible thing to say about Ethiopian women who were very beautiful and didn't need anyone's approval on underwear etiquette.

Robin almost came to tears.

"Fuck it, Robin. No big deal; it was a long time ago."

"Then how come I can't get it out of my mind?"

"Have you told this stupid story to anyone else? Does Dave know?" and Myrna laughed the question to lessen its importance.

"You mean about the Ethiopian guy …"

"No, I meant about the shoplifting."

"No, no, I could never tell this to David. You know what a tight-ass he is. He would never forgive me."

"About the Ethiopian guy, or about the panties?"

"Same thing," laughed Robin.

"I have no idea what you're talking about right now," said Myrna.

"Big, black guys with big dongs," laughed Robin.

"All these years and you've never told him?"

"Nope!"

"Have there been many?"

Myrna was just as curious as any human being. No response.

"Big, fucking David Calder; he thinks he's so important because he's a banker. A little man in a big bank, that's what he is," Myrna said about Robin's husband. She wanted to cheer up her friends. "If it weren't for you he'd be nothing."

"There was a time when I could've told him my secrets, but no more."

"Change is good," said Myrna.

*

The daughter of a self-made millionaire and founder of Pioneers Bank, Robin grew up without the usual infectious teen anxiety or concern. Both her mother and father were contented people who spoiled their daughter with worldly goods and kisses. Kindly Robert and Helen Sargent led a soft, sweet life, heirs to expensive comforts. They easily lolled in the limelight of their sprawling wealth. Robert was the son of an immigrant French bank accountant, Bernard Sargent, who had been transferred from the

Grenoble branch of the Toulouse Continental Bank to its small branch in Chicago at the turn of the Twentieth Century as its manager. A dour and determined man, he hated fun-loving Chicago, full of the braggart Irish politicos who ruled the city, and convinced his superiors back in France to move the branch to Los Angeles, "the future of America," he had rightly predicted. When the Continental Bank of Toulouse went belly-up during the 1930s, Bernard begged and borrowed and bought the LA branch of the Toulouse bank and immediately changed its name to The Pioneers Bank of California. The bank flourished at the same rate as California and Bernard with tenacious humility quickly dropped 'of California' and The Pioneers Bank became Pioneer Bank and totally his baby. It was this baby that only son Robert inherited from his Rhone-Alps immigrant French father.

When their one and only child was born, Robert hovered sweetly over proud wife Helen and their baby daughter and glowingly said, "She looks like a little robin in her feathered nest."

From a little girl, Robin wanted to be a poet and to her parents' great joy she was a prolific writer. Her poems and stories were rich in imagination, full of inspired everyday reality for a young person of her age. She wrote about love, the universe, and above all else, she wrote about poor people, especially the homeless people of California, and India, and Africa of whom she had read so much about, and of whom from a distance she greatly sympathised and loved. In her stories, the poor were loyal to their promises while the rich were always duplicitous. When she got to high school, it was an easy jump from the homeless poor of the world to the many more millions of closer at home impoverished blacks, or aka African-Americans of Watts and East LA, and the vague South of Stephen Foster's 'darkies'.

All through high school, Robert and Helen tried hard to remind Robin of her French heritage but it was soon apparent that she had become obsessed in what they thought was an adolescent, confused way of thinking, one hundred and eighty degrees in contrast to their own values of proud French inheritance.

"Hopefully she'll find her way," confidently Robert would periodically remind Helen.

"Well, she's fixing her own bed and let her lie in it," Helen, the stringent realist would insist, unforgivably confused by Robin's intransigence.

"She would make such a wonderful doctor," her father would insist.

"Don't be fooled, Robert; your daughter is a little bitch," Helen would lovingly reply.

They loved their one and only daughter and neither wished to abandon their one and only heir to their vast family banking fortune because of silly adolescent blabbing.

All through high school, Robin kept her literary thoughts to herself fearing that if she showed any sensitivity to social problems in class she might be thought of as a geek, or worse a socialist. Such is the curse of American high schools that they crush their students into stressed out cool dudes and babes full of awkward hang-ups instead of geeks. Manipulated by a strained environment into almost open hostility, well fed young men and women at the prime of their lives shun their intellectual instincts in favour of purposeless, bogus adoration of meaningless high school football. Stupid fucking Neanderthal high school football played nowhere else on earth other than in tough America. Fear of not being accepted, of not being part of the in-crowd keeps ambitious young people dumb-silent for four years and then more. Very few, if any, American high school students want to show that they might have a mind that's different from the opinions expressed by their teachers who faithfully mimic the opinions of the media least they lose their jobs – permanently! And all the school incompetent counsellors meekly advise that it is desirably normal not to want to be different, and the beloved gym teachers smile their speeches on how sports build character. Teachers of literature and thought have no chance against the wisdom of coaches of American high schools.

So it was with Robin, a most abnormal girl, superior in all things intellectual and beautiful, squeezed on all sides to fit her high school counselling normal. She was beautiful, with sensitive blue eyes that gave way to a deep crystal clear sea of enormous promise in their sparkle. Throughout her high school years, a baby's unspoiled complexion framed by thick, sun-yellow long hair emphasized her erotic woman's pink lips and beautiful face. She was impeccably campus beautiful as were her three best friends: Sharon, Kitty, and Myrna. Yet, during all four high school years she was needlessly wary of being grouped with the geeks. And every time she entered a classroom, she did her damnest to be counsellor normal, though male teachers did stare. She prayed that she might not be called on, though she knew that she knew the answers to most questions.

*

Absolutely unravelled by four years of a typical unchallenging American educational experience in Magnolia High School, Robin never really recovered her teen eagerness even after four years of college, two years in the Peace Corps in Ethiopia, and a marriage to a very handsome ex-Peace Corps Volunteer, David Calder, who likewise served with her in Ethiopia. Anticipated enthusiasm away from home gave license to Robin to do things that she would never have dreamed of doing while growing up in Sherman Oaks. Far away from her weary upbringing, she dove into a love affair, actually a daily after work fucking period with a light skinned Ethiopian, but the affair was much too bold for Robin's white conforming soul. Her imprinted upbringing was morally squashing the good things of her Protestant class and culture. Overwhelmed by her stubborn past she dumped the Ethiopian and returned to her breed in the safe arms of David Calder, a man most Daddy familiar. Unfortunately for David, Robin was the wrong woman for him and ultimately it led to a wrong marriage. For two years she strayed naked for a skinny, light skinned Ethiopian who, he in love, managed to liberate her ego from its infantile memories and bring semblances of happiness into her life. But her Ethiopian affair was a tale to a cheap novel because she and her lover were two people whose cultural gap was wider than the Rift Valley. He taught her that it wasn't necessary to wash after every lovemaking, or just water was okay. They were two people of different color and she was incapable of overcoming her racist upbringing, much as she might once have thought that 'to marry them' was the answer. She had been deceitful to both David, her American sidekick lover, and Taferra, her honest Ethiopian lover, neither of whom could focus beyond her beautiful face.

After returning to the States she found it difficult to make the adjustment to the American way of life she had known. She would find herself mentally alone, silently protesting a life not to her liking, though she knew that for her there was no other. She developed a way of not looking at people straight in the eye, a limited glance that was misinterpreted even by her friends as an unfriendly expression. In time, her voice became masculine rough and when she spoke everyone stopped talking, an effect that she didn't like because she didn't want to be the cause of it. She disliked herself and found an unfamiliar, foreign, peace of mind only when she was with her best friends who had the soothing effect on her of making her voice revert to her femininity softness of long before. Without wanting to, somewhere in time, probably in the course of her Peace Corps years, she had become the cynic she didn't want to be. Poetry, her one-time love affair, had repressed to a confused story in her uninspired mind, thoughts of beauty bringing no joy. Mentally devoid of any medical explanation as to her lethargic post PC behavior, it was nonetheless very nice that her bed of thorns was handsomely transformed into lovely roses by her Daddy's millions.

The post Ethiopian angst invariably faded and within years they disappeared as the familiar scenes of being back home overcame the silly thoughts of somewhere beyond the sea. The agent to the reversion was the huge libidinous secret hidden deep in her unconscious that surfaced again, actually, had never left, and, she knew, would never go away. Since her sophomore year in Magnolia High School, Robin had been in love with star quarterback Hank Merker, best friend Sharon's then boyfriend and now husband. The lustful chronic desire to fuck Hank, even after all the years since high school, twisted physical and emotional pain in her fantasy face. And when in the real presence of Hank, now days somewhat rare, her feelings for him produced nude behavioural distortions, generating unadorned frustrations and naked anxieties in front of other people around her, but especially with her best friend Sharon, and terribly exposed her unfortunate real feelings for husband Dave. The heart blinked and skipped retreated and, terribly, every time, made her lapse into unintended comparisons between the two current males in her real David, and her fantastic Hank, life. And even after all the sexual exuberance of Ethiopia, painful feelings for high school Hank increased instead of fading away. The pain of not possessing him became more acute, and in the process of her greed for Hank, the love and friendship she had for Sharon became disconcerting, confusing her love for Sharon with the dark secret desire for Hank who had become the golden trophy she couldn't have. When she tried desperately to repress her feelings for Hank, more powerfully they would bounce back and invade her mind. Huge lumps of Hank would fire from her unconscious, and without wanting to, thinking of him, her best friend's husband, immense guilt would invade her soul. Fighting to hide her emotions, over the years she became arrogant, anti-social, and at times hostile to her friends, unnerving them and everyone else present. Since high school, being always blinded by high heat for Hank, she consciously diverted her attention away from boys who showed interest, and later on, unconsciously, away from interesting men, whose contact she feared would make her tongue stammer away and maybe reveal her secret to the world: that all she wanted to just one time fuck Hank Merker. Not until she joined the Peace Corps did she, for spastic moments, without regret, allow herself to forget handsome high school Hank, the love of her adolescent life. It was in Ethiopia, far away from trite Magnolia High School, did she momentarily discover grownup love, that Robin briefly forgot the corniness of the unrequited puppy love that she had been nurturing for Hank. Unfortunately, sadly engraved in the white, blond world of her youth, and though far, far away from home, Robin still lacked the willpower to seduce a life of basic, animal, instinctual, sexual adventures full of the intensity that nature had meant for her and of which she repressively desired.

"What were some of your interests in high school," innocently asked David one night as they lay in separate beds.

"You mean like boys," her mind stuck on Hank.

"I was asking more about intellectual or artistic interests," he said trying to make talk. "But if you want to talk about boys, I'd like to hear about that too."

"Well, I did have a crush on Hank Merker," she tried to smile away the pitiful, deep-seated neurosis.

David grinned a silly smile, like he couldn't have cared less; it would have been perfectly natural for a young girl to have a crush on a boy, though her smile did stammer something more than a just a typical teenage crush on a high school Hank Merker.

"Did you ever fuck him?" asked Dave.

Without a second thought Robin slapped her husband hard.

He was surprised by her reaction. He had met Merker once and thought him empty.

"That's ok, Robin. You can fuck Hank as often as you wish," he said laughing. "You can fuck him as much as you want. I don't care. You fuck everybody else so why not him?"

Robin could not have cared about his words. She decided that her secret was still safe because her husband was too much of an egoist to have understood what she had just confessed, the punishing secret of her life. In her mind, it was preposterously unlikely that her dumb husband would publically admit that his wife had pent-up sexual feelings for her best friend's husband.

"I hate you," she said. "I wish you were dead."

Robin was hurt. He could've said go to hell, instead.

"Maybe we should seek professional counselling," she said after a few minutes of nauseating silence.

"I don't give a shit what you think we should do. As far as I'm concerned you could just get the hell out of my life and go fuck Merker or anyone else you want any time you want to. I'm staying with you just for daddy," he said most unkindly.

"Fuck you," she said.

"I'm now going to get a beer," he said.

The man did not mince his words in articulating her position in his life. Crushed like a cockroach being stepped on, she thought that maybe someday she could be forgiving towards her greedy husband, though she knew that she could not ever come to love him. She smiled in her bed because for a long time she had known that her marriage was empty, and if she wanted happiness she would to dance her nights away in scummy discos full of strange sensations.

And many nights, before she fell asleep, she would imagine what a wonderful couple she and Hank would make.

Sharon and David would also make a lovely couple, she would think, to be fair and then fall into a sound sleep.

Chapter Three

Myrna Lambert rinsed the last glass of the morning's breakfast and haphazardly shoved it somewhere on the upper tray of her dishwasher. She then clicked the dishwasher door shut and pressed the third button of the picture-coded panel depicting the 'wash/rinse' cycle, the number 145° F for water temperature, and sequentially the smiling sun for 'hot dry'. Such conveniences, she thought; such a happy way of doing the breakfast dishes. If only life were so straight forward, so comprehensibly uncomplicated. Though the dishes were a chore, and honestly, there weren't that many other chores in her present life – what, she and her two daughters only - she could've easily done the dishes by hand, but the modern, high tech dishwasher made her feel that she was part of a bigger, more youthful world. She was part of the world of the rich, and she could've had two dishwashers if she wanted. She wondered if there were still people in America who did dishes by hand anymore. She shuddered at the thought of being common, and she had her first thought of a cigarette. Her father had been a real estate man, uncommon in his instincts, a salt of the earth American.

She looked at the clock on her microwave oven and it read 8:37 am. She had already been up for more than two hours and rightly felt tired. Her legs had started to swell, as usual, even this early in the day, and she wasn't even forty yet. The only thing she wanted to do was to get off of them, sit down with her feet up on the next chair, and have a leisurely cup of coffee, or two. As she lit the first of her day's many cigarettes, she had no clue as to what she was going to do to fill her day, a daily dilemma that she hadn't been able to resolve since her husband had left her, actually abandoned her, with two permanently hungry teen-age daughters.

Fuck him, she thought.

A woman wants a man who's in touch with his inner self and not some whiner like her ex-husband Phil, the weasel.

Daylight hours baffled her and she had meant to start a diary just to keep track of her thoughts, and not just of him.

My two women in the making, she proudly thought of her two beautiful daughters whose good looks probably came from their father, the moaner weasel, she conceded. It's a well-known fact that daughters get their looks from their fathers, she hated to admit, because she hated the bastard. There was no denying their playful sisterly antics; they were clone feminine copies of her soft husband's frolicking shit.

The loneliness of her divorce snuck up on her and generated feelings of personal rejection, and stomach aches. After almost twenty years, he dropped her like a one-night-stand stranger, walked out on by an indifferent pig, as if she were some wrinkled woman, though barely over thirty. He ditched her, and she felt like any woman would - jilted.

Women like me don't come every day, and if there was a bad apple in the marriage it was him and not me, she couldn't get her mind off the shit

Thoughts like these led to exhausting days filled with aggression against everyone, and life in general, though she tried to be cool. So she passed her days in frustrating monotony wishing she were dead, but not seriously. It all led to further frustration and sleepless nights full of hot flashing anxieties. Her pissed existence was slowly draining the little energy she had left as a single mother without a husband. Other women had been divorced and had moved on in their life without hating men. But Myrna's common enough divorcee had loudly invaded her life, insidiously tormenting her thoughts with dark loneliness and hatred. Her mind twisted sick as a dog, scaring her of early death, she would sometimes fear. Other days, when the sun shone brightly, she thought that her life had come full circle and that she might be in some ridiculous loop unworthy of repeat. Still, as much as she tried to dismiss her husband's absence, there remained the fascination of having been married that she couldn't overcome. The bastard Phil was everywhere around her; he just wouldn't keep away. So she swallowed her solitude into an emptiness of being a proud divorcee which was a lie because she cared too much about what her friends were probably saying behind her back - that poor Myrna couldn't keep a husband.

"I could keep ten husbands if it weren't for the gossip," she blew out the smoke, swaggering in defiance to their gossip-mongering.

"I never want to become some puny hysterical little bitch in heat," she said to herself, and Myrna wished she could overcome the stinking thoughts; forget the jerk who had been her husband, who had left her without good cause, behavior not normal for an American marriage. Other women had suffered the indignity of a divorce and had survived, and so would she, she told herself trying to regain some sense of ego-respect

Her mind persisted with false arguments as she tried to overcome her disturbing predicament of a beautiful woman without a husband complicated by the presence of two teen age daughters. She might not have a husband in her current life, but Myrna was grateful that she at least had her two daughters, proof without debate that one could be a complete woman even without a husband. She had put on a little weight, but her daughters' presence were a wall to shut away the rumourmongers and do away with any thoughts of depression and suicide. Her daughters' company, in her otherwise lonely divorced life, had the sustaining satisfaction for her to face the world with pride, knowing that her two girls were magnificent beautiful creatures. The girls neutralized her neurotic thoughts that sometimes struck panic in her lonely heart: thank God for her lovely daughters.

There was a bitterness to being a divorcee that just wouldn't go away, though she was convincing herself that she was much happier without her hanging-around-her-apron ex-husband, weasel Phil. The unpardonable, lamentable, Phillip Lambert, a champion ass hole!

But as much as she loved her lovely daughters, there were moments when perhaps unfairly, she thought that they, in a way, might have been responsible for both her loneliness and Phil's exit from her life. They did test her patience, and probably his, with their teenage shenanigans, but she loved them for the pleasing moments they literally screamed into her life. At times, she would admonish herself for loving them too much, as if that were possible for a mother to love her children too much. But then no mom is perfect.

The loneliness she felt was most obvious during the hours of the day when the girls were in school, or when otherwise away from her. Fear and uneasiness about her darling daughters' future trailed her every thought, and without wanting it, less than pretty pictures about Justine and Meredith crossed her weary mother's mind. The girls were growing up spectacularly fast and independent of her; lively daughters of the Southern California outdoors who seemed to care more about their long glistening in the sun legs and silken golden hair than their mother. And when they ran their quarrelling antics through the house in their innocent but indecent half-naked ways, Myrna's fears and frustration at the naked sight would scream stronger than the day before because, it seemed to her, there was no way of subduing her daughters' vigour, or muffling their filthy slang, and that she, alone by herself, was incapable of providing any direction for them.

Other than shopping and cooking, there isn't much else that I can do for them, she would think. And to her dismay, they didn't seem to care what might be bugging their concerned lonesome mother.

"I'm gonna tell mother what you do with Wally Austin in school every day," smilingly Meredith would threaten her older sister.

"You do that and I'll tell her what you do with Andrew Cotter, and he's eighteen," Justine would fire back, and in the distance Myrna would pray that neither of them tell her anything, because having been there, at their age, she knew what every mother knows.

They were healthy girls, full-bodied and strong, and their fast approaching separation from their loving mother had already cast its presence. Even now, they didn't ask anything more of her than a comfortable house and tasty food. It frightened Myrna to think that her daughters found more involvement outside their home, that they came home only to eat and sleep, and she wondered how long even that would last. She wanted to do more for them, but they never asked for more; they didn't have to; it was always handed to them before they asked; they weren't as needy of her, as she would have liked for them to be. Even without their father she continued to spoil them; and they deviously thrived in it.

She was curious and had misgivings about her fast developing daughters who seemed awfully liberated these days, and her curiosity would get fumbled in the fascination of the changing features of her pubescent daughters, but her mind would always retract to the safety of "what else could I do?" and she meant it; as a single mom she had her hands full just dressing and feeding her always demanding, carefree beautiful daughters. She didn't know what to do in this modern age of child rearing and she didn't want to stifle her daughters; it would have been a shame, because they were so sexy beautiful.

Difficult as it was for her to think about it, she had concluded that if Justine, her older daughter of sixteen, was sexually active, well, it was okay, because, well, it had to happen sometime. Myrna was sure Justine was becoming sexually irresistible to her high school boyfriends, just as she herself had been years earlier when she was in school. From the time she was a baby, there was no denying Justine's beauty with her long legs, blond hair straight and soft, shining even in the dark with her incomparable full smile. And there simply was no minimizing her upright breasts - always a focal point for imaginative mama's boys hanging out and sniffling around her beautiful daughter. She had seen Justine recently naked and she had feared her good looks because she knew that Justine's innocence wouldn't stop some obscene older teen bastards from fucking her. From her own experiences, she knew what high school boys were capable of.

Like a good mother, she wondered about her daughters' possible involvement in drinking and other addictions like drugs. She didn't know which of these thinks was the worst, thought she felt that sexual addiction was the least offensive, as long as safety precautions were taken. She must check with Justine.

Justine was definitely developing into a hot young woman and Myrna couldn't help but compare her to her beautiful friend Sharon. Like Sharon's, Justine's young face was a flawless symmetry of faultless features. Crudely, in Myrna's motherly estimate, Justine had already become a stunning piece of ass. Sexuality radiated all around her freshly coloured lips, always perfectly outlined. They echoed a smile that was a young girl's vanity for approval of her devastating good looks. There probably was too much stimulation all around her, and it would have been most natural for her to want to fuck. It would have taken superhuman effort for Justine to resist the temptation. She had it all, and what an unforgivable sin it would have been if no one stooped to sniff. And Myrna ached that it be no more than a sniff, for at least a little while longer, though she knew from experience that sooner or later someone was going to invade her beautiful daughter, without regrets all around. Blame it on DNA or what, the girl simply exuded sex as she moved through her teen space. What a flirt, she's too much, thought poor Myrna, but what was a mother to do?

While Justine was busy busting out like springtime, Myrna was having a lot more difficulty accepting the possibility that her thirteen-year old Meredith might also be fucking boys, probably much older than herself. Two beautiful nymphets dancing through her house, Meredith was filling out just as lovely as Justine; she loved fitting into her older sister's clothes. There was a lot of sensational imaging floating around the dinner table as the girls would tease each other while salaciously licking their spoons.

Who am I kidding, the ugly thought kept buzzing in Myrna's ears. She was scared to death to ask, for she didn't want to know, because she wouldn't know what to do.

Anyway, now days, everybody was doing it, she would think. God, let them not get pregnant. Was it her fault that she had beautiful daughters? Well, maybe, because she did bear them. What was a mother to do? Scar their faces as in the days of old, or as in some scary uncivilized countries of today, mutilate them even worse, drown them, she would frown in riddled ambivalence.

Alone, with no one to discuss the issue, she didn't know what to make of her daughters. She was so proud that they were so rare and beautiful but scared to death that bad men would take advantage of them and contaminate them pregnant. She thought of making them carry prophylactics in their backpacks along with their school books but the necessary instructions of when and how to use them scared that thought. Same for pills; what else was a mother to do with two such totally fucking desirable daughters?

Mothers with ugly daughters are the lucky ones, she thought.

One day as she watched Meredith step out of her shower, Myrna's heart melted away at her daughter's pink, luscious body.

Out of love she said, "Why couldn't you be a little uglier?"

She caught her breath and hugged her daughter and Meredith knew that her mother loved her but that she was a little wacko.

Worrisome as the thoughts about her girls were, Myrna was delighted that both girls were very popular in school. Justine was going steady with a senior on the varsity football team. He was a handsome boy named Doug whom Myrna approved of because he reminded her a lot of young Hank Merker, her best friend Sharon's husband whom Myrna also had fucked when they were in high school. Myrna had witnessed Justine's and Sharon's evolving big girls' best friends' flirtatious bonding and she approved, for Sharon was one of her best friends that she could forever trust. She was happy that Justine confided her boyfriend secrets to best friend Sharon. She knew the story of when uncle Hank had been a varsity quarterback, like boyfriend Doug, and when Hank and Sharon and Myrna, like best friends, shared love in high school.

Doug was a good-looking young man but a bit on the shy side, not very talkative, just like young Hank, Myrna recalled. It seemed to her that Doug was from a solid, wealthy family. Whenever he came to the house, he hurriedly mumbled his greetings to her, as if he had places to go, and off he would rush with Justine to her room. They seemed to like each other a lot and Myrna was happy for her daughter. What else could she do? It would never occur to Myrna to snoop into her daughter's private affairs. Jesus, that would take her back a couple of generations, an age before soccer in America.

Meredith didn't have a steady, yet, but she was always an exhausting thirteen year old going on eighteen when every day she would recounted all the school juicy gossip to her mother. Who was going steady with whom, suspicions as to what girls in her class were doing it already, and on-and-on with the latest fads, like which bad girls were coming to school commando. All the news were daily similar to Myrna's ears: unending, exhausting adolescent blether. But Myrna did love the glow on Meredith's face and her melodious voice that rose with each wide-eyed revelations as she disingenuously related stories about the 'stupid boys' in her classes. Every day there would be tons of phone calls from many boys for both girls. Without doubt, the girls were very popular, and definitely part of the in-crowd. When you're popular, you got it all; and when you're very pretty, you're very popular. Boys always want to cup a feel and grab your breasts when you're pretty. Having your breasts and ass felt by boys in your class is always a good indicator of how popular a school girl is: the more they cup and feel, and the more they grab, the better the girls feel and more emotionally secure they become that they're popular and on their way to a satisfying life. And when you're a pretty popular girl, you can't wait to run home to happily relate all the day's events to your over-the-moon mama, except about your own felt pinches, or about the removal of your panties in the girl's bathroom before attending classes.

What the hell, Myrna had concluded; she herself had been twelve the first time it happened to her and she survived the lift-off ok. I have to stop worrying about the girls, she thought. I'm sure they'll find their way. We all do somehow.

*

"Here I am with so much free time to do all those things that I use to think I would want to do, and yet not much stirring in the brain," she stared out of her bright kitchen window. "I am so brain dead," she said to the world.

41

Even gardening had become a chore. Lately, she had begun having fantasies of negotiated affairs with pick-up strangers at the supermarket or even in parking lots but had rejected the thoughts as bad form if her teen daughters ever found out. She hadn't had sex for many weeks now, ever since before her husband left her, and rarely did they fuck even then when he was around. Phil wasn't much of a lover and she should have cheated on him, then, but he had given her such beautiful daughters, she found contentment in them instead of him. And in her lovely fantasies of sexual exploits, one adventure repeated time and again into her uninhibited mind as she silently puffed away alone in her handsome house. Time and again, ever since high school, her mind would drift to handsome quarterback Hank her secret lover whom big tit Sharon, a discarded waif, had beaten her to. She would have given anything to be with Hank, to make love to him, to be married to him. And now that she was free from the cloistered monk that once had been her husband, her mind would wildly channel the possibilities with handsome Hank and to hell with best friend Sharon. In the sweetness of her mind, every night Hank would smilingly visit with Myrna for long bouts of reckless love-making. Remembering about him, though, wasn't like the real thing, she concluded one night after an arduous exercise of sexual fantasies. Many a night Myrna, the Beloved one, would reset and enjoy Hank as she once knew him.

"We lived the hermitic life," she would smile with conviction to friends about life with Phil. "But now no more, no more. I'm free and available."

"Say no more, Myrna, my beloved," Sharon would laugh, and Myrna would wonder if Sharon could read her mind.

She had been a good wife but she should have cheated on the bastard, when they were married, when he was the wit with all the girls. And the thought would come crashing into her brain with a vengeance: It wasn't too late to cuckold the son-of-a-bitch even now after he had flown the coup. Two-time him now with lustful fantasies of lurid sexual encounters with young lifeguards and high school champion athletes. She loved the thoughts of champions humping her. Warm, early morning mellow fantasies to dust anew the lovely memories of once hot, immaculate, teenage salacious sex with Hank. Hot fantasies of lustful encounters with strangers and not so strangers, sometimes would come fast and furious, and felt awfully good, as silly daydreams often do, assuring her that she still hadn't dried out.

She took a deep drag to calm her revving mind away from all the sex shit.

But the real thing of being pushed hard against the wall by some tall basketball champ, or even a footballer, would be so much nicer than any fantasy, she would wiggle her handsome ass in punishment of that bastard ex-husband who so dastardly had dumped her.

Fuck him, who cares, let him mildew in some cave, she thought.

She poured herself another cup of hot coffee, lit another cigarette, and became restless again; still no thoughts to occupy the young day. She liked her coffee like her father did: strong and dark, no sugar, no cream. Her father was a beautiful man, strong and silent. He made a lot of money selling real estate in the Van Nuys, and Sherman Oaks areas of LA.

Funny how every time she thought of her dead father her eyes would tear up and she'd go into a momentary trance. She couldn't help it. He was one of the greats; an all-American guy who made it big by the strap of his will. Bob Lawson started out as an accountant in Robert Sargent's Pioneer Bank. He made good and after a few years of hard work he was put in charge of Mortgages and Loans where he became a true believer of capitalism. He left the bank, after being assured by the bank's friendly management of special help in getting easier mortgages for his prospective buyers. He quickly made a bundle and opened a plush real estate office determined to mentor his son, Robert Jr., in the all-American art of making big money. Bob Lawson believed that making money was God's greatest invention to mankind. And he and Junior made a huge fortune. Unfortunately, and in spite Myrna's unbounded love for her daddy, All-American Bob's plans did not include daughter Myrna in any meaningful way, she being a girl. As a father, he loved her as any American father loved his daughter and he spoiled her with girly things all the time, and when she married Phil, the Lawsons were all too happy, and very generous to Myrna: Daddy Bob bought her an expensive six thousand square feet house in Brentwood, and smiled good riddance to the female. Eerily, the morning of Myrna's wedding, Bob's stressed out body gave way to a massive heart failure, and two weeks later, his widowed wife Alice died of a broken heart. The whole affair was too much for Junior who proceeded to blow his brains out leaving Myrna an unexpectedly huge inheritance.

Even dead, Bob Lawson was always in Myrna's mind. Like a little girl still worshipping her daddy, she often recalled the last night before her wedding: she had spent it with her fabulous father. It was in the early morning hours when they had returned from an exaggerated pre-nuptial dinner that Bob had hosted for his one and only daughter. Exhausted, Alice had gone to bed but father and daughter had continued the celebration at home enjoying clean vodka martinis.

"I love Latino music, don't you," he said to his daughter.

"Well, Daddy, I think you mean South American music," and she gave him a little peck on his chubby cheeks as he pretended some sort of cha-cha in their bar-room.

"Mostly Brazil," he smiled delighted in his luxurious condition.

He had been to Havana when he was eighteen and had brought back two albums, "Havana at Night One", and "Havana at Night Two" which he always played when he was making merry.

"No city in this entire world is as exciting as Havana at night …" he danced the night away back in fun loving Havana, now happy to bring another closure to his successful life.

"Besame, besame mucho … love me forever and ever … this last night together…" he danced and drank the night away.

It was the very next day that his heart blew up while he was sleeping the day away.

"Too many martinis," said Alice.

"You're a horrible wife to say that," said Myrna.

"Go fuck yourself," said the heartbroken mother who was now confronted with a wedding and a funeral at the same time.

Life is so strange, thought Myrna, recalling the sad episode.

*

What to cook for her daughters came back to bug her. Pissed off at her every day annoying routine for the need to cook, she stood up, coffee in hand, and walked around her spacious sunny kitchen in deep empty pissed off mood. Finally, after innumerable loops of endless intentions, she decided that she would plan her menu as she shopped, later that morning, soon after her coffee, on her daily browsing of the supermarket aisles. It was too early after breakfast to start worrying about dinner for her two out of control daughters who pretended not to eat very much but ate everything they could forage in the house. Sometimes she felt like in the myth of the children eating the parents – or was it the other way around? Who the fuck cares about stupid myths? As if reality isn't disturbing enough, she sighed.

"I need some myths to push the loneliness out of my life," she continued talking to herself like she was nuts. "Maybe my daughters will eat me as well, and I can disappear from this dizzy boring life."

She puffed and puffed and walked the counted steps around her spacious home.

They are young and insatiable, easily persuadable by deceptive seducers of young girls sweet-talking them to have sex … these guys never think of marriage, only of sex, she rambled on without an ending.

"Idle cats lick their ass," she recalled her daddy saying.

Better yet, laughing to herself, she remembered her daddy also saying "When the Devil has nothing else to do, he fucks his own children."

*

When her dentist husband Phil lived with them, planning menus and cooking dinners were easy undertakings reminiscent of pioneering beef stew recipes that resided in Myrna's DNA. She loved cooking for him because he was always appreciative of her efforts. In her kitchen she felt like one of those master chefs that come on TV in the early mornings to share ideas with their friends at home about the day's meal. She was rich, but above all she wanted to be a good pioneering wife preparing meals at home.

Like unbelievable Rachel et al what's her name.

But cooking for two daughters, only, had become an annoying drag. Unlike her Phil, who had been easy to cook for, her daughters always complained of the meals she prepared for them. Duplicitously they complained after gulping everything down, though, admittedly, the menu had pretty much shrunk to half-cooked, white only no spices, chicken breasts, and supermarket pre-tossed spinach salads, and what's her name could go to hell.

Lazily and without aiming to, her mind wandered to recall Phil's favorite breakfast. It was a yawn, and she giggled at the thought. He would daintily scramble two eggs, sandwich them between two pieces of whole-wheat toast, with dollops of ketchup on top, and purposefully chew each byte slowly and deliberately unaffected by his wife's and daughters' presence at the table. She remembered how he would finish the ritual with a series of graceful sips of hot sugary decaffeinated coffee. He was a good simple man, quiet and shy, she now thought; but she still could not forgive him for so callously out-of-nowhere abandoning his family. Every time she thought of him, it pissed her off royally. It was beyond her how a guy like him, always exquisitely extending his little finger away from the rest, could father such beautiful daughters like hers, and then walk away.

She again filled her huge mug with strong black very hot coffee, which was the way she drank it now days, like her daddy, bitter and hot, and hoped that it wouldn't whack her too much. She drank the black coffee in a tenacious battle against her drooping ass and multi-folding layered waistline, and damn her high blood pressure. Not very elegant the way she drank her thick dark coffee without any sweetness. She didn't care; it was simply something to do to pass her indifferent day away.

From the kitchen window of her very expensive home, a gift from her All-American daddy, she could see the two tall palm trees, each inside the opposite corners of the privacy wall of her huge well-trimmed yard. They had been planted by her husband soon after their marriage. Growing powerfully straight and tall, they reminded her of her two daughters, especially in the spring. Like her beautiful daughters growing tall, the palm trees glistened in the morning sunlight as determined breezes swung them back and forth, and then straight up they stood to meet the blue skies and boundless heavens during the freshness of the day. The odor of the coffee and the thought of Justine and Meredith, the palm trees, and the brightness of the early Southern California spring morning mesmerized her. Everything in her back yard was in full blossom. Looking at her exquisite drooping racemes of sweet pea flowering in purples and pinks, and climbing wisterias against her privacy walls that were competing with the jasmine bushes for cover, brought smiles to her early morning still without makeup face. Like the cool fresh flowers of her garden, it was an attractive face, hardly touched by time even at forty two, she thought, imagining her lovely natural complexion that was emotionally reflecting the sentimental moment. She watched two blue jays fretting on her expertly trimmed green grass, dumb happy for the day's sun, and envied their untroubled life. A teal blue hummingbird implausibly weighed in the air, fluttered in and out of her red and yellow hibiscus shrubs, and tears came to her eyes, and she wished that she were twelve again. She loved her back yard and every day she would spend a lot of hours carefully cultivating its year round romance when not too busy daily tending to her two daughters and once upon a time to her husband's feeding frenzies.

She wiped the tears and went back to the kitchen table, took another sip of coffee, and thought how very much she loved her daughters. It suddenly occurred to her that her happiness was totally depended on them; a discomforting thought, but true. Maybe it was the idea of love that, out-of-nowhere, brought another flood of tears to her eyes. She put the mug of coffee down because she was trembling. She couldn't understand this sudden outburst of choke in her throat so early in the morning.

With her shaky hands she again picked up her mug, but the thought of one more swallow of black coffee made her want to vomit. She ran to the bathroom to splash some water on her face and when she looked in the mirror she became sickly aware of the many faint wrinkles on her throat and face. Those fucking wrinkles; they were there before but only as minor distraction, a dirty fake disturbance, a not so subtle sterility on the surface of life. Inexorably they showed their ugly shadows without pity.

Jesus, she thought, why so soon? Where does fucking time go?

She cried hard and wanted more time to flush out the tears but there was no more time to be had; she had to pull herself together to go do the day's grocery shopping. Trembling, she told herself that it was probably the strong black coffee, and too many cigarettes, and that maybe she should cut these out, but her mind revolted at the thought of growing old, of aging, and it made her cry even more.

"God forgive me, but I'm just not that old to have to give up everything. If I give up cigarettes and coffee, and doing my yard, and all these other little things in life, what's left?" she sobbed her getting older into her hands.

"I feel sorry for my daughters," she said out loud. "They don't know anything."

She filled her cupped hands with cold water and splashed it again on her red face. She cried a few more tears and stared harder at herself in the mirror, a wishful attempt to retrieve her not so long ago youth, but even that juvenile attempt at revival wasn't coming out right. Too vain, even in tears, the concern was more with the appearance than in the distressed sobbing, she had to admit.

When I have spent so many years carefully cultivating my back yard, why the fuck can't I be buried in it? Weird thought, she thought, but didn't care. After all, it was her well cultivated yard that she wished to be buried in. But not yet … too soon.

But who would buy it afterward; only her daddy could've sold such a melancholic piece of real estate.

Parents' gift houses are full of sounds and faces of dead people, mostly theirs, and their grandparents, and everyone else that had passed on their way to nowhere, always tripping you up with dead memories, she emptied her dark coffee in the sink rather inelegantly.

Burying herself in her back yard stopped the tears dead. The thought of death was a little too early in the day and definitely cheap melancholia, she concluded. She had a long life ahead of her and she wasn't going to be intimidated by the presence of a few stinking wrinkles. She put on a tight dress and went to the supermarket.

Chapter Four

Kitty was the oldest of the four friends by almost a year. Making up for the lead time which had begun to show itself grey, she dyed her hair pure yellow blond and didn't give a hoot that her hair did not match her brown eyes. Front-runner that she was, she loved the trendy contrast between her true dyed blond hair and her greenish light brown eyes because the clash, as she was fond of reminding herself, made her appear so much smarter. Like her hair, she exuded highlighted confidence. Fashion was her rage and she flaunted it. In spite of her small stature, five-four she would claim, she was fearless and wouldn't let anyone push her around. Yet, in high school, she was everybody's sweetheart. A loud minimalist in her style, she had an aptitude for winning people's attention with her large collection of colourful tight Brooks Brothers shirts that highlighted her magnificent tits and buttock hugging miniskirts. Everybody accepted her fanciful efforts, and she in turn loved everybody in kind, and made sure she never lied. It was beyond her vocabulary to say mean or ugly things, but she did love a good joke. She would never insult anyone's feelings and Christian-like she relished the moment of turning the other cheek. Even in high school, Kitty had happily fucked several men from various happenstances in her life; yet, she was the perpetual virgin who would always blush with the telling of a dirty joke. Her favorite song was "…touched for the very first time…" which she flirtatiously loved to sing to Sharon.

"Sharon, do you ever turn the other cheek for Hank," she would tease her friend.

She hid well her intimate affairs in high school, and never succumbed to a steady boyfriend, though she had no problem making out with dirty little boys even when she was wearing braces. She was very attractive by any measure, but her beauty registered imprecise by the damning expression, 'she's so cute', that hung like a cloud all around her. To be known as 'cute' was the bane of every girl in high school who wanted to get laid. Nobody took a 'cute' girl serious about wanting to get laid. So, she displayed a quirky personality that was inviting, appeasing all boys, and making it easy for them to think of her as a "good piece of ass." To Kitty, all the boys were comparably nice to lightly flirt with, in the hallways and classrooms but, when pressed to come clean, the only thing she wouldn't admit that she was slightly nympho and would laugh away that "all the boys were just nice boys, except one," she would giggle to her friends, and all knew whom she had in mind. All wished that a boy named Alex, who was on the wrestling team, might have been the one pinning her with a few crotch lifts because Kitty liked sports guys and she would always walk to physics class with him, but nobody knew for sure, and Alex did look like a dork. Among the four friends, it was common knowledge that Hank was corking Sharon, Myrna was always going steady with someone new, but none too serious, and there was faint suspicion that Robin might be a dyke. Kitty was beyond reproach; she was just too cute and nobody fucks 'cute'; she knew her grownup secrets were safe.

Although only five four, she had big breasts for her size and all the boys would talk and fantasize about playing with them, but Kitty was, naturally, very particular of the very few whom she had allowed to press against her breasts - female organs always prized by teen age boys. Those allowed to touch them were usually the star athletes of the school, and even Hank Merker had lifted them from behind a few times, in the presence of best friend Sharon, naturally. Neither of the best friends minded Hank cupping them because he was the star quarterback. Anyway, of all the boys, Hank did have huge hands and could easily fully cup them which made Kitty always feel full-sized excited. And when morality muddied her thoughts, she would tell herself, "What am I supposed to do with them? Hide them?"

"Stop that Hank; I've told you many times not to ever do that again," she would giggle her cute smile when they were in the presence of one of the friends.

After Hank and Sharon married, somewhat suddenly, thought Kitty, she had a long summer's sexual encounter with a married man whom even to this day she knew only as Ray, of Mexican or Italian descent, she wasn't sure. Ray, as she would demurely call him, was six four and all summer long he secretly fucked Kitty, away from her friends' possible reprimands, pretty much every day. Ray was a produce manager at the local Alfa Supermarket and got off early in the afternoon when he would pick her up and take her to a shithole motel owned by a friend of his. After that summer long fucking experience, there wasn't much that Kitty didn't know about fucking from all possible sides. She was giggly grateful to Ray whom she never forgot, though very indifferently she remembered him as her first full-time, substantial lover. One day, Ray, for some sadistic reason, directed perhaps against Kitty, or maybe against his wife, but known only to himself, or maybe not, insisted that Kitty meet his wife and his two children and he took her to his very nice homely house. The whole time that Kitty was with Ray and his family, that day, she had an uncontrollable desire to laugh, which she nervously did, impolitely every few minutes, throughout the uptight evening soiree. Later that night, when Ray was about to take Kitty home, she was approached by the wife who callously said to her, "I know my husband is fucking you, but I don't care."

"No hard feelings, but it's me who's fucking him," smiled Kitty.

Inevitably, after that celebrated evening with the family, Ray and Kitty parted company as dispassionately as they had met. After that practical satisfying affair, Kitty felt functionally adult happy, a ripe young woman, and no longer the childish, cute girl.

During those wonderful summer afternoons full of sex, she also enrolled for a summer session of Italian at UCLA. It wasn't that she was particularly fond of Italian but she had nothing better to do to pass the mornings away and Italian was the only freshman course that fitted her summer schedule. She found the sounds of the Italian language sensually melodic, like herself, and she decided to continue with Italian. Motivated for the first time, she enrolled full time for the fall semester at San Jose College to major in Italian.

"You are a natural with languages," said her young Italian instructor at San Jose who praised her as they huffed and puffed away on his bed, and he convinced her that she should take a trip to Italy, which she did the very next semester and almost never returned to the US. If it hadn't been for the memory of her three best friends she might have stayed forever in Italy.

"I didn't raise you to traipse around Italy, of all places," her father would write her, and threaten her with cutting off money. At one point he even funded a handsome young blue-eyed, blond, American young man to go to Italy and maybe persuade Kitty to return with him to Southern California. Unfortunately, by then, Kitty had gotten into the habit of Continental ease and she would laugh at everything not to her style or taste, and when she saw the young man get off the plane at Leonardo da Vinci at Fiumicino she laughed a little too much and after fucking him over a weekend, she quickly convinced him that he should return to California alone, without bagging her. This, however, did not stop her father from hopelessly continuing the practice of sending handsome young Southern California types to regain his daughter from the madness that had engulfed her to want to live in Italy instead of California. They were all handsome boys and she excitedly fucked every one of them before returning them to Daddy.

"There is a fortune to be made in herbal medicine, and this could only succeed in the US," he would beg his defiant daughter to come back home.

But Kitty had fallen in love with Italy, travelling throughout the medieval and classical sites, mostly from a base in Rome. She was a young woman on the make, and there is a direct relationship between the distance from home and the joys of love: she loved to walk the edge and thought herself invincible. It was the romance and familiarity of Rome that made it easy for her to cope after her hilarious divorce from weird, first husband Milton. For two full-fledged happy years she toured Rome and Southern Italy during which time she found solace from the guilt of straying away from home knowing that her best friend Robin had also made the decision to lose her way in the Peace Corps, drifting overseas for two years.

Kitty often thought of Myrna, and Sharon, and Robin while in Italy but the friendship that she once felt for her best friends had become a bit hazy and she often wondered whether it had ever been as binding as it once felt. Fucking her way to maturity with a variety of sun-burned Italian strangers, she no longer had those needy feelings that once touchingly felt that without her friends' friendship there was no meaning to her life. Being there, full of excitement, every breath she took of that eternal Roman Bernini air, energized every thought in her mind and every morning she longed to live on Italian air alone. She would have wonderful moments walking the glorious memories of sunny Italy, day after day, after day, and lost in her love affair with Rome she began to have doubts as to whether friends, or more accurately, best friends, were necessary for a happy life. Yet being typically a confused American, she couldn't quite reconcile her love for Italy for her love of Southern California; the schooled feeling of betraying America was always there driving her crazy with regrets. It wasn't her father that made her unable to get Southern California out of her mind, but the sweet enticement of once again fucking sterile Hank Merker, silly high school quarterback, the love of her life.

And then quite incidentally, like most single women travelling alone in Italy, she met her real true love. His name was Claudio Albiona.

*

At the age of twelve Claudio Albiona began scavenging through garbage bins and city dumps in Palermo, Sicily, for things he could sell, like aluminium cans and other metal scrap, to support his mother's booze and drug habits. Daily he searched through huge garbage heaps and found treasures, like not-so-used books, small saintly artefact, and discarded clothes that he could sell in the flea market. He was never finicky of the scrappy provisions dumped for him in the daily fresh piles of garbage. He had no regard for those who frowned on the scrap he gathered, which often times were enough to buy his mother polluted pills cheap off the street; poisoned stuff that kept her moaning at home instead of roaming the streets looking for tricks in the alleys of Palermo. Two years after he had quit school, nobody cared, his mother died of exhaustion, natural causes they said, but probably from the tainted ingredients in the adulterated pills that he lovingly provided for her.

Handsome Claudio, dramatically mysterious with his Nordic blond hair and blue eyes in a land of olive skins and dark hair, grew up with the reputation that he must've been the bastard son of some German tourist who had paid a few visits to his attractive poor mother, herself, a stray away from a humbled home. Disgusted at the profane indignities heaved by unkind people upon his mother, he refused to publically accept his good looks as an immoral encounter between his kind mother and some unknown Nordic.

One hot Sicilian summer's afternoon, at the ripe age of fifteen, though he looked much older, almost prime for his age, a not so young and a not so beautiful young Greek woman tourist, in her forties, who was sweaty hot, out of nowhere, paid him one hundred dollars to fuck her. It wasn't his first time at love, but it was his first money fuck behind an ancient ruin wall of an ancient Greek site.

"You're a Greek God," she said to him; words that imprinted hugely in his mind.

Alone in the abandoned ancient Greek ruins with her, out of sight, during that long hot summer afternoon that unfolded all over his sudden grownup innocence, she couldn't get enough of the boy; she clung to him all wet with ripe perspiration and dripping desires of aromatic, flavourful lust that he very much glad to be part of. She kept caressing his face and squeezing his muscular body between her legs, and he loved it. All afternoon she kissed him but all he could remember were her immortal words, "You're a Greek God".

After that happy summer chance encounter, and with 'you're a Greek God' always in mind, he accepted that he was good looking. Silently he thanked his mother's good looks that were a blessing to him, and though God only knew who his father was, but bless him too. He very quickly realized that women paid good money to fuck him. He was young and full of libido and his sun-burned muscular arms glowed under the hot Sicilian summer sun, and the durum wheat bread, dipped in extra virgin olive oil, that he daily ate. He rubbed his hands with sand to purposefully keep them rough the way his women liked them. He wore light blue shirts, and his pants and shoes were always pristine white; he was a proud rooster and all the hens around him were eager to be part of his roost. He was a strutting cock who quickly learned as a young man to easily satisfy two or three lays a day. His reputation as a lover hardened with each new rumour, and infirm husbands made appointments for their frustrated wives. It was also whispered that fathers had brought their not-so-pretty daughters to him. He was especially sympathetic to those semi-pretty girls who always came back for more, and to the silent loving daddies who dutifully paid the cost to see the happy smiles on their ugly daughters' faces.

By the time he was nineteen, Palermo had become too provincial for Claudio; there was no privacy to be had there; everybody knew him and the friends he kept, and he decided to move to Rome where obscurity was the norm and where there were a lot more women willing to pay a lot more money for his services. Full of expectations, he took the plunge and moved to Rome.

Unfortunately for Claudio, it was the wrong move: Rome was flooded with Romeos full of the cosmopolitan sophistication and neat unbuttoned good looks that he, the provincial, lacked in spite of his superior looks. His competition gigolos had the manners and the speech to go along with the name. More incredible, dark hair was the gigolo mode in Rome where thin-nosed Nordic blonds, both male and female, pursued their Mediterranean fantasies of their Scandinavian desires. Olive-skinned lust was on their pizza menu. For Claudio, it was the complete opposite of what he had known in Palermo. He tried his best to imitate the Med-dark competition, drank espressos, and took up smoking, open shirts loosely to the belly, but the experienced gigolos had a way of making their bullshit taste like gelato to their hungry Janes, and poor Claudio couldn't shed the hick. For five years he worked the side streets of Rome, mostly as a waiter in subdued trattorias, once in a while hitting on unfortunate middle-aged tourist women travelling on a budget. For a while he even learned to strum a guitar and play a grating version of *Yesterday*.

When he began to like his guitar he cried.

One lazy autumn afternoon, while hanging out in the Piazza Navona, he was approached by a pretty American young woman who offered him one hundred dollars. Holding hands they took a taxi to her hotel room at the Excelsior and she quickly undressed. She was petite but solid to the touch with perfectly well-defined legs that joined at an amazingly tight American well-fed ass whose dimpled lilywhite buttocks were made to withstand prolonged hard massaging. Her breasts were fabulous.

There were no moral dilemmas running interference in Kitty's mind that afternoon and throughout the whole fucking affair she said nothing, pretending fragility with her soft ah's, a super virginal tactic for a young woman fucking in a foreign land.

It was easy for petite Kitty to feign fragility.

"Is this your first time?"

"Yes," she lied, but who could tell, and Claudio didn't care.

When they were finished, they fell asleep next to each other.

She could not sleep. Exhilarated by his love making, she dreamed wide awake. She got up from their bed to better view him. He was a very handsome man and she thought she fell in love with him as he lay there naked.

She felt giddy and wanted to see her naked body now enveloped in the intimacy of the late hot Roman afternoon, and looking into the mirror she became aware of her splendid whiteness. There's nothing more alluring than the lustful body of a young white goddess, she thought and smiled at her image. She went back and lied next to lovely Claudio, her body glistening in a strong desire for more sex.

He was twenty three, and it was his first encounter with an American woman.

He's the dumbest fucking idiot I've ever met in my life, thought Kitty.

It was then that she decided to marry him and to hell with Milton and little Albert.

*

Her husband, Claudio Albiona, handsome Claudio to his friends, formerly the glory of Palermo, Sicily, and all of Italy, and currently the splendour of Los Angeles, ran a very profitable fast food and restaurant grease gathering and recycling service. It was a dirty job that few wanted to do but he accepted it as a blessing. He was good at recycling grease, like he had been good at recycling garbage. Thanks to Robin's father, banker Robert Sargent, who, at Robin's pleading, provided the initial loans, and Hank Merker from whom Claudio collected his restaurants' grease for starters, plus some quick and easy Sicilian, *una razza, una faccia*, influential connections, street wise Claudio in time came to manage an eighty percent monopoly on Southern California grease gathering business with a fleet of over two hundred trucks criss-crossing LA and Orange Counties. He made many friends in the restaurant business, including Hank Merker, who in addition to his restaurants, was also lovely Sharon's husband. Good looking Claudio did covet Sharon's body, and he still hid the Sicilian hick beneath his easy smile, but Sharon was never one to like pretty boys. So Claudio made easy friends with Hank and hopelessly kept a proper distance from the rest of the best friends. He liked them well enough but he was uneasy around Robin's amazingly stacked body, and he thought Myrna a bit weird; still, there was no denying all his wife's best friends' flawless beauty. It was always a pleasure being around them, especially distant gorgeous Sharon. The four best friends and their husbands would often get together at expensive restaurants and thanks to Claudio's connections, the treat was always on the house.

Kitty was proud of her handsome husband because in such a short time he had become very successful. It was a huge accomplishment and not just the usual success story of immigrant making good in America, though Kitty thought it incongruous that such a good looking blond-blue-eyed, tall, thin Italian should be involved in such a sticky, gooey business like collecting restaurant grease, wealth generating as it was. She would have preferred if Claudio had been a hedge fund manager, or perhaps in real estate, from maybe Oregon, or Massachusetts, but Claudio was as always well focused on a reality that made lots of money. The opportunity, greasy as it might have been, was all over Southern California and the ambition in Claudio easily cashed in on the American dream.

Easy enough, Claudio's street-wise innate marketing genius was soon evidenced in the Brentwood Village sixteen thousand square feet mansion that he and Kitty lived in, and in the numerous trips they took abroad, now rarely together. Their trips were anxiously awaited and bragged about, and when afterwards related to their friends, the adventures were full of sweet intrigues and discoveries, away from each other. As Claudio would laughingly boast about their separate trips, "I can't keep up with her anymore. She likes sightseeing everything, while I just like sitting around bars and cafes enjoying another beer with my Southern Comfort."

Such commentary usually embarrassed Kitty not because of their revelations but because country bumpkin immigrant Claudio thought he was being witty. Besides, how do you say "Southern Comfort" with a Sicilian accent?

"Not to worry, Kitty, nobody is really listening to Claudio," Sharon had once sarcastically volunteered for the whole gang. Sharon was always afraid to look Claudio straight in the eye so she made wicked little remarks about him while pretending she didn't care.

"He's so pretty," she would say, and all the friends would laugh with her sarcasm.

"He looks so much like a blond Marcelo Mastroianni," said Myrna.

"It's a lovely name Claudio, but Claudia is so much prettier, like Claudia Cardinale," sipped Robin past her martini. "It's not Cardinale, it's Martinelli … shit, who cares?"

"Isn't there some character name Claudio in some famous play," asked Myrna?

"Life is one surprise after another, a sunny country road full of new discoveries," Kitty would counter her husband's embarrassing accent with her own stories of "luxurious hotels" and "ill- mannered Negroes" all over the Caribbean who always looked like Harry Belafonte with strange fetishes. Her friends always blushed every time Kitty, speaking graphically under the influence, revealed each treasured insight; and they would all laugh, together, also under the influence. Mischievously she would then recount stories of her naughty Claudio's rogue confessions of his adventures while traveling abroad solo.

"He always travels to Cuba for the 'big-assed broads' and to the Philippines for 'the tight twats'," she would laugh quoting her husband.

There would be a brief hesitation between the extravagant stories she would relate about her Claudio, and an involuntary inflated giggle right after; and then, she would ask, of no one in particular, "Can you understand that?"

"She's such a tight ass," in the meantime, full of pride, Claudio would indulge his wit, jesting about his understated wife, to all the friends, in attempts at harmless humour.

"You mean anal, dear," Kitty would accommodate at her loving husband.

"That's right, Kitty, just like you and your son," Claudio would laugh faking naivety of language. His DNA was of ancient grandeur, and glorious blood flowed through his Sicilian veins, he was proud when need to be, forgetting the possible Germania connection. The ancient Greco-Roman link was the only thing that he never forgot. He was of splendid stock in spite of his blond hair and blue eyes and after his greasy success story the only sensation he felt when in the presence of his newly found friends was the ever-present desire to fuck Sharon.

Kitty's son, Albert, now in his early twenties, from a previous marriage to a college romance first lover, Milton, then, as now, a bipolar social worker, always recovering from barbiturate overuse. About the same time his father dropped out of everything, Albert, now somewhere in Oregon, had dropped out of college during his freshman year, and for several years had been working calving cows in a breeding farm in southern Nebraska.

"He's delivered thousands of calves by now," Kitty would applaud her son's audacious triumphs in a blush of self-deprecation.

Sicilian Claudio didn't give a shit about Albert but at the behest of his beloved Kitty he would splendidly provide monthly support "for the bastard" as he unkindly referred to Albert.

"Hell, we're probably eating one of his babies right now," Claudio had once insensitively shouted at a bar-b-cue affair and Kitty never again fed another straight line about son Albert and his line of work in front of her fucking dago gigolo husband.

"He had all the makings of a gynaecologist," Myrna had pretended sympathy and had picked up on Claudio's medleys of stepson Albert.

"Long, skinny arms perfectly suited for insertion up a cow's…"

"Shut up and go to hell, Robin," Kitty would feign anger at Robin.

"I feel sorry for the cows," said Sharon her sarcasm keen.

"No need to, Sharon, his arms are long with girth," Claudio hugged Sharon who sensed revulsion at the uninvited incursion.

"That's what Sharon meant, Claudio," said Phil.

What a jerk, thought Sharon.

Chapter Five

No wars occurred in California during the best friends four years in high school. Sharon, Robin, Myrna, and Kitty, the best friends forever, felt good about their lives though at times, like for all people, emotional disappointments would invade their days, often unjustly they would think. But because they had each other for support, gracefully they suffered the unfairness of social setbacks including the constant interference of familial crises that were always an embarrassment. Most importantly, there were the banalities and scandals of high school social gossip to be carefully avoided. Thanks to their determined love and friendship for each other, the best of friends had become impervious to even unfair prejudices from obvious rivals who ultimately registered as jealous annoyances. Their four souls had combined into one firm firewall, and aside from the usual teenage angst of crossing into womanhood, the four friends' friendship had matured as solidly and as satisfying as had their still girlish beauty.

Sharon felt the high school anxiety more than the others, unable to rid her mind of her parents' loveless union, but she hid her wounds in the love she found in her girl friends' arms. She knew she would never overcome her parents' stupidity for being what they were, and she wished they weren't so; and she thought that in time she might perhaps be able to forgive them and get over her secret despair. But that was far removed from the horror of being viewed as a geek in high school. All her effort was focused on being 'normal', just like everybody else.

The other three also felt their parents' meddling into their affairs, but noted it as normal. Myrna felt a bit slighted by her father during these years but then he had always slighted her, his son being a lopsided favorite. Robin adored her father because she thought she had to; after all, he did own a bank. Kitty's main concern, all her life, was that the boys wouldn't like her because she might be too short. She had a smile on her face all the time, and a tremendous need to be loved, something that had not been forthcoming from her parents' maternal and paternal instincts, which was ok with Kitty.

The girls friendship during high school reassured them that they weren't alone, that they had steadfast friends to confide in and share their anxieties, particularly when periodically hormonal disturbances of sexual tensions surfaced. But even for best friends, the sexual stuff had their own perverse discomfort, and often each of the girls went her private way. Rarely did they raise arguments of intellectual content during their periods because they couldn't count on the stable state of their mood swings; nobody wanted to pick a fight out of nowhere. But even innocent thoughts and talk about boys came under the heading of sexual activity, and no matter how close the friends had become, personal, opposite sex feelings were out-of-bounds, non-committal, neurotic secrets that simply could not be shared without the possibility of argument, which nobody wanted. Though they tried to be open and honest with each other, their secret desires sometimes clashed with their public displays, particularly about a boy that they all might have liked beyond the feelings of "he's cute."

"I think Darryl is cute."

"I guess you'd fuck anyone wouldn't you, Kitty."

"That is not fair; not just anyone!"

"What about Hank Merker?"

"Hands off Hank, Myrna. He's Sharon's boy."

"You can have him anytime you want, Myrna," and Sharon wished it, and meant it, and hoped it, but nobody would believe her.

"Do you think they go all the way," Robin would inquire Kitty, over the phone, about Sharon and Hank.

"Isn't obvious? I can even tell you every time they do it."

It was a game they played because they knew it all, though they pretended ignorance.

"She's such a tight ass," Kitty would say, and they would laugh.

"Sharon, what'd you think of anal sex?" Kitty had teased one time.

"I don't know, Kitty. Do you like it," Sharon would hit back.

"Bull's eye," Robin said.

"I don't, but Robin does," Kitty said.

"No I don't."

"So you've tried it. Who was the lucky guy, Robin? Does Daddy know?"

"It's probably with one of her daddy's vice presidents," and they would all laugh.

"I think she likes Mark more than Hank," over the phone hopeful Myrna would say to Robin who also couldn't understand what Hank saw in tight ass Sharon.

"Well, she is very pretty," Kitty would always remind the friends and do away with the jealous shroud that might hide conflict.

"Admit it, you like him too, and it shows," they would scratch each other.

Hank would be the touchy quadrangle topic of sexually annoying arguments between the high school friends that was to be avoided at all costs. Invariably, references to Hank made for unfriendly fears that might have led to revelations of true confessions of complex, or even sour psychological entanglements.

It was during their high school years that the best friends' natural urge for sex that the friends lost their holy virginity. As in times immemorial, it had to happen sometime, and in Twenty First Century America, Sharon, Kitty, and Myrna, but not Robin, were deflowered in the course of intense libidinous sensations that were part and parcel of Friday night high school dances. So powerful were Robin's feelings for Hank, that she preferred to stay away from the Friday night dances, rather than find herself in Hank's arms. For the rest of the friends, the desire for sex, free of STD, hygienic among neighbourhood boys and girls, who knew each other to the point of almost incest, did naturally rush the senses to find release among partners, who found love in each of his or her own conventional private fucking world, with the tacit understanding that all had to remain secret. Sometimes these secret affairs were nothing to brag about and they quickly dissipated after the first time; other encounters were such a conquest that they had to be shared, especially about boys on the varsity of anything. But unlike boys, bragging is rare among girls who rarely want to admit about unwholesome, amoral sex. Still, sometimes, for those that do not brag, the love and sex they find in high school does turn to lifelong sweetheart marriages.

None of the secrets held by the girls were so offensive as to be anywhere near offensive to their friendship. Such was their beauty that it multiplied when they were together and the attention they experienced, for being best friends forever, was almost as satisfying as their private fucking exploits. And when at last the senior prom came, there were very few secrets left between them, and they were ready for America's ultimate spring festival.

*

"Who you going to the prom with, Ord," yelled across the gym locker room Josh Keller the non-stoppable grinding muscular ape fullback on the Magnolia High Varsity Football Team. Jimmy Ord, the 300 lbs middle line backer didn't bother to respond knowing that Keller was an asshole trying to josh him.

"He's taking Connie Joye," said Mark Freeman, Hank Merker's trusted wide receiver. Mark was a good man, liked by all, both on and off the field. Most observers held that Mark had a good chance to make it into the NFL because rarely did he drop a football.

"She's a good kid, Jimmy," continued Mark to his affable teammate Jimmy Ord.

But everybody knew that Joye and Ord were a gross mismatch, she being only a ninety pound, five feet two "short stuff", which was what every one called her.

"Everybody is going to the Prom this year," said Josh. "It's going to be a blast this year. Who you taking, Mark?"

"I don't think I'm gonna go; no girl wants to go with me," said Mark with a grin on his handsome face.

"He's taking Sharon Langdon," somebody yelled from the other side of the lockers.

"You're crazy, if you think that. Everybody knows that big Hank has his hands all over Sharon," came the reply from the same side.

It was true, the whole school knew that Hank and Sharon were a serious couple and that it was a foregone conclusion they would be dancing together at the prom. And no one had to say it, but they all knew that big Hank would score that night, and that greased the way for all of them to do it too. The orgiastic festival would smell of wine and green grass as soon as the temple dance was over. All the pent-up excitement and familiarity of four years of high school would explode into lustful naughtiness on prom night.

*

"I guess we all know who's taking Sharon to the prom," said Kitty as the best friends were walking to school one bright morning. Wistfully, in the distance they could see the junior varsity team in spring training. Like the seasons, the endless list of super high school athletes just keeps on coming.

It was hard to believe that four years had gone by so fast. It seemed like yesterday, when they were giggly little girls on their way to becoming big girls. And for sure just before their senior prom, just before their high school graduation, they were mature, serious girls.

"Who you going with, Robin?" said Kitty.

"I don't know," said Robin. "Mark Freeman asked me but his heart didn't seem to be in it. So I don't know."

"He'd be a good fuck, don't you think so, Robin? He's a momma's boy, good looking, and you seem to like those types," said Kitty.

"Kitty, is that all you can think about? If you think he'd be a good fuck, you fuck him," said Robin.

"What did you tell him, Robin?" asked Sharon, thinking that it would be great to double with Robin and Mark. She had been nervous, full of apprehension, she didn't want to be alone with Hank on prom night.

"I told him I'd think about it," said Robin.

"Please, please, please, say yes," begged Sharon trying to be pleasant without showing uneasiness. She wanted to double, which normally wouldn't have been unusual, but a bit strange for a prom night.

"Relax, Sharon; it's not like any of us is still a virgin," said a confident Kitty.

"I know you're not," said Robin.

"I know you're not," said Kitty.

"Kitty's right," said Myrna, "this prom shit is overrated. Maybe a hundred years ago our grandmothers would have been full of trepidation at the prospect of maybe being deflowered on a park bench but we all know what it's all about and if you want to know my opinion it's no big deal. It's all a slip-slop …"

"Myrna, are you still going steady with Ronnie?" asked Robin wanting to move on, away from sudden unpleasant discharges.

In the old days princesses pretended to be deflowered when the occasion called for, especially when they had already been deflowered.

"Yes, and he's asked me to the prom and I've already accepted. I know he's not a super football jock like you guys like, but I think he's very handsome, and he's very sweet. Did I tell you guys he's been accepted to Johns Hopkins? He's going into pre-med, he says."

"Well look at you," said Kitty. "Girls, our Myrna is going to marry a doctor."

"Probably a proctologist," said Robin, and they all laughed.

"Fuck you, Robin," said Myrna feeling good.

"Who you going with Kitty?" asked Sharon.

"Well, I was gonna keep it a surprise, but Josh Keller asked me and I said yes," said Kitty. "He was so sweet and so nervous when he asked me."

"Kitty, he's gonna rip you apart. The guy has a reputation for being an animal," said Sharon, good-humouredly.

Josh was six-three and Kitty barely five-four.

"That's what you think," said Kitty.

*

Sharon Langdon and Hank Merker were married two months after their high school prom. During the last quarter of her senior year Sharon experienced a series of gastrointestinal disturbances that medical treatment could not alleviate. Doctors couldn't find any physical damage and Sharon understood that her problem was emotional. She didn't say anything to her parents or friends thinking they would think her wacko, but she did find some comfort in being with Hank. Her pain would subside while making love to him and she persuaded herself she could find remedy in a life with Hank. Well aware of her parents' unhappy marriage she nonetheless decided to hold her nose and risk it. She had read in some magazine that life is a series of repeated patterns which scared the shit out of her because she simply couldn't stomach being like her mother. Still worse, the prospect of an obnoxious continuation of the familiar high school fruitless days led her repressed mind into the prospect of a similar future full of fear and uncertainty, like her mother's. During moments of neurotic clarity she saw her life filled with psychosomatic disorders provoked by sad-sack images of her mother. She thought she could break the pattern with Hank. Her mind convulsed like her stomach when she sought relief in the arms of the man who had raped her.

The decision to marry was viewed as barely this side of common law marriage since her heart really wasn't in it. The two of them swore eternal union at Sherman Oaks City Hall with Hank's best buddy Mark Freeman being the best man witness to the signing of the civil ceremony certificate. Honeymoon was a night at the Van Nuys Village Motel where they also had lobster and fillet mignon for dinner in the proud presence of a perspiring bottle of Moet Champagne. After a bashful dinner with Mark, the newlyweds went to their room to "fuck our brains out", was the way they worded it, and best man Mark gave them his blessings. Whereas ages before, the night of the wedding might have been a sacred time of miraculous discovery for bride and groom in the presence of gods and angels to witness and chant the consummation of breaking the hymen, there were no rituals or mysteries to be had that night and even the fucking was just a formality. Years later, reflections on her wedding night always transported Sharon to memories of her prom night which in her mind had registered as her real wedding night.

As was the thing to do, Sharon had formal sex with Hank during the night of the prom. It was formal because Hank wore a tuxedo and Sharon a lovely pink gown. It's a sign of our times that most high school kids have had sex often more than once by prom night. Unlike years before, the enthusiasm now days is somewhat subdued because the sex is all too familiar. Still, there is something special about having sex on prom night, the boys being formally dressed in tuxedo and tie and the girls beautiful in their gowns; it's almost like a prelude to the wedding that's not far off into their future. The anticipation of the occasion, with proud parental approval, induces powerful shameless appetites for lustful sex the moment the corsage is neatly pinned on the breast of the girl, very carefully not to prick her, right there, in front of mom and dad. It is a magic moment of daddy pride, of pretence that his daughter is still a virgin, though mother knows better, as he approvingly takes the unforgettable photo that signals to his little girl that it's ok for her to fuck that night. Plump, skinny, tall, short, pretty, not so pretty, smart, dumb girls, they all get daddy's tacit approval to fuck on prom night. It would be naïve to think that daddies don't know what happens on prom night; as naïve as not knowing what happens on honeymoon night. It's understandable, then, why tears are sometimes shed as the dainty daughter walks out of the house in her expensive gown holding her beau's hand. You can prick me all you want, she smiles at him as he gently pushes the corsage against her swelling breast.

The pinning of the delicate corsage rushes in colours that make all girls feel that their favorite fantasy is about to come true. They will make love that night and the delicate corsage will be crushed beneath the weight of all those years of waiting to be fucked without guilt. And what is true love but the feeling of doing it for the first time every time you do it.

No male, least of all Hank, could have resisted Sharon's smile, or face, or her perfectly pinned breasts, or, in brief, her whole God-given rose-lovely-in-the-June-moonlight seventeen year old breath-taking body that night, even though her father hadn't taken any photos, and the only thing her mother had said to her daughter was, "Be careful, and don't come home too late", as if she didn't know.

The exit scene from the Langdon house, as Hank led Sharon to their prom, had all the distasteful force of two young people bound in tragedy. Sharon's heart and mind were in her stomach; events were proceeding with the fury of all the fears now storming her insides. Incoherent prompts to protest blocked all thoughts of reason for Sharon who felt that pockmarked Hank was dragging her to a huge despair. A clamorous plea between her ears screamed for her to drop her hand from his and to turn back and go home. More than ever, that prom night, as they were walking hand in hand to his car, she had come to despise silent, Hank, the man who had raped her times before, and she wanted to scream to him, "Go fuck yourself" and start all over. Like the bride who changes her mind as she walks to the altar, she wanted to rip off the corsage and turn away, but there were no guests to cheer her on. The distance from her porch to Hank's car seemed unforgiving and all the time the idiot had this twisted smile and bulging eyes grossly disproportionate to the rest of his face, like an exaggerated cartoon out of Loony Toons. She felt faint and looked back to catch a glimpse of her parents but all she saw were dark windows. She lifted her gown and got in the car away from Hank who reached and squeezed her breasts.

Throughout the evening Sharon became more and more despondent as the night of pretended ecstasy proceeded. She acutely realized, on that prom wedding night, that Hank was the wrong guy to permanently commit her body, soul, and mind. Despairingly Sharon felt sure of this, she had no doubts, and she didn't want to do it, though it would not have been possible now alone with him, nor for the first time, but what else could she have done when everyone else was doing it in formal attire? On the other hand, Hank had no idea what Sharon was thinking that prom night, and more importantly, he didn't particularly care as he groped time and again for Sharon's unbridled breasts. Even as they were copulating, the love that Sharon was desperately looking for behind her tightly shut eyes was that of the boy on that field trip of long ago whose dreamy, wonderful translucent smile did gently surfaced in spite of hurried Hank's powerful attacks of incomprehensible humping in the back of his dad's Buick.

What was his name? She reached again and again to remember, still with her eyes closed while Hank unloaded away; such a beautiful, tantalizing face, irresistible, she found all the comfort in that smile. She kept her eyes closed during her prom night and all she wanted to do was to just keep looking at that beautiful boy. Unlike growling Hank's, the boy's face was an unblemished miracle, its presence so much more powerful than any prom reality during the various climaxes of the horrific night. Unbeknownst to Hank, on that prom night, and forever and ever after, he was indeed, at best, a depressing second choice.

*

If untimely independence from home and mother comes with anxiety for many young women, the possibility of no marriage frightens them into panic. This is especially true when there's unhappiness at home; then, it truly becomes difficult to think straight about what's best for you. Regardless of your home setting, when you finish high school, you're supposed to be some kind of an adult making serious decision about your future. For a high school graduate, single girl, very few things are more serious, more adult like, than the constant brooding over marriage possibilities. For many, marriage is a more important preoccupation than even college, or a career, or just a job. It's well known that parents often send their daughters to college not for a degree but for a husband; and sadly, forced to become a waitress condemns a young woman to a life of groping by insensitive greasy owners. For Sharon there was no dilemma about degree or husband: she knew where to get the husband. She wasn't sure if he was the best of choices, but then, really, what choice did she have?

Shit! Marry Hank, and be like my mother, or wait for my boy-man who most likely will just forget to show up in time for the wedding. Or maybe I could get a job as a clerk at some bank or supermarket, and pass my days away waiting for the weekend happy hour; or marry one of the Kennedys, Sharon would ponder the night away trying to reassure herself that miracles do happen.

Deluded by fears of loneliness, she made the furtive decision to marry Hank Merker and not go to college. The less than loving union was further sealed when Hank was denied a football scholarship at San Diego State, thus crushing him to East LA Junior College. Ironically, there was comfort in the thought that they were playing in an even playing field now: no huge expectations for Hank; both were equally losers. Disillusioned, they put up with each other knowing that neither of them had on advantage over the other.

It was a huge setback for Hank, from the high school days of glory and a promise of a possible NFL career, to the lowly East LA Junior College; the disappointment slowly seeped throughout his body emotionally numbing him. Events nowhere near his expectations, he dropped out of East LA, and after months of drooling over his past glories, he borrowed money from his father, who had been supporting him all along, and bought a pizza-by-the-slice, hole-in-the-wall carryout near an East LA high school. It was a dump sold to him by a run-away Mexican immigrant for two thousand dollars. He was barely making it when out of nowhere the high school was converted into a community college that stayed open till ten pm with many more hungry students taking night courses after work. In attestation to the free market forces, and the many hungry undergraduates, at the encouragement of a friend of his father's, he introduced Italian Beef and Italian Sausage sandwiches that immediately became a huge success. Unexpectedly, he quickly made a killing grossing hundreds of thousands of dollars within a year. Over the next few years, in a chain reaction, one fast food place led to another of several beef and sausage franchises throughout LA high schools and colleges, and very quickly lucky-in-love Hank became very rich. With a newly discovered entrepreneurial savvy, and a little investment capital and consultation from Robert Sargent's Pioneer Bank, thanks to the intervention of Sharon's best friend, Robin, Hank soon moved upscale to expensive 'downtown' restaurants and luxurious suburban homes.

Unhappily, as fast as Hank's investment restaurants were reproducing, Sharon wasn't. To her great grief she was diagnosed as incapable of getting pregnant due to an infection she had contacted sometime in her youth, probably from Hank, she had concluded, very likely on that fateful prom night, or maybe in that boys' locker room. There had only been Hank, she couldn't believe her great misfortune. Such was the blow of her great miscarriage in life that Sharon cursed unfeeling fate that had brought such sorry fulfilment to a beautiful body such as hers. One man, for goodness sake! Nature had been kind in its promise to beautiful Sharon, but most heartless in denying her a baby. Deep in her saddened heart she found only guilt that she had somehow, sometime sinned against the Lord who was not being very merciful in her need. It should have been Hank who should have been punished with not having babies, but as far as she knew, he was probably having all kind of babies with all those young bimbo waitresses shoving their round asses on his lap.

It would have been a most beautiful baby, in spite of Hank's pock face, Sharon would cry in silent anguish.

Nothing after that clinically diagnosed barren day had any real meaning for her.

Long were the days and longer the nights that followed in familiar long silence between Sharon and her husband. Nothing that poor Hank did would provoke any reaction from her. No asides, no diversions, no digressions were to be had from his lovely wife in life. Finally, Hank lost interest in screwing beautiful but emotionally barren Sharon and sought relief in "…other fish in the ocean…" as he would periodically remind Sharon who would laugh at the metaphor. During those long intervals of non-intercourse, she surprised herself at the liberation she felt from being unchained from dumb Hank. With ambivalent feelings she accepted the dark pleasure of separation, a most personal private affair, which was her empty marriage of no love. There was no love and no baby which might have been God's testament to their love. In a most mindless leap, in time, she found salvation in her bareness believing it to be God's way of demonstrating His presence to her. Here was the revelation that one needs nothing more than God in his or her life. And only God knew what the future would bring. At last, she understood that like her mother she too was destined to be alone. With distaste she had come to rejoice the physical and emotional divorce from her tongue-tied husband. The separation was not total because they continued to live openly together and once in a great while they would also have a bout of old-time sex. She blamed their odd moments of marital intimacy on the ferocity of the sun's hot light which, as it did to the birds, bees, and weeds in springtime, also made her temporarily receptive after the many months of vindictive abstinence. But there was nothing more to their coupling than some leftover splenetic grind of primitive instinct, a mere pointless remnant of the menstrual female. Not even the hot sun, thank You Lord, could warm her or her husband to any prolonged amorous sensitivities, and their temporary intimacy would numbly subside to its customary everyday back to emptiness. Other attempts at reliving the once animated memories, like conversation with her not too bright husband, ended as they began: with grunts, and long passages of time, on both sides of the bathroom.

But then, who could figure the ways of the Lord, Sharon's thoughts slowly began to flow into her passion. Only He, in His infinite wisdom and compassion, only He knew why He had brought the two of them together in an anaesthetized marriage. In the matter of her dead marriage, she had put her faith in the unquestioned wisdom of the Lord.

Thanks to the presence of the Lord now in her life, the estrangement from her husband had become a no big deal to Sharon. Thanks to the variety of painless tranquillity readily available, she found easy comfort in the abundant prescriptions conveniently affordable at any drugstore. Happily she had discovered uppers and downers in a vast selection of pharmaceuticals that make possible an infinite number of doors to a variety of realities and perceptions. It was easy to subscribe to the seductive little pills' invitation that any marriage, or lack of, or any relationship, was just another door to another perception, within another relationship in an ever repetition of unending ceremonial days. Everything was meant to be. It was senseless to suffer pain, from whatever the source, when relief was a short reach, now and forever, amen. And every time she reached into her medicine cabinet to find cheer, she demanded the relief to be immediate, with one pop of a pill after another. Faithfully, she would walk the valley of darkness alone with her pills and her Lord.

> *"Now, and forever, and from all ages to all ages,"*
> *"Amen."*

Now and a painless forever were to be found within the arms of the medicine man, and the greatest of pharmacists was Jesus, Sharon felt reassured. In the house of the Lord where Jesus caressed away the pain with a medley of pills and prayer, she prayed and wished for the painless day to come while she was still young. She didn't want to grow old in pain, O Lord, for she knew that without her youth and firm looks, there would be only pain. And in her melancholic prayers she would ask herself, where was there sweet love for her. There were many pills and just as many prayers but no soothing love except in that long ago memory of that beautiful boy on the fieldtrip bus.

Chapter Six

"Are we going to have food today or shall we stick to our neat martinis?" said Robin.

"I'm gonna have a burger with my martini," said Kitty. "They have great Angus burgers here, even though they're a sushi bar."

"You're such a little pussy, Kitty," said Robin.

"Kitty, did you know that in England old ladies are called pussies?" said Myrna.

"Up yours, Myrna. I don't want to get plastered again," said Kitty. "You can have that sushi shit if you want. That goes for all of you. I want some good American beef."

"You mean like Claudio," said Sharon, and they all laughed.

"Did I offend my little pussy willow," said Robin. "Pussycat, pussycat, I love you … my little puss, pussy, pussycat, pprrrr."

"Keep it up my little bird Robin and I'll eat you up, right now, meow" purred Kitty.

"This conversation is getting too dirty," said Myrna, as she took her place at the table.

"They're just talking about pussies, Myrna," smiled Sharon.

"Sure they are, and any minute now they'll start licking each other," laughed Myrna.

"Get your mind out of the gutter, Myrna," hissed Robin.

"She meant 'licking' as in 'scratching'," laughed Sharon.

"Screw that shit. Let's have a drink," said Kitty.

It was a fifteen minute drive from UCLA to Sooky's in Santa Monica where the four friends periodically met for lunch and a few martinis. Sooky's was a regular hangout for the best friends and the management there always welcomed them because the girls were heavy tippers. In return the four friends made it a point to look stunning in their expensive fashions and they succeeded every time. There was a glow to their high cheekbones after a martini or two and they loved the warm effect on their boobs. They crossed their fabulous legs this way and that way, always a bit exposed away from the salmon coloured table cloth, and their mood was relaxed, receptive to easy talk; their eye makeup never smeared, and their nail polish never faded, because they were the best of friends, stretching all the way back to middle school. The aroma of their expensive perfume ostentatiously mingled with the virile taste of the vodka sweetening their words that euphoniously rolled out of their artfully painted lips.

As Claudio had noted to Kitty one night about the four best friends, "You all have libidinous lips," and she smiled a luxurious smile.

"You can go without marriage, or justice, or honor, but friendship is indispensable to life," gently quipped Myrna as she quietly tipped another long stem to its bottom.

"Do it again, Myrna," said Sharon, and they all laughed.

They were used to the vodka. It would take quite a few martinis over a few hours to get them over the hump that reached beyond feeling.

"Friendship is the cornerstone of society. In friendship there is universal warmth," slurped a joyous Kitty.

"This is what's happening here," said Sharon. "When women can't have an honest relationship with men, they pour their hearts out to other women."

They all looked a bit annoyed at her. The observation was unnecessary, too close, much, much too close to sobriety, draining the sunny afternoon of the jibe that called for a lot more handsome well chilled martinis.

"Words without vodka are never enough," sneered Myrna and signalled for another round of clean vodka martinis.

"It's unnatural to go without men," Robin hid a slight slur beneath a deep sigh. "It's in the risk of being denied that the sweetness of love lies," she quickly recovered.

"Great emotions are felt only in the fear of betrayal by men," sighed Sharon who then gulped down her chilled vodka, her rosy cheeks matching her violent lips.

"What the fuck is going on here?" said Kitty as she slurped another huge bite into her bloody thick Angus burger. "Let's all get serious and enjoy our drinks as we discuss current events according to the UN."

"Good one Kitty. The UN is an American joke," said Robin, recalling her Current Events, Middle School editions.

The martinis were having their congenially rosy effect. Amusement was everywhere, kind of dull present, but after a couple of vodkas, Grey Goose, please, it was not unusual for the Sooky skies to get a bit foggy. There had always been ample informality between the friends and there was never any need to wean fucking words. They had become accustomed to the sound of their voice and words and there was no need to search for meaning. So they talked to each other with the ease of children: every empty thought was permissible because they weren't there to solve the world's problems.

"Kitty's right," said Myrna. "We all know and we all like a good lay. I mean a good man; and what's a better lay than one with a friend? We all would like to share a friend … and that's damn good friendship. Who among us wants to fuck an enemy?"

"Say what you mean, Myrna," Sharon tossed down another one.

"She's right, Sharon. Let's all fuck our friends. Nobody wants to fuck her enemy?"

It must have been Kitty.

"There's many ways of fucking your enemies, but only one way of fucking your friends," said Sharon who was beginning to lose her sense of humor.

"The problem with American high schools is there are few true friendships …"

"You are so right, Sharon," interrupted Robin. "In Ethiopia there are true friendships there because all the people there are friendly and they fuck each other without guilt."

"Above all, friendship is a racist class line," Myrna came back strong.

"Four coffees black," said Sharon to the waitress.

"What do you mean, Myrna? I'm really curious. I've never heard you speak about race," said Robin who was pissed at Myrna's sudden interest in race and sociology. She looked probingly past the long stemmed glasses into Myrna's words.

"You especially know what I mean, Robin," she smiled, and there was a sharp tone to Myrna's voice that the friends rightly understood as unnecessarily aggressive.

"What's up Myrna? Don't hold back," said Robin.

"You know, many white girls might have relationships with other classes or other races but rarely, if ever, do they have true friendship like ours, because we're alike," responded Myrna. "In all truthfulness I don't think that I could have a true friendship with a girl of a different race. What would we talk about?"

"What about a man of a different race, Myrna? Do you think you could find something to talk about with an African-American male, for example?" said Robin.

"I know white men find a lot to talk about with black women," smiled Sharon.

"I know you do, Robin," said Myrna.

"You're pathetic, Myrna. The least you can do is pretend, like the rest of us."

It was too much for Robin who quickly shook off the vodka. Once again Ethiopian memories now rotting quietly in the background of her unforgiving mind released their stink. How could she befriend a person like Myrna who had such racist thoughts?

Suddenly the air conditioning in Sooky's felt frigid. There was a definite break away from the teddy bear hugging friendship of moments earlier. It was one of those sobering moments that once traversed could never be recalled regardless of remorse or regrets. Myrna, with her racist remarks, had overstepped the bounds of polite familiarity, even for best friends, and everyone there knew it; but she was tired of the baroque bullshit that all these years had passed for friendship; tired of relationships that could not withstand the adult sorrowful cries of rage. She didn't care; all good things have to come to an end sometime, she felt the moment's rage, and screw Robin and her African friends. There was no turning back; there was truth in the clarity of vodka. Flashes of her pain confused her personal misfortune amidst the runaway celebration. It was no use; the dam had burst; she was in no mood to plug up the hole with more social lies. She sipped her martini and all her best friends for a minute melted out of sight.

*

After her husband Phil had left her, (out of the blue; it was thought he had gone and joined some monastery in Illinois), she was no longer thrilled. She no longer had the dedicated desire to meet with her friends and partake in the weekly gin and vodka pickling that passed for renewal of girlhood friendship. Down, down, down, she went.

The departure of her husband had been a personal funeral for Myrna. She briefly thought of suicide but knew she was made of weak stuff and what would her friends have said: that she was a wretched coward, and rightly so. Ironically, she found warped comfort in the thought that there might have been another woman in her Milton's life. It would have shown her friends that she had been married to a stud who sought out women, but she quickly remembered that Phil was simply a two-faced weasel, and that nobody who knew him would have believed the stud story. She could not suffer her snake-in-the-grass husband's deceit even to her close friends. The shame of having to continuously make excuses as to why her rat husband had left her had become vile gossip in the mouths of all who at one time or another had envied her. The bastard monk Phil didn't deserve the cover of depressing excuses.

Actually, she didn't know why he had left her; to be a monk of all fucking things.

"It's got nothing to do with you," he had said huffing and puffing on his way out.

It was an ugly thing to say and an uglier thing to do, and it hadn't stopped ringing lily-livered loudly in her head from the day the shithead left. It was a miserable explanation, "it's got nothing to do with you." More for left-over conversation, with her friends, who most respectfully had found Phil's abrupt departure most intriguing.

"So, why did your Phil leave you?"

"It had nothing to do with me."

She would seek no pity, make no apologies about her despondency, and she would accept no patronizing bullshit, ever, from her three more fortunate, still married, friends! No more commiserations about bad luck and fate, no more feelings of rejection, no more pretended humiliation from the loss of a weasel, for Myrna, she after a few martinis at Sooky's she then resolved to drop out of all the piss-eyed glaring bullshit society that sadly included her long-time best friends.

Fooling herself to a solitude away from people, to be left alone to her own coping, not to be disturbed by unhappy thoughts, Myrna initially found comfort in unrequited fantasies; she went from one to two packs a day, and drinking endless cups of dark coffee to wash down the tar in her mouth, but most appallingly, she also took up drinking excessive amounts of gin daily. The gin was warm and relaxing and had the agreeable effect of emptying her previously complex life to its bare social necessities.

"It's either gin or gardening, and I say fuck gardening," she would say to herself after an early couple of gins minus the tonic.

*

Sitting at Sooky's with her friends, somewhat inattentive to what she had been thinking, not caring about her friends chatter, the sole concern that had remained a constant in her mind that afternoon that had started out with pleasure, and being a single mom, was whether her two beautiful daughters were still virgins, though, being a woman, and having been there, her daughters' virginity was not a particularly heavy complication to her presence this vodka amiable afternoon with her friends. In her moments of booze clarity, 'they have to get fucked sometime', was a truth eternal. To be sure, she was motherly curious, but she didn't particularly care to ask.

"They have to fuck sometime," out of nowhere, she loudly announced to the friends in Sooky's, and Robin opened her eyes wide and forgot her anger.

It was an embarrassing moment for everyone, especially for the smiling Mexican busboy bringing the black coffee.

"Myrna, be nice," said Sharon. "After all, the good Lord doesn't object to fucking. I know and I can assure all of you, if you don't fuck here and now on earth, you'll never fuck in Heaven."

It was nice to have Sharon around because with one ridiculous comment she equalized everything. And the girls laughed in an attempt to regain the happy hour feeling of pre-Myrna sulking moments earlier.

"Give me a break," insisted Myrna, almost looking for a fight. She didn't like Sharon's easy drunken fancy always turning toward religion. "I believe in Jesus and Santa Claus like anybody else, but beyond the seven day prologue to the grand opus everything else is beyond reason. Let's face it, it's all a mirage."

"Well, I too grew up without religion," Kitty tried to tone down the turbulence which was now violently churning Myrna's stomach, "but sometime during my life, I opened up to Jesus and the rest; and good or bad, I'm now a believer. It's nice."

"Good or bad, or neither good nor bad, that's the way it is," said Robin, who showed great restrain in not taking offense at Myrna's earlier attack, one way or another.

"What does she mean by seven day prologue?" Sharon asked.

"She means in the beginning," Robin volunteered, and then, "...oh screw it."

"Don't mock the Lord, Robin," said Kitty.

"The Lord is within everyone's grasp after a few martinis," said Robin, blinking her eyelids in Hollywood fashion.

"'I believe in every drop of rain that falls, a flower grows, a flower grows ...,'" Kitty light-heartedly tried again.

"Lucky for Eddie," Myrna cynically reminded Kitty, "and not so lucky for sometimes dopey what's her name."

"You mean Liz or Debbie?"

"Like there's a difference?" Kitty pretended to be Jewish.

"We'll have an eternity to stuff ourselves with spiritual love, but right now let's drink to carnal love, the way the good Lord meant it," said Sharon, which was unlike her.

Probably the Grey Goose, they all thought.

As if from some unconscious world, Sharon was suddenly overwhelmed by a mental infatuation of an image, an illusion, of beautiful Justine. It was pure magic.

What beautiful young breasts, and that perfectly firm ass, she secretly thought of Justine to herself, troubled that she wasn't getting it right. Alone for one moment away from the friends, she imagined Justine bare assed and bare chested. Sharon's face glowed with the same tint as she fantasized Justine's ass. It was a glow that unglued Sharon from her friends.

Robin was the only one to perceive the strange fixation in Sharon's eyes. For some time now she had noticed that Sharon out of the blue would become quietly removed from them. She didn't care what the others thought of her and she spoke her slow mind as though she were in a prolonged dull-witted state of psychosis. Her eyes seemed to slowly drill into a distant space giving a dispirited sense of other worldliness. There were too many Biblical references carefully dressed as insights during her hypnotic states. Inhibitions, once Sharon's hallmark, had slowly given away to pulpit like commands and weird repetitive pronouncements of hearty events and truths to be recalled from some distant era in the mind.

"To think that you know yourself is the same as self-deception," said Sharon still focused on the holy Justine icon.

"Or delusional when you begin talking to Jesus and he to you," said Myrna.

"Your personality is pretty much arrested in adolescence, either in junior high or high school, when you're told to educate yourself to be what you will become for the rest of your life," continued Sharon, smiling for relief from Myrna.

"I agree with you, Sharon," said Robin. "Our corruption started in junior high."

"I don't feel corrupted," said Kitty. "Do you Sharon?"

"Especially for young girls," said Myrna, her tortured mind always on her daughters.

"Well, they say that education is the process of denouncing pleasure and happiness," said Kitty. "So, until we do that, I suppose we're all corrupt."

"I wonder what people are saying about us now," said Robin.

"Well, Robin, people will always talk about us but who cares anyway," said Kitty.

"No, I mean people will say about us that even though we're privileged, still, we've no careers, no children, nothing to show. Other women become doctors, lawyers, architects, yoga instructors, or even whores; but not us; we're nothings," summed Robin.

"Well, being nothing might be something sayeth the Buddha Sharon," said Myrna. "Anyway, we're happier than most."

"Other women drop out of careers to have children, but not us … we're barren," continued Robin.

"Speak for yourself," said Myrna.

"Look at it this way, Robin, no one can accuse us of having it all," said Sharon.

"Hell, we do have it all," said Kitty. "Rich young husbands, above all our friendship, which makes us well connected all the time – what do you mean not having it all, Sharon?"

"But we should have had children, if not careers," said Robin.

"Yes, women are supposed to have children, otherwise they're not natural," said Sharon, sensing a familiar melancholia invading her heart. It was difficult to tell whether she was playacting in front of her friends, or she really felt the loss.

"We're screwing up somehow, but not because we're not having children," said a thoughtless Myrna who, unlike Sharon and Myrna, did have two beautiful daughters.

"To that having it all, don't forget to add ageing skin, alcoholism, and divorce," said Sharon who was beginning to feel aggression towards Myrna whom she thought dishonest.

"You're right Robin. Let's face it, no career means never having amounted to much," said Kitty. "We've never had to toil for a personal sense of accomplishment, which is a lot different than simply inheriting the wealth."

"No children, no maternity leave for Dave, no school plays and parties," laughed a faux wistful Robin.

"I say screw the children and careers; just give me my caveman quarterback," jeered Sharon and the friends were lost in her irony.

"Without the children who will take care of us when we're old," said Myrna.

"You're kidding, Myrna," said Sharon. "Our money will take care of us much better than our children; just like we take care of our parents," and again everyone laughed knowing that the money had come from the parents.

There was silence. It was the silence of truth, the time to recharge.

"Suppose one of us found out that the other is fucking her husband. For example, you, Robin, fucking Hank; would that stop you from being friends with Sharon," said Myrna.

"Bullshit, Myrna. We're not capable of adultery; we're not sexual adventurers; we're not promiscuous predators, we're nothing," said a wound up Robin.

"We blur the line between sex and friendship," said Kitty out of nowhere. "Sex for us is an expression of affection and of eternal friendship, and must be kept private."

It was Kitty at her best: lovely words meant to reconcile but only in her mind.

"Is that what Claudio tells you," said Sharon, "that he keeps it private?" and everyone had a hardy laugh again at Kitty's expense for surely this time everyone understood the irony in Sharon's words.

Kitty didn't mind because she truly loved her friends.

"He tells me that we all want to be loved by all and not just by friends; which I really don't understand what he means, but I do love him a lot," said Kitty.

"Well, are we lovers or just friends," asked Sharon.

"The blurring of friendship and love allows us to be friends forever," smiled Robin. "Like flirting, there's always some sex involved in friendship."

"Some people can't separate sex from friendship," said Myrna, the beloved.

"We should intensify our friendship by having sex with each other," said Robin.

"Including our husbands," said Myrna.

They were all talking at the same time. As usual, what was registering was the happy chatter of their voices and not what they were saying.

"There's got to be more to our lives," said Sharon in an arresting tone.

"Be careful what you wish for, Sharon," said Robin who was always attentive to Sharon. "The more you wish, the less you get, and when you don't get what you wish, you go mad, bonkers, crazy, like lulu-head," she made up the last word.

They all came to attention.

"So, let's all of us be like the millions of other American housewives from all over TV-land. Let's just pretty ourselves all day long and wait for our men to come home from work to screw us," said Kitty with a satisfying smile.

"And some of us might be able to pick up a lover or two in the gym where we pretty our bodies and wickedly commit mental adultery," said Myrna.

"Yeah, isn't that exciting!" said Robin. "Really, how many of us get the chance to commit adultery? And even if we did, how many of us would commit?"

"Most of us, I would imagine; even the not so pretty women of the world can easily commit adultery," said Sharon. "That particular Commandment has gone by the wayside during our cloud-filled matching days."

"Let's put it this way: how many American women have known only one man in their lives? A small minority," Myrna answered herself. "So what's the big deal about adultery?"

"You're a loose woman, Myrna, and if you continue to believe that adultery is not a big deal the Lord will not allow you into His Heaven," said Sharon.

"Sharon, you are mad," said Myrna who loved Sharon as much as she loved Hank.

*

When the friends parted company and left Sooky's, all, except Myrna, went straight home to rehydrate and sleep it off. Myrna drove to West LA where Hank Merker was waiting for her with his buddy Larry in his Five Palms restaurant, a specializing sizzler of char-broiled steaks and sirloin burgers. They were sitting in the restaurant's bar where old Larry, he was over seventy, was a daily guest of Hank's. Larry was a lush who was being preserved by the large amounts of alcohol flowing through his veins. In spite of old age and booze, he could still appreciate a beautiful woman.

Myrna Lambert casually walked into the Five Palms restaurant. It was early afternoon and there weren't many customers in the dining room. She was greeted by the head waitress, Roberta Denise, a statuesque African-American lady in her early forties who had managed to maintain her young girl's figure as if she was still a cheerleader in high school, and whose long legs met at a fine protuberant ass highlighted beneath her satin black waitress uniform. She moved hard and had the air of a very desirable hot woman. For several years Hank had been screwing Roberta and had had a son by her. Though both Hank and Roberta were tall people, their son, Adam, who had been named after Hank's father, was short and frail. The boy lived the scary world of uncertainty and insecurity. Both Roberta and Hank tried hard to be loving parents to Adam but it had yet to show in his delicate demeanor. Hank had spent many Sundays teaching Adam how to throw a football, just like Hank's father had taught him.

"Hello, Rob," said Myrna.

She saw Adam sitting by himself and went over and hugged him.

"Hello, Miss Myrna," mocked Roberta.

"How you doing Robby?"

"Come for your bi-weekly dose, Miss Myrna?" she pooh-poohed.

"Go fuck yourself, Roberta."

"At least I don't have to drive to get mine; and mind you, I get mine daily."

"Here she comes again, you lucky bastard," said Larry. "One of these days you have to give your old friend Larry a piece of that beautiful ass."

"You're too old," smiled Hank.

Hank met Myrna as she approached in the bar. He put his hands around her hips and slid them down her ass and gave her a nice kiss which she readily accepted on her still perfectly glossed lips. Her breath still had hints of vodka. He then walked her to his office in the back of the restaurant and, as always, fucked her on the special leather couch that he had purchased for that purpose. With the exception of Larry, Roberta, and perhaps fast fading ex-Phil, they believed that nobody else knew that they had been secretly meeting and fucking in the back room for the last two years.

First Hank came out, walked to the bar and poured another bourbon and coke for Larry. Nobody said a word. It wasn't necessary. The deed stunk of cum throughout the bar and there was no need for details.

She came out of the office straightening her dress and slowly walked and sat next to Larry. She had a hard time climbing the bar stool because her dress was too tight on her.

"Can I get a kiss, Myrna, or are you saving it all for the quarterback?"

"Sure Larry," and she pecked him on the beet purple bloody cheek.

"I mean a sexy kiss on the lips," said sloshed Larry.

Myrna looked towards Hank as if to ask for permission.

"Go ahead, Myrna, take him to the back office," said an insensitive Hank.

"No, no," said shaky Larry. "A mere kiss on the lips will do." And then apologetically said, "I wish I could do you, Myrna, but I can't."

"That's OK Larry. I couldn't do you either."

She tossed her blond hair back and left the place feeling like a bar whore. But she knew that she would be back.

Chapter Seven

S haron Langdon was a very bright high school student, and even though her grades did not reflect her true abilities, she understood that, for her, life after high school was not going to be as easy as that of her wealthy best friends'. They had lots of money; she had only beauty, and beauty in Southern California was an abundant commodity. All through her teen years she felt defenceless against the casual Orange County high school wealthy ways of skating through the merry American way of life. Unlike her best friends, she came from a middle class parents who were struggling to keep pace with their upper middle class surroundings: her father had lost all ambition and would forever be a pharmacist, and her mother felt fulfilled as a student counsellor at the local college.

Most of her girlfriend schoolmates had few doubts that good things awaited them after high school, especially the anticipation of college, and the far away from home freedom with all its handsome love affairs that would inevitably lead to rich choices of husbands. For Sharon also, her powerful intellect promised an out of the poverty of her high school mental stagnation, and fooled her with beautiful dreams of college. Unhappily for her, fears stemming from memories of a dysfunctional childhood discouraged her from openly embracing the excitement of going to college, of being free and away from home. A home life full of hostility did not make for wholehearted support for her from her unhinged parents who were too involved in their own bitterness. Feebly, her mother tried to show some enthusiasm about college, but was loudly drowned out by Anton's violin. Unable to organize her thoughts, even as high school was coming to an end, she diffidently avoided any thoughts of college fearful that socially she couldn't make it anyway. She had the looks, but so did her mother, and look what that got for her. As much as she wanted to be like her friends and rejoice about their fabulous parents, it was always difficult for her to let go and fully trust her parents; they had messed up their own lives and it wasn't so apparent that they had learned anything from their own shattered experiences that daily played for beautiful Sharon; they hardly spoke to each other and there was no advice to be had from the home team.

Bright and pretty as she was, Sharon found little reason to believe that suddenly the sun would shine bright just because one day she would be a high school graduate. Angry repressions of lost childhood happiness clouded any promises of sunshine days, or of college romances, and even of reasonable social life, let alone of a brilliant and enviable career, because during her high school years, Sharon absurdly hated her parents for not being happy and rich.

In the mental harshness that dominated her life, even more than her parents, she hated the smell of her high school ex-boyfriend now husband who then and now fucked her just for the fuck of it, though admittedly with all her neurotic permission. She had become indifferent to his assaults, and every chance he got, he manhandled her, and she dumbly never protested. Overanxious Sharon had an apathetic complex, and mindlessly she had prepared herself for the darker side of an inconsequential life. Quietly she settled for the easy adoration of mediocrity, and stupidly she pissed her high school years away.

*

Hank drove his Honda Civic and picked up Sharon waiting for him in front of her house. She got in and shyly and kissed him on the lips, a ritual she impulsively hated, but one that Hank casually expected.

"Hi, babe," he said in his manly guttural star quarterback voice.

"Hi," she said and feebly smiled his way.

"You wanna go to the golf course?" he said.

"If you want to," said Sharon well aware of what Hank had in mind. It would have been ridiculous to have refused him because they had been there many times before.

"I heard you had a funny thing in history class today," he said.

"Oh, it was nothing important," she said. "He asked me how the US had supported the Allies during World War I and I said, 'money, materials, and manpower.'"

"That's so fucking great, Sharon," laughed Hank with his manly approval, and Sharon felt good that she brought pleasure to Hank.

They drove to the public golf course as the sun was setting. They walked to the man-made pond and on its banks they made out, as they always had done, until dusk set in. Hank then fucked Sharon for the umpteenth time like all the other times on the golf course. She got up off the ground and dusted her skirt off. She felt like a lump of meat when she pulled up her panties; a pretty lump of meat, but a lump of meat nonetheless. Still, she had to admit that like all the other times, juicing Hank was pretty good.

There wasn't much else to do or say as she watched Hank skip flat pebbles across the pond's surface. When she finished straightening out he drove her straight home without saying a word. She smiled goodbye in front of her house and he took off to meet his buddies.

Sharon walked into her house scared, that her parents knew. She felt huge gulps of guilt as she walked past her dumb parents who looked at her but never said a word. She went to her room and read her Bible.

*

Well into her marriage, thoughts of her school retarded memories, which invariably included her husband and his long time high school beer-drinking buddies, released strong hatred that manifested as dry, sticky saliva into her mouth and throat. Even before she married Hank, her husband's friends were loudmouth oafs without the tiniest hint of humanity in any of their brains. From their carefree high school days, she thought them freaks but held her tongue least she offend her star quarterback boyfriend Hank. The clothes they wore then and now hung loose, too low and too loose, in imitation of janitorial society, and strangely fashionable, and mostly for Sharon's eyes. They didn't care about the impression they were making, and in her mind she would vomit at the thought of them; she couldn't take them. But they couldn't have cared about her feelings and showed little concern whether they embarrassed her when in her presence. His buddies, always his buddies, were unbearable in their bad manners, and she had nauseating thoughts about them; they sucked vile. Her temper would explode when complaining to her husband about his idiot buddies, but Hank would still not say or do anything to control his friends' meaness.

One day Sharon finally noticed that cool Hank's pants also hung too loose and low on him. And it was because of her husband's and his friends' insulting manners in looks and dress, and above all in their vulgar vocabulary, that she began to intensely hate her husband as much as she hated his friends, for they all rode their crudities in tandem to her disgust. For the first few years she put up with her husband's pack behaviors until she realized that he was still married more to them then to her. When she complained that it was unnatural for his friends to hang out at their house so much, Hank gave a confused story about the meaning of friendship, and what good friends his buddies were, and that they liked Sharon even more than they liked him.

"They're low class and have a mouth that's filthier than a sewer," she would protest.

"You don't have a fucking clue of what true friendship is, do you Sharon," he would try soft persuasion on his gentle wife. "It's about team and sticking together; that's all there is in life – team!"

"If at least one of them was married and could bring his wife with him for me to keep company while you assholes drank all night long …" she didn't know what else to say.

They were all prodigious beer drinkers who pissed all over, in and out of her toilets.

"They're rotting the toilet floor with their beer piss," she would say. "Next time, you clean that fucking floor."

"It's just beer … dear," he would laugh at the pretended rhyme.

It was as if she were the queen in heat and they were all spraying their stinking sweat all for her. Choose me, my once and always lovely queen, they all biologically screamed. Even when they were merely staring, Sharon could feel their filthy hands all over her. The rushing roar was everywhere, and made cornered Sharon a frightened prey, scared at the thought of cheap assaults, and she hate her husband more and more, as his buddies' drooling looks repulsed her deeper into fear. And her husband, former high school star quarterback, now successful restaurateur, accepted the atrocious behaviour without a word to his high school menacing stupid buddies.

The dysfunctional ambience in her home cast dark memories of a wasting life and reminded her of the wasted four years of Horace Mann high school education, when Hank was a jock, and she was terrified that she might be lacking in the high school graces that were so essential for all the school's beautiful people to nicely fit into the smiley, in-crowd, which invariably, as in all high school in-crowds, after graduating into the real world time, turn out to be the out-crowds, forever stuck in the shallow memories of nowhere to be found again adolescence. The need to fit in with the right crowd has forever been a powerful addiction to a myriad fantasies of millions of high school students all over the US; and as beautiful and intelligent as Sharon was, she too had become part of the crippled herd that found ill-comfort in the pack. She sobbed, but couldn't deny it.

*

The tearful make-believe graduation farewells quickly wilted into loneliness. The many tenuous friendships that had once passed for best friends forever in the classroom quickly diminished into the scary world of unending hard to get used to pain in the ass menial work, the freshness and vitality of youth withering into crass everyday existence. Being a stranger to any kind of humble work, Sharon found comfort to always look back and recall the loveliness of the days of her once teen innocence; and shudder at the thought of honest work. In her perverse recollections, she found comfort in the exploratory fondling of probing hands of boys, innocent, loving little boys, stupid lovers streaking through the crowded empty halls of her mixed up mind. Alone in her kitchen, she remembered the days of the dimly lit library book stacks where goosing girls was a favorite pastime for boys goosing girls, and girls giggling pretended indifference, and how she too partook, loving being goosed, her lovely ass to be part of it. Every time she looked back, sadly, she got most of her goosing from Hank Merker. Rare was the brave boy who dared to put his hands where Hank's hands had been? On the other hand, she knew she wasn't the only one that Hank was forever goosing, for he was every girl's dream to be goosed by the starting varsity quarterback, typically near the boys' gym where Hank was lord of the realm and where some of the girls made it a point to hang out.

Hank was a powerful gooser, as she now recalled, the memory hurting now as it did then. More than goosing, he loved fondling her breasts pretty much every time they were alone on and off school property and she did timidly allow. He pressed on, and pressed on, every time, in sexually assaulting her; he couldn't get enough. But high school years were weird times of discovery and Sharon kowtowed to the unwholesome deeds only because Hank was the star quarterback and he could've fucked any girl he wanted; and all her friends knew how lucky she was that he chose her to relieve himself, a quarterback full of testosterone. It wasn't love but it was the accepted thing to do with a star quarterback. She wasn't sure what she was doing; she knew that other girls in the school did envy her and that included her best friends, especially Myrna and Kitty, who were also goose favourites for Hank, and who always wanted to know, "Are you having sex with him?"

As if they didn't know.

Nor could she remember any of her high school teachers as having had the least relevance in her life. Kitty use to say, "He's nice," or "She's nice" about their history teachers, or their physics teachers, or their geometry teachers, but for Sharon, teachers had minimum contribution to the formation of her character.

*

She had long ago forgotten, if she ever knew, what, in the first maddening place, had made her like, let alone fall in love with, her pockmarked faced Hank. Cynically, she now contemptuously recalled her husband's pockmarks which in their high school days showed up as glitter in her brains.

"It must have been that unblemished complexion of the star quarterback that attracted me to handsome Hank," she fanned herself to laughter.

"And I'm feeling good," she would sarcastically chastise herself.

If she could do it over again, like every other now grown-up disenchanted housewife, she would have been less eager to be airhead popular. If she could go back, she would make friends with the few boys who, in spite of their teachers, were good in math and science and who actually understood poetry. Boys who grew up and now appeared on Sunday morning news programs, and on late night discussions of current affairs and politics. Successful men who became Senators and Congressmen and Wall Street executives. But no dumb athletes, thank you.

The thought of successful men would bring sad images of her father Anton, and she absolutely knew that she didn't want any more 'stars' like husband Hank, and daddy Anton, in her unhappy life. The disconcerted thoughts of her Daddy and Hank in the background, rattled her mind on a daily basis now in her stupid married life.

"You die when your heroes die, and they die awfully young," out of nowhere, one day, the brash thought interrupted her usual nonsensical preoccupation, and frightened her.

She had conditioned herself to suffer her dreaded insecurities in the privacy of her home, alone. Alone was preferable than being with her friends who did love her, but continued to think of her as being so lucky to have landed Hank, as if he were a pizza.

"I don't want to die young," the thought occurred to her in the pain of her loneliness. She wasn't sure which was worse: to die young or to live alone.

But then, she herself could have been one of the stars, one of the silent valedictorian people. She too was good in math and science, and everything else as well, but had stupidly held back in favour of being part of the insipid in-crowd. If nothing else, if she hung out with the serious, nerdy types who wore glasses because they read a lot, she could have developed a more interesting mode of conversation, like beautiful celebrities on TV, for there was no denying Sharon's beauty. Instead, she had felt the school pressure to hang out with fucking jocks who even then, she knew, definitely did not make for lively conversation. Not to be too unfair, but still fair, let's face it, rare was the high school jock who had any imagination beyond some reefer coach infected childhood expectations of ridiculous big time glory and a herd of beautiful women.

Pathetic little fuckers, Sharon thought.

"Jesus help me; you make one fucking mistake and it haunts you for the rest of your life," she protested trying to exonerate herself from disorders.

"What might it be like," she now wondered, "to be married to an intelligent person, a non-jock, a college graduate, perhaps a PhD, a gentle man who would whisper dreamy words into my ears in the wakening minutes of our pillow-talk."

"A thing of beauty is a joy forever,
Its loveliness increases ... " she recalled from a poem she liked.

It didn't do any good to cry because time had passed her by; she was grown up now.

*

She went into her kitchen and got a Lady Godiva dark chocolate bar, slowly returned to her bedroom and lovingly licked it for a long time as she quietly lay on her bed.

It was delicious though not too sweet.

She thought of a drink but decided to stick with licking the chocolate.

"What would it be like to be married to a person who does not continuously slurp cans of beer? To a man who could go for days without the mention of inane sports stats, but found pleasure in sharing pretty thoughts?" she heard herself say.

She stretched her lovely body on her soft bed. The dark chocolate was getting to her, making her hot, so she undressed, a nude queen with melted chocolate on her fingers.

In the vicious magic of her mind she saw her husband Hank as an old man, dour, dumb, and nude of any grace, staring at her, lying next to her on their bed. His eyes were slowly bleeding out the evil of fear and failure that had been contaminating every pock-mark of his fading face. If he had had any dreams left, he had managed to undermine their youthful simplicity and beauty. The fate that had fed his high school silly dreams of glory, his young man's honourable ambition that he could've been someone important in football, had long ago crushed the man and his dreams. In the cruelty that fantasies often play ugly tricks on people, Hank's prize was beautiful Sharon instead of a stellar football career.

Not fair, she thought, thinking of herself only as some common trophy wife.

She had sacrificed everything to be in the right crowd.

"I was afraid, then, that I might have been thought of as an undesirable geek. I didn't want the world not to like me. I now wish I was ugly."

Her recollections were all tasteless bluster.

Frantically she tried to keep her feelings and emotions under control.

She pushed her lovely hair back.

She dry-cried at how pathetically average she and her friends had thoughtlessly been moulded into brainless popular clichés of endless excuses.

Depressed boys and girls, who grew up to be depressed men and women, where the good was bad and the bad was good, still unable to utter a single intelligent idea and risk being thought of as a fool, or worse, a geek.

"I didn't want to be passed by, and be married to the wrong man, like my mother has been," she stupidly thought, for that was exactly what she had done.

And all too often, the fucking thought haunted her that she was still traveling the same trip, now husbanded into a living emptiness, with the same in-crowd losers of her not so long ago high school days.

She got up to take her morning shower because the very thought of those people from her past, now and forever, again as ever before, made her feel hopelessly lost in a quagmire of immense insignificance and boredom that had become her present life.

Chapter Eight

Ever since she published her first and only novel, Judith Langdon had been consumed by disappointment as the book had come out to minimal fanfare. Fame, public acclaim, reviews in learned journals, even recognition among friends and relatives, never came as she had dreamed. No publicity, no praise to clear away the dust of obscurity, no television appearances, and even less worldly goods, like money. There it was, a book bound with all the trappings of authorship, including her name in big letters on the cover to prove it was hers, but it might as well not have been there at all. Sometimes she wished she had never written it, and wondered if it was worth the cost of the paper that it was printed on. The whole fucking world was totally indifferent to it and her existence; not a single glance of what might have been construed as recognition came her way. Stupid people at work who couldn't write a single page on anything still greeted and walked and conversed with her as equals. So she hid the disappointment of her artistic debut with an emotionally twisted smile on her lips. The effect of her let-down was to shadow the whole family.

A good-looking woman, Judy worked as an Admissions Counsellor at East LA Junior College. After completing a Master's degree in Guidance and Counselling, she married Anton Langdon, a onetime violin child prodigy. Anton was a shy fellow who had always felt uncomfortable with his genius. Intimidated by the thought of becoming a renowned musician and having to perform before audiences, Anton chose to eschew great recognitions for the easier route of becoming a pharmacist, an out-of-the-way steady profession with minimal conceit. Langdon and Judy had one child, Sharon, who was nine years old when her mother published her book. Until that eventful day, the Langdon family life had been one of a moderate existence, full of Christian amenities. It was a sharing life filled with natural goodness, until that muted reception of her book that unpredictably smeared their happy home, and fed Anton's jealousy, the Langdon house, that was once crammed with laughter, crumbled hard and crushed the three of them who were once one big happy family.

*

Every afternoon, as soon as Anton got home, usually before Judy and Sharon, he would take off his coat in favour of a loose vest, lovingly pick up his pricy Italian violin that he had bought on a trip to Vienna and solemnly play his favorite, Pachelbel's *Canon in D Major,* endlessly. His soul found peace in the natural redundancy of the piece. But even more than Pachelbel's masterpiece, he found unbound tranquillity in the Song of Seikilos, an ancient Greek epitaph graphic dedicated by Seikilos to his beloved dead wife:

> *While you live, shine*
> *Have no grief at all*
> *Life exists only for a short while*
> *And time demands its toll*

Endlessly, the simple words, when alone with them, would bring tears to his eyes. In them he found the peace that comes from the absence of human ambition; a gentle stillness that manifestly also resided in his soft and lovely violin. During these infinite moments when he was alone with Pachelbel and Seikilos he easily forgot Judy and Sharon who, after all, were simple mortals.

Even before marrying him, Judy, an inexperienced but intelligent young woman had figured out Anton for the emotional cripple that he was. Unfortunately, her own hang-ups made it difficult for her to overcome her social inhibitions so she accepted a first blind-date fix with stranger Anton, a promising professional. Having had minimal exposure to boys and men before Anton, she innocently thought, and wished, that all males were tough, full of testosterone, and always walking around with a hard on. At first sight he wasn't a bad-looking guy and when they first started dating – simple stuff, like movies and popcorn, and lots of diet coke which made it difficult for them to make out later on because they both wanted to piss a lot - she bravely gave in to her emotions and yielded to date again and be alone with a strangely nervous Anton; also she stopped drinking coke as did Anton. The first time she kissed him, he had been too shy, almost afraid, in their intimate moment and she wished that he had been a bit more aggressive, more confident in his groping of her; she had to guide his hands to her breasts. Every time she kissed him, she wished he was more impetuous, reckless, unthinking, qualities which, unfortunately, were also lacking in her own reticent personality. In spite of her bountiful brains and undeniable beauty, ever since she was a young girl, she had exhibited inhibitions that she conveniently rationalized away as simple shyness. It was an even match with Anton until she became most aware of his insecurities, and in return, her self-confidence intensified making her more adventurous and almost foolish in assaulting him. Later when they had progressed to regularly making out in the dark, she badly wanted him to touch her everywhere but he never did, until one day she took his hand and guided it to her crotch. For Judy the invasion was a first, and she was not to be denied that night in the old Dodge as she pressed acquiescent Anton on. She had allowed no other man to come that close and touch her, and she was not going to backtrack now; and though poor Anton might not have been the most desirable of sexual partners, that night he scored.

Having been brought up as a good Catholic girl, she could not in all good faith forget the moment of her deflowering as church normal, so she politely accepted her damnation and selected to confuse the morality of the act for some good fucking. Fearing of being pensioned into the pasture of old maids, of frightening gossip, of being alone in years to come, during their next several months of courting that followed, she and shy Anton experienced the sweet agony of repeated, most memorable, sex that obliterated all Godly commandments even for faithful Catholics like Anton and Judy. Though the two were shy well-mannered Catholics, theirs was a love story based on insatiable sex.

Their lovemaking was excruciatingly good and won out all other emotions by a mile. For two shy geeks, their sex was most honestly direct with minimal of the schmaltzy romance of chocolates and roses. Entrenched in the pleasurable dilemmas of premarital sex, she made the decision to heed every girl's immemorial advice and take the dive, and deny her own genius in favour of Anton's so-so, so that he might feel superior and marry her. So she smiled that twisted smile that he thought as fantastically wicked, just for him, and he accepted her resignation as smart accurate, and he took her up on the tacit proposal. The rejection of her personality in favour of an introverted marriage had the additional benefit of erasing all the guilt feelings from their Catholic minds. Marriage was the moral equalizer to a sinless mind for both.

Fear of being tainted in the eyes of God, she never wished to acknowledge the possibility of other suitors, and made a wrong choice in her young life and married Anton Langdon, former violin child prodigy. She had felt extremely annoyed and impatient in the frustrating thought of waiting for the right man, so she respectfully accepted, Anton, her partner in sin, as her mate in life. In his stubborn eyes, she was the compliant woman, and it made him feel the winner.

Until she published her book, *"Gainsay"*.

For years she feigned a happy marriage and disingenuously pretended that her husband had the brains in the family, with her every response to his requests always being, "Yes, Dear." But after *"Gainsay"*, things changed. She glowed proud of her accomplishment, for it's not easy to write a book. The tingling experience of being an author invaded her whole being, from her toes, through her heart, to her neurotic brain. It was exhilarating to think about her book with all its clever scenes and intuitive characters leaping through all sort of contradictory excitements. She had joined the ranks of special people, undoubtedly geniuses all, who write books. For once, her excitement superseded her husband's hackneyed violin outmoded recitals, and he was jealously jolted back permanently behind her. In her mind, the book ranked perhaps even a bit higher than the birth of her daughter. Unlike Sharon, the *Gainsay* was an offspring of more than nine months gestation. Wanting to share her happiness, she sought recognition from those around her, convinced that she deserved it. Joy invaded her smiling face and she discovered a new assertiveness in herself. She displayed an easy happy outlook at home and work. She was glad she had written her novel, even though it didn't get any reviews that she would have wished, and thought it deserved. Nevertheless, the love that filled her heart from the reality of her book extended to everyone around her, and was reflected in a pleasing smile that she happily shared with her daughter.

Unfortunately for Judy, her husband had nowhere near the same sense of pride and happiness that his wife had about her published achievement. His reaction to the book was a restrained, "I hope you write many more." It was obvious that he was uncomfortable with her sudden rise to stardom.

One late sunny afternoon at the dinner table after one of his Pachelbel sessions, Anton thoughtfully shared his state of mind. He had been moody for several days and neither Judy nor Sharon had any particular desire to ask why. There hadn't been anything light about the man in recent years and they had become accustomed to his sulkiness.

"Have you ever thought of the significance of 'from dust thou art and to dust ye shall return,'" he addressed the space around him, looking up at the ceiling, though both Judy and Sharon were with him at that moment.

It would have never occurred to Anton to pinch Judy's ass playfully, in view of Sharon's impressionable eyes, and thus reveal his humanity; that it was perfectly normal to show his young daughter that married couples did pinch each other's asses, even outside of their bedroom. But to recite uncommon poetry, or tweet strange vacuous thoughts, like dust and death, he exulted in.

"More salad, dear?"

"What the fuck are you talking about, Judy? At a time like this and all you can think about is a salad?" and before Judy could admonish him for his language in front of their young daughter, he would burst out of the kitchen dropping his napkin.

What an asshole, she finally gave in, after years, to her true feelings.

From that day on Judy had very little meaningful conversation with her uptight, anal retentive, psycho husband.

"I'm so disappointed with my book after all the months I had spent on it …" she recalled having said to him one day.

"It's just a fucking book; write another one," he had dismissively snarled at her.

It was so inconsiderate of him, she had cried. He was the stranger that she had first met who, in between then and now, had conveniently, more like sexually, provided both of them with a sorry religious reason for being married. Even Sharon, their beautiful, bright little girl was insufficient in their eyes to give meaning to their lives. The green-eyed envy had cruelly surfaced from the grave. It had materialized as a book and had infected the Langdon household and there was no ointment to be had. Like caries, it had chewed away at Anton's bones for years until it now drained him of any love, and his marriage to Judy suddenly crumbled like a butter cookie, crushed to make crumbs for a bitter pie pan.

Whether it was the world's unenthusiastic reception of her novel, or her husband's envy and lack of support for her accomplishment as an author, for a long time, Judy Langdon felt sorry for herself. Her emotional state deteriorated to a variety of tranquilizers and other helpers, and for one modest moment's temptation to walk on the wild side of life, just once, without the baggage of piety, Judy Langdon had a brief love affair, a lovely semester's juvenile tryst with a fellow instructor at the Junior College. It was no more than a tempestuous erotic affair with a married man, ten years younger than her, who was feeling his vanity outside his bed. It was a neat, pleasurable little affair that was carried on during work hours in empty classrooms and in the broom closets of the empty hallways of the school. Returning to her adolescent laughter, she found pleasure in her newly uncovered feelings, and daily anticipated her fucking embraces. Innocent enough as it was, Judy could not bear her secret two-timing, and realizing that the affair was going nowhere, that it was too commonly irresponsible, she childishly confessed her transgressions to Anton. Humiliated once again, in the darkness of his mind, by another deceit, another insufferable treachery of the many that were his lot in life, the duplicity of an adulterous wife whom he always suspected being lasciviously over sexed proved his suspicions. Jabbing him behind his back and painfully making him the laughingstock of her infidelities, Anton Langdon decided to punish his adulterous wife by not speaking to her. So demoralizing to his fragile ego had been Judy's extramarital affair that if Anton had not been brought up as a good Catholic, and had there not been a Sharon, he would have immediately divorced his wife, or even worse, he would have angrily applied the Bible's terrible punishments against lascivious wives of stoning the whore to death. He was convinced that everyone knew of his wife's cheating, performed, undoubtedly, on a garbage-strewn, worn out, classroom filthy floors in the back of darkened rooms, in front of angels and God, and all would have approved of his stoning of her.

And Sharon saw and felt every shaft of incomprehensible hatred that darted between her parents' poisoned behavior. Repressing all that she saw and heard, she was too young, too polite, too fearful to protest, to scream, or say anything that smacked of the parental pain and embarrassment that was suffocating her into silence. Hoping for a miracle in her parents' relationship, she chose to turn away from the cruel reality that had invaded her young life.

There followed a long period of mental abuse between Anton and Judy Langdon wherein Anton's true character of a jealous man revealed itself in its full ugliness. In his mind, his wife's success as an author, most modest as it were, highlighted Langdon's own failures and made his stomach churn and distend full of noxious gasses which he sickening burped continuously. Where once there had been subtle pleasantries in the daily social graces of the family, the double whammy of adultery and authorship brutally cancelled all communication between the couple. Silent grieving took over the house. Like the low barometric pressure that invades before the storm, a depressing stinking silence trumped all family activity in favour of morose reading to fill the vacant evenings.

The muted stillness of a house gone mad made little Sharon fearful of the loneliness she was sensing. There were no words to buttress the walls and ceiling of a home defrocked of love. She began to dislike her parents for the selfishness that they exhibited in their hatred for each other, and for their psychological abandonment of her. And every so often, Judy Langdon, sensing her daughter's loneliness, would try to console her and herself with readings from the Bible.

While Judy sought sanctuary in the God of her Bible, Anton's disappointments forced him away from his Catholic beliefs.

"It's all lies," he would cruelly say to Sharon whenever he overheard a Biblical conversation between her and her mother.

Everything was a lie, her father had said. Nothing was real, there were no boundaries. For Judy, it was the myth of the Old and New Testament that shielded from Anton's hatred; for Anton all life was full of lies. Their lives had become a perverse reality wherein nine year old Sharon had to choose which of the parental muddled thoughts to follow. Out of fear she decided to live in her mother's reality, though that too, she no longer believed as real, being obviously makeshift. She wished it weren't so, but in her preadolescent existence, Sharon resided in the dumps.

Constant frustration and love deprivation led Sharon to constant fear and a distorted personality. She covered up her craving for affection by sneering at the idea of love and outwardly presented herself as defiant. Being young, it was safer to line up with mommy than the empty bleak world of Anton. She chose her mother's God righteous path without fully understanding that girls instinctively cling to psychic entanglements with other women friends, and especially their mothers. A sullen mix of anger and melancholia followed her thereafter, and filled her heart with resentment for the rest of her life.

These were confusing days for nine year old Sharon, and for many hours she and her mother would sit alone, more like hide in her bedroom, and read passages from the Bible. She understood little of what her mother was reading but found comfort in being alone with her, away from her father whose eyes sank deeper and deeper into their sockets and grew darkness around them as he tried to make the world disappear. Together, Judy and Sharon, memorized passages from the prophets about the Kingdom of Heaven. They read of the miracles of Jesus who made wine out of water and many loaves of bread out of fish, or fish out of water. Together they prayed to Jesus, Son of God, who ascended from the dead, while all the angels were singing "Alleluia".

"Holy Lord, Holy and Strong, Holy and Immortal, please bless our souls," Judy would pray to God, more for Sharon's benefit than for her own worthless self, and Sharon would hear the angel's melodious songs.

"You know, Sharon, God loved humans so much that He sacrificed his One and only Son for our salvation. He especially loved children," Judy would smile and Sharon would uncomfortably tighten her belly in fear of the Lord. Still, it was His Son He sacrificed and not His Daughter, and Sharon would smile and be glad that she was a girl.

But in Sharon's young mind, the lines that she loved and were forever embedded in her memory were from the most beautiful Song of Songs, as her mother would say, and her imagination would wander.

"I am the rose of Sharon, and the lily of the valleys ... "
"Thy two breasts are like two young roes that are twins, which feed among the lilies ... "
"How beautiful are thy feet with shoes, O Prince's daughter!
the joints of thy thighs are like jewels, ... "
"I am my beloved's ... "
"Thy two breasts are like two young roes that are twins... "

Sharon loved the baffling words like 'roes' that are like breasts, though she had no idea what roes were, even after her mother explained. Did she dare ask if she was the rose of Sharon? But above all she loved *'how beautiful are thy feet with shoes, O Prince's daughter!'*

Judy tried to explain that the poem was about physical love, which is just as beautiful as any love, but it was too much for little Sharon. She only heard the words.

Still, the words carried such intimate emotions for her, as she envisioned her feet with and, or without shoes, naked, walking across the dew green grass of evenings in some bejewelled Biblical garden, being watched in the moonlight by an equally romantic young prince. Young as she was it was easy for her to understand its meaning as she pleased, for it was meant for young girls: it was an amorous song of young breasts, and joints like jewels, made by God, right out of the Bible; breasts and thighs just like hers that already she could see were jewels from Heaven.

"Like mine, mother?"

"Yes, like yours, O Prince's daughter," her mother would caress her.

"Am I a Prince's daughter, mother?"

Poor Anton; he had become the butt even of their jokes.

"No my beloved; you are a princess of Jesus and I am the queen, your mother," and they would both laugh to the complete exclusion of asexual Anton.

"Is this poem about sex, mother?"

"It's more than that; it's about love. It's about the love of a man for a woman, and the love of people for God, and the love for nature and for all of God's things. Only the hypocrites identify sensual love with impiety," sighed Judy.

"But there's also sex in those words, isn't there?"

"Yes, it is also about the beauty of sex."

"Do you and father also have beautiful sex, mother?"

"I don't know, my beloved," and two tears washed out of Judy's eyes.

Sharon looked at her mother and tears came to her eyes too.

"Tears of my eyes, what have we done to you?" Judy cried and looked lovingly at her daughter. She took Sharon in her arms and

they both cried hugging each other, as they sometimes did when they prayed together.

"I know that you and father hate each other, and I'm sure you and father don't ever have sex anymore. I mean like in the poem. Is it so horrible for you, mother?"

"What do you mean, Sharon?"

"To fuck your husband; is it so horrible for you?"

"I'll tell you when you're older, but for now, don't use such foul language," said Judy.

"Why foul? Even the Bible says it's ok," said Sharon. "Are you at least friends?"

"You'll understand everything in its right time."

"I think you've had sex with another man. Did you, mother?" asked Sharon, long having suspected foul play.

"Yes," said Judy.

"How could you mother?"

There was no denying the truth, for Sharon was a bright girl. What would have been the use of hesitation and searching for lies to tell her daughter?

"I'm not going to have beautiful sex with many man other than my husband when I grow up," she said forcefully.

"You mustn't be so judgemental …."

"Why? What does the Bible say, mother."

There was no denying the rose of Sharon.

"You must always remember that the most important of the Lord's Commandments is, *'Thou shall not commit adultery'* ".

"What does that mean?"

"I hope you never have to find out," said Judy, too aware of her own mortal sin.

"I know what it means," said Sharon. "In today's world adultery is an anachronism. Not to worry mother, I suspect that even then it was an anachronism."

*

The overpowering daily silence coupled with recurring Biblical readings produced psychoneurotic introspections of uncertainties in Sharon. Thoughts that she might do terrible things, without realizing it, overwhelmed her daily existence. Threats of disapproval from her parents unsettled her life continuously. School phobias followed her for years and the temptation to do 'bad' things, usually sexual in reference, became unbearable and for some reality relief she shut her personality deep into her unconscious so that the temptation might go away. Screaming emotions of familial hatred juxtaposed with Biblical love stories echoed bipolar moods in her and drove her deeper into mental isolation. For years she looked down when she walked, and sat in the back of the classroom fearful that she might be called on when she feared she wasn't ready. Then, one day, just as it happens to all princesses, as she was walking through the unlit high school hallways of her mind, future husband Hank Merker, most unexpectedly, blessed his smile on her. She was first embarrassed and then thrilled, the envy of all her friends, and though still lacking in self-confidence to understand the pressing, she understood that she was as she had suspected – beautiful! She was too young to fully appreciate how devastatingly beautiful she was, but from that magic moment of recognition, her whole being tingled with thrilling sensations because, after all, he was the star quarterback, and for many days thereafter, Sharon floated on the vast American cloud of high school football legends. Before Hank's eyes fell on her, she was barely coming out of early adolescence. She had felt modest in her estimates of herself; shy and hesitatingly pretty in her mind, she thought that perhaps she might be a little more than just plain; at best, merely one of many budding beauties that American high schools are full of. But for Hank, like all the other pretty and not so pretty faces blossoming and competing to be mated by a star, she too emotionally spread her skinny legs, for the star quarterback, because she thought she was in love. She was sixteen and suddenly life burst into spring; he chose her and what could she do but say yes to his fondling smile. They walked hand in hand in the crowded hallways of Magnolia High School, in Sherman Oaks, California, constantly smiling but not ever saying anything. Sharon was shy, and shyness makes people dumb, or at least makes them appear dumb because they say nothing; and though they know they appear dumb, there's usually nothing they wish to say or do about it. Spiritually, she felt like a virgin out of the Bible, struck dumb by the Lord for her lewd thoughts about handsome Hank. To her relief, neither did Hank have much to say. He just smiled a lot, and flaunted his perfectly whitened teeth.

During their first school social date one Friday night, determined Hank took Sharon by the hand and led her to the big boys' gym dressing room, familiar ground to the all of Magnolia High sport jocks, just off the main Gym. While everybody else was dancing the night away, he spread eagled her on one of the benches between the metal lockers, her feet trembling on each side of the wooden bench. He lifted her skirt and stared down at her as a wild predator might stare before the charge. She was speechless, motionless; mesmerized, she obeyed his every move without the tiniest of protests. Suddenly, everything that was happening was terrifying for Sharon. She didn't know how to react, and he brutally raped her without mercy. There was no foreplay, no petting, and no gentle soothing words. He fucked her without even taking her panties off. He was an experienced big boy quarterback with a huge penis, while for her, it was her first time, and she had no idea how to protest his powerful hurting thrusts. Without pity, he nailed her on the cross that was the bench. He was relentless in his attack and he hurt her without thought or care. She was in too much in pain, too timid, too shy, to protest the brutal rape that forever became her cross to bear.

She asked for it and she will remember this for the rest of her life thought macho Hank, the diesel hung star quarterback of Magnolia High. She wasn't the first girl he had raped in the boys gym lockers.

It all happened too quickly. She stood up and tried to straighten out her clothes, but her mind could not comprehend how she had wound up spread-eagled numb on a wooden bench and how someone who she didn't know very well had so easily fucked her. Emotionally, she could not feel a thing, though later that night, alone in her bedroom, the humiliation would surface excruciatingly hard, both mentally and physically.

When he finished washing his dick in the gym sink, he returned with some paper towels for her to wipe herself. He then smiled at her and took her by the hand back to the dance floor in the Gym.

For the rest of her life, Sharon felt disgust with herself recalling how effortlessly Hank had crushed her virginity and soul, one evening, soon after they had met, fucking her in a stinking boys' gym locker room.

He walked her home after the dance without saying a word. He kissed her hard on the lips on her front porch. She remained stiff and speechless while he tongue-kissed away. Energized by the lopsided score, in two leaps he bounded down the five steps of her porch, fast disappearing in the night's sidewalk. He would have wanted to make out some more with easy Sharon but his friends were anxiously waiting for him in Abe's Pizza Tower to hear of his conquest of lovely Sharon.

The whole porch scene was watched by Anton through his dark living room window, but he didn't want to make an issue of it.

She entered the house and was surprised to see her father still awake. She followed him into their kitchen and she sat down by the kitchen table somewhat in fear that her father might have guessed what had happened to her earlier.

"You want a coke," he politely asked.

It was unbearable, being there alone with him. She was sure he knew.

"No thank you," she said, and she got up to go to her bedroom.

Unbeknown to Sharon, there was a small blot of blood on the back of her skirt and also on the kitchen chair she had sat on moments earlier.

"Sharon …" but she didn't turn around to her father's calling.

Must be her period, he thought. Definitely unprepared but what do you expect from a dumb mother like Judy.

At least she's not pregnant, he smiled to himself, alone again.

He felt very proud that he now had a grown daughter, a beautiful menstruating young woman. If only he could tell her.

There was a burning sensation to the injury she felt as she washed the blood away in her shower. She hadn't felt the pain when he was raping her but now she felt a stinging wound as if there had been a cut deep inside her. She washed for a long time; there was a lot more blood than she had been led to think about sexual intercourse.

Unbeknownst to her at that moments, it was the beginning of her hatred for Hank.

The bastard injured me she thought and bled in secret silence.

Alone, it was that night, as she lay sleepless in her bed that Sharon wrote her parents out of her mind as if they had never existed.

They died in the swamp that had become her muddled mind.

Chapter Nine

"Who would have ever thought that an ex-Peace Corps Volunteer would have been such a cruddy little bastard," half-heartedly smiled Robin thinking about her husband David Calder. She liked strolling around the UCLA campus because it reminded her of happier days when she was an undergraduate, and later, when she trained there for the Peace Corps. Looking back, they were naive days, uncomplicated by the duplicity of adult deceptive words and actions; happy days when she still fancied herself as the next Emily Dickinson, though by her sophomore year in college she had stopped printing her poetic crap in favour of concentrating on world social awareness issues like the outbreaks of malaria in the underdeveloped countries, overpopulation, and global pollution in the irresponsible overdeveloped. Annoyed with herself at having been so naive, she now couldn't imagine that once upon a time she actually believed that she could really make a difference in the world. Hers were heroic fantasies of triumph solidly imprinted in her youthful mind; ideas to which she had faithfully adhered to in sublimated pleasure to cover up her ignorance. Now grown up, she viewed her youthful politics as amusing little white lies intended to combat her insecurities. From the very beginning, they were feel-good promises to a pretty little girl, from mommy and daddy, so that she would always be a winner. And so she remained a virgin to the world until she was invited to train for the Peace Corps to go to Addis Ababa, Ethiopia and teach English. She was twenty one at the time and knew that somewhere beyond the sea there was a world for her to conquer.

She stopped and sat in the grass in front of Royce Hall on the UCLA quad and again found the beautiful Mexican-deco, pink-coloured building, pleasing to look at. The warmth of the building lovingly passed through her entire body, and she felt the afternoon sun melting on her. She looked straight ahead and tilted her head slightly up at the bluest of skies and felt the vigor of her youth. She breathed in the scent of the recently mowed fresh green grass and sensed the world as her own. The scene was one of calm, and she felt relaxed in its familiarity. It was the same picture she had often seen in her dreams. It was a scene recalling the calm and happy days before complications to prove oneself had set in. In her dream she was sitting on the green grass, like she had done so many times during PC training, when she wanted to feel alone, Royce Hall on her right. Like in her dream, she was now looking straight ahead at the warm setting sun, felt free of all the world, and she longed for the feeling of the fading day not to end. After all these years she still felt clean and memorably twenty-one whenever she walked the cool grounds of UCLA.

Tired memories of the young men and women who had been invited to the training program at UCLA that would eventually take them to Ethiopia swept through her mind. She couldn't help it: the Peace Corps experience had been pivotal to what and who she now was. If she could, she would now re-invent the group as more normal, more flawed, in-the-raw human beings rather than the fragile bright-eyed people just out of college that they were then, full of uncertain idealism and nervy theatrics about maturity, and middle age, and old age, and endless other opinions. It was that silent fear of the real world that made them, "including myself," huddle into the cloister of Peace Corps volunteerism, she thought. For some, the fear of what lay ahead evidenced itself in an insecure laughter that betrayed confused clumsiness and improbable assertiveness. She recalled how some, including herself, would gather around the dorm's lounge piano, just before suppertime, and sing the tearjerker

> *"Go tell Aunt Molly the old grey goose is gone;*
> *she died in the meadow, the old grey goose is gone.*
> *The gander ..."*

How stupid, she thought.

*

The sound of pre-digital alarm clocks would go off at six am, or earlier, in the June-gloom Southern California marine layer rolling in each morning, and by seven a.m. various training classes would begin. With bright shining faces they were all in their places complaining of the ungodly hours but not too loudly lest they be cut from the training program and be send home, a bizarre possibility full of implied failure, compliments of Peace Corps administrators.

Robin was thrilled to be part of the laughter and gestures of the group, and quickly succumbed to the grand exhibitionism of the new and still exotic responsibility that was just beginning. She would pretend to be startled, and girlish jump, at every tepid touch from one of the more bold male volunteers. And still desiring to be part of the in-crowd, weird laughter of familiarity, unreal, would surface on her lips and fill the acquaintanceship of the big deal gentle poking of her ribs, an act of intimacy as close to her breasts as common etiquette allowed. Weird with informality was her friendly reaction to the newly recognizable fellow travellers' probing intimacy.

How embarrassing, she would think to herself; she had never behaved so stupidly before, never allowed anyone to poke her ribs, or anywhere else. Though unsure that her newly acquired PCV behaviour was acceptable, she did conform to the magic of being part of the group, of starting out as an equal, of not having to display all past baggage, good or bad; in effect, she shut her eyes and travelled incognito, in spite of the silly PC psychological testing. She desperately wanted to prove to herself, her best friends, and above all, her daddy back home that she wasn't a freak, a nerd, or a geek loser; that she could make lots of friends like everybody else could. She would have done anything and everything to fit into the PC group and not be cut from the program, an event that might be construed as unforgivable failure by herself and all those around her. There was incomprehensible fear to have volunteered two years of your life to do noble work but to have some indifferent bureaucrats question your commitment. Worse, the unfathomable possibility of being removed from the program because of incompetence was particularly scary.

Five days into training, a disturbing storm swept through her body and mind: to be cut from the program would mean devastation; it would amount to smudging her ass black for the rest of her life; she had to go to Ethiopia. She knew very little of Ethiopia but suddenly she felt that her future as a productive human being passed through the highlands of Ethiopia.

It was a turning point in her young life, though she was too young to realize that imposing training programs, like stupid schooling, was simply one of those recurring events that are common but insignificant in life. She buckled down and made the PC training particularly significant, envisioning it as something full of the excitement that somehow would trash her insubstantial past and push her to grasp on to a most exciting future. So she excelled in everything the program called for, and poking of the ribs be damned. She had to go where her life could find a new start, a new continuity, and out of nowhere Ethiopia beamed quixotically at her. She became a best Volunteer not to be cut from the program. And with all her beauty, who could deny her?

It was on this road taken that she met her future husband David Calder, Dave to the group, whenever he would honkytonk on the lounge piano in Myra Hershey Hall, where the group had been housed. Immediately she had recognized that he was everything she wasn't. In any other environment she would have pissed on him and walked away. Dave was one of those good looking boys whose rosy face was a pass to any convention. But for Robin, the ethical road having been cleared of compunctions by the need to fit, the ghost that might have protested to a more acceptable choice for a companion had been conveniently effaced out of the moral mind by the need to go to Ethiopia, and if plucky Dave would claim her as his girlfriend, he being a critical member of the training social group, then she would be in with everyone, including the daunting Big Daddy Peace Corps.

For several days she side-stared Dave, literally for the fuck of it, trying to find some unique quality in him, but to her dismay, all she could see was a vague immaturity, that in her mind, echoed nothing more than surface deep 'nice guy', but which somehow mysteriously led her to the sure and easy way to Addis Ababa, which at the time, was exactly what she was looking for.

It was another first for Robin to cautiously move in a continuous direction towards bubbly Dave who easily bounced around Royce Hall with his groupies, male and female, always in attendance. The guy wore sneakers before his time, which turned Robin off, but she found it curious that she attracted him. His head turned when she was around. His lustrous blue eyes, like a baby's, evoked nothing but mother's love for the world, and she had to admit they were sexually enticing. He was not the one that played the staid Aunt Molly tune on the piano; he was histrionically jazzy, which she likewise found amusing. Already his hairline had begun to recede and the crown of his head had lost most of his strawberry blond hair, "indicative of larger than normal amounts of testosterone", his female friends would be in awe of him. Between his tennis shoes and his red nylon wrinkle-free windbreaker that reflected brightly on his white face, Dave took all the Peace Corps girls' breathe away. But to Robin, he was an easy mark. He was too easy not to pass up, still an adolescent, and Robin was much smarter than he. She supressed all feelings of indifference and charged to charm Dave.

"Hey, Dave, you want to come up and see my bed?" one spied, brave, alone, afternoon moment, Robin teased that Peace Corps laughter out of sparkling Dave.

Everybody wanted to see Robin's bed.

"What about your roommate?"

"Risk it, David," she said as she led him to her room.

Robin locked the door behind her even though she knew that her roommate had an extra class that day and was at least an hour away.

It was more for Calder than herself.

She undressed quickly and stood tall in front of him smiling all her tantalizing purity to the lucky Dave. Her white nakedness shined like a Grecian statue in the twilight of Southern California afternoon. It wasn't so much that she wanted to fuck at that moment as much as she felt she had to. She wanted to get it over as quickly as possible; what the fuck was the big deal? A tear came to her eye as he fucked her to a quick, silent climax. In his lucky afternoon he was never aware that it had been her first time, that he had deflowered a most beautiful girl. When he finished, she was surprised that it hadn't hurt; she went and showered, and when she came back he had left the room.

It was that easy.

*

"You mean to say, Robin, that all through high school and four years of college you stayed a virgin?" Kitty had asked in disbelief one day years later.

"Yeah," Robin said to her trusted best friend, "and it still pisses me off that I had saved myself for so long only to have been plucked by an insensitive asshole like Calder," she confessed about her now transparent husband in that strange laughter that was becoming more masculine with age.

"Oh, Robin, I'm so sorry; we never knew," commiserated Kitty. It would have smacked of pity except that Kitty had a keen sense of sarcasm.

"What a bull-shitter you are, Kitty," laughed Robin who never really needed Kitty's expressions of sympathy.

"Of course you never mentioned anything about your sex life before, though we all assumed that you had to be doing it with somebody, from junior high times even, because you're so beautiful, and we all thought somebody was corking you, because you've always been so secretive …"

"'fess up, Kitty, when was your first time?"

"I won't tell you!"

"I bet you all thought it was my cousin …"

"Well, no, we thought it was your uncle; you know, the thin nosed lawyer," and they both laughed.

"I won't tell if you don't tell," said Kitty.

"At our age, we brag of such boosts, Kitty, so do tell," said Robin.

"I'll tell the others to call you Miss Chastity from now on," giggled Kitty.

"Screw that scene, Kitty. After the first time all other times become only one other time. And I can truthfully tell you, Kitty, that there were many, many, other times. Every night the trainees would pair up and fuck their stressed-out brains. Whom you paired with was not ever an issue; we were all one great, big, happy family. It was almost incestuous. We fucked each other like kindergarten children playing in the toy-room."

"What about the Peace Corps people? Didn't they know what you were doing?"

"Sure they did. Some of the younger, gamier instructors, including the Ethiopians joined in the nightly fun."

"Is it true what they say, Robin? That once you go black you never come back?"

And once again Robin's mind wandered to the days of Addis Ababa, the 'new flower' days and to the tall and slender lover, Taferra, who simply would not fade away and whose huge loving eyes, over the years, continued to look into her heart; and each time she would have given anything to be with him for one more time.

She stupidly looked over her shoulder hoping to see his childlike face.

For two Peace Corps years he had been her beloved, courageously giving every sweet cell of his body and soul to her, but she always withholding, racially resisting, out of fear of his non-white skin.

"Hey, cuckoo bird; are you still with me?"

"Bullshit, Kitty. I went black, but I never left white, and did marry white, as you know," Robin wistfully recalled.

"I was just wondering," Kitty dissolved her curiosity.

"And let me tell you. The fucking didn't stop with the training period. For the next two years we continued to fuck each other without concealment, thanks to the free condoms, courtesy of the Peace Corps. And every so often, we would stop by the Swedish Hospital in Addis Ababa to check our levels of syphilis and gonorrhoea."

"All right Robin, that's enough of the bullshit. I now think you're pulling my leg. There's just too much fucking in your story!"

Robin couldn't stop laughing at her friend's innocence. Sure she had exaggerated a bit, but Robin had never fucked as much as she did as a Peace Corps Volunteer.

"You know, Robin, Myrna's sorority stories are no different than your Peace Corps stories; while you were fantasy fucking away in the PC, everybody was fantasy fucking each other in her sorority as well. You'll never hear those kind of stories from me, though," summed Kitty with a bit of phlegm in her voice.

"Well, what are friends for?" said Robin, after a moment's exasperating delay, thick with discord, her eyes still focused on the sweet eucalyptus odors of Addis Ababa. They were masculine words, loaded with heavy feeling and short of friendly sentiment. They came out forcefully between Robins teeth and blew Kitty emotionally dry. She didn't know why Robin said what she did about 'friends', the way she did; for her, friendship was a corny great big hug, an act of confessional openness. It wasn't something to choke on. Friendship for Kitty was not a point of one-upmanship for selfish gain; it was an act of binding people in pleasure. She felt as if she somehow had offended Robin.

"If you want to know what friendship is, Robin, it's the deep feeling of pleasure you sense when you are with your friend," said Kitty.

"Oh Kitty! You are a great friend and I love being with you because you do give me great, great, deep, deep, pleasure," smiled Robin in all honesty and took Kitty's hand in hers, all hostility disappearing from her voice.

They took a cab to Sooky Rawko's Bar on Pacific Highway in Santa Monica to meet Sharon and Myrna for vodka martinis, sushi, and sashimi delicacies, and always a half dozen oysters for Sharon.

*

Later that evening as she lay awake next to her husband she couldn't get her Ethiopian lover out of her mind. Taferra had been a history teacher in the same school she had been assigned to teach English. He was young, no more than twenty five, and he walked with the superior peacock grace that the Amhara people have carried in their genes since the time of Solomon and Sheba. Robin had been amazed by the easy Ethiopian good looks when she first got to Addis Ababa. She, like most other Europeans, was pitilessly abused by the fine features and perfect complexion and colors of the Amhara and Tigre people. They walk with ease and when they sit it's as if they're sitting on flowers.

He instantly intimidated her. Tall and Ethiopian skinny, he fixated on her soul the first day he saw her shyly sipping her tea in the teacher's lounge. She felt his intense presence and immediately understood that inevitably, soon, they would become lovers. The premonition was strong, they belonged together; she thought it was the appeal of the exotic that was unsettling her tummy. She was thrilled at the irrational, which made the prospect of fucking the Ethiopian more appealing, but not for one moment did she forget that she too was beautiful and that he had to acknowledge her presence or he'd be out of luck. She thought it ridiculous the way he carefully covered himself behind his always buttoned-down suit jacket faking it as blazer.

For the first month or so, the strange exchanges were limited to sparse side-glanced eye contact and greetings of "Good morning" and smiling "oops" whenever they bumped into each other in the school's hallway or stairs. But there was no mistaking the powerful attraction that was sizzling between them. She sensed the delicate beauty of his light brown skin and every day that she saw him she couldn't shake her persistent longing to be embraced and to be made pregnant by him. They both knew it was a matter of time.

One evening her doorbell rang and when she opened it he was standing there holding a passionate red rose. With a most serious hesitation on his face he waited for some seconds and then unabashedly walked into her life. She was terrorized by his unannounced presence.

He was as much in fear as she was.

"Where did you get a rose in Addis," she broke the silence, and with those words she immediately became part of the family.

"Addis Ababa means 'new flower' in Amharic," he said. "It was either an apple, or a new flower for the new teacher," he said, the words trembling on his lips.

He was like a lost little puppy in her doorsteps. She couldn't stand it any longer and took his hand and led him to her bed. They made up for the long anticipation of awaited lovemaking until the wee hours of the morning and in the end, when he parted, she was certain she was in love with him.

For the next two years he was the not so secret lover for whom she had travelled beyond the sea to Ethiopia. During that time that measured as a lifetime while it lasted, her heart was flooded with love full of tranquillity and cheer. She found the luxury to believe that she was in love with an Ethiopian, a stranger, lovely Taferra. She was enthralled by his gentle assertiveness, which made her forget her faraway American competitiveness; she was convinced that she had found her soul in his embracing laughter. His skin was beautiful to her touch. His lips and eyes became ancient springs of kindness that always pinned her with their liberating smile. Not until her Peace Corps tour was near the end did she see her white skin resurface again, that hers was not brown like his. She cried that day realizing that the Ethiopia Volunteer thing, including her Taferra, was but a whimsical adventure paid by Uncle Sam. It was a lovely love affair that for sanity's sake had to be extirpated, lovely as it had been, with all the surgical innocence of an intercontinental flight detachment.

If Taferra was her special weekend flavoured lover, David Calder continued to be her everyday American lover, full of the playful sexuality that continued uninterrupted from the days of UCLA. And they weren't the only two for whom she covered her bed with passion. She didn't care. When the opportunity presented itself, often, because she was beautiful, she gleefully bit her lip and uncovered her breasts to another capricious adventure. She was far away from the disapproving eyes of those who might not have approved, like her parents, and she felt free; being sexually desirable was an opportunity not to be dismissed. Hers, too, was every young woman's fantasized wish for many lovers to attend her infinite appetites. And for her, her fantasies were coming true, far beyond the sea, as she had often imagined as a young girl. She was young and beautiful and what was she supposed to do with her youth and beauty? The days of PC idealistic voluntarism were also of pure uncomplicated sexual happenings as well. It was as nature, and her immense beauty, had intended life to be. The libidinous exploration was a welcomed pleasurable landscapes of audacious freedom to be savored away from the discomfort of parental prying; prurient desires were to be enjoyed before the inevitable conforming to one, servile, crushing husband in a social marriage of the rich, most often negotiated by daddy and others around her, presumed to last a lifetime. The holy tradition of a wedding that none would be able 'to do apart', were thoughts to be visited on a later date, after Ethiopia. And like the new Addis Ababa flower that she had become, she opened up her corolla with its precious petals to show the world what she had, a beauty to be cherished and abducted every time, far, far, away from home, where the deer and the antelope played, and no one could pass judgement on her.

She balanced the world between her long legs, but in her dreams and daydreams, Daddy would intermittently appear with the same pained face that she knew as disapproval to remind her that he was shadowing her everywhere she might be; that Ethiopia was not that far removed from his California world that she could hide from him. And in that sexual rebelliousness that was her PCV world, her best friends would also appear in long letters, and she would wish she could forget them, but she could not. Shame was a forceful tormentor to all her innocent pleasures which should have been hers without regrets. The easy Peace Corps affairs, in time, became a bipolar world, voracious in her extended appetites, but laden with guilt; and she prayed that she be able to consciously keep the two apart without losing her mind.

The thought of Daddy humbled her and when alone she would cry knowing full well that sadly he would not approve of her "coarse behavior" as he would invade her mind. In all her vulgar fucking, Daddy was ever present, compounding her sins and sorrow with the unhappy thought that her white reality had David as her only means of accepted atonement. She knew well that no Ethiopian, no matter how bright or virtuous, how worthy or respectable, could match the sanity of David that Daddy would accept. Conceding her neurotic self to the recesses of her lovely mind, she found comfort in the lie that there were only two lovers; that she was fucking Taferra out of love, and David out of daddy necessity only. Unfairly, she thought David stupid for actually believing that he was the heir apparent to her heart. But in moments of clarity, during the darkest moments of her bipolar mind, she knew that she had no huge love for anyone.

"Fuck them all," she would say. "They're driving me crazy."

Six weeks before departing from Ethiopia, Robin found out she was pregnant. She told David of her condition and he was at first stupefied, then confused, and after very little consideration, all too thrilled to share in the great portentous event of the birth of his first child. There was some ambivalence on becoming a father so early in his life, but here was proof positive that his receding hairline was manly stuff. Proud of his physical strength to father children, there was no hesitation at the thrilling prospect of Robin becoming his wife, promiscuous as she was. Recalling that first time at UCLA, to David Calder she was a woman most desirable. He just wished that she had been a little more careful with whom she paired, but there was no longer fear of being dropped from the PC program, because they'd be going home soon, anyway.

They both politely swallowed the very little pride there was left, and they made plans to marry as soon as they returned to the States.

"I wonder if it's a boy, or girl?" he would stupidly ask.

"Let it be a mystery to the end, David," smiled Robin who then gracefully touched her lips on the dolt's forehead.

For both David and Robin the two year Peace Corps tour in Ethiopia was the turning point in their lives. That experience brought misery to Robin and, soon after his return to the US, great wealth to bouncing David.

She never said anything to Taferra, but she knew that the baby was his. There was nothing to be said other than it would have been a beautiful mulatto. Their two year affair, tender and passionate as it was, she now understood, could never have ended happily in marriage, or in a prolonged pathetic romantic love affair fatefully doomed to tragic failure. Lucid now that her departure was nearing, she saw no room for Taferra in her American world and way of life. He was too delicate to survive outside the bewitching beauty of bloated Abyssinia. He could not be far removed from the miserable dirty little side streets of Addis Ababa that were nightly cleared of garbage by scavenging hyenas. He would have been swallowed alive, as she had done of him, by the anthropophagi of the free marketers of capitalist America.

Softly she sang the song he had taught her:

> *Antchi lidgi, wadda kouchi*
> *Antchi degamo, wadda gini*

"I love you too Taferra," she cried to herself, on the plane, all the way to America.

Years later, when her mind had stabilized into the familiar reality of her traditions, the thought occurred to her that all memories are reworked fantasies, the censored wishes for a pleasant world. She realized that the Ethiopia of her Peace Corps mind was not a geographic location but the remnant fantasy of a twenty two year old easily impressionable American girl; that she could have as much return to that faded fantasy, as she could have once again become twenty two years old.

The fantasy did linger on mostly without Taferra. It was a touching sentiment without hope of realization because it was illusory and, as any psychologist will tell you, illusions are there to fool you; that what once might have been passionate realities, in quick time they fade away into ill-defined hallucinations, as assuredly as lies tend to become truths the more you continue to repeat them.

"What a fantastic world, to freeze your life into illusions," she often thought.

*

Though she knew whose baby it was she at the time said nothing to David. She needed a husband to keep the faith with Daddy and David qualified; it was a no brainer, that as soon as she got to California she would abort her fetus, which she did right after the wedding.

Stressed out to almost panic condition, for a few days after her wedding to David, she kept throwing up every morning. Everyone happily assumed that she was pregnant, which she miserably was. No one suspected her unhappiness except, perhaps, her father who half-smiled a curious sideward glance halfway down the church aisle; but it was much too late to wonder. 'For better or for worse, in sickness and in health … till death do us part …' It was a wretched wedding. Throughout the ceremony, and the expensive reception afterwards, Robin kept thinking of the embryo inside her and how to get rid of it. Dumb David was far, far away, from her mind, while Robin was temporarily mired in the Ethiopian within her.

And all her best friends kept hugging her and saying how happy they were for her on her luxurious wedding. Only Sharon felt Robin's uneasiness.

The day after her honeymoon, secretly, with the help of her friend Myrna, who understood her friend's condition, Robin had an afternoon abortion in an assembly line abortion clinic in East LA. The morning after her abortion she woke up in a pool of her blood that had warmly soiled her silken sheets. It was assumed that she had naturally aborted though nobody bothered to look. Compassionately, upon seeing the bloody misfortune that had befallen them, David comforted his wife and assured her, not to worry, that the Lord would bless them with more pregnancies.

There never were more pregnancies and though Robin didn't deserve that fate, the good Lord working in His many ways, and unbeknownst to Robin at that time, and for a long time thereafter, medical second opinion sadly confirmed, time and again, that she would never again get pregnant. She tried to be defiant as Daddy would have wanted her to be, but a gnawing remorse painfully cluttered her pretty personality.

Two years after her abortion and still unable to adjust to her post-PC lifestyle, and against her husband's and every friend's advice, Robin decided to return to the source of her confusion, like all confused ex-Volunteers want to do.

She bought a ticket to Addis Ababa.

"I have to see Taferra," she said.

"You can never go back, Robin," was David's admonition.

She landed at Bole International Airport in Addis at six in the morning after a long flight from LA via Kennedy Airport. Once again overwhelmed by the clarity and freshness of the Addis air, she remembered the first time she disembarked at Bole as a PCV and felt the same eagerness and anticipation, as before; that she was doing the right thing to be there.

By the time she got to her hotel, she felt very alone. Though exhausted from the trip she was much too nervous to sleep. Suddenly she didn't know what to do, she didn't know where to look. Fear struck her in the midst of a strange African City, when Big Daddy Peace Corps wasn't there to protect you, or to pluck you out and gently carry you back home in case of an emergency. What if something silly happened to her, like falling and breaking her neck? Who would take the time and effort to do the right thing on her dead behalf? She recalled the true story told to her by Taferra of Malcolm X, in fear of his life, being holed up in the same hotel years earlier, when he had fled Cairo after arriving there from Jeddah, Saudi Arabia, believing that CIA agents, or somebody equally unfriendly, was out to get him. He holed up for days in the hotel trusting no one, never eating food until reassured it wasn't poisoned, never going out, until the CIA, or trusted Ethiopian officials, or friends from Washington, or maybe the Peace Corps, assured him all was ten four, and that he could return to the USA, where safety awaited him.

Thinking herself naïve, or worse, succumbing to paranoia, she decided to go out and test her shaky knees.

On the walk to the Piazza, once the meeting place of 'who was who' in middle class Addis, excitement set in, mingling with the memory of having been there so many times before. She was hoping for a chance encounter but when she got there she found the Piazza more barren than she wished or remembered, and distraught, she went emotionally dumb. An old waiter in the St George's Bar recognized her and with joy on his face, with full and happy gestures, was asking her many questions. Overwhelmed by the different reality than the one residing in her memory, she couldn't utter a word to his cheery welcome.

She felt ridiculously tongue tied. She wasn't afraid because she too recognized the old waiter but her brain was empty of any words, not even a *"tenais talling"*, a simple hello. She thought of asking if he had seen Taferra, but there was a long delay in even recalling her lover's name. She stood before the old waiter, alone, feeling brain naked. After several dumb minutes, she walked away lost in an emotional abandonment of an Ethiopian fantasy that was once a wild, beautiful reality, but now jumbled and obsolete.

With welted eyes she walked away from St George's Bar. Empty of feeling, she sauntered around the familiar filthy streets recalling and brutally relinquishing every romantic thought of the murky two year affair with an Ethiopian whom she now felt had been rightfully a stranger. Walking in the eucalyptus sweet smelling air of Addis, it became obvious to her that she was in the wrong place with a leftover romanticized hangover for a man who should have never existed for her, hard as she tried to imagine and be kind in her thoughts about him. Their affair had been a short fictitious story whose monotony made for barely existent memories. Taferra, as was all of Ethiopia, had been a fictional figure who one time long ago had been expressed by her wishful young girl's mind into an unlikely love affair. How unfair she had been to Calder. She had to find Taferra and once and for all get him out of her mind.

After regaining some calmness, and her hands no longer trembled, she took a taxi, to the all-girls Princess Gennet Boarding School where she had taught English as a Peace Corps Volunteer two years earlier. The privacy walls around the school's compound were as forbidding as she remembered them; they were there to protect the young female boarders whose favorite national pastime, as they liked to remind Peace Corps Volunteer Robin, was sex. When she entered the courtyard of the school, it took only seconds for the students to recognize their former teacher, and there were hugs and kisses and screams of happiness as all the girls rushed her with an enthusiasm reserved only for rock stars.

Again Robin was speechless, this time dumb with happiness, unable to respond to her former students' stream of unending questions. They are such happy children without a chip on their shoulders, without an axe to grind, she thought. They were as she remembered them: all beautiful, with a tantalizing brown red hue complexion that made each and every face sparkle flawlessly. Such beauty, such exuberant comradery, such girlish innocence, such enthusiasm, such genuine friendship – what lovely Ethiopian qualities, she thought, as she finally reached out to touch her students.

Sadly she remembered her own high school experiences at Magnolia High in Sherman Oaks where she and her three best friends clung together in constant anxiety, lest their friendship, that timidly bound them together, but artlessly lacking the savage passion of endurance, might dissolve in stinking emptiness. That familiar timid love affair contrasted with the fiercely uninhibited Ethiopian welcome she was encountering. She recalled her own high school pathetic football pep rallies every fall, cheered on by dumpy coaches and dumb depressing unimportant high school 'athletes' who in monotone, cacophonous voices 'led' the school gang in inane 'school' songs intended to inspire school spirit. They were tragic, pitiful acts, tedious in their badly rehearsed annual fall repetitions; Friday afternoon minor celebrations that couldn't compare to the spontaneous, unrehearsed Ethiopian students' enthusiasm now rushing before her with yelling and screaming to shower her, their former teacher, with love.

Strengthened by her ex-students' expression of love, Robin found her way to the Principal's office, an Indian woman of modest credentials.

"I wanted to ask you if Taferra is still with you," shyly said Robin.

"Haven't you heard? Taferra died soon after you left."

Everyone, including the Principal were aware of the illicit affair between Robin and Taferra. She had silently disapproved then of her staff's fucking on the side and she now gave the deadly news with relish.

Robin's brain drained to her stomach and she fainted.

After she was revived, the lethal news continued. She was told that after she departed Ethiopia, Taferra became depressed, and soon after deranged, disoriented in speech and behaviour. He began to use foul language and even verbally molest his students. Whereas before he had been vain, he was now dishevelled and soon became fat from indifference as if malnourished. One fateful morning, as he made his way to school across an open field nearby, he dropped dead. It was said that by the time he was found amidst the weeds by a passer-by his bloated body was covered with millions of flies.

The image was too horrific for Robin's mind to grasp. The fly infested stinking bloated body was too foreign for her memory of a once beautiful man, for no matter the previous thoughts, a lover decaying in an open field covered with buzzing flies became too appalling, too perverse, an image. She didn't want to retain anything of Ethiopia.

"How stupid of me," she said to herself as she walked away from Princess Gennet School, wishing never to return again.

"The whole Peace Corps thing has been an abortion," she did not fail to see the irony.

The next day, she flew back to Los Angeles, aching only to see her best friends again. Sweet Southern California where the best fiends' friendship could honestly be sustained by Grey Goose vodka and the many reds and whites of Napa and France.

*

David Calder did tolerantly suffer all Robin's bullshit because being the son-in-law of Robert Sargent, owner and CEO of Pioneer Bank, was a cool position to be in: his father-in-law graciously had promoted him to Executive Vice President, Human Resources, after his marriage to Robin. After returning from Ethiopia, in his altruistically soaked bright mind there was some ambivalence in his seemingly Peace Corps idealism, and the greedy capitalist contradictory shit, but he was enough of a realist to accept that morality had more to do with politics than with some antagonistic notions of right and wrong. Like sex, everybody was doing it, so he too dropped the altruism and became a capitalist. He also knew from historical accounts that all women everywhere throughout the centuries had been considered morally inferior to men. To think otherwise would have been abnormal. Shit, you could've tested David a million different ways, as Peace Corps had done, and he would have always come out normal.

Chapter Ten

Blessed are those lucky few who have nothing more important to do than to just get together and shoot the bull and lick the bone together with loving friends. One call here and one call there, and the response is always "Sure, I've got nothing better to do," and off they go. Usually, the place of gathering is not important, though it's always nice, because the camaraderie is always perfect. Friends loaded with excess love to share with each other thrill at the prospect of getting together one more time. There is no agenda to be touched upon, no planned topic of conversation worthy of anticipation other than the drinks which are a given, and the finger foods which are an annoying cover-up for the drinks. The tall stem crystal glasses are always close to one's heart giving grace to the friendly digs and disagreements that are coated in loud laughter. It's all a play, a familiar game, acted out by bosom friends having a good time.

"Do you guys think we're gay," asked Kitty as she tipped her clean vodka martini past her newly lusciously crayoned lips. "I mean sort of like Phoebe, Rachel, and Monica?"

She left a thick mauve trace of her lips on the tall stem lip.

"Were they gay?"

"No because they liked fucking men. They were always fucking. Once a week they fucked! But now with the reruns they're fucking every day, all day long," laughed Myrna.

"But always off stage, as they say," said a proper Sharon.

Pretty much all of Sharon's comments were off the mark, kind of off stage, but even though she wasn't rich she was the most beautiful of the friends and had been part of the group since elementary school. It was her bluest eyes, or her kissable lips, or her lovely cheekbones, or maybe everything. Anyway, most of the things she said fell into a hole never to return, because the friends were all looking and not listening. But they still loved her.

"Well, most fucking does take place off stage," said a thoughtful Robin who always felt the need to be supportive of Sharon.

"So, we all like to fuck men, Kitty, and therefore were not gay," said Myrna.

"All of us, except Sharon, like to fuck men, so we're not gay," smiled Robin towards Sharon.

"Fuck you, Robin," said Sharon and she flipped the finger to her friend.

"Seriously," said Kitty, "friendship is like love, you have to cultivate it."

"Like eggplants," laughed Robin.

They were stretched out on lounge chairs in Kitty's back yard next to the pool. Robin stood up to look for the marinated radishes and ginger slices, which both, she now thought, were the perfect accompaniment to a vodka martini.

"Where the fuck are the radishes," she said, pissed. "Kitty, you haven't been cultivating your red hot radishes," and all laughed.

"Really, do you guys think we might be gay? Like we've been hugging each other since middle school," said Myrna.

"No, we're not gay because we like to fuck guys," insisted Kitty, whose house it was.

"Except for Sharon who never fucks anyone anymore," said Myrna.

"You'd like to fuck me, wouldn't you Myrna," said Sharon.

"You got it wrong, Myrna. Sharon likes to fuck, but only her Hank," said Robin.

"Hank and Sharon, Sharon and Hank, forever," laughed Myrna, which was a mean thing to say because she was also fucking Hank.

Sharon knew, like every wife knows about her husband's infidelities.

There was a brief moment of respite as everyone lifted their glass.

"No, really," said Kitty. "Friendship is a powerful mover of human emotions. We're lucky that we've been such good friends for so long."

They were all moving around the pool now, getting refills and digging into the shrimp, and parmesan, and smoked salmon, and grapes, and raspberries and blueberries, and breaded chicken wings.

"Hey, you wanna do some skinny dipping," said Robin. They had done it before.

"Not without our husbands," said Myrna.

"But you don't have a husband right now, Myrna," said Sharon. "Maybe you could call Justine and Meredith to come and join us in his place."

"That would be very cool, wouldn't it, Sharon," said Robin, uneasily.

"That would be very sick," said Myrna.

"I know what you mean," said Kitty.

"Then we could all be best friends forever," wickedly continued Sharon.

"Count me in," said Robin.

"This conversation smacks of disease, as in deep-seated psychoneurosis," said Myrna.

"Like I said, friendship and love are all over the literature and poetry," said Kitty.

"Oh, fuck you Kitty; you're always trying to avoid the unpleasant. Sometimes, you really are a chicken-shit," said Robin who was into psychoanalysis.

"Exactly, Kitty! Even the Bible talks about … well, mostly about love," said Sharon.

"Yeah, now days love is mostly gay love, like Sappho and her Lesbian dykes," Robin kept the sexual theme going.

"This world is getting sicker by the day," somebody said.

"Freud definitely was a lot more interesting than the bulls and cows of Wall Street," somebody else said.

"Bulls and bears," corrected Robin.

"I've heard that athletes have the biggest hard-ons, don't they, Sharon," smilingly said Myrna. "I understand they get it up, spread your legs, and let you have it."

"How would you know, Myrna," Kitty to the rescue. "You married a dentist."

"He told me," smiled Myrna, coquettishly.

"Truisms from the mouth of a dentist's wife whose husband drilled her without mercy," laughed Sharon, now somewhat boozed up.

"Sharon, if you have something to say …" Myrna didn't finish.

"You're all envious of Sharon because she's married to a big hunk athlete; a big hunk dumb ex-athlete," said Robin, and Sharon laughed, and almost choked on her martini.

"OK, everybody stop it. Let's do something more serious than this silly small talk," said Kitty who as hostess was obliged to move on when things dragged, or got too vicious.

"I like small talk," said Robin. "We all seem to like small talk. We four best friends love small talk."

"Don't pay attention to Robin, Kitty. Go ahead, you start us on more important things than hard-ons," said Myrna. "Come to think of it …"

Kitty cut her off, when suddenly she said, "Barb, my mother, was a sad illiterate woman. Happy, maybe, but definitely illiterate."

"In those days, it wasn't necessary for housewives to be literate," quickly added Myrna. "The only thing expected of them was to pop out babies."

"Come on, Myrna! It wasn't all that long ago. We're talking about our mothers."

"Well, not quite, Myrna. Like today, some housewives even then, could read and write. Most of them went to school you know; but not my mother," Kitty was almost in tears.

"Your father was an ophthalmologist, wasn't he, Kitty?" said Myrna.

"Yes! Doctor Michael Davenport, Ophthalmologist, his sign at the door read. His office, or I should say his business, because he made all his money from eye herbal medicines … was out of Santa

Monica, Wilshire Boulevard," and there was a sparkle of deep pride in Kitty's eyes.

"What about your mother, Myrna? What did she do for a living?" asked Sharon.

"Sharon, stop bugging Myrna," said Robin.

"My mother was a saint, Sharon. She loved her husband dearly; so much that she died – I don't remember exactly – but I think it was about a week after my father died. I don't know. Why do you ask, Sharon? You were all at the funeral."

"I meant in so far as schooling … but never mind … I'm sure they're both in Heaven, dear," said Sharon, and she meant it.

"Both your parents and Kitty's parents had the foresight to leave each of you with a huge fortune," said Robin and there were deep sighs from all the friends.

"Did you guys know that a long time ago people thought that the deep sky was Heaven and all the stars were saints?" said Sharon. "Well, that was before we discovered that the blue in the sky is really a reflection of earth's oceans, and that just beyond the blue skyline there's nothing but deep darkness?"

Everybody's glazed eyes looked up and quickly dried. There is small talk and there are tall tales. Sometimes it was difficult to understand when Sharon was small talking or when she was tall telling. But then, none of the friends was particularly careful of the words they chose to express their not so profound tales. They were long-time friends and they didn't have to be particular about their vocabulary or their intonation during party times. Familiarity and vodka gave license to blunt simplicities and uninspired talk. They were all champions at hiding the gnawing memories of their jolted minds which required elusive performances to fend off words that they might accidentally utter and reveal their pedestrian ways.

"You know, we could write a book if we record all the things we say," said Robin.

"What about you, Robin? Was your mother literate?" smiled Sharon.

"You all know that my mother spoke French and therefore she could not have been illiterate, for your unkind suggestion, Sharon," said Robin who was never offended by Sharon' beautiful face, which she viewed as innocence.

"Your parents are leaving you a bundle, aren't they," half yawned Kitty, now deeply mellow. She really didn't care.

"Well, they are big time bankers; but there are rumours that your father is double timing your mother. Is there any truth to that, Robin?" said Myrna.

"Get your mind out of the gutter, Myrna."

"It's not me, but you, who's in the gutter, Sharon," said Myrna.

"*Pas de probleme,* Sharon. Ever since Phil left, Myrna hasn't been getting any, and she's been cranky ever since," said Robin. She quickly downed-the-hatch her martini, and hurriedly got another; she was feeling gooood, and she didn't care.

"You have no idea, Robin. I bet I get a lot more than you," said Myrna.

"I bet you do, Myrna," said Sharon. "Do you know Larry?"

"Larry who?"

"That's too bad. But I know Larry," said Sharon.

"It's your turn, Sharon. Tell us about your mother," said the hostess.

"My mother was a father fucker," said Sharon, and she almost threw up from frenzied paroxysms of laughter. Vodka came out of her nose.

"That's why I love you, Sharon," said Robin who was also laughing very hard.

"What does that make you, Sharon," said Myrna, who wasn't laughing; she was pissed that Sharon knew.

"Right now, I'm a little tipsy and I can't tell whether it's the vodka or you Myrna, my beloved, whom I love too much because you're putting up with some heavy teen upbringing, what, with two vivacious teen-age daughters who might or might not be having coitus ..." and she again spit out some of her vodka in uncontrollable laughter.

"Don't change the subject, Sharon. We want you to share your thoughts on your mother. Each of us knows each other's mothers but right now we want you to tell us about your mother," said stupid Kitty, who chose to bypass a threatening good story.

"Go ahead, Sharon, share with us," laughed Robin.

"My mother is a great author. She writes books, so she's very literate, unlike your mother, Kitty. Nor is my mother sad. She loves to read and is an expert on the Bible and Christian religion in general. She finds joy and happiness being in the loving arms of Jesus," and she again almost gagged in laughter. "She's a true believer and thinks that Noah and his ark were real as were all of Jesus' miracles, because they're all in the Bible," and here again Sharon almost gagged on vodka and laughter.

"Aren't you a believer, Sharon? For a long time I didn't believe, but now I do," said Myrna. "How could I not believe when my husband is a monk?"

"Coitus you Myrna. Just because your ex-husband joined a monastery …" said Robin.

"He's still my husband, Robin. We haven't divorced yet, unlike you and your husband who haven't touched each other in years."

"My parents have been in love from the first day they met," said Sharon. "And after all these many years, they're still in love. They're Catholic, you know."

"Isn't it strange that we all had loving parents," summed Kitty.

My God, she's unbearable they all thought.

But Kitty was doing it on purpose because, after all, she was the hostess.

It was after five pm by now, the best friends were all boozed up, the chicken wings had been consumed, but no one had the slightest intention of abandoning such late afternoon stimulating conversation with all the nuances of artful dialogue on the classical path that leads to beauty and truth. They had all emptied their bladders a few times which made Kitty's back yard smell fresh, and again inviting to the outdoor conversation. Besides, there was nowhere else better to be than Kitty's garden.

"There's nothing strange about it, Kitty," said Robin who was slurping her stories a little bit less than the others. Sobriety had given way to fluency of speech. "We think we have loving parents because, we, like it or not, to us, they have managed to raise us just like themselves. It' called replication, my dear Kitty. From the moment we are born, every mamma's whole objective in life is to raise her baby, especially her baby girl, to take care of mamma when she ages. It's like we owe it to them."

They all down-the-hatch another.

It was a sobering thought. Each took a minute to rehash what they had just heard, lightly scratching their heads. It sounded a little bit too personal, too Robin-like, too much bullshit; but on second thought, there might have been some truth to it. To be brought up to be like one's mother was not out of reason, and it probably had been noted in some book or other before. I mean, what is a mother supposed to do? Raise her child like it's not part of her? Also, it's got to be the mother that raises her children to be like her, and not the children who raise the mother to be like them.

"There's definitely an intricate entanglement between mothers and their daughters," said Myrna. "Being a mother, sometimes I think it's my daughters are raising me to be like them instead of the other way around. I'm just kidding. Let's face it though, mothers definitely tend to know everything that their daughters do because they had done the same things when they were young. I suspect …"

"I hate my mother," another sudden burst from Sharon.

It wasn't as bad as it sounded. The girls were too far gone to be impressed.

"Hate is a bit too strong of an emotion for one's mother, isn't it, Sharon?" said Kitty.

"Illiterate, illiterate, illiterate …", they all tossed another.

"Oh hell! It's true enough, I couldn't wait to get away from mine either. She was suffocating me with her servility to my asshole father. She was his manservant – or I should say, woman servant, abject to every one of his gutless wishes. I don't know whom I hated more, Daddy or Mamma."

"That's why we're all such good friends and have been for such a long time. It's because we all hate our mothers and don't want to be like them when we grow up. Jesus, that's why we've been together since we were little girls," said Robin full of Freudian insight. "We became friends because we hated our mothers."

"More than my father, I hated my mother," said Myrna, unversed in Freud.

"Whoa there mamma Myrna. Think about your daughters," said Robin. "Do you think they hate you?"

"What about you, Robin? Did you hate your mother?"

"No, I never hated my mother. She's such a pathetic little creature totally obsequious to my arrogant father. There isn't much of her to hate. But him I hated and went all the way to Ethiopia to get away from. He smothered me and followed me all the way there, far away from him, but he continued to make my life miserable. You know, every time I take a shit, I think of him," they all laughed.

"Freud says that it's boys that have problems with their mothers. He said boys have psychosexual problems with their mothers. Can you imagine that? I never had any sexual problems with my Albert," said Kitty.

"But maybe he did with you, Kitty," said Sharon.

"Are you serious, Kitty? Isn't Albert currently calving cows in Nebraska?" said Myrna.

"Nobody knows the trouble I'm in, nobody knows my sorrow …" Sharon sang in faux cowboy baritone.

"He still calls me the apple of his eye," Robin blinked her eyes.

"You guys are getting too serious. You want to switch to wine," said Kitty?

"Just kidding, Kitty. You know we all love you very much; just like Albert," said Robin.

"Well, I love you all as much as you guys love me," said Kitty.

"Kitty, is it the vodka or do I note a little sarcasm in your voice," said Myrna, smiling.

"Just kidding," said Kitty. "I really do love you guys."

"Which brings us back to the original question: are we friends or just lovers?" said Sharon. "Kitty just said that she loves us as much as we love her. Does she love us because we are good friends or because she lusts after our ass?"

"Nobody lusts after my ass," said Myrna.

"Sharon, sometimes you are goofy," laughed Robin.

"Well, Robin, your stale mouth is corny to the point of exhaustion," said Sharon.

*

Having consumed a good amount of vodka and an even better amount of white wine the four best of friends joyfully succumbed to the mellow spell of the Southern California warm afternoon caresses of Hypnos, the god of sleep, who had arrived just for them from 'beyond the gates of the rising sun'. Together with Morpheus, he took them up to Venus' Mount, otherwise known as Kitty's back yard, and they were soon merrily running and dancing alongside the nude mad Maenads of Dionysus. Robin, being the most amenable to happy dreams, was leading the way. Morpheus pointed them out to her, and she saw Claudio and Hank fast furious following the best of friends, clawing their way up to catch them with their panties down, and she understood their lustful intentions. In a heightened sexual desire, in her poetic dream, she persuades her best friends to tear their husbands apart and devour them, including David who now belatedly appeared. Like ferocious lions, they attack their husbands and rip their heads off. They then feast on their husbands' remains. This lasts a lifetime and reaches an intensity that can only be satisfied with uncontrolled bouts of sex. They were four beautiful brides of the woods who in the fury of their lusty excitement and in the passion of their wantonness, any male would do, though the more acquainted the male, the more receptive the rage. And there among the sweet odors of the pines there came a procession of big hunk athletes from the fantasies of eternal time. Brainless big hunks like Zeus and Hercules and Hank and Mark and David ejaculating low IQ semen into the orgiastic screams of adolescent virgin princesses, the daughters of kings, and other nobles, who naturally want the lust to last beyond the reality of the event. And like in all dreams the most pleasurable of moment was the climax.

*

Snoring on their deck chairs, and deep in their intoxicated sexual frenzy, oblivious to any reality, Claudio arrives home and is pleasantly surprised by the sprawling scene. He takes a couple of minutes to size up the situation: showing all, buttocks and breasts, the girls are all commando. Sharon's breasts are hanging out defiantly, most inviting, and there are bare thighs and asses galore; bottles and stem crystal glasses everywhere, a true Bacchanal orgy. He smiles and immediately understands the festive occasion that preceded it. At first he wants to wake them up but changes his mind. He goes into the house and brings out four silk bed sheets and, carefully not to wake them from their deep drunken stupor, covers the girls.

He then goes in the house and calls Hank.

"Hank, your wife is passed out on my deck," he laughs lightly.

There's a slight hesitation at the other end.

"Did you say that my wife is passed out on your dick?"

Hank liked to make fun of Claudio's sometimes Sicilian accent.

"Yeah, maybe you like for me to take care of her," suggestively laughs Claudio.

Another hesitation on Hanks part.

"Claudio, if she says it's OK, it's OK with me too," said Hank.

"Maybe we could swap sometimes," anxiously suggested Claudio.

"Well, Claudio, with that swap, that'll leave only Robin out of my snare," said Hank. "That bitch is never in heat."

"You dirty dog! You mean you've been humping Myrna too?"

"For a couple years now."

Every woman knows that true friends have no secrets.

"Does Sharon know?"

It was almost a rhetorical question.

Shortly thereafter, in holy Dionysian lust, Claudio decides to fuck Sharon. He undresses nude and tippy toes quietly, quietly lies behind her, and cups her breasts ecstatically. Sharon comes to for a second, recognizes Claudio, but still too drunk to properly grasp what's going on behind her, says nothing, and falls into the arms of Hypnos again. Totally under the influence of her drunken stupor, she dreams of stomping on purple grapes. The sweet purple grape juice beneath her feet slowly rises to above her waist on its way to her breasts, and in the depths of her dream, she feels Claudio slide deeper inside her. Dreamingly she gets on her back and makes herself more open to his manly body and to his experienced hands that are making her feel like the narcissist that she is. It was a gorgeous meeting of two beautiful people. She was the personification of a beautiful woman, and he was very handsome. At that moment, they were young lovers, two strangers meeting for the first time, which made their lovemaking most pleasurable. It was the stuff that dreams are made of, and she was happy to be in it. For the first time in her life, Sharon felt the delight of her womanly instincts, and she was loving it. She felt the warmth of the dream, as he drilled her, and being in a dream, it was all free of guilt or sin, and she wanted more. She half-consciously made herself even more available to Claudio who wondered how he was going to repay all this kindness, and how Hank, the hunk, would get even with his Kitty.

For one brief second Kitty came to, saw that Claudio was fucking Sharon, goofy-smiled, and fell back asleep.

Later, when she woke up, Sharon found herself all wet, vaguely recalled Claudio, and realized what had happened.

Humiliated, the next day, she called Robin and told her what she suspected.

"Fuck it, Sharon. You can't go back to change things."

"But Robin, he raped me," said a still clouded Sharon.

"Does it hurt?"

"No," said an almost inaudible Sharon.

"Then fuck it," said Robin. "And listen, make sure you say not a word to Kitty. It would kill her if she knew."

Chapter Eleven

She was in her house, feeling naughty in her brand new Max Mara. She wanted to be indulged like all pretty girls do. Lounging in one of her velvet chaise chairs in one of her spacious game rooms, she coyly licked the rim of her martini glass, self-consciously trying to fit another hopelessly mindless evening into her lovely expensive dress.

It was another insipid poker night at the Merker mansion. Like every other Friday night, once again, happy Hank was hosting his leftover dumb high school football teammates to endless rounds of poker, lots of finger food from his restaurants, and all the beer they could drink. Every other Friday night, the boys of old days would get together and feel good about their socio-economic status, rolling up the cuffs of their old-time janitor-like loose-fitting pants. It was their way of recalling the simple joys of happier times of their high school varsity days when they could and did get any cheerleader they wanted. They were happy Friday nights with endless finger-licking barbeque Buffalo wings, compliments of the house. Hank especially enjoyed these poker nights when he could show off his good luck and fortune to his former football teammates.

There was alwasy an open invitation to Phil, Dave, and Claudio to Merker's poker nights, due to Sharon's insistence who wanted some people with brains around. Dave, however, rarely joined the group feeling out of place with all of Hank's high school jocks, something that he never wished to be. Occasionally, Claudio and Phil would show up; Phil to keep Claudio company, and Claudio mostly to enjoy Sharon's presence. He had figured that it was worth the few bucks at the table to cop a few stares at Sharon, the game's hostess, a role she hated but forced on her by host husband Hank. Some of the nights, one or more of the girl friends would also show up to keep Sharon company, but tonight she was alone.

"Sharon, have I ever mentioned to you that I'm an artist?"

It was Claudio, her other rapist of a few weeks before, whose assault had reaffirmed in her mind that she was right to have detested him from the day she had met him. In reality, the attack still somewhat pleasant on her mind, had left no damaging wounds on her, and with the exception of Robin, only she and Claudio were privy to the event. Accepting that no harm had been done by his unscheduled raping her, she excused the whole tasteless affair as nowhere near as horrible as that of husband Hank's rape in the boys locker room years earlier. It was quite possible, she had considered, that in each case it might have even been her fault; certainly some of it. She had accepted Robin's advice not to make an issue of it.

She barely acknowledged Claudio, her rapist with the dupe's smile. A feeling of weariness and boredom made her look his way for one second. She felt revulsion recalling that in a dream there is no sin, except, she now knew, that it hadn't been a dream. She stood up from her chaise to get away from his glare and her legs involuntarily spread apart to keep her steady. She walked away and felt her whole body reluctantly parading against her will. She felt ridiculous, trembling in her own house. She was awake now, not under any influence, and the fucking Dago was not going to intimidate her.

He was not impressed.

She regained her form but still somewhat lightheaded she spread her thighs hard against her Max Mara evening blue form-fitting dress and gained confidence against its support to steady her stand. Form fitting, stiff against her firm buttocks, and just for the fuck of it, she once again was commando that evening, and everything next to that dress rubbed tough and unassailable. She felt impregnable in her stunning dress and in response to the idiotic question she had just heard about his artistic credentials, she exhaled a wicked little laugh. She gave Claudio a daring look with her huge angry blue heavenly eyes, and immediately regretted it. She felt open to his stare and felt disgusted with herself for initiating such numb conversation which he obviously loved.

Kitty's artless husband Claudio, an artist? A rapist maybe. At that moment she loathed the presumptuous bastard; sneaky fucking foreigner; they're all sneaky; can't trust any of them; poor Kitty. The memory evoked by his presence had already begun to spoil her evening. There was never any hope of mighty Hank coming to her rescue because he no longer cared.

Bored and agitated by the European odor of his presence, she again stared at Claudio, an unlikely quarterback, and wished that somebody other than Claudio, would surface and touch her stupid breasts, braless beneath her tough dress. She wanted an American male to let the Dago know that he was not the one for her. She read his charge very well; he made her feel naked, and she wished that someone other than Claudio would appear and touch her everywhere to cleanse her of his stares. Squeeze her firm breasts and bring her out of her dejected gloom. Even Phil would have been acceptable.

"Claudio, I feel sorry for you because you're a fucking idiot," she half whispered.

She watched him for a minute as he laughed that twisted affected laughter that all foreigners are known for. She understood that the stupid laughter was intended mostly to put at ease all those within hearing range.

What the fuck does he want, she thought to herself? He couldn't possibly think that I would want to fuck him?

Immediately she regretted calling him an idiot and she hoped that her remark was understood as more coy than aggressive.

His smile never left his face, and everywhere her mind went, he followed.

"I know you think that about me, but it's not fair. I suppose it's your American way of thinking non-Americans as just fuckers, as you say, that you've always thought that about me, but I'd like the chance to prove you wrong," smiled Claudio who really didn't give a shit what Sharon thought about him, or about anything. To Claudio, Sharon was a lovely piece.

"You guys want some more beers, or something …" yelled out Sharon to the players shuffling their cards under the hot overhead light of the poker table in the adjacent room of the great game room.

"From you, I'll take the something else, Sharon," came the typical rude reply from one of the guys. It pissed Sharon off that her husband never defended her by showing some minimal disapproval at his filthy-mouthed friends' bad manners.

She left Claudio and walked to the poker table and tried to put her arms around her husband's shoulders. It was a dismal gesture signalling to her dumb husband that he needed to run interference and save her from Claudio's charges. True to form he heartlessly dismissed her in preference to a pair of fours. Behind him, hanging prominently on the wall was a huge poster of Johnny Unitas.

"Later," he said, and all the boys laughed at the innuendo.

"OK, Hank!" they shouted. "Show her who's the boss."

"Later," said Hank, and that too brought down the house.

She knew there would be no 'later' that night because she didn't care to be alone with her depressing husband. But Claudio, even in her denials, had aroused her beneath her tight dress and she was feeling a bit upset, uncomfortable, and vulnerable. She felt her tight form fitting dress flawlessly hugging the dimples of her buttocks and felt hot, sensing all the testosterone around her. She also knew that as much as she might have wanted to make love that night it wasn't going to be with Hank because he couldn't handle losing and he always lost on poker nights.

Frustrated and feeling neglected, she walked back to the bar area, distastefully flipped a finger at Claudio who was sitting on an upholstered mahogany chair against the wall, patiently waiting for the sure thing. She thought she saw an idiotic smile on the face of a fool who wanted to impress. Sharon misunderstood the stupid smile as intellectually void, similar to the expression she had come to recognize in Hank and his cerebrally damaged friends. His smile was an exaggerated display of teeth whiffing for the right smell, same as that of her husband's, and his friends'. She thought the devious little smile on his foreigner's face, familiar to her since adolescence, was displayed only by her husband's stupid friends whenever they thought they had something to look forward to. And here was Claudio displaying like them; like an ass in heat. Annoyed, she looked into his rough face and it reminded her of the learned posturing that children put on when being photographed.

"You know Claudio, most artists die young. They die without children even though they have many mistresses and marry when they're young."

And then she lost it, talking to herself more than to Claudio.

"They die wrinkled, and are buried in their village grave where they remain harmless dead, as ordinary nothings; as nothings, as when they were alive," she mustered her hostile, leftover venom, full of vengeance, to dump on Claudio's face for having taken her for granted.

She felt relief and hoped she had hurt him.

"Grave thoughts, there, Sharon," said Claudio, still grinning, trying to impress that he was attentive.

"I still haven't told Kitty on you, and if you don't behave, one day I will tell her, and she'll spank you," Sharon stupidly smiled.

He laughed, determined as ever to fuck her that night.

They were in a great room warmed by stained-glass ceilings and a huge granite topped mahogany bar with eight upholstered mahogany bar stools in front of it. Before the bar, and behind the bar stools was the billiard table. At the opposite side of the bar, looking out to the poker room was a Vegas size craps table. Along the walls all around were hand-carved side tables. High school quarterback Hank Merker had done very well as a restauranteur.

"Sharon, I have to say, it's so nice being here with you. I much rather be here with you than out there with your husband's poker buddies."

"You're too dumb to understand," she said, "but at least you can still breathe."

It was another unkind remark to wish him dead, and incomprehensible even for her. She had no idea what she was saying, or why, except maybe in reference to his assaulting her. She couldn't help it, but it was uncalled for; even after his assault, he didn't deserve it.

She couldn't believe that she was beginning to have feelings for Claudio.

Her husband deserved such hateful outpourings more than Claudio did.

"Trust me Sharon. You deserve someone better than Hank." He was trying to stupidly convey to her that nothing she could say would frighten him away; that she had no way out, and that Hank was in on it.

I see you now and I see you as you were when you were sixteen, you pretty little pussy cat in heat; thrill screeching to hide your lovely tight ass, then, as you are doing right now, pretending that somehow you're different than the others, he held back.

"In the Garden stood a maid, beautiful as life could be." He smiled timidly trying to rhyme a poem for her, but it was obvious that she was insensitive to his wit. Stuck, he wanted to sing it to her but there was no melody ringing in his mind.

She rolled her bluest eyes and her mind travelled to the Garden of Eden, and she immediately wondered if Adam and Eve did it in the Garden with all the holy angels chanting heavenly songs as they watched.

"Dirty little angels," she said. "They have to go to confession and communion."

"I, for one, like dirty little angels," said Claudio. He didn't care.

"Have you told Kitty?" she said.

She went behind the wet bar and again spread her legs hard against her tough form fitting dress, a perfect eight, sensed her tough thighs against it, and felt that things were under control. She chilled more Grey Goose and poured it in her glass with a lemon twist. Normally, she liked un-pitted fat green olives with her martinis but she felt like a hard-on at that moment and added another twist.

"In your honor," she said to Claudio and added an olive anyway.

She felt good, angels beginning to buzz above her head.

"If you want to get another drink come around and fix it yourself," she said to Claudio.

Going behind her to pour himself another scotch, Claudio purposefully brushed his hand against Sharon's well defined ass clearly well rounded within her tight dress. It was a good exploratory feel without being too obtrusive.

So that's the way it starts, she thought. Go ahead asshole, get your cheap thrill, because that's all you get tonight.

She said nothing.

"I mean, after Kitty and I got married and I set up my company, when I stopped driving around to pick up restaurant grease, and I had more time in my hands, I didn't know what else to do and I thought I would try doing some writing, which I did, and I've enjoyed ever since."

He took another large gulp from his Johnny Walker Black.

Talking about Kitty made Sharon uncomfortable. She changed the subject.

"I thought you said you're an artist?"

"That too," said Claudio. "I have never told you that, have I?"

"Told me what, Claudio?"

"That I'm an author?"

"Well, now you have," smiled Sharon in affected interest as she licked her lovely lips alluringly around another martini olive and in unison with her tongue coyly batted her crystal clear eyes. The vodka had snuck up on her and she was feeling good.

Claudio raised his eyebrows and nodded his head; he was feeling his scotch erecting.

"You are full of surprises tonight, aren't you, Claudio? I'm so glad you've made me one of your secret sharers, Claudio. You know, an hour ago I hated you, and you know why, don't you? Imagine, our Claudio, an artist and an author these past some twenty years, imagine that," she teased the prick.

Claudio smiled the proud smile of recognition.

She's so beautiful, he thought.

"Who would have ever thought," Sharon smiled to herself.

She felt another confusing moment of delectable vodka. She was alone at a time when she needed a friend to tease her feelings, or maybe cry on her shoulder. There were all sort of indistinct emotions blending with the vodka. Unfamiliar stuff surfacing from the depths of her stomach, it seemed; distressed light headedness that could only have been safely played out and shared only with a good, good friend.

Or a priest, she thought.

She wanted to sit but there was no chair behind the bar.

And at that moment Claudio once again from behind reached for a gentle touch.

She didn't feel a thing. She was too distant from Claudio's senseless fondling. He was not a familiar face to whom she could extend an approving smile, or a warm kiss in response. He was merely an acquired nuisance, her best friend's second husband. Stupid ass; as if touching her ass meant happiness in his life; or hers. There was no way of registering his emotionally empty groping as anything meaningful.

"That's my boy," she said, and feeling sorry for him, like an adolescent, gave him a gentle insipid kiss on the cheek. It was an afterthought meaningless kiss, and just like Hank and his buddies didn't care about what she was doing behind the bar, so, she didn't care what Hank and his poker buddies were doing in their good times poker shit game.

She felt pity and shame for herself.

Death crossed her mind.

Bad luck, she understood exactly what Claudio was after. She didn't know what the fuck to do as he gently pressed against her dress and to go into a swoon would have been too melodramatic. All at once she realized that no moral defence could stop Claudio's drive to a good fuck. He was determined and she felt weak against his pressing.

"Odd thing is that I've always thought of you being there as the single most person of goodness away from certain corruption and to this day I could never find out why…" it was Claudio huffing and puffing in her ear.

What the fuck is he doing, she thought?

"Hey, Claudio and Sharon, what are guys up to in here?"

It was Mark Freeman, her husband's best friend wide receiver, in a surprise come-to call for Sharon. In one of the rare time, she was happy to see him.

He had been part of the team, inseparable buddies on the Magnolia High School Tigers varsity football team, and ever since, Sharon knew that Mark badly wanted to screw her. Once, she had danced with him on the school gym, on a Friday night school dance, and he held her tight and made sure that she felt his hard-on. It was a long slow dance and she remembered it as very pleasant. In a different happening she would have been ok with Mark. Too bad for Mark, in deference to the buddy system, you did not hit on a best friend's girl. So with reverence to his best friend Hank, who had gotten there first, and who had been screwing Sharon for some time in prelude to their marriage, Mark had learned to honourably keep his distance. There definitely was honor among friends in those early years of high school acquaintance. But as the years went by, the prowl instincts among the best of buddies became more determined, and stealthily they approached uncomfortably closer to her. And Mark wasn't alone: all of Hank's best friends wanted a piece of Sharon. Imperceptibly, lust gave way to indiscretion and crude familiarity. Of all of Hank's friends, Mark was the most discrete as if by chance always appearing at the wrong moment with the wrong words. She found herself between distraction and disappointment as she felt Mark's honor code on every pack occasion to rut into stupid touchy-feely, pardon, accidental pawing of her. And the more Hank's interest waned in her, especially the last couple of years, the more solicitous Mark had become towards her. Stale odors exuded from an ignored wife whose body language had long ago blocked all sexual invites to amoral behavior among the dumb crowd including Mark. Bit by bit, though, the long-time high school buddies casually confused their once proper behavior with gratuitous little ass pinches and wanton hugs on an outwardly unmotivated Sharon who detested the physical attention of all of Hank's high school buddy-friends.

There was no such expression of empathy on Claudio's part. Unlike Mark, he, without solicitousness, wanted Sharon without the hang-ups of best friends.

"We were talking about art and the artist," said Sharon straightening up her dress. "Did you know that Claudio is an artist, Mark?"

"And an author," said Claudio exiting from behind the wet bar agitated by Mark's sudden appearance.

"Who's winning, Mark?" said Sharon.

"Well, your husband is getting drubbed as usual, but he's got the mullah so it's good for us poorer poker folk."

"Mullah?" asked Claudio.

"You know, money, c-notes," proudly said Mark.

"What'll you have, Mark?" asked an irritated Claudio.

"I'd rather hear the request from Sharon's lips, if you don't mind Claudio. Anyway, who made you the boss of this house? I'm gonna tell Hank, Sharon," grinned Mark.

"I know exactly what Mark wants," said Sharon. "He wants what he's always wanted, a double bourbon neat. Right, Mark?"

Mercifully she actually poured him a double triple bourbon.

"Whatever you say, Sharon," said a dejected Mark realizing he was not welcomed.

He took his double triple bourbon and crawled back to the poker table. First hand, he got a full house and the excitement killed any thoughts about Sharon and what she might have been up to behind the bar with the Italian Dago.

Claudio and Sharon were once again alone, behind the bar, out of hearing range from the poker room where Hank and friends were in the throes of another Texas-hold-them poker night. Not far from the boys' action, in the Great Room, powerful sexual feelings were smouldering in Claudio who had already confirmed with his best friend Hank that it would be OK if he screwed his Sharon. It had been a long wait but he would not be denied this night. Encouraged by the low lights hanging over the circular poker table with Johhny Unitas cocking to unload a bomb for Hank, and with all the buddies concentrating on the game, Claudio saw the score coming.

She was more receptive to his hands now which he skilfully maneuvered playfully around her waist, disrespectfully dropping them naughtily across her tightly-dress-fitted ass on his way to fucking her behind the mahogany bar well out of the way from the intense poker game. He was saying nothing, barely breathing trying to keep it quiet, she too quietly feeling mischievous and seeking an out from the boredom of the night. He stared most forcefully into Sharon's eyes and she was momentarily mesmerized; but she recovered quickly. In a macho stance full of the tired cool, Claudio's wandering hands sensually drifted across her back.

Sharon was at first surprised and then bemused at the puffed trousers, all too familiar, no more than the usual outrageous sexual excitations that all of Hank's friends had at one time or another stupidly exhibited since high school. In her mind, Claudio was just another dumb friend of her husband's whose charge, like all the others', would invariably be blunted by the adherence to the ubiquitous code of best friends restrain. They were all lightweights, easily forgettable, her husband's friends, including Claudio, in spite of that night, and after all these years she still could not bring herself to take any of them seriously. So emotionally removed had she been from all their jumbled displays that she was never unsettled beyond the initial surprise of rudeness.

For one last moment Claudio thought of stupid Hank and in his mind he saw a foolish man enmeshed in his paltry poker losses and out of touch with his beautiful wife, cursing his bad luck. With both hands he held her gently by her waist and looked into her face and all thoughts of friendship with Hank went to hell. He was on an emotional peak and all he could think about was spreading Sharon's legs, and fuck Hank. He was sure Sharon was lubricating just for him, and from the feel of his searching hands knew that she was commando tonight. Any protests from Hank would have been met with violent punches, and screw the friendship bullshit. At that moment she was worth ten thousand friendships. Once again he fantasized about the feel of Sharon's naked breasts against his unshaven, manly face, and damn the sin.

Problem was that Claudio was still the village jerk, terrifically inept, a jock without a strap; so disorderly that he lacked any semblance of charm to incite a woman to slide into seduction even when she went commando.

What a hopeless dolt, she thought.

"Imagine that; our Mark, a published author at that!" she deeply sighed, and like a practiced queen moved slightly beyond his reach.

"Claudio, Sharon. The name is Claudio, a famous Roman name," he said coming down with a smile. He was in heat and nothing was going to interrupt his irrepressible charge.

She thought of her father, but no support there; nothing would come of it; he had long ago violently disowned her when she told him she had married Hank. And her sorry Judy Anton mother was nowhere to be found. She then thought of Kitty and said "Don't" to herself and Claudio thought she was speaking to him.

Irresponsibly, Sharon decided to play along with Claudio's sniffling game for lack of anything better going on in her husband's poker get-together, one of the many boring evenings she had suffered many times before. Most other poker nights she would have secluded herself into her bedroom until the friends had left. But on this particular night she had decided to join the boys even for a while. It was the dress; the damn tight fitting Max Mara dress had turned her on and she wanted the world to see her fabulous tight fitting ass that night. So, between the easy to swallow martinis with huge green olives, she flirtatiously fluttered her eyes and toyed with Dago Claudio, wickedly smiling directly into his face.

Slightly frustrated but still determined, Claudio tried to perk up his courage in his golden scotch and went and got some more.

She went around the bar and peeked into the poker game and saw her husband's thick neck half-hidden in the dense cigarette smoke all around him. He was half drunk and definitely more interested in the poker game with the "Hi there" gang of best friends than at what might have been going on with his wife behind their wet bar in the Great Room. She had no blazing thoughts about that particular moment in her life; everything was registering as everyday dull normal. Back behind the bar and mentally pressed against the liquor with little space between them, and her ass wet against the bar sink, she really didn't care one way or another, and she shoved her knee between Claudio's semi-spread legs and smiled.

She felt as surprised about herself as much as Claudio looked stupid.

It was vengeance, and she too decided to play it stupid.

It wasn't difficult to play stupid because Sharon had many years of practice after many years in high school with her stupid husband Hank. She thought she loathed what she was doing, but being in close contact with Claudio's knees was by far the activity of least regrets, other particulars to come still vacant in her eyes. All tangled up, she felt exposed, like meat dangling on a butcher's hook, and too late she wished she was alone in her room away from the punishing shambles of the poker night. It was an awfully awkward moment, but she felt she could out-manoeuver dumb Claudio as she had done with others many times before. She knew that she had been fantasy-fucked by all the men she had passively met during the course of her life, from a young girl on. If Claudio was revelling in his amoral fantasies, that didn't make her a slut; and if it did, then all the world was made up of sluts.

High behind her bar, she felt Claudio's rush on her cheeks as an unfolding adolescent play, a minor sexual embarrassment empty of threat. Shoring up her befuddled mind with a sip, the maddening thought occurred to her that it was probably her husband that had put up dumb Dago Claudio to this predatory pretence to test her out. She couldn't believe that Claudio had the balls to put a rush on her behind her husband's back, or Kitty's, for that matter. Pissed, she took a good gulp of her martini and viewed the event as sexual role-playing among the wooden marionettes being manipulated by a vengeful husband getting even with a wife who wasn't giving anymore. Unhappily, she knew that even if her husband was watching, he would not have strongly protested Claudio's rude behavior towards his wife.

She decided to play out the dumb scene; after all, how long can one fend off the charge, and, anyway, what are friends for, if not for sharing, she thought?

Once again Claudio did dare, like a sixth grader, to reach and feel Sharon's ass.

"So you write?"

Like an adolescent, he was quick to withdraw his hand, not giving her time to disapprove. He felt stupid, as if he was on a first date.

"Well, I do write and I've been meaning to ask you, if you have some spare time, and if you wouldn't mind, to read some of the things I've written," haltingly mumbled Claudio. "I would really appreciate your critique and opinion, because I know you like to read a lot, and Hank was telling me that you're into religion these days."

She covered her mouth to keep from laughing out loud and discovered a leftover drop of vodka under her tongue. It was extra smooth and gave her pause to see that friend Claudio was really dumb. There was a stupid smirk on his sterile face and the crowd was anteing up one more time. There was not a single stir of recognition from the low profile poker crowd to her impolite laughter at Roman, or more classic, Sicilian Claudio. It was one of those wet nights when no one had anything better to do than to let lust play out.

"So when do you want to do it?" he said, his eyes welting.

"Do what?" she replied, somewhat surprised.

"Get together," he said.

At last, the waited charge of the tomcat pressing the queen, complete with near misses. The slow dance and posturing had occurred time and again between her and one or another of her husband's pointless wide receivers in any of a thousand nights of extended, clan celebrations. For countless times, the lingering smell to fuck Sharon by one or another of her husband's friends was always just short of its intention, because the boys were essentially dumb. But tonight's reach by Claudio had touched a chord in Sharon's ass and she was interested. Even in playacting, a good actress sometimes will put her soul and heart into it, and for one second, Sharon thought she wanted it. Morality was fast disappearing in the presence of powerful libido urgings with nothing but an inconclusive husband to block the heat. Her heart pumped a couple of extra powerful beats and she was sure there would be no consequences to the act. Not for her, anyway! She only hoped that the dumb Dago wasn't playacting out some sort of misplaced neurotic macho fantasy bet with her husband, "bet I can;" "bet you can't," that he, and maybe others, God forbid, had made with her perpetually smiling mindless high school days in-crowd husband.

Fuck it! Who cares, she thought. Fuck'em all!

"Well, bless my fucking soul," hushed a licked Sharon as she puckered up her over-crayoned luscious lips, "our Claudio, a writer! What do you write about, Claudio?"

There was a long pause and Sharon was disappointed.

"I write about all sorts of things. I've bought a lot of notebooks and I write in them all the time. Especially at night, just before I fall asleep. I find so much tranquillity in fantasizing about a lot of things and I fall asleep," he grinned a baby smile.

She smiled back a reserved smile, like one for children who say cute things.

He was mindless now, his sexual charge having scrambled his mind, mingling Sharon's powerful odors with his Johnny Walker Black.

Jesus Christ save me from this idiot, thought Sharon, and all previous thoughts of hanky-panky gave way to the unadulterated simple feelings that she always had for Kitty's second husband. A faint tear full of vodka rolled down her right cheek in fear that her eternal woman's timeless defences might now be crumbling too easily. She wiped the tear ever so carefully not to smear her mascara.

Got her ass now thought Claudio aware only of the perfect tear that had rolled out of Sharon's blue eyes, an eternal sign of female capitulation to an irrevocable invitation for sex.

"Don't worry, I won't hurt you," he said.

"I mean what kind of writing do you do, Claudio? Is it fiction, or history, or maybe you write about romance ..." she desperately smiled and touched his hand.

She finds me irresistible, he thought.

He took the irreversible step of manly interrupting what up to now had seemed to him to be Sharon's feeble attempts to hold back the long awaited score. He purposefully stared disrespectfully deep into the divide of her gifted breasts, rolled his tongue out, and licked his chops that were her breasts. Like a prey before the predator, poor Sharon was indeed mesmerized into shameless submission. He wasn't "gonad fuck" around anymore, as he was known to say during serious moments such as this. He took a large gulp of his scotch, tried to control his penis rising, and articulated his natural born gifts as an author.

"I write about tits, Sharon. I write about big tits like yours."

She felt the booze rush into her brain dulling out all other sounds.

"My tits are much too big for you, you fucking prick," she said. "They're a handful for any man and definitely way beyond your reach," uselessly she tried to protest, lest she seem too easy, though her words were awash with the sweetness of the Grey Goose.

He smiled the wily smile of the alley tom knowing well enough that the more she protested the least she would resist. It was simply a matter of finding the right moment for a fierce piercing quickie, so fast, that nobody would notice.

"Everything about me is big, Sharon, including my mouth."

It was a gross display of hormonal rage as he reached for her crotch. Simultaneously, her hormones persuaded her mind that no harm would come of it; that it was most natural and that it wouldn't last forever.

He raised her tight fitting dress above her waist gorging on her nakedness. He entered her with ease because she had been ready and she caught her muted scream between her teeth in time for others not to hear her belatedly pained soft, "don't."

Powerful sexual urges, pulsating from somewhere within, most unfamiliar to her, enveloped her whole being. She was wide open, and he was out of control, and she had only herself to blame. For what had seemed to her a long time, for only God knows how long, Sharon let Claudio fuck her, and with muted approval, and freed from her tight form fitting dress, she gave in to his long-time built-up powerful thrusts. Breathlessly, she spread her legs and stood still as any ready princess would. She took it all in, not succumbing to dumb Claudio, but to the overpowering sex urge that shocks all reason, and for long powerful minutes, she let him have his way. It was a lusty scene full of vigorous plunges and she couldn't deny the trembling moment. He was all over her and she almost passed out with each and every charge. It had never, ever, been so good with Hank.

"Are you all right," he said.

"Yes."

And then like a little girl she said, "Thank you, Claudio," and meekly off she went to her room.

Claudio too grabbed his jacket and took off not saying good night to anyone.

"What fucking luck!" bellowed across the room the unbearable yell from former varsity line backer Curtis Don May, now highway toll booth operator.

"It's uncanny," screamed back Mark. "That's the third inside straight you've drawn tonight, Hank. I've never seen anyone as lucky as you."

"Especially tonight," said Curtis.

"Me neither," said another of the players. "Ever since high school Hank has had all the luck," and pissed, he tossed in his hand.

"Thank you, guys, you've made daddy happy tonight," smiled lucky Hank.

Everybody at the poker table guessed what had been happening in the Great Room and enviously became convinced that Claudio had scored. But if Hank wasn't budging, if he didn't care, why should they have cared. There was nothing to be said. They did wish they could've seen the action, or maybe have gotten a piece of the action themselves, but that would have meant betraying Hank's friendship; and his trust in them was more important than a piece of ass, as good as Sharon's was. On the other hand, Hank felt relief in front of his trusted friends that he no longer had to think of Sharon as some virgin angel, that she had finally, in full view of his world, joined the ranks of common folk. Perhaps now he would not bear all the blame.

*

Delightful confusion sweetly followed into Sharon's mind; there was something appealing to Roman Claudio this unexpected night. His was the gentle love without the grunts, and he was kind. This was the way it should have been from the very beginning, and not the ugly way that Hank had offensively assaulted her the first and all the other times. The impromptu act was so good that it left no room for stray regrets. Something short of a miracle had happened at the bar. For the first time she had sex that she didn't think as dirty.

She thought of Kitty and felt sorry that she might have betrayed her friend. She shut her eyes, turned away, not wanting to see Kitty's face which had now snuck into her bedroom. Once again she agreed with Robin's advice not to say anything to Kitty. She had to keep it to herself. She didn't care if Hank knew.

Suddenly, she had a splitting headache and laid on her bed hoping to rest it away. She took two aspirin and cried heavy tears, alone in silence, wishing she could talk to her mother who long ago got tongue tied to a frozen husband. She shut her eyes to dull the martini pain and thought of the magical moments of her Biblical Sunday school days and felt the recurring need to once again lose herself into bright happy thoughts. If only she could go back to those Biblical moments, just one more time, long enough to forget the merciless vodka pain throbbing in her brain so she could fall asleep and take that other bend on the road, to find a different path to a more normal life.

Sleep was nowhere to be found that night. Contradictory thoughts pleasing and distasteful hovered rudely in the darkness of her brain until she understood that she really had no control of either her body or her mind; that there were many strange but natural feelings of love; yes, many different types of love that reigned over human beings.

And then like her mother before her, she asked for God's forgiveness.

"We could have been so much better if we hadn't been such misfits" she tried to wipe away the loveless memories of her parents' pathetic relationship that passed for marriage. It wasn't a blessed union; but then, it was no one's fault.

Again she thought of her intransigent parents.

God bless their souls, she thought, and with her mouth wide open like a fledging waiting to be fed, she slowly faded into sleep.

Chapter Twelve

That very same night, Sharon had a very strange dream.

She was walking down a narrow ochre-yellow, urine-smelly dirt road lined with muddy light brown huts in a dead place, somewhere very foreign to her mind. Out of a movie, perhaps, her unconscious mind ventured into the uncensored scene, probably in some blazing hot lifeless desert in the Middle East or Africa; or maybe out of a Bible study picture book. It was a curious amalgam of desert colors. In her dream were scenes and shades of shimmering yellow and orange pastels, lovely, silent, pastel waves filling her eyes canvas. Everything before her slow moving sight was shiny silent.

Silent stillness everywhere including the imperceptibly shifting tiny grains of sand that inaudibly seemed to move in harmony with the yellow heat of the glistening air. It was a forsaken landscape eerily barren of life, except for the flood of yellow, the color of death, she thought. The straw-mud huts barely endured against the desert wind. They resembled crumbling tombstones in some forsaken ancient cemetery. They looked like they had been shovelled into the ground to wait a second coming. Time had eroded most of the huts back into their deadest grains of sand and dust; their walls had mostly crumbled; they smelled of the dusty death from ages immemorial, tedious all around, the inexorable sun having scorched the last drop of water, of life, out of them.

She looked up and the whole dream, place, earth, and sky, blended into blinding yellow. The high noon sun was glowing intensely unbearable challenging the dead tranquillity of the cast beneath it; its heat was energizing the fine dust in unison with the whispering wind to gust tiny funnels all around, fiercely blinding her and forcing her to lower her kerchief to shade her eyes and block the light, so she could see past the storm. For the first time, in her dream, she realized that too much sun, too much light, can blind a person. She began to hate the sun that now disturbed her dream and sought the comfort of the protected shade and went and sat next to a crumbling hut. Full of uneasiness she found relief in taking deep breaths to lessen the chocking pain in her chest. The gasps of dry air and the blinding stillness of the place worsened her fears and made her want to scream and wake up from what was now becoming a nightmare. Leaning against the ruin, she felt afraid not knowing how to get out of her misery. The puke foul odor of urine was everywhere and the revolting stench was compounding her difficulty in breathing. Again and again she gasped for air, breathing hard through her mouth, for it seemed to her less obstructed and less offensive than breathing through her nostrils. She felt weak and very tired as she tried to make her way out of this improbable dream built out of mud and hay and held together, she was now sure, by nothing more than the fear of emptiness which sometimes is discernible in dreams. Bewildered by the stupidity of her mess, her unconscious brain released ever more shades of color to allay the fear that had trapped her. She frantically gasped to find an exit from her unlikely state but to her terror there was no visible out of her intense surroundings. The strong fear emitting from the deafening filthy dream was exhausting her and she wanted to cry out loud and end her desolate nightmare, but could not.

Ominously, everywhere, including up, and everything all around, raged stupefying yellow, the color continuing to register panic in her mind as the precursor color of death, which was strange because for most of her young life she thought dark, not light, as the color of death. Bright yellow from the life giving sun was what she grew up with; why now death? She felt trapped and wished she could run away or somehow be carried out of this stinking deathly yellow quandary.

Out of nowhere, in her dream, she saw a strange otherworldly figure enveloped in a princely white robe, his head covered, his eyes barely revealed through an opening slit in the folding of a golden mantilla.

Even at a distance, the eyes, those eyes, were disturbing, reminding her so much of eyes she thought she knew. The alien apparition was fast galloping towards her on a powerful white stallion on top of low flying small white clouds against the bluest of skies.

At first she was startled, but then even in her sleep a smile slowly came over her face, and she sweetly thought, this obviously is an act of God; the ghostly appearance should not be so upsetting, nor so unexpected, or so sudden, and for sure not so unpredictable, for surely it's a sign from God. She felt the power of the insight, and calmly focused on the apparition which was furiously swinging a sparkling sword above its head, powerfully reigning in his steed before her as it floated on the aura of white light, now all over the desert sand.

Though she welcomed the spooky visitation of the holy figure, which blended in her mind as familiar as a member of the family, yet it might have been death itself, and she remained fearful in her dream, and tried hard to turn away from it, but could not move, bound as she was on her bed. It was becoming a crazy scene and in her desert bed she was perspiring hard and suffocating under the weight of her miserable jam. She felt trapped between her sheets, stuck without clothes on, nude in an infertile desert with its crumbling mud huts all around her. She might as well have been in some cheap motel anywhere in Los Angeles, stuck in the jaded world of her unconscious. The gagging scene was a scary encounter full of the sin, its only salvation being the Lord's forgiveness, her rapid eyes aimlessly fluttered. The ghostly sight is a bad omen, an early warning of disaster, possibly of death, her sleeping mind searching opaquely for the shore.

It was no use, only prayer could now and forever save her wretched soul from the immoral Acts of Magnolia High School's insipid culture, once again retching up the foulness of her barren life with Hank and his dumb friends, ever since high school, always trying to hump her in warehouse sex.

And in her nightmare, her heart filled with the fear of Hank and his friends, and of Claudio at will with her, and her liking it, in the warmth of her luxurious bed. Her best friends, Kitty, and Robin, and Myrna made cameo appearances in her dream, their shinny faces smiling and full of love, together, outside of the warehouse.

But the unforgiving white knight viciously struck his sword close to her face, in full stride on top of his pure white horse, hurling her to the ground before the frowning silence of her mind's floating illusion.

Alone once again, she was in the middle of a desert wilderness with nothing but lifeless sand dunes as far as her eyes could see. In desperation she prayed for the Lord's forgiveness and, strangely, as it often happens in dreams, although the sun was as blinding as ever, and the air as hot, yet, the inhospitable surroundings changed with the prayer on her lips, and suddenly the hot orange sand beneath her barren feet felt fresh and cool. And in the setting of the sun she breathed fresh air again and was no longer afraid of being alone in the wilderness. Soon she was walking the invigorating cool breezes of the dusk desert air and in their midst she thought she heard a most melodious song. Or, rather, it was more like a chant, a most heavenly chant, up from above and all around, sung by the sweetest of voices. Like a holy vestment, it engulfed her body and soul and she knew that she was before a blessed presence. The mesmerizing chant followed her for what seemed to have been a long time, though Lord only knows how actually long. It was soothing, and soft, and sweet, and it touched her heart like no other melody before. She vaguely recognized it as one of those full of humanity Byzantine chants that mystically induce a lingering air in the minds of people who have heard them. And although the language of the chant was foreign to her, yet she understood its meaning, which was of love and forgiveness.

A new vision, like a shimmering mirage, now commanded her attention high above her tired eyes, eclipsing everything else around her. Her unconscious mind focused on an iridescent face of what she paradoxically knew was a young beautiful monk. He was undoubtedly the angel sent to save her from her sins. His handsome elongated face was covered with a sparse long light beard that was proof positive that he was of holy rank. He was sitting alone on the windowsill of his monk's cell in a monastery perched high above the world on a rock-solid cliff. Looking towards the setting sun, he sang in the most pleasing of voices, stirring her mind and capturing her soul, repeating softly his embracing chant which in rhapsody reverberated magically within her captive heart:

> *Those who have been baptized in Christ*
> *In Christ they shall be resurrected,*
> *Alleluia…*
> *Those who have been baptized in Christ*
> *In Christ they shall be resurrected,*
> *Alleluia…*
> *Those who have been baptized in Christ*
> *In Christ they shall be resurrected,*
> *Alleluia…*

Like delicate wind chimes on a muted windy night the chant encircled her mind for hours, so it seemed, before waking her to a disturbing but most pleasing emotion. She lay quietly in her bed, totally unaware of her husband sleeping next to her, recalling the words so powerfully inscribed into her consciousness by a dream. She silently repeated them, *"baptized in Christ"*, *"resurrected"*, *"alleluia."* They were pleasing words, mysteriously soothing. She felt the warmth of their presence, smiled contentment, and fell asleep again.

*

The very next morning, Sharon received a bouquet of thirty yellow roses accompanied by a love note from Claudio.

> *"Last night I saw a thousand stars*
> *Passing before my eyes*
> *Bearing hope and love*
>
> *Hope that you will love me*
> *Until all the stars of Heaven*

In everlasting eternity
Pass before both our eyes…

Nobody has ever cried for me…

Tears came to Sharon's eyes but for reasons that Claudio would never understand. Never again would he get a chance or an explanation from resurrected Sharon. There could be no Hank, no Mark, nor anyone else in her life, after the sweet faced Monk's song. She felt spellbound by the holy message dream from heaven and the beautiful face of the holy monk and other saints. She cried and wished and prayed for a life more substantial, more connected to the Lord's wondrous world. She felt the emptiness of her soul and wanted to be somebody, she told herself. If she couldn't have children of her own, maybe she could find a more productive life in helping others. Yes, be a good self-sacrificing Christian. She would search her soul and begin to understand, love, and give of herself to those less fortunate than herself. She thought of her friends and happily concluded that there was room for help there. She decided that she would be God's instrument to help her friends.

Perhaps unkindly, though she didn't think so because she did love them, in thinking of her best friends forever, she wished that she too could be less sexy, less attractive, more like them. If only she could trade her bodily beauty for something more spiritual, more intellectual, something on a par with the excellence of her splendid buttocks, she smiled the worldly smile that was her trademark. Unfortunately, looking at her fabulous self in the mirror (she couldn't help it) only made things more confusing for her: why couldn't she be more normal? She didn't want to think of herself as only beautiful. If she weren't so wonderfully blessed, maybe she could have been an art teacher helping children to see the beauty of the Lord's world; or maybe by adding works of art to His creation through her artistic efforts, or something as equally, but non-sexual, gratifying.

*

The more she stared the more she wished; and the more she tried, to find fault with herself and bring about blessed change, the more things stayed the same. Trapped in a married life of greasy restaurant rich, she would fret the dissatisfaction with minimum penitence. And in the loneliness of her barren life, time, fast pacing her existence, had become a hateful presence. Weeks went by as fast as days, months as fast as weeks, and her anxiety intensified as her mortal ass began to gently sag below the support level of her youthful vanity.

Jesus, if only she could stop that frigging time.

The passing of time is simply a shortcut to old age and death, for one uncertain moment she hesitated her crippling thought.

She began a futile cosmetic struggle to at least slow the weathering tear of time; she tried fantasizing feelings of love for her husband, an attempt to retrieved love from a time when once she thought she loved him. For one instant replay moment to stop fleeting time and trick it back to youth. It was no use, her husband's presence having long ago become invisible to her. He was gone, forever and ever, vanished from her life. Instead of slowing time as she would have wanted, the thought of her husband only highlighted the waste of stupid time.

Thinking of the years since high school was, like, only yesterday; the years had disappeared as if with one touch time had been deleted from her brain. But when there, now, alone, in the fucking present, time was dragging its ass like a whore the morning after. Years go by quickly, but the seconds endlessly torment.

Her husband and his friends suffocated her as she wilted away in her tortured brain now full of sin. Yet, much as she displayed her dislike, for all of them, at every opportunity and encounter, for all practical purposes, she knew, there was no way she could divorce herself from them. Where on earth, at her age and time, could she make a new start all by herself? She felt stuck with her dumb Hank and his friends as much as they, like frightened, clinging lemurs, were stuck on her. As loathsome as were her silent, inarticulate high school days' silly admirers, beautiful high-flying tits like hers, after all was said and done, demanded the adoration that she had become accustomed, God forgive her, from her frivolous dummy devotees. As much as she hated to admit, there was heart breaking comfort in being part of a crowd, unpleasant as it might have been, but anything less, than the amorous glances eyed upon her by the boys of her life, would have made her everyday boredom even more agonizing. Loneliness was a cruel companion, a constant shadow in the gut that ached her days to zero.

And as the days and weeks and months and years furiously rolled by, Sharon became more and more aware of her terrifying solitude. As distasteful as her daytime thoughts were, they were nowhere near as frightening as was the darkness of the moments before falling asleep when the ghost of time would appear and whisper in her ear, "is that all that is? Is that all there is?" Even with her eyes shut, she could see that everything she had was so pathetically predictable in her modern woman's urban easy life, so full of the obvious nothing, traveling ever so fast, to more of the same nothing. In her frightened soul, feelings of anxiety and depression smothered any decent thoughts; that indeed in her case that was all there was, irrespective of her beautiful still high saluting tits. Like the transubstantiated red wine that she loved so much and which was so lovingly morphing her into an alcoholic mistress, she wished that she too might be morphed into a more soothing spirit.

Like Myrna and her gin, Sharon sought salvation in the red, red, wine in which she sought relief from insufferable loneliness. The sweet red wine would grease the memory trails retracing thoughts from the almost forgotten but joyous childhood years. And the recollections would often lead to the love of her Sunday-school days. Such pretty yellow dresses full of the petticoat and Mary Jane red shoes hopping through her mind's crispness, and of the spring's many sunny Sundays. Every morning, of those memorable Sundays of her childhood, was full of the sun, full of the everlasting glorious light, and full of the blessed song of Jesus Christ that always warmed her heart to glorious gladness and rapture, young as she was. Oh, wistfully would she evoke those lovely memories of the eternal promises full of gentle love in the beautiful blond bearded face of iconic Jesus. Recalling those wonderfully blessed days of Jesus and the Old Testament tales of justice and joy, of faith and forgiveness, of marvellous miracles and cherished love, was now the only way that she could fall asleep.

*

And in the absence of an intelligent lover, Sharon found in herself the love she sought. Her mental health and happiness flourished in the privacy of her bedroom where like other young women she too found her own way to panting orgasms. In her spacious pink bedroom she rubbed and stroked, selfishly excluding all real intrusion from what she thought was the wilted world she was living in. Alone each morning she felt the impulse to rub her naked belly on her silk sheets and artfully masturbate. Alone she found happiness in her very private self-absorption. Daily she found pleasure in babying herself all over until her whole body was consumed in the sensuality of her own adoration. She loved every bit of herself, narcissistic bawdy as it was, and found no disparity between rubbing her baby soft ass on milk white silk sheets and pillows while looking up at the ceiling with eyes closed to find her fate in the heaven of saints. Her God given beauty demanded the attention she was heaving on herself. The morning matins of ritual self-massaging were not an adolescent's hysterical worship of the temporary body, she had convinced herself, but rather the true adoration of eternal love, even though, more often than not, she found her exhibitionist tendencies to be gestures less than darling. Everywhere she touched, she loved as one loves the first immorally persistent memory, relishing the feverish temptation to repeat. During these sinful moments, her soft hands became playful, depraved, luxuriously elegant enchanters, escorting her whole being to sensual little nonsense meant to tactfully appal. More than ever, she was now looking inward and turning away from the world that had been her husband's, and her parent's, even her friend's, but scarcely hers. Alone in her thoughts she was indulging herself in an irreversible selfish love of her constant loneliness.

Is there such a thing as love for oneself only, beautiful as one might be?" she would occasionaly think. Could a person love only oneself and none other? Is there such thing as love only for oneself? Can there be love when one is alone as Adam was before Eve? Or even as Adam and Eve were, alone, just the two of them? Or perhaps the three of them? For they say there was a second Eve for the three of them to share each other's blessings. Could there have been true love with all the sensual pleasures that must be part of love if there were only one, or just two of them? The sweetness of love is surely more tempting, more exciting, more burning, in the presence of more than two lovers; it was a seductive thought, tempting. For love is a holy gift to be shared in community with others, as the Lord Jesus had meant it. Doesn't love involve sharing one's world with another, or better yet with many others?

The thought was persuasive; truly that must be what Heaven is like, she concluded.

Such pleasures standing naked before her full length mirror conversing with her galloping mind in search for relief from incessant self-pity. At times she chanted her inquiries with angels and saints, oblivious to the inanities aborting in a mind not firing with all neurons. Her sanity was intellectually masked with fierce questions as to who she might be with no easy answers forthcoming. There was the reality of the fabulous body struggling to morally reconcile her consciousness to the sordid tendencies of an unstable personality. As Jesus would have wanted her, she indulged in steady spiritual but also improper reflections, confusing her mind; the mess mostly making for unhappy times. She was sad at times that there was never enough time to fully comprehend such pious signals of love hiding somewhere in her mind. Confronting the paradoxes of her lively self, she skipped to more pleasant thoughts of time enough for all of God's wishes, to feel good about her spiritual self and her undeniable beauty, which also was a gift from God.

Too much thinking produced wrinkles in the brain. It was a waste of time, for who really knows what love is. Sadly, after all the years that were her life, Sharon could not say who she was, or that she had any inkling of what love was. Her one worldly stable element in her life, she was thrilled, was the love of her friends. And every so often, without surprise, the ghostly apparition of her dreams, would appear before her cabernet cloudy eyes, and slash his sword through her air, as a reminder.

*

When at times in the depths of gloom, she very clearly thought that time had no place in her heart. It was no use, she could not run away from time, even though time was fast leaving her behind. During those moments of unhappiness she could feel time crumbling everything around her. Time was making her old faster than she could measure. It was fast killing her and she had no time to figure out how it was that the ticking of the clocks was racing her breathless to unreasonable depression. Deep in her heart she knew it was time, of which she felt she had very little left, that was exhausting her, making her miserable and confused as it whirled inside her head like other short term thoughts that faded as quickly as they arrived, leaving her in disputations. Carelessly she would dress and undress, try on different colors depending on the time of day, and drink lots of white and red wines in the privacy of her bedroom to keep away the thought that maybe she should join some tranquil nunnery, like Phil and his monastery, and have the time to devoutly think of the meaning of time in her present haphazard life of untested friendships, and an empty husband. Time was sweeping away all the fast food plentiful riches and the uneasy serenity of the many splendored pills and tonics, all of which now seemed to her the equivalent of accumulating blank days in an empty mental archive never again to be visited. Ingeniously she gathered her days into clever miracles of timeless observations that only she could detect. Events in her life rhymed without reason, leaving her empty.

Is time the same as conscience, she heard herself say.

She wasn't sure, because in time there seemed to be conscience.

A spark from some undefined sphere within her soul had delivered the unsuspecting message that life is temporary even for the Lord's most beautiful creations, such as she was. Though she would tease herself, touch and feel good about what she was touching and feeling, she was tortured by the fear that even she, more beautiful than anything else currently on this earth, was nothing more than temporary. Everything is temporary, and temporary is a tiny slice of time which is eternal, she thought.

Alone, she cried perfectly clear globules of uncontrollable tears to no effect.

Everything was temporary. Between the beginning and the end, everything was full of madness; thank God all things are temporary. Even marriage, contrary to the impossible commitment, till death do us part, was too silly not to be temporary. They had ninety-three wonderful years together, before she passed away, Sharon coldly summed to herself, thinking of the billions of ghosts now floating alone in the vastness of time immemorial. Everything, regardless of the duration, was temporary. There was never any time to plant, and no time to harvest; actually, the harshness of life is that people think they have time. Damn unrelenting time! It respects nothing. Why did God have to make time? What a horrible reminder and cruel tormentor of all living things, but especially of youth and beauty, is time.

Too soon, too soon, the seasons come and go, and darling Sharon, cry as you may, all the soons are soon forgotten, and there are no seasons left; holy words to bet on, she cried.

She looked in the expensive Florentine mirror and sashayed across her bedroom in full naked length noting her lilywhite buttocks, so familiar to her.

Above all, she thought, time is the enemy of all things beautiful, like her alabaster buttocks. Ugly, hateful, pent up time, unmercifully released by the gatekeeper sun to insult youth, her face flushed in anger at the damn light.

Anyway, there was tremendous comfort in the thought that there is no time in Heaven; no clocks, no time; that's what makes Heaven so worthy of the sacrifice. It couldn't be otherwise: for Heaven is eternal, and it makes no sense to keep track of eternity. God does not want you to keep track of time; it was a comforting thought.

She put on a yellow Polo knit, soft perfect over her firm outstanding breasts. She would never wear a bourgeois Polo in public but it felt pleasingly soft in her bedroom and she indulged in its comfort, in her bedroom. A little polo pony above the tip of her nipple.

"I love you, I love you, and I'm slowly melting away, and I don't know what to do," she said to her body. "I love you and I just want to die as I am this moment."

Her preoccupation with time was somewhat new to her. Not completely new because everybody keeps track of time, and all her life she had a watch, and she was aware of the cliché to be on time. But her recent out of nowhere anxieties about time were strangely curious and not like other times. They surfaced during the weirdest moments, intense and atonal in their determination to disturb at times when her mind was already uneasy. She had no idea wherefrom the timely thoughts invaded her mind, but she didn't mind, and initially she found strange excitement in her obsession with time. At first she was a bit reluctant to acknowledge the truth, that the reality of her married life came shrouded in time, as did all other weird thoughts that out of nowhere rode on time to irritate her mind, but she eventually accepted the repetitive beat of time as unavoidable. In the beginning, time had been a neutral subject before it slowly became the dominant challenge in her life.

But then, it wasn't as if she had anything better to do.

The problem was that in time, reality and time began to clash. It had become a mystery to Sharon how something innocuous like time could occupy so much of her time. Finally, she concluded that the meaning of time was an explanation of life, an important revelation transmitted into her brain for a reason, by higher sources than she, and were meant to be uttered as a prophet might reveal and preach his holy visions. She began to like the forcefulness of these bewildering apocalypses, because they gave urgency to her life, a sense of participation that was lacking before their visits. At the very least, they made her feel smarter, charged with inspirational mysteries impassioned with poetic promises of wonderful future events, undoubtedly more interesting than those of the unhappy past or the regretful now.

She looked at her digital clock, set it to digital noon, and unplugged it. It would always be noon in her life, she mused. Noon time would never invade with dark shadows to disturb her looks and mind. Not wanting to, she couldn't help but think that there wasn't much after beauty, a creation of time; except maybe madness.

Time and its associates, light and madness, are gravely waiting on the side line to desiccate my life, she would think. I hate the hipster sunlight that floods my days, and she would sob her way to another red.

"Light is time and time is light, and light is the beginning and end of all. This I know; time is green jealousy, full of envy, for why else would it destroy all things beautiful?"

Alone in the house of Hank, cluttered thoughts streamed across her consciousness sending her mentally back to find comfort in the loving days, when she was with her mother, and light and time did not exist. There she found pleasant thoughts. Immense happiness reappeared the deeper she ventured into her childhood with her mother, and strangely, time disappeared out of her present. Even though she thought she hated her mother, the enjoyment she found in the more and more frequent emotional visits with her had a soothing, stabilizing effect, allowing her to function in her minimum daily chores and affairs without displaying any crazy manners or changes to her personality, so that no one could have perceived any odd behavior. Nothing that she did or said could have been misconstrued as being abnormal because that's the way Sharon had always been: simply beautiful in all her goofy flaws.

It would be something to live in some Scandinavian country where it's dark nine months out of the year. Surely the darkness there slows down time, she often thought. And sometimes Myrna would come to mind, and Sharon understood that probably Myrna was of Viking descent because she didn't seem to be affected by the passing of time. And then quite often, from sunny Sicily, Claudio would pay a quick mental visit, but she didn't know why, didn't care, and she wasn't going to waste her time on Claudio.

It was the Lord that made light and time, including Claudio who was a much better lover than Hank, she immediately cursed the offending thought, darker than the darkest sea. But it was all true, He had made all things, including Claudio, good as his cock was.

What strange sensations were these thoughts? Her eyes would sparkle huge more than ever, as each ridiculous mental revelation emerged evermore on a daily basis. She could be doing anything, anywhere, and joyously they'd pop into her brain.

She became convinced that there definitely was a purpose to these vividly illuminating visitations, whose meaning had yet to be made known to her, but it was coming. Surely there was profound intelligence behind the graceful stream of extraordinary beautiful words entering her mind and energising her.

"Without a doubt, the sun is the fast processor of this hurtful life," she took another hit, obviously derived from ancient lineage.

She waited for the next burst.

"Death starts out yellow," she heard herself say.

It was a marvellously succinct thought. She liked it very much.

The successive, pedigreed-inspired revelations, and they must've been, because they weren't cogitated by her highly not so bright mind, must have originated from a Higher Source, which made Sharon feel special, that she was who she was, but, at the same time, somewhat confused about becoming what she was becoming. Cheerfully, that Higher Source was now brilliantly in Sharon's mind. A few yesterdays before, she had been less confused, but felt worse at what she was, because being young and even younger, she still had no sense of what she might be becoming.

Being chosen, like others before her, was very satisfying to her soul. She could not deny that perfection lay before her mortal life, which was full of sin, and could only be cleansed with saintly devotion, as apparently demanded by the Lord. Subliminal thoughts focused her eyes on Heavenly realms where the ultimate reality transcended the base existence she was leading. Salvation lay in the Holy Spirit of the Bible. Some use incense to lull the spirit home; some use wine; and some use both incense and wine, for the shades of grey that grace the mind are very dull without the unlimited variety of saintly spirits.

When she was younger she subscribed to the importance of the body's external looks, as youth is naturally inclined to do. But as she matured and time kicked in without respect, she wanted to believe that she was more spiritual, more cerebral. Certainly more intellectual than her husband's laughable IQ. She wanted the world to see that she was more than just a fabulous piece of ass. If only she could match her physical beauty with the erudition that was there, inside her, to shock the world and her friends with witty comments, that showed the brilliance of her Godly gifted brains.

And as is the case with too much thinking, every rambling thought was chocked with the malevolent curse of time, which was making her brain smooth and her skin wrinkly. Gratefully, Sharon thanked the Lord for the expensive skin care products and multi-vitamin regimes that pitched in to help deny and keep at bay the not so subtle deathly reminders, like stupid crow's feet.

Ah, that youth be twice, no three or four times, she thought, and old age never, and she gingerly took another sip from her bloody red savage cabernet full of the Holy Spirit. She had read that cabernet sauvignon increased longevity and it made sense to drink it.

Though her breasts and buttocks were still as firm as ever, there was no denying the evils of light; but the evils of time were even worse. Decaying time was warping all her dreams, and she spent a fortune trying to check it, day in and night out, with creams, serums, and moisturizers. But nothing could blunt the chronic emotional agony of Satan inserted light. Light was evil, and there was evil everywhere in her world. She hated light, especially the morning's light, because it woke up time. It made her do things when she didn't want to do anything, like get out of bed just because it was light. Without light the new day would never start and her cheeks would remain forever firm. Even the small amounts of yellow light shafting through her windows were enough to whither her blind. Like twin grim reapers time and light had always been there, every day, and although it was too soon, much too soon, to acknowledge the odors as anything more than pre-pre-menopausal angst, there was no escaping the persistence of the cursed sun and its light in this evanescent life.

"There's no denying that it's the damn sun and its daughters, time and light, that make the skin wrinkle and remind us of our mortality," another delightful gem hung full bloated in the twilight of her untiring mind. If no sun, then no light, and no time, and no aging.

She loved the beautiful way she had discovered to pass her time away, pretty much every day, since she had nothing else to do, and her husband was simply too dumb to keep up with her way of thinking.

Was it the passing of time that brought to light the rising sun, or was it the light of the sun that measured the passing pulse of time? Light had a pulse as it daily arched across the heavens, and time had a measured beat to Sharon's heart and both were heartless half-breeds, floating in the universe, she was pissed. Thank God for red wine and green leaves, she thought; and, it's the green leaves that make the tree. And the villain of the lot was the seething bastard sun. It's true! It's not the trees that make the leaves but the leaves that make the trees. Sharon had begun to dislike the sun with its life sucking light as the harbinger of inevitable death. Fuck, everybody dies; even trees and other animals, though they don't know it. No seasons without life! The sun and its light were not the source of life, as the silly scientists would have us believe, she cleverly denied its importance.

> *In the beginning there was the Word ... no!*
> *In the beginning there was light ...*

The silliness of the claim astounded her as she lay in her bed. She had put on her silk kimono and she tucked it between her legs to feel sexy. In a fetal position, she was also sucking her thumb. Light definitely had to come after the beginning, she fancied, because if there had been no beginning, then, there could not have been light. Light, then, must have been preceded by time. Time, was the beginning, then, but for how long before light? So, time was first and light was second. Unless, of course, light is the beginning in the sense that it comes before all other things, which essentially means there was nothing but a void, which means there's no beginning, or anything else in a void but an endless nothing.

She wondered what color was the void.

All this, naturally, revolved, like the sun itself, around the existence of life since without life there is neither time nor light. Unless, of course, light and time were the same, which Sharon was now inclined to believe that they were.

You could go crazy with such thoughts, she thought. Sometimes things that don't make sense seem very clear to an unassuming mind. Speaking of unassuming, she thought of Claudio, but the stupid ass quickly disappeared

The beginning is much more inconceivable than the ending, she continued. As if the melding of time and light was the answer to anything. Everybody knows the ending.

She switched to a more intoxicating vodka martini from her beloved red and tipped another double in search for a different more dramatic scenario to revel in her mind, alone, in the emptiness of the daylight darkness of her expensively decorated bedroom. There was a praying mantis barely hanging from her ceiling. It wasn't unusual these days for many coloured animals, large and small, to blur the shadows of her ceiling. She could make out lots of nice animals in the play of the light. Familiar visitors, they were her friends.

It was definitely that damn light.

"Without the sun there is no life, frightened and tired prophets of science repeat with fuzzy vision, as they lean on their staffs, and watch the sun set," stormed ahead Sharon. "Stupid old men waiting for their time to pass. Without the sun, without light, there is no time, but assuredly there is life. In death there is no light. For Heaven and Hell don't care one wit about light or time. Young people, mostly children, who bring home the light, while old people bring nothing but darkness.

She smiled because she didn't like old men.

Forever and ever, amen!

Damn light makes people old and go mad.

How strange that people are born with wrinkles and they die with wrinkles, she sipped another thought. It's only between the wrinkles of birth and the wrinkles of death, that there's a little stretch. All life is nothing more than a little stretch, she felt proud.

To her praise, there were times when Sharon thought she was going mad.

When thoughts of madness crept into her delicate mind she sometimes gave in to them so as not to lose her mind.

Too many thoughts, too many regrets, lead to insanity she was certain.

"I don't care; I have no regrets; there are farts and then there's thunder," she tittered.

She breathed easier believing that there was nothing bizarre about her peculiar thoughts, other than that she had been perhaps notably blessed with the rare gift of prophetic visitations. Without regret her thoughts were full of curious insights of an unknown but friendly source, which stirred her lonesome soul. And who wouldn't have likewise thought these feelings of sadness as a blessing, these intriguing outbursts of profound insight? For there you are, one minute admiring a most gorgeous still exquisitely firm titillating body, and the next minute your neurons jump to synoptic probing of strange thoughts that seemed to have no obvious purpose, quirky, yet most coherent, peculiarly there to inconspicuously drive you mad with happiness. Could it have been that her inquisitive mind was searching for some sort of explanation to the ages old question of "is that all there is?" And not until these curious thoughts escaped her unconscious, and intellectually became part of her soul, would Sharon begin to fully understand them, and free her body of sin, and find peace of mind.

Humbly, the insight and the desire to find peace arrived almost imperceptibly but most naturally. It was kind of strange, simple, and yet, to her, it had been there all the time, ever present. It was as if in some mysterious way the secret code had always been there, linked to the question, and that every time her mind now asked the question, "is that all there is?" the all-encompassing response would pop up, in triptych.

For the Lord is truly Holy, and Strong, and Immortal.
For the Lord is truly Holy, and Strong, and Immortal.
For the Lord is truly Holy, and Strong, and Immortal.

"How beautiful these words are, how full of truth," she smiled, still on her soft bed, eyes half shut in disdain of the Satanic world sometimes blinded her.

She saw a shaft of morning sunlight swaying with the movement of her silk window curtains, and she buried her head into her silk pillow. She could no longer enjoy herself while that triptych was erratically trembling through her still half-naked mind.

For the Lord is truly Holy, and Strong, and Immortal.
For the Lord is truly Holy, and Strong, and Immortal.
For the Lord is truly Holy, and Strong, and Immortal.

That ever, damned, morning sun splashing through her bedroom's wind-blown curtains startled her sapphire eyes, shimmering to them the cruel perception of those ever-present yellow lumps of death splattered across her ceiling. Streams and streams of light splashed through her windows, invading her privacy, and bringing gloom and shame to what used to be an undisturbed life. It seemed silly, and at times she would wonder about her state of mind, but Sharon had come to dislike, even hate, the intensity of the morning glow, through her pink curtains, of the tiresome sun. She had come to think that there was nothing worse than starting out a day with bright bursts of morning bright sunlight intruding into her soul. It was as if her mind were being X-rayed to relentlessly remind her of all her fractured and forgotten thoughts. She wished for dark grey days in tune to her cloudy mind, and heart, and soul. She was certain that the exasperating morning brightness would one day unfold the end of her imagined existence. Full of remorse, she wanted only the quiet darkness that must have been before there was the damn light. She remembered the darkness of her yesteryears as the soothing flat line of undisturbed childhood and she ached to relive it again. It was the infantile years of easy tranquillity that she sought while the pulse of light now emanating from her brain was the terrible biological forerunner of inevitable death, a tediously recalled monotony of a foolish past.

Dawn is so beautiful, it fools you into thinking that you will never die she ached the pain of un-fulfilment. When I was young, I too thought that I would never die because I am so beautiful; as beautiful as any dawn spread across the sea, she stretched on her silken spread. Beautiful people should never die.

"Draw the damn blinds, leave me alone," she shouted to no one in particular, for, again, she was all by herself inside her luxurious bedroom, a loving presentation from her dumb-witted husband.

"Keep that damn light out," she cried in a half-hearted voice full of disappointment.

She looked up and across her ceiling and as in a psychedelic state she saw a rainbow of colors dancing in slow motion. All the colors of the hateful light were flooding through the prism of her senses diffusing in all directions in the room. All the colors of the universe were streaming through her windows, bouncing off the walls of her bedroom, reflecting up from the mahogany floor, even rising from underneath her bed. She could see every shaft of blended and unblended green, and red, and blue, but mostly jarring yellow dancing across her ceiling. Everywhere within the firmament of her bedroom's empty space she saw pastel photons dancing on top of air-born dust molecules and though the music was inviting, it frightened her.

"The sparkle of sunlight against the swaying green leaves of trees in the spring coolness of dawn," she sighed in a tiny moment of upper clarity. "It's a bedazzling display but totally depressing, because like all fireworks, leaves dazzling in the whispering sun are simple acts of transpiration lacking any mystery and are thus common and devoid of any significance."

The betrayal of her lovely green leaves immediately rushed in another attack of loneliness collapsing her into the warmth of her very own neurotic reality.

Lovely, but damn it, all was happening too damn fast and there had to be more.

"Jesus," she cried out loud again to no one in particular, "how can anyone have a private thought with all that fucking light streaming across your eyes"?

That boy, that boy, that boy, such rosy cheeks, such hot red lips, that boy will never die, he will forever kiss my lips, she replayed the magic image of her memory over and over, again and again, and tried to overlap the boy's face over Jesus' but it was no use there was too much light, and Jesus all too powerful.

"Have you ever been kissed on the lips by a boy on a moment's lark and liked it," she asked the world?

She got out of bed, dropped her kimono, and before she put on any clothes she fumbled for a pair of sunglasses to dark out the light and tone down the glare that was bouncing off of everything in the wild bedroom of her mind. Groping for something, anything, to calm her strange anxiety, she thought she saw a stretched spot of skin on the back of her otherwise smooth hand and she violently sobbed at the unfolding wrinkle. No more glowing bedrooms to shock the shit out of your senses and rip your nerves to the frenzied edges of insanity. Thank God for the ever-increasing grey pollution with its dark smog and clouds enveloping this sickly world. That global gook ought to burn some retinas and cut out the blasted morning sun.

She thought of Kitty – just for one moment.

"Amen" she said out loud.

"And in your soul let there be Peace," she heard her mind respond.

She had come to the conclusion that

The Lord works in mysterious ways.
The Lord works in mysterious ways.
The Lord works in mysterious ways.

The scattered insights, flashing lightning-fast more and more frequently now, were surely of mysterious ways, and had to be the portents of things to come, for the Lord surely was their source. She could not predict the sudden outbursts of their appearance but welcomed them and prayed to encourage their visitations to make her day.

Like all the saints, she prayed. Praying reminded her of home, and she found comfort in her prayer, which she understood as true connections to the Holy Spirit; they were not some false neurotic manifestations of brain cell receptors and neurons firing and misfiring at each other at chaotic sequences determined by hormonal adjustments which themselves were predetermined by pre-dispositions as governed by one's DNA helix.

She interrupted herself to look in her mirror.

She smiled and unabashedly did a twirl in front of her mirror. The mirror smiled back and threw her a huge kiss.

> *I love you with all my heart*
> *Only you do I adore*
> *And to know that you love me*
> *Only makes me love you more*

"I am so beautiful," she wanted to cry. "I could fall in love with me."

> *And to know that you love me*
> *Only makes me love you more*

*

Weird thoughts jostling for attention against tiresome everyday boredom came and went, unabated, and Sharon walked her lonely kitchen, more and more unable to grasp the logic of their force. Ambiguity reverberated in her mind, but as she tried to reconcile her thoughts to more natural explanations, the whole perplexing lot took flight towards Heaven, and never looked back. High it flew into the sky, and it became much easier to simply curl up on her silk sheets bed and suck her thumb, like other people do when in bewilderment. So, in cadence with other thoughts and pleasures, which were perhaps common to all human beings, to all human behavior, might not these private thoughts be also natural adjustments to the various realities that were possible, thanks to modern day wonder pills and other pharmaceuticals? The free will choices available to human beings surely would not exclude the blessings to select from the Lord's inventories of gentle comforts. In the Lord's infinite varieties, that could have meant recalling the wonderful teachings of the New Testament, or munching salsa and corn chips with a variety of partners, mates, husbands, or wives, while fondling one's self. For sure there were all those and other choices all of which were simply God's gifts to man and woman, meant to bring happiness to one's brief and, God willing, perhaps blessed life. No one ever needs to suffer the loneliness of the heart knowing the presence of the Lord Jesus.

Oh how she hated Hank!

Pray and you shall find salvation within your heart.

Please be kind and understanding
Love me more day by day

The joy of prayer is so rewarding because it's so frightfully easy.

I direct my prayer toward my salvation,
oh Lord, my Destiny,
I direct my prayer toward my salvation,
oh Lord, my Destiny,
I direct my prayer toward my salvation,
oh Lord, my Destiny,

Three times the prayer touched on her lips as she joyously combined the Jesus thoughts to her morning hot shower.

I direct my prayer toward my salvation,
oh Lord, my Destiny,
I direct my prayer toward my salvation,
oh Lord, my Destiny,
I direct my prayer toward my salvation,
oh Lord, my Destiny,
'Lord, my Destiny!

What did that mean, really?
You are my destiny…

She recalled the song and began singing as loudly as she could, the perfumed water trickling down her lovely breasts and all around to her coccyx bone.

She repeated it again … *you are my dhe-e-e-e - stiny …*

She sang to the pulsating hot shower, in pleasing pain screaming, *"You are my destiny."*

It was no use, for there was no consolation in the stupid lyric meant only for the adolescent heart. It was depressing to realize that the adolescent silly songs totally lacked the Lord's eternal destiny. Such a stupid pop song fraudulently directing generations towards ungodly love! You, boyfriend, girlfriend, are my destiny? It had no saintly salvation. No human being is another human being's destiny. Human beings are simply too minute to secure each other's destinies. Only the Lord Jesus can be another human being's destiny. Every man and every woman's life can have meaning only in their heart-felt love for Jesus. He and only He can be our destiny. For destiny, as well as all things, comes from the Lord, and the Lord alone is one's destiny, for He is the All. Only through the Lord Jesus is life eternal, as the Lord has meant life to be. Destiny manifests itself only through the will of Jesus. Without Jesus there is no destiny; with Jesus only there's the All. It is in the All that destiny resides, in the union with the Lord Jesus, and not in pop music.

She hesitated; hot water was distending her arteries and increasing the blood flow to her brain making for clearer thinking. She wasn't sure what 'destiny' actually meant, or was. Damn Horace Mann American high school shit that passes for education.

Reluctantly, she got out of the very hot, hot shower that always made her whole body glow with the odors of the wild *'fleur de printemps'* body gel she loved to use to make her lovely body tingle. She always felt rejuvenated after a hot shower, pumped up like a virgin looking forward to the first time.

Get a hold of yourself, Sharon, she laughed. She dried herself very quickly and dropped her towel. Walking through the house butt naked and half wet, she wished she could drop her strange thoughts as cleanly and casually as she had peeled and dropped her white bath towel cooling off her spotless pink ass. As she walked through her house, she fantasized a handsome blond, blue eyed Viking from the dark North entering her from behind, somewhat like Claudio had done. She felt his rough hands fondling her all over her hot naked body.

"It's all wrong," she said. "It's all so wrong."

*

It took Sharon less than twenty minutes to drive to Magnolia High School, just as the students were being let out. All excited, Justine ran to Sharon's car, like a child running to her daddy after a long absence. Her face sparkled the cool freshness of a beautiful teenager. In one hurried act she opened the car door and jumped into the seat next to Sharon. She turned toward Sharon, and her eyes were two breathless pools of blue, her cheeks blushing rosy pink, and her smiling lips wore fragrant baby's breath, all framed in the teenager's tossed carelessness of her blond hair. She leaned and gave Sharon a long tongue kiss, and out of sight, gently squeezed Sharon's perked up breasts. In a response that had become a habit, Sharon moved her hand up Justine's cool, perspiring thigh, all the way up to her panties. The girl was wet with anticipation.

"Let's get out of here before someone sees us," said Sharon.

"I don't care," said Justine.

In Sharon's silk covered bed, long legs intertwined with long legs, and roaming hands found the pleasures of the female front and back. Tongues stretched deeper in each other's mouths and lustfully slurped each other's juices. Like no man could, they sucked each other's sweet tasty nipples and gladly arched their backs for easy access. Oh what a beauteous thing it was, their frequent lovemaking. They were two immortal, wedded women together bound with all the passion and desire for hot sex. Sharon and Justine were of true legendary beauties, and not to have been loved, in all ways, would have been a sin that nature, and perhaps the good Lord, would have never forgiven. No one was going to deny them their lovemaking that day, so they fucked their brains out, as they had on the many previous occasions. With all their senses, they felt the insatiable lust for each other's bodies because they were so beautiful.

"We should go," said Justine, after several winning climaxes.

"Don't worry, my love, my lovely love," said Sharon. "I told Myrna I'd pick you up after school and bring you home a little late. She won't be concerned knowing you're with me."

"She's fucking out of it," said Justine of her mother.

"Don't say that, Justine. Your mother is a good woman."

"That's right; she's an old woman."

"What do you mean? Your mother and I are the same age."

"Yes, but you're a little nymphet running through the woods in search for the wild anemones," said Justine. "My mother likes only young boys."

"Are you saying she fucks a lot of boys?"

"No, no, no; she's very discreet and particular with whom she keeps company," said Justine, very adult like. "I'm sure at times she's listening in on Doug and me when we're alone in my bedroom."

"Justine, you don't fuck boys, do you?"

"No, they fuck me."

"You should wait until you're older before you get into boys, Justine."

"I'm not into them, Sharon. They're into me," she laughed rudely for a young girl.

It was late and this long day's affair had gotten a little tiresome.

Chapter Thirteen

S omewhere between subliminal faith and delusional fantasies Sharon lost her mind. Unable to withstand a life fast emptying, the vacant road before her smacked of insanity. It was paved with sadness, and the only way out was Jesus. Everywhere she looked, there was Jesus blessing her with an inviting smile right out of her childhood Biblical memories. She found relief in those comforting memories, and being an honest friend, she decided that the time had come to share her Jesus joy with her best friends.

"This is my blood," she would murmur with every sip of red Bordeaux, "drink of it to sooth your sorrows away into a happier life," and another tall glass of red would slowly take a dive to sooth Sharon's sorrows, her red lips wet with the wisdom of all ages.

She is so beautiful, all her friends thought; her face is like a Bernini statue, its beauty way beyond the words it utters.

And everything that she so prettily spoke, the best friends were only too glad to gulp down in jolly red unison and recognition of its divine origin, because it did come from Sharon's perfectly sculptured lips whose scented perfumes kept the best friends enviously breathless.

Actually, nobody cared about what Sharon had to say; but it was an irresistible treat even for lifetime friends, to want to stare into her biteable flawless baby pink face.

Nor was it only the face and lips that held sway among the friends, or any crowd in any presence, but also the magic light that darted from her bluest eyes when she would celebrate the Lord's words, and at the same time, touch each of their lonely hands on the holy altar of various restaurants and bistro bars throughout LA. Yes, the joy of communion, the joy of sisterhood and friendship, made the girls want to plunge recklessly into Sharon's gorgeous halo and drink of her soul. Like a prophet's out of the wilderness spellbinding sermons, the girls would tirelessly listen to the words coming out of her bloody rich mouth, and pleasingly get lost in her miraculous face.

Everyone, that is, except Myrna, who at some unrealized past moment, had fallen in love with Sharon. Physically in love; she dreamily fantasized lying next to Sharon, the two of them naked. Two beautiful, glamorous, best friends fucking each other; just the two of them. It was weird. When she didn't have to listen to her, when she only looked at her in silence, when she would mute her out, Myrna couldn't help but erotically desire Sharon. In Myrna's fantasies, it wasn't the spiritual Jesus love that she wanted from Sharon but unbounded sexual intercourse fucking, and not the silly fairy shit she was sharing with her friends. This ungodly desire became especially lustfully powerful after Myrna's husband had left her. Quietly she would tune out Sharon's words and stare into her face feeling the excitement of her astounding longing. When near Sharon, she would breathe out slowly, nervously hiding her secret desire, so that others might not pick up on her mind's yearning. There were breezy guilt feelings associated with the fantasies, but the illusions were too, too dreamy, and difficult to deny. Powerful shit like tits being squeezed and orifices being plugged. And sometimes, she would fantasize the threesome: Sharon with her husband Hank, and herself.

The girls were killing time, enjoying the view from an outdoor chic café on the Third Street Promenade in Santa Monica. It was early afternoon, a little after one pm. The lunch crowd had given way to the window shopping and café strolling crowds, mostly easy going, rich-local, long-shiny-haired blondes, and hip-skinny tourists from Japan enjoying the out of nowhere spontaneous Indian piping music by real natives from the mountains of Peru, and other jazzy cultural ragged groups up and down the promenade.

"You sure are spiritual at times," Robin lovingly smiled at Sharon.

"She should be; she's glowing full of Bordeaux," said Kitty.

"Drink for this is my blood," Sharon reverently raised her red to her lips.

"Sharon, Honey, this isn't the Last Supper," Kitty tried to keep her friend in tune with the New World music from Peru.

Don't listen to her; just look into her lovely face, Myrna smiled.

"You know, guys, time harms and eventually kills all things," said Myrna.

"And don't forget the fucking sun," said Sharon.

"Myrna, I think you've been listening to pea-brain Sharon for too long," said Robin. "Stick to hugs; she needs hugs more than existential bullshit."

"They work so hard," an elderly lady was commenting on the street's musicians, to an equally wealthy old friend, as they elegantly strolled by the friends' table. They were showing off their ten carat emerald rings from Columbia, solidly mounted on globs of twenty one carat gold. Probably widows who had inherited tons of money, the Promenade would have guessed.

"All I know, Robin, is that if time heals all things it also spoils all things including friendship," said Myrna, insisting past the courteous widows of Santa Monica.

"I have a feeling this is going to be a long afternoon," laughed Kitty.

Kitty was a genius who could have easily done commentary, on all topics, better than any CNN, or any other chit-chat media reporters. She could be wicked.

All four friends had spectacular legs, and they knew it. They were displaying them in the best possible crossed-legs exposure for all passers-by to sideways glance and enjoy. The sun was reflecting bright off of their sexy shinny shins and their revealing knees below their short skirts, catching all eyes, and the girls were feeling good. All beautiful women love to display their beauty; it's called vanity and the friends were proudly very vain. They were rich and vain.

"Rare, if any, are the lifetime friendships, especially those of long time high school friends, like us," said Myrna, vainly trying to add substance to their afternoon.

"I don't agree," said Sharon who lately seemed ill at ease around Myrna. "Friendship like ours has been nurtured by all of us, from our grammar school days. It's real and has love at its very core. It's the love within our friendship that binds us together. Without love, friendships are of temporary ties; they are mostly binds of convenience, really; invariably they exhaust themselves as quickly as they are formed."

It all sounded very wealthy but it didn't matter because airhead Sharon had said it.

"*'Love is forever.'* Anything without love is nothing," said Sharon.

"How did you get to be like this, Sharon," said Robin ironically appreciating Sharon's observation on love, an uncomfortable topic for all the friends, who naturally assumed its validity without the need of particular attention or argument.

"Well, there are friendships and friendships," said Myrna, looking at Sharon and dismissing Robin, and she crossed her legs on the opposite direction from Sharon's. "There are those friendships that last, and those that mentally, or most often, physically distance themselves. You know, people move away from each other, while others seem to fondly keep the heart humming, but on closer examination, friendships are rarely more than comforting affectations, a kind of crutches."

Everybody was surprised at Myrna's unexpected harsh elucidations on the character of friendship. It was a first time any of them had thrown enlightenment on the nature of friendship, particularly their own, and Myrna's words smacked of suspicion. Was she referring to their friendship? If so, Myrna was way off the mark with her comments, and in unison they all criss-crossed their legs in the opposite direction from hers. It was odd they thought that Myrna never mentioned love in her comment on friendship.

"This is especially true of adolescent friendships, something close to our bosoms, a condition most always forgotten, but familiar to most friends," she continued. "Different needs, at different times, efface the simplistic ties of youthful friendship. Other people, like lovers at first sight, interfere to steal the glow of friendship from the best of friends. But worst of all, is the sudden inexplicable love, *coup de foudre*, as they say, the lightning bolt that strikes out of nowhere from strangers, the hormonal mutilators of friendship, who rip your heart out, make you lose your mind, and heartlessly drive you to impulsive choices that you invariably regret, leaving the adolescent friendship sprawling on the sidewalk of memory."

There it was, an unexpected wounding of some sort of friendship love sprawled out by Myrna on the extensive sidewalk of the Promenade. Too incontestable for an afternoon's martini run on Santa Monica's Promenade. For sure, Myrna was beginning to be a drag.

"Myrna, you're beginning to sound like Sharon," said Kitty who always found a polite way to hit the nail on the head and knew what to say. "To me friendship is a great big hug that gives pleasure as long as it's good to hug. You lose the hug and all is gone."

"Thank you, Kitty," said Robin.

"You're right, Kitty," said Sharon who for some time now had begun to feel removed and unsympathetic to her friends, almost indifferent to what they might have to say, which she knew was always more of the same. "But, as Myrna just reminded us, the warmth of friendship more often than not depletes over time. It cools off the summer heat of youth, slowly giving way to fall and winter blues, until the good-time memories fade and slowly disappear. Sadly, friendship all too often dies of exhaustion, and incomprehensibly gives way to sneaky, not easy to admit loneliness. Without friendship there is no love; yet without love, friendship is a tepid trip. Life, existence, is that interaction between friendship and love in men and women, and in any combination of these. Even in loneliness, there are the many memories of life's loves, and the many varied friendships. But time has no pity, and old loves, and old friendships, regardless of their old fire, do give way to hoary age. Such is the deceit of friendship that even the best of friends do not realize it's waning, until it's over. But for those lucky few that find it, true love lasts forever."

Beautiful words coming out of beautifully articulating lips. To Myrna Sharon's lips were more humming than articulating; such sexy lips.

"Sharon, you're crazy, girl. Where did you get all that shit from," said Robin. "If you're pretending, it's ok; but if you're for real, we're going to take you to the looney bin."

"Well, what's your definition of friendship Robin," Kitty asked?

"She doesn't know what friendship is, Kitty," said Myrna.

"I don't know and I don't give a shit," said an angry Robin who felt that her afternoon had been pissed on by Myrna and Sharon.

"I think, Myrna, that you're probably the one who doesn't know what friendship is," said Sharon. "What the hell, who cares! That's about all she rode, isn't it, Myrna my beloved, my beloved, Myrna?"

It was a slap in the face and only Myrna suspected where all the resentment was coming from. Robin and Kitty looked at each other and wondered about the recent antipathy persisting between Myrna and Sharon. Whatever it was, it stank of bad blood between friends. To be best friends forever is no easy task; it's a full time job and it cannot be subordinated to any one's ill feelings. Myrna had become a bit too abrasive for the long time best friends.

"Listen Myrna and Sharon: cut out your little scratching. It's ok to be crazy, just don't get goofy!"

*

Communication between the friends had thus broken down into two camps: Myrna on the one side and Sharon, Robin, and Kitty on the other. The split was not a seismic fault caused by a moral weakness on her part, Myrna had judged, now whistling in her mind of her afternoon rendezvous with hung Hank. It was Sharon who was to be blamed for Hollywood Hank's infidelities. For sure it was Sharon's fault that Hank had stopped fucking her. Of this, Myrna was sure. A man fucks around only when his wife ain't putting out, as everyone knows. In spite of her dalliance with Hank, whom she now recognized as the jerk he had always been, and who would never love her, in her heart there would always be a warm spot for Sharon.

She had often wondered if the others knew of her involvement with Hank. She didn't care. It was just a stupid little coquettish affair, a hangover from high school days.

Stupid Sharon! Still hung up on the high school quarterback, she thought. Why the hell doesn't she divorce him, like Kitty did to her husband? Or like I'm about to do to Phil, my homo monk husband? We're all hung up on the meaningless high school quarterback, but we don't want to admit it. The guy is a hopeless prick, and we're all hung up on him.

She wondered if it was ever true, that for most women, no matter how much they might deny it, a prick, and not a brain, is still the biggest sex organ on a man. They certainly flaunted that way.

Though she continued to pretend there was room in her heart for Sharon, Myrna slowly withdrew into a world less loving towards her best friends. Tormented by her loneliness and need to be with Hank, she sometimes regretted her weakness at betraying her friends. She realized that the desire to be with Hank had been there for a long time, undoubtedly from high school, for shame on stupid her. But what was she supposed to think of her three friends who had never grown up, and as if underprivileged, were incapable of comprehending the world beyond their roka salads, the dear hearts. Worse than hers, their immaturity was also still loitering in their high school days of feel good hugs, their desires now to be fucking like big girls quenched by vodka and wine consumption.

They are still virgins, Myrna thought about her friends who, she was sure, were stuck on the addictive wine. Wine and vodka simply hid their repressed desire to have high school sex preferably with the quarterback. What woman has ever wished and thought of fucking the valedictorian in preference to the quarterback? For the friends, just like it happens in make-believe movies, sex with the quarterback sometimes became a reality, otherwise the wine would have to do. It was all Sharon's fault who didn't want to share, that they all had to keep it a secret. No doubt about it, Sharon was non-fucking goofy; no wonder Hank had stopped fucking her.

Untimely feelings that she now had for Sharon aside, Myrna's love for her persisted. It's not easy to just walk away from a true friend even though you're fucking her husband. Recalling Sharon's gorgeous eyes as she spoke her gospel, while Robin and Kitty giggly-gossiped aimlessly, Myrna at times regretted that she had succumbed to an adulterous affair with Hank. She had long known that Hank was the wrong man for Sharon. Confronted with the dilemma of whom she loved most, Sharon or Hank, Myrna could not make up her mind, a condition which definitely was a leftover from their high school days, when, even then, she thought she loved them both. And when she had that thought of shared love, she wanted to hug Sharon and kiss her on the mouth. Still, every time Sharon opened her mouth to talk religious crap, Myrna became more and more convinced that Sharon was definitely goofy and by default she felt Hank was hers. Sharon's single-minded attention to the topic of love, always cloaked in religious shroud, was as absurd as baby-babble, and it simply didn't jibe with her substantial tits. It was as if baby-faced Sharon secretly wished to revert back to being a virgin; that she was looking for a new start. Myrna recalled how Phil had told her that in mythology there were many stories of deflowered princesses and goddesses bathing in holy rivers and mountain springs and being renewed to their virginal intactness, many times throughout their debauched lives. Aware of her needs and desires, adulteress Myrna knew that Phil was no prince, and Sharon was definitely not a princess, and there were no magic springs nearby. Her annoying arguments, and not so subtle reminisces of loneliness, would unhappily remind Myrna of her estranged husband now cloistered in some damn monastery somewhere, probably trying, like Sharon, to find his own holy John the Baptist to cleanse him and regain his purity. Ridiculous, thought Myrna.

"Totally incomprehensible," she would say to herself and laugh at the sad-sack character of her ex-husband and of her still best friend.

Maybe Sharon was still a virgin, metaphorically speaking, and was searching for a new man, perhaps one of those Greek semi-gods who bleeds onto the lap of lovely maids and transforms them into wild breathless anemones, pristine luscious flowers, swaying in the spring breezes. Or maybe she unconsciously desires a wild bull beast that rips you apart and sends you to your Hades; or maybe a visit from a mad stinking ram to lip-nibble on your anemones, laughed Myrna fondly of her friend.

"Sharon, you definitely need a bull," Myrna had said to Sharon, one time after she had been with Hank.

"She has Hank," Kitty had set the record straight, she herself having known Hank's bullying on several occasions in high school.

It was no use; the get-togethers had lost their flavour for Myrna. Nasty images of silly Sharon trying to recover her virginity would now come to her every time she looked at her beautiful friend who might have been her daughter. Copulating images of Sharon with all sorts of super-human and mythical creatures, in ancient woods and vales, followed by scenes of Sharon scrubbing her pubic hair in magic streams would float before Myrna's green eyes, and she would narcissistically smile into the mischievous projections of her mind, distancing herself from her long-time friends, who were beginning to think unkindly of her.

No matter the arguments on love and friendship, Sharon still had those exquisite pointed breasts and Kitty and Robin, like Myrna herself, were definitely simply asides to Sharon's stared at beauty. She was the magic that kept the group together, but with Phil's unexpected and most awkward departure, not even Sharon could keep the magic of the foursome going. The cultivated mood of adolescent chatter was insufficient for Myrna. She had realized that with Phil gone there could never again be the best-friends-forever sisterhood of the four, regardless of Sharon's upstanding tits. Fucking Phil had crushed her and she would no longer be an aside to anyone. She knew that the long friendship journey was coming to an end, and Sharon's feeble attempts at holy renewals, and finding grace in Jesus, of her spastic attempts at some sort of delayed recovery of puberty, had no spiritual remittance. The best friends' periodic get-togethers, like her pride in her marriage, had become exaggerated social bubbles that had irreparably burst.

*

But for Sharon, and Kitty, and Robin, the camaraderie of breaking bread together, of sharing a laugh and of maintaining the friendship, still held worth. It was still a delightful symposium to celebrate the natural human need to be in physical proximity with one another. The party was easy because the girls were at ease with each other. They got along very nicely because cheap familiarity had never set in. It was a friendship that had unfolded most casually at a young age, and it had never evolved into vulgar intimacy, though the girls had outgrown their pristine years. Even without Myrna, the lunches continued to warmly unite their otherwise disjointed urban lives. In a way, Myrna continued to be with them for they always wondered about her metamorphosis, expected her to return to the fold, and never accepted her change as a rejection of them. Their door was always open to Myrna, for nothing as common as words could permanently separate good friends.

In gin, Myrna had found a different door to perception, of a reality more unfussy than the one she had led in her earlier life with her now ex-husband, and her now becoming ex-friends. It had been sad for everyone when Myrna dropped out of the group and their weekly luncheons to become an addict to her gin. For, it was not the food, nor the drink, obscenely expensive as each was, that brought the friends together, but the ritual of the communion, which they so badly needed to fill in the huge abyss in their uncontemplated mortgaged life. For Myrna, that communion, like her underhanded husband, had begun to straggle untidily across their luncheon table. The get-togethers no longer brought peace to her demoralized soul, and so, she had, for the time being, cut out of the gang. After Phil, she had found the expensive luncheons to be discouragingly insufficient, and she didn't care to be part of them. Sadly she had decided that the future would be as empty as the now, or the fast disappearing past, regardless of the friendships. But for the umbilical cord still binding her to her daughters, everything else was becoming one unmemorable void. At a solid middle age of forty, there was no time to fuss over lettuce and roka leaves served with retarded mixed-up champagne dressings.

Chapter Fourteen

Devouring time does not torment the rich as it does the poor. The rich have the power of their money to delay the angst of time by leisurely waiting it out. They never have to work, they never have the daily routine of a pointless job to go to if they don't want to. The rich can afford to just sit around and shoot the bull, as often as their little old hearts' desire. Of course, in their minds, the bull they shoot is so much more potent than the arguments that common folk debate. So compelling is their money that it actually slows time to the intoxicating pace of unending rounds of wining and dining, and shopping for expensive things, like many gold watches to check their time until too late they're too old. Day after day, the rich rejoice in their good fortune of never having to rush things, like running off to work, without finishing their cup of coffee. Triumphantly they stretch their days as if owed to them. Rich men's wives gossip about social affairs; they don't talk about money, or, God forbid, politics. But, sometimes, in the conscience of a good woman, whether rich or poor, disputes invade from depths unknown and equalize the playing field of life. In the world we all live in, regardless of one's birth status, all human occupation is always checked by reality. Good fortune, always welcomed as a gift from the gods, also brings doubts with it, and some, few sensitive souls, wonder if they're worthy of the gifts. Scepticism sets in and the search for answers invariably, for most people, leads to God. An unconscious struggle then ensues to fit reality within their conscious bounds, and the battle often lasts a lifetime. It is here that the rich think they have the advantage.

Desperately trying to hold on to their edge they run into a wall that is time. Time becomes a consuming illness, and rushes in tormenting thoughts about 'is there all there is', even to the rich, who seldom want to be reminded that they too are mortal.

Sharon had begun to understand the plague of her mortality. But in the confirmation of her sins, which ever since she was a little girl shadowed wickedness and anguish, she also discovered the means to her redemption. Or rather, she re-discovered the love of Jesus that had the powerful healing effect to forgive all sins and lead the way to peace and tranquillity. In rising from an empty life, in Jesus she found her days being filled with thoughts of beauty and truths that had been in her soul the whole time. More than anything else, Sharon wanted to share this obvious truth with her best friends in the hope of saving their rich asses from a meaningless life. She had finally seen the light that, in reality, that was all there was.

*

They had just sat at their table at the Seven Seas of Beverly Hills to unwind a little, to dust away the hangover of Myrna's stupid withdrawal from the best friends' powwows. As always, it was another informal to chase away the blues that too easily got the better of their idle souls, and the last thing they wanted this day was to be harassed with world important mumbo-jumbo. Just a cup of the grog to smoothly slide the time away, while they conspicuously displayed their brand new dresses. Yes, that's all there really was.

"Poor Myrna," Sharon reminded Kitty and Robin, once again, about Myrna's breakup with her husband. "To be alone is like being a lonely flower in the desert. No matter how robust and pretty, it quickly wilts and dies because it has no other plants to shade it."

"If you're gonna start that shit again, Sharon, we'll leave right now. You're driving us crazy with your goofy allusions from nowhere," said Robin.

"Or for it to give shade to others. Healthy people need to be around other people all the time otherwise they whither, wilt, and die," she puckered her perfectly painted lips nonplussed by her best friend Robin's seeming irritation.

"Well, I have to agree with Sharon, Robin. Myrna must be pretty lonesome, all alone without a husband's shoulder to cry on," said Kitty. "Sharon said what she said about Myrna because, after all, what are friends for?"

"What makes you think that she doesn't have shoulders to cry on, Kitty," laughed Sharon as if she had a secret.

After observations like this, Kitty and Robin would look at each other and wonder if she knew that they knew; but who could have matched her ample upright breasts and perfect lips? And who cared that after all these years Myrna was doing Hank.

"One of these days, too much love might kill the superstar," Robin and Kitty had envied over the phone.

"Why Sharon Langdon! Do you have some juicy knowledge about Myrna that we don't? Come on, spill it."

What rich bullshit!

In truth, the three friends were all blessed, physically gifted, and they just didn't go to a restaurant like the very upscale Seven Seas of Beverly Hills just to gossip, nor for the food, good as it was. Above all, they went to the Seven Seas to be seen, and what better sights to catch wandering eyes than their rosy cheeks, their perfectly rounded Giotto buttocks exquisitely fitted in Dior dresses, and their always at attention breasts? Ever since Middle School they had known that the world loved them, and every so often, to enhance the sensation of their narcissism, they would double the action by going commando. They outward lived the sensation of the cool refreshing Pacific air through their opulent arrogance.

In spite of Sharon's overworked babble, they calmly enjoyed each other's egotistic good looks, the friends especially loving Sharon's Hollywood entrances, whose smile twinkled little sparkles in any room. For Sharon, the weekly midday get-together was a treat, an illustrious moment to show off, once again, her God given gifts in all their worldly splendor. It was a moment to repress ugly thoughts about Hank and all that past stupidity. The attention afforded Sharon's good looks by her friends, and the always admiring crowd at the Seven Seas, was most pleasing for her, the clientele there being of a much higher social and intellectual level than her husband's grunting high school greasy, ugh, buddies. You could sense the energy of a very successful crowd, and she bathed in the public stares and smiles that were never enough. From an early age, she understood the exaltation of her loveliness, which justifiably fed her vanity, unlike Robin, who for a long time had known that vanity smacked of unholy self-love, the other side of self-hate.

Unholy or not, Sharon knew that in any get-together, she was fucking it. Except for an unhappy marriage, the girl had it all. Yep, that was all there was.

"We are the beautiful wives of successful men, Sharon. Let's just enjoy our blessings today without your preaching," said Kitty. "We like you for what you are, and not for your fucking erudition."

"Nice one, Kitty. I sure love your learnedness. Did you get it from classical Claudio?"

"Fuck you both," said Sharon with confidence. "I say something, and you guys think it's preaching; you say all sort of crap, and you call it erudition."

"Such ferocity," said Kitty, and they all laughed.

The three friends were intent on enjoying each other's company even without Myrna who had perhaps misdirected her love from them toward what or whom only God knew, and who had thus foolishly if not untidily withdrawn from her best friends, Sharon, Kitty, and Robin, they of the green leafy full of varied vegetation salads. It was her loss. Holding no ill will against Myrna, they wished she was still with them, as they merrily continued to meet every Wednesday at their celebrated hangout at the plush Seven Seas Restaurant for roka leaf salads seasoned with the finest extra virgin olive oil, delicate Balsamic white vinegar, and plenty of clean, white, juicy gossip to chew on.

"You're married to a restaurant tycoon, Robin's married to the president of Pioneer's Bank, and I'm married to the baron of recycled grease," continued Kitty, happy to be part of the Seven Seas society of the rich. "So let's all be happy and enjoy our bread and wine."

"It's Pioneer Bank, and he's Vice President of Human Resources," corrected Robin. "Kitty, you're a sweetheart. You've always had a way with kind words, unlike Sharon who's always waiting for Jesus to show up," laughed Robin.

"Well, Robin, in Sharon's mind, Jesus probably shows up in the red wine," said Kitty and Robin nodded her head in mock understanding.

"There is love in the sharing of a good red wine," Sharon volunteered.

"You start preaching again and I'm out of here, Sharon," said Robin, but Sharon knew that Robin didn't mean it. She hadn't moved out for years and she wasn't going to do it now.

"I didn't say anything," said Sharon.

"Sharon, honey, let's not preach today, we're drinking your wine, your fine red wine; what more do you want?" said Kitty.

"Probably more red," said Robin, and they all laughed in wealthy loud agreement.

Taking a cue from Myrna's excesses, and recalling all the media shrill about fatty livers fast desiccating into grey stones on hard liquor, they had decided to drop it a notch, for a few days, anyway, to give theirs a rest, and skip the gin and vodka in favour of the delicate French wines. Today, at Sharon's insistence, they were enjoying a Saint-Emilion Grand Cru Rouge Sec full of the subtle French summer sun that engendered it with love.

She took an easy sip, held her glass daintily between her long, thin, fingers and said, "For had not Jesus said, *Love one, another,*" and a sweetness came out of Sharon's lips.

"Let's get out of here before it's too late," said Robin, pretending to stand up to exit.

"Sit down Robin. Sharon was just joking."

"No I wasn't," said Sharon, again smiling the sweetest of Saint-Emilion.

"Your waiter will be right with you," said the Mexican busboy as he tipped their glasses, already pretty full, with icy cold water. In a toast to the busboy, they all took a sip and agreed it was good water. You taste tap water anywhere else and it's like they forgot to rinse the glasses; you taste it in Santa Monica and it's like it just arrived from the Alpine mountain tops of, well, Mt. McKinley.

"Have any of you heard from poor Myrna," asked Kitty.

"I heard, and don't ask from whom, that Justine is pregnant," said Robin.

"That's a dirty lie, Robin," said Sharon spoiling for a fight.

"Hey, calm down, Sharon, no need to get riled up now; we'll know for sure in a few months," smiled Robin. "You know, it's not the first time some teenage girl gets knocked up. Anyway, who cares? It's got nothing to do with us."

"That's right Sharon. After all, she's not your daughter," said Kitty.

"Anyway, we all know that sooner or later all daughters get screwed," laughed Robin.

"Poor Justine, she had so much going for her!" said Sharon in a voice genuinely affected with muted sorrow.

"Well, Sharon, she's about as old as you were when Hank drilled you, so you ought to know that it had to happen sometime, so why not now? She's a pretty enough girl to be attractive," said Kitty trying not to make a big issue out of something she thought common enough.

"I wonder who the lucky bastard is, because she's a beautiful peach," said Robin. "She looks a lot like you, Sharon. Anyway, she can always get an abortion, now days."

"Really, Sharon, we've always wondered, did you screw Hank when we were in high school?" smiled Kitty. Everybody knew.

"So did you, Kitty," said Sharon.

"Deflowered at such a young age, violently bruised by a deformed beast with a hard-on that shows up out of nowhere to spill his sperm all over her thighs ..." burst out Robin in pretended Shakespearean monologue.

"Fuck you too, Robin. Just because you were such a tight ass and didn't get it ..."

"Whoa there Sharon. Justine's seventeen and it's not unnatural for women to have babies," said Kitty. "You know that in the old days women had their babies as early as fourteen of fifteen. And let's be fair, we all know that all girls and young women must have their sex, or else they quickly get fat."

"Talk about babies, there's only one between the three of us," said Robin.

Too late, Kitty had blurted out a touchy subject that Robin tried to cool: It was so insensitive of her to bring up the painful matter of Sharon and Robin being barren. It was a cruel thing to say knowing that Sharon and Robin couldn't have babies. It was too late for apologies, though. True friends don't apologize like strangers would for stupidity.

"Even gays have sex, but they adopt babies," said Robin. "Ever thought of adopting maybe an Ethiopian baby, Sharon."

"Is that sexist, or simply not politically correct," said Kitty? "These things are so confusing these digital days."

There was an awkward moment of silence, and then, no one wanted to make an issue out of a stupid comment about gays and adoptions.

"Being pregnant is a process of renewal, dear," smiled Robin, the words directed at Sharon, she herself still hoping that she might someday get pregnant again.

"Being knocked up is a quick jog to death, into a darkness never to return again. I know, we all know," Sharon strongly affirmed to her friends her understandings of pregnancies. "I know that son-of-a-bitch boyfriend of hers doesn't love her. He just wants to fuck her all the time. Poor Justine, too stupid to say no."

Eyebrows were raised and silence interfered for a moment or two.

"Cool it Sharon. I'm sure Myrna hasn't taking it as badly as you. You're becoming weird, honey, and you'll get stretch marks on your teen face before you age," said Robin. "We should all be as lucky as Justine to hook up with some oversexed teenager. I'm sure she'll do fine."

"You'd like that, wouldn't you, Sharon? I know I would," smiled Kitty half-jokingly.

"Men are so damn stupid. They lug around with a hard-on and they'll crush everything that's in their way for a piece of ass," said Sharon. "Stupid asses is what they are."

"How old is she anyway?" somebody said.

"Is she going to marry him?" asked Sharon.

"She says she wants to keep her baby and marry the guy, and that Myrna supports Justine's decision," said Kitty hoping to end the Justine saga.

"Jesus! I hope not for either of those reasons," said Sharon. "You know how those things work out. All too soon they'll wind up divorced, and Myrna's too old to take care of a baby. So, who's gonna take care of that baby? Or what's the sense of marrying?"

"You know, you get on board this Ferris wheel and go round and round, and up and down, and …" and Robin could not finish the thought.

"Never underestimate mothers and daughters, and daughters and their babies. They are the fabric of every society, my dear," said Kitty, and, too late, she was sorry again.

"Teenage sex is adulterous, and dirty," said Sharon.

"They're both single," said Robin.

"That's when it feels dirty," she said.

She just wouldn't let go, but her choice of words were interesting, so Robin and Kitty let her go on. It was understandable that barren Sharon might be a bit jealous of Justine.

"Sharon, do you know the Mickey Mouse song?" said Robin.

"Still, Myrna should have been more Christian-like with her daughters," continued Sharon puckering her lips with cranky emotion.

"Cut this shit out; no more tears of self-pity, Sharon. You're not responsible for getting Justine pregnant," said a pissed Robin.

"Think about it, Robin. Myrna simply doesn't have the money to support an extra mouth … or two, if we count dumb-ass, bloodsucking son-in-law," said Sharon.

"You're full of shit, if you think Myrna is having financial problems, my little pussy willow," smiled Kitty, and she looked around for the waiter who was fast approaching with that savage cabernet.

"You're the pussy, little Kitty, little pussy Kitty-cat," said Sharon and they all laughed.

"Well, maybe Myrna wasn't so very religious, but hubby Phil sure was," laughed Robin.

"Now Robin, these things happen," kindly offered Kitty.

"Speaking of Myrna, I too didn't take the Bible too literally, as my poor mother had," volunteered Sharon in another remarkable flip-flop, "until one night St. John came to me in a dream…"

"Which one, dear," Kitty said, and gently poked Robin on the side.

"What do you mean," asked Sharon truly befuddled.

"She means there are several St. Johns, as you of the Bible Sharon know. So, which one came in your dream, I mean," Robin continued the tease.

"Shame on you, Robin," giggled Kitty.

"I never thought of it, but you're right, Robin. Let's see; there's John the Baptist, and John who wrote the Bible, and John of the Apocalypse and …"

"Never mind, Sharon, let's just get a drink," Kitty dropped the subject.

She reached out and touched Sharon's and Robin's hands.

It always amazed the friends that they actually had things to say. Maybe not profound conceits to throw light on the void, but conversations above the usual rich ladies gossip. It was not uncommon of them to proudly attack the unfamiliar.

"You know, fellow Americans, we should all be very happy because we are all very successful millionaires. And more importantly, we've never had to struggle to be successful. That's why we don't have to prove ourselves; we are born successful millionaires-asses, with beautiful assesses," laughed Robin, who had a tendency to laugh at her own doggy humor.

"It would have been nice if Myrna was with us right now," said Kitty trying to change the subject. Sometimes Robin's humor was a bit too bitchy for ladies.

"And maybe that's why poor Myrna is no longer with us. They say that even though her father sold a lot of insurance on the internet, he wasn't very fond of Myrna and left her very little money and that's why she married a poor dentist," said Robin.

"Mr Lawson sold real estate and he made a lot of money, Robin. And after her brother committed suicide, Myrna inherited everything," said Kitty. "Of course she isn't as rich as you, but then who is; but she's rich enough not to have to cook every day, sorry Sharon."

"She says she forgives Phil but will forever hate him for dumping her," said Sharon.

"Which definitely smacks at a major paradox," said Robin, "for how could she forgive her husband and not love him? Doesn't forgiveness come parcelled with love?"

"Poor Alice, she died of a broken heart too," continued Kitty in memory of Myrna's angelic mother. "They say that life is all patterns."

"I wonder if Justine ever thinks of how poor they are," Sharon's mind relentlessly lamenting Justine's pregnancy predicament. She thought it "awful" and "stupid girl."

"Well, it has nothing to do with us anyway," said Kitty. "You know Myrna was always careful to sidestep any soul searching stuff."

"It might have burst the dam," said Robin.

"You are blessed to have such a loving husband as your David, Robin," Sharon enviously complimented her friend. "He is a giving person, volunteering so much of his time, as the Lord would have us all do. He is so fortunate to have found contentment in his life, thanks to you, Robin."

There were times when Sharon showed a very keen sense of sarcasm. Robin wasn't sure if this wasn't one of those times. It wasn't; Sharon meant the compliment.

"And he's soooo good looking," Robin mockingly blew the words like cigarette smoke into the Beverly Hills expensive air trying to neutralize Sharon's words.

"Yes, he really does have the love magic, doesn't he Robin," said Kitty. "And he is soooohhh good looking, and never seems to get old …"

"Well, you two, sometimes I think you two love handsome David more than I do, which is a waste of time on your part, because everyone knows that David and I are lovers forever young," Robin smothered the words with the fine cabernet. It was delicious and smooth as it travelled down the throat; not a hint of tartness.

"Remember Robin, first you love the Lord, God, then you love your husband, as you would love yourself; but always God first," Sharon reminded her friends.

"You can't go wrong with that," quickly interjected Kitty. "But always remember the first time."

"Where the hell is that Dago waiter?" whispered Robin.

The friends were now slightly buzzed.

"Let's switch to that white dry Bordeaux, in the meantime," more calmly called Robin, as she tried to adjust to the quick presence of the rushed maître de.

"No, let's have more red wine this week," sharply cut in Sharon. She was determined on the red and was not about to be derailed by anyone this day.

"Why bother, they're all the same," smiled Robin trying not to appear agitated.

"Just for me, Robin, let's celebrate with a red today," insisted Sharon humbly.

"OK. Make it a blinding red and bring us some blindfolds," said Robin as she turned to the maître de and twisted her lips to mildly protest Sharon's insistence for a red.

"Except for Sharon; she has her darkest shades on already. She views the world from a monk's dark wine cellar with her shades," Kitty shushed a quirky smile.

"Make it a bottle of your finest red Bordeaux," continued Sharon, more determined, "and I don't care about the price. Do you have a thick Bordeaux?"

"A bloody thick Bordeaux from the finest vineyards of Bordeaux just for you, Mrs Merker," smiled the maître.

"I don't mind the Bordeaux," said Kitty, "but no shades for me. I like to see what I'm drinking. I also like the color red, fiery red, like the dark red poppies of the field …."

"We're talking about wine, Kitty."

"Color is what we like, and being a long-time good friend, red we shall all have, forever and ever, Amen," smiled Sharon.

"You know what they say about color, Robin? Don't knock it till you try it," Kitty tried to show Robin that she could keep a secret.

"Naughty, naughty, Kitty," smiled Sharon. "Have either of you ever tried it, Robin?"

"Sharon, Robin's spent two years in Ethiopia, duh," said Kitty.

The topic of race was always a bit grouchy; so they quickly skipped over it.

"What're you going to have, Sharon," said Robin.

"I'll have what Sharon has," said Kitty; food wasn't all that important.

"Kitty, you'd try lamb's brains if Sharon ordered them for you," huffed Robin who was taking out her anger at Kitty for the Bordeaux that Sharon had ordered. "Go ahead and ask Sharon to order you some brains. It's on the menu."

"Just like you eat lamb's balls you order all the time, ha!, Robin. Ugh! If you like balls so much you should order bull's balls." Kitty smiled into the distance.

"I like sweet breads like any other healthy woman," said Robin, carefully acknowledging her haute cuisine preferences while also blushing her high cheeks. "And by the way, their proper name is mountain oysters around these parts. Have you ever had them around these parts, Sharon?" She quickly recovered into the warmth of comradery.

"Only while they were still hanging, I bet," said Kitty.

"No, really, Robin, do you use knife and fork with them?" asked Sharon pretending innocence. "Grilled, sautéed, a la stir-fried …?"

"Stop it, Sharon; you're cracking me up," said Kitty.

"Such daintiness; you're so damn fastidious in your personal tastes, aren't you Sharon," said Robin, who could knife with a smile. "I suppose if anyone knows about balls, it would be you, like footballs …"

"Did you guys know that orchids means balls, as in testicles," said Kitty, again calming the storm that sometimes sneaks in when the conversation turns to rambling personal.

"Kitty, maybe you shouldn't have any of the Bordeaux today. You seem testy enough already," Robin fondly smiled at her friend.

No matter what Kitty said, the best of friends knew that it was free of meanness.

"I bet Sharon could finish off a couple of bull's orchids all by herself," Kitty flirted aimlessly among the rare flowers.

"We will all partake of the red Bordeaux," Sharon gently put her hands together in front of her as if to offer a prayer.

"Fuck it, Sharon, there's no going back. Let's just enjoy our time now. It's a privilege being part of Beverly Hills, just like the hillbillies," Robin tried to amuse the crowd away from Sharon's wasting nonsense. She suspected that Sharon was about to go off the track again. She wanted to hug her but not in public.

Sharon was suddenly no longer interested in what Robin and Kitty thought about bulls' balls, or had to say about silly, girly things, and so she mentally dropped out of their mindless exchanges. This immediately became apparent to Kitty and Robin and for a moment the two friends looked at each other and tried to guess what Sharon might be up to, first insisting on the red, then holding hands, then dropping out, but searching for meaning to her words and actions wasn't important since the wine was great. It was the call for more wine and not the prayer stance of holding hands that held the girls' afternoon attention. It wasn't the first time that Sharon had reached out to hold hands, so they were used to it. Ill-mannered as the thought might be, it was Sharon's flamboyant tits that made her good company, and not her holy demeanor which simply didn't jibe with those breasts mostly outside the barn.

The girls were having fun hanging out.

"Drink ye this red, for this is my blood," Sharon opened her eyes to Heaven. She would be unstoppable now.

"Sharon, have you been shacking up with saints again?" said Kitty.

"You buy and I'll drink of this holy Bordeaux any time," Robin expertly swirled the delicious blood in her mouth.

Sharon, more than ever, became convinced that her friends needed help. Once again they were blathering on, without purpose, to nowhere in particular, Lord help them. She would have to interfere and get them back on the right track.

"The thought occurred to me," said Kitty, "if lamb's balls are called sweet breads, is there a special name for ewe's udders?"

"There is for Sharon's," laughed Robin.

"And, more importantly, are they edible?" inquired Kitty.

"Well, Kitty, I've never seen any kind of tits as an entry on a menu, though I'm sure Sharon's are very edible, probably most rare," said Robin snapping her mouth for a huge bite.

"Most succulent," said wide-eyed Kitty.

Sharon finished her glass of red, gave a side glance at Robin's shy breasts and uttered, "You wish you had tits like mine, Robin."

"A lot of good they do you, Sharon," said Robin, tit for tat.

The thought of Kitty speculating about ewe's tits, and Robin wondering whether her tits were gourmet entrees, made Sharon blush and her breasts swelled purple. She privately mused at her reaction to her friends' humor, and like an adolescent girl's early encounters of heat, the intensity of the feeling radiating from her breasts startled her. Ever since that day on the bus, her tits ruled. It was strange how on occasions like this one, with hot-like flashes flooding menstrual emotions, her thoughts always travelled to the boy on the bus who first made her aware of her breasts. How could she feel so hot and bothered at a long ago memory? Of a little boy, handsome as he was! She took a drink of water to cool down, away from the wine, but her mind's easy trip was still making her blush hot. She was fast losing touch with her surroundings over a silly reference to an adolescent boy and her breasts, and she struggled to regain control of herself. Everything was becoming a simmering desert yellow wave, the air too hot and dry, catching her imperceptibly short of breath. Her whole body, especially her belly and the inside of her thighs and crouch were profusely perspiring. She lowered her head slightly and dabbed her upper lip that was wet from tiny drops of perspiration. Slight nausea surfaced in her unsettled stomach and she put her hand over her mouth and gently bit the inside of her cheek to keep from sliding into a faint. She was afraid to look towards her friends least they think badly of her, though to Robin and Kitty her behavior seemed Sharon normal-abnormal and they didn't bother to ask. She continued to lower her head slowly as if to look into her lap, and her mind inexplicably went into another private swoon, the heat in her face reminding her of her morning's shower. Spinning head still down, she saw herself standing under the hot water and she suddenly raised her mystified face up to meet the splashing water. Weirdly all in her hot brain now, the shower was pulsating huge gushes of water on her face until it got unbearably hot and she gulped for air and she turned the knob for cold water and relief.

During this strange semi-trance, Robin and Kitty continued their dawdling chitchat unaware of the turbulence in Sharon's silent misconduct. Acting as if nothing unusual was happening, they thought it best not to say anything until the empty stares from Sharon's eyes filled up again.

Other customers in the restaurant witnessed the bizarre behavior, saw that the two companion friends had everything under control, and decided not to be bothered by the theatrics. In the crazy world we live in, to flash bipolar was, like, statistically cool these days.

Seated among the snobbish Beverly Hills restaurant crowd, Sharon again shut her eyes to sooth the din all around her and under the muting cool water of her hallucinating mind, her dizziness began to retreat to normal.

Under a different influence now, she thought it strange that Robin should have alluded to the Da Vinci's Last Supper in her earlier moment of Bordeaux pique. It was as if her intention was to bring the Lord's Last Supper to their attention, comparing it to their insignificant luncheon, perhaps, and by some extension, wishing it to shine some light into their dreary lives. What a lovely reference to bring the Holy Icon of the Last Supper to their table at the Seven Seas Restaurant. Robin's indirect reference was surely an act of charity, a gift from God. The importance was the presence of God; the Seven Seas venue was irrelevant, thought Sharon. The benevolence of a sermon really doesn't matter whether it occurs on Golgotha or in a Beverly Hills restaurant; it's the good news of the message that's important. She and her friends were simply God's instruments of tuning in to eternal love. Allusions to powerful images of, well, God and Da Vinci's intentions, just don't surface so serenely, as Robin had just casually done, unless inspired by, well, God, as Sharon was surmising. How divine of Robin, thought Sharon. How beautiful of her to bring up Jesus' last supper with His disciples, who were His friends, except for one.

Ever since her desert dream that was filled with magical chants from monks and angels, Sharon had been trying to figure out a way to recapture the moment and share it with her friends. She was certain that the dusty desert habitat of the handsome monk had been a glimpse of Heaven, for the sensation of the dream was still Heavenly, and that she had now been called on to share the privilege.

Curiously, now out of her deep shower delusion and absorbed by Robin's inspired stillness, with trepidation Sharon searched for the crucial moment to share the joy, with her friends, of the bread and wine, which were of the body of Christ. In humility, with eyes lowered and with love in her heart Sharon most softly, most clearly, recited of Jesus to her best friends from her beloved days of youth. In a soft voice full of delight she shared with her friends the love that came from Jesus.

> *Drink ye all of it;*
> *This is my Blood of the New Testament,*
> *Which is shed for you and for many,*
> *For the remission of sins.*

Away from the Heavenly desert and back into the posh world of Beverly Hills, Kitty and Robin could not deny their ears. Speechless they stared at each other. Once again their beloved friend had transcended well above the wonders of their easy fashionable world. Not knowing what to do or say, they made funny faces at each other, looked around the restaurant, and wished for an alarm to go off and wake them up.

"Sharon, are you having fucking problems with Hank again and it shows. Is he not screwing you enough, dear?" said Robin ready to slap some sense into her friend.

Sharon was lost in her Eucharistic moment and heard nothing of what Robin had said.

"This vampire talk has to stop or I'm leaving," once again threatened Robin.

"They do say that red wine does wonders for your health," said Kitty.

It was an unorthodox moment and anything said would have been wacky.

"Where is that wine?" puckered back Robin. "Get another red."

"Good for the heart, say the French, and obviously good for the soul according to Sharon," said Kitty, who then took Sharon's hand.

"Red makes you more sociable, Sharon," kindly smiled Robin, who then also reached out and gently touched Sharon's other hand.

There was only one explanation: their beloved friend Sharon was in dire need of professional psychiatric help.

"Sharon dear, you need help. It's either psychiatric help for you, or losing you to the priests," said Kitty. "And I'm serious. Man, snap out of it!"

"We love you, Sharon," said Robin not knowing what else to say.

They loved her and wished they could help but didn't know how. Besides, now was not the right moment to dig deep into the psyche and neither of them had schooling in psychology.

"Robin, we'll just have to put up with her bullshit this afternoon, and she'll have to find her own way out of her obviously repressed sexuality," hushed Kitty. "It's obvious she's not getting enough, if any."

"Go fuck yourself, Sharon," said Robin and the two friends laughed at her expense.

Extending herself beyond her friends' best wishes, Sharon continued to focus on the words in her now translucent mind and quietly began to reflect on their meaning. She wondered what Robin had meant when she previously had referred to "bloody red?" Not so clear the bloody red. She opened her eyes wide and there definitely was ambiguity in "bloody red" when referring to wines. Her mind retrieved those simple words in syncopated bursts – blood, bloody, red, blood, bloody, red - until in unison, like a jolt to the frontal lobes, she felt their powerful meaning. Instantaneously her heart swelled with harmonized rhythmic composure at the profound beauty and meaning of Jesus' last words to humanity just before His crucifixion. And since time immemorial it has been the true prophet's burden to speak his vision of Heaven to this troubled world, so it befell on Sharon this day to share the message of Jesus with her beloved friends. And what better way than with Jesus' own words? It was all so obvious. Suddenly, she stood up in her place at the table, steadfast and seemingly in full control. It was as if the Lord Jesus was there with her, directing His eternal words through her as she now softly staring into the distance pronounced them to her friends,

"Drink of this my blood and you will find salvation."

"Sit down, Sharon, you're embarrassing us and making a fool of yourself in front of all these people." Robin had lost her patience at Sharon's going wacko, in public, before her eyes. "What the hell is the matter with you? Are you out of your mind? Right now you're the weirdest."

"Stop it, both of you," nervously hushed Kitty.

She took Sharon's hand and forcefully sat her down.

Robin and Kitty suddenly broke into a long quiet giggle. They both looked sideways away from Sharon and slowly regained control of themselves. Together they realized that Sharon preaching in Beverly Hills wasn't as weird a scene as it might have appeared because more bizarre things take place every day in the Hollywood environs of LA, and the crowds are rarely impressed. After all this is fantasy land.

"Where the fuck is that Bordeaux," once again demanded Robin.

Seated again, but still mystically removed from Robin and Kitty, Sharon's mind remained focused on Jesus' words which unsurprisingly again led her to the picture of Leonardo's *Last Supper.* In it she could see Jesus' undeniable Godly demeanor as He calmly pronounced the words

"Drink of this my blood and you will find salvation,"

Beautiful words that floated in her mind carried by the beacon light that crossed the bright yellow desert sand, which at that moment, in Sharon's mind, was more beautiful than any crowded restaurant.

"Sharon, shut up! You're not Jesus, and for your information Jesus didn't literally mean that the wine was his blood. Yuk, can you imagine drinking blood, even Jesus'?" said Kitty.

Deaf words as far as Sharon was concerned who was still visiting with the Last Supper after her brief foray into the empty desert.

"It's a good painting, but most inadequate to Jesus' words," continued Sharon to her friends, still in a desert of her own. And then,

"Drink of this my blood and you will find salvation,"

"Compared to the words spoken most sweetly and lovingly by our Lord Jesus, Leonardo's *Last Supper* is a very gloomy expedition. It lacks the eloquence of the eternally more powerful words of Jesus" she said.

Not Robin, not Kitty, and for sure no one in the restaurant gave a damn on what Sharon had to say. Unsurprisingly, Sharon had more to say.

"Much as we love it and praise it, it's not a very good painting," she said out loud. "It fails to capture the passion. It depicts Jesus as just one of the gang, a good old boy betrayed, and not the Lord that he is."

"This Bordeaux is excellent, Sharon. Take a little sip; it'll do you good," said Kitty.

"Yes, Sharon, listen to Kitty. Who among us has not sinned?" said Robin, who then quickly covered her mouth, not wanting to laugh too loudly at her slip of the tongue, which let the cat out of the bag, that she had fallen into Sharon's trap of pretending a presence in the Lord's Last Supper, or at a minimum, some Christian Sunday mass.

"Next thing you know I'll be going to confession," laughingly said Robin.

"I'm trying to save your souls, but you both continue in sin," said an angry Sharon.

In her unruffled mind, Jesus' words were much more direct and comprehensible than any of the paintings of the Last Supper by the many artists over the centuries, which were full of staged melodrama, such as the one by Leonardo, a man who really didn't know what he was. In Sharon's mind, there was no comparison to the words.

"The words easily win out over the melodrama of the thirty silver coins buried in the dirty leather pouch. Unlike the stillness of the painting, the words are full of the energy, of the promise of salvation, and who can deny their everlasting power," said Sharon now seemingly in control of her mind.

"Sharon, what are you mumbling," said Kitty.

"Drink of my blood,"

Sharon answered honestly, retaining self-control at her friend's silly question.

"Don't talk to her, Kitty," said Robin, "and order her a plate of locust."

"I can assure you both, blood is the only route to salvation," said Sharon.

"Sharon, I can tell you that we're all marching straight to our death and no words, beautiful as they might be in your troubled mind, can change that prescription," said an unkind Robin, passive-aggressively warning Sharon to shut up.

"And here He means dark red blood wine," insisted Sharon. "They are hard words full of dripping red warm blood, easily digestible by even the humblest of human beings, for God forgives all. Drink my blood and you will be forgiven your sins. Drink it and all of your sins, for all you wretchedly poor, and all you rich alike, all the time, for all time, for as many times as you drink my cleansing blood, you will be forgiven your sins no matter how horrible these might be," Sharon, full of smiles and grace, looked into the future, and held her empty glass high.

"I think space cadet has abandoned us again," noted Robin who had faith that Sharon would return as soon as the bloody red Bordeaux once again resurrected.

"Where the hell is that wine?" Kitty was furious and she saw Sharon's eyes pop open.

"Just kidding, dear," she said to Sharon not to disturb her beyond the present.

"Sharon, what's eating your ass, for God's sake," said Robin.

"It's definitely not Hank," said Kitty and she and Robin had a good laugh.

Both Kitty and Robin were beginning to lose their ladylike poise. The wine was great and Sharon was buffoon silly. They were using coarse, foul language and they were beginning to abandon their friend to her bizarre illusions.

"What the hell; we all lose it sometimes," said Kitty.

"Yeah, it happens to all of us. Fuck it! It's no big deal," said Robin.

"What other Words touch our hearts to give so much salvation?" Sharon passionately continued on her desert revelations. "Unconditional salvation! Fear of dreadful death, deathly death, and its aftermath eternity in horrifying hell, once and for all stomped on, forever destroyed, gone, by the simple act of the drinking of Jesus' blood symbolized by a sweet blessed red wine."

She had thought her words carefully and had understood the truth in them. Of this she was sure, for she had caught a glimpse of Heaven and knew that deathly death had forever been destroyed by Jesus.

"Mark me, oops, excuse me, my goodness," she had burped a sweet smell, "these words make for brutally powerful images. But then, the universe was not created by the meek, but by God Jesus," happily continued Sharon to her friends. "There is no denying these words. Above all, they work all the time."

Believe in the redemption of the blood of Jesus, and in the end, just before you sail into eternity, you say the words,

'God forgive me',

and you will sail into eternal salvation."

She was outwardly calm now, and no one wanted to deny her sermon.

"Those who have been baptized in Christ
In Christ they shall be resurrected,
Alleluia…"

"Never heard that one," said Kitty.

"Were you baptized, Kitty?"

"Can you think of any simpler words to neutralize the pain, Kitty? Listen carefully to what I have to say: those who don't believe in His words will spend an eternity in darkness suffering in dreadful deathly death," she sweetly reminded her two sisters in Jesus. It was just a warning; she really didn't wish it.

"Now and forever and from all ages to all ages."
"Amen."

"If you don't stop this shit, I'll never come to your party again," said Robin who then excused herself to go to the ladies room.

As Robin was walking away, Sharon thought she heard her cry out, "Please help me Sharon. I need the Lord's help".

Though the whole mystic retelling of Jesus's evangelical words lasted only a minute or two, the scene, in all its reverence, was definitely an overstatement for a Wednesday afternoon lunch, Sharon had to finally admit, as she watched Robin walk away, and saw Kitty sitting there atypically numb, most unusual for Kitty.

Slowly she came out of her trance as she witnessed Robin nonchalantly returning from the ladies room. And as she sat there, at the Seven Seas, tears came to her eyes, when she saw her best friends dumbfounded by her words which were the words of Jesus. The tears were for Robin and Kitty both of whom she loved very much. She suddenly realized that both friends were now asking for her help. Especially, Robin, who, she could tell, was full of pent-up secrets ready for relief.

"We all need help, Robin," said Sharon who took a long drink of the red wine while still a little dizzy and weak; she leaned over and kissed Robin on both cheeks, while climbing out of her hot shower.

"What is the matter with you?" gasped a startled Robin who hated being touched by females let alone being kissed in public.

She saw in Robin's ungrateful reaction to her tender prelude to salvation a reflection of her own avoidances to reality and it startled Sharon back to the restaurant. She touched her Channel pink suit skirt, bordered with its grey braid, to make sure she was real and not out of her mind. Awake and filled with love, she looked at Robin only to see a severe face where a friend had been there before. Understanding the saints' struggle with the flock, it occurred to her that like the giving of help, forgiveness, where none is sought, was no easy task; sometimes people don't want to be forgiven. She realized that she was weak and incapable of helping anyone, including herself, and she wished that she were stronger. She wanted to convince Robin of the red wine and the blood of Jesus but felt inadequate and lacking in inspiration. The thought crossed her frail mind that maybe it was she who needed the help but would not admit it. She thought of Myrna, and her mind became even more confused.

"Where the fuck is that Bordeaux," Sharon repeated Kitty's words in an attempt to re-join her friends and spike her heartbeat.

It was the unexpected shock of the word coming out of Sharon's lusty lips that made them rejoin and laugh together.

"It's about time you started acting normal again. Stop your mumbling shit and act normal," said a relieved Kitty. "Stop saying those things like you know what they mean and stay put in your chair. They're going to throw us out of here for good if you don't behave and stop saying that shit."

"It's only because I love both of you," ached Sharon.

"Jesus, Sharon, some of the stuff you've been repeating are signs of mental illness. You know what I say: piss on earth," Robin tried to bring it home with some down to earthy reality.

"If you have true faith, get up from your bed and walk away, was the way Jesus had put it to a poor man who had been a cripple all his life," humbly Sharon felt the need to preach just one tiny bit more. She was exhausted and wanted to get off the mount.

Without warning the lame thought crossed her mind that she was the cripple, without the moral strength to walk away from an unhappy lot that was her life. And as beautiful to behold as she was, she very much felt that she was a hopeless cripple.

"We are all cripples," said a pissed Robin, to her best friends, as the wine luncheon progressed somewhat in unexpected silence and unanticipated pathos.

"Sorry for the delay, ladies; I'm ready now. May I take your orders."

It was Gianni their favorite handsome Italian waiter.

Gianni's arrival was not a moment too soon. The establishment purposefully delayed taking orders knowing that the ladies liked their wine. He was in good spirits and his face had a radiant smile, his eyes were bright, his whole disposition a contrast to the unusual gloom of the three good friends who were his favorite customers. He quickly glanced a happy smile to each of the girls and waited for their usual merry greeting.

"I'm ready any time you are, Gianni," winked an always cheery Kitty, and the massive weight of Christ's bloody words were quickly set aside.

Gianni's smile was infectious; they all responded in kind. He was one of the best in his slick job. Give him a couple of millions and he would be exceptionally good-looking. The girls liked him a lot, except for Robin who would never admit that she too found him attractive.

"We'll have three Roka leaf salads with the boiled squid and champagne dressing, and a double order of goat feta, Gianni," said Sharon quickly adapting to the good-spirited moment at the sight of Gianni.

Like a little girl playing outdoors with her friends, she found excitement in Gianni's presence, and she beat everyone to the punch to rush an order for the three of them.

"Who made you the head chef," smiled Kitty, happy to have Sharon back. They really didn't care about the salads which they rarely ate anyway; she could have ordered anything and it wouldn't have made any difference because they were never hungry.

"Make sure it's goat feta, Gianni," Sharon gesticulated familiarity by waving her finger.

"Why not get the good kind?" kidded Robin, happy again that they could make jokes about the food which was really nothing more than an accessory to the afternoon. That's why they were there: not for the food, or the expensive wine but for the pleasure of bawdy friendship served over a layer of hot gossip.

Robin's sarcastic comment about goat feta sailed happily over their heads.

"For the benefit of Robin, I meant feta from goat's milk, Gianni," and Sharon seemed to be back in her voluptuous smiling best form. She loved to play Gianni.

Gianni was a good man, worth every penny of his pourboire.

"We always serve the best goat feta to our preferred customers, Mrs. Merker," Gianni welcomed the entry to flatter. Being Italian, he could never understand how a beautiful woman like Sharon could have fallen for a pock-marked faced jerk like Mr. Merker.

"Say Mrs. Merker again and no tip for you, Gianni," joked Sharon loving the relaxed informality of his casualness.

From the many female customers sailing the Seven Seas, Gianni had learned that in flirtation there's always sex. Unfortunately for him, Sharon didn't know how to flirt.

The get-together that afternoon had been a messy confusion and Robin and Kitty found relief in the teasing manner between Sharon and chivalrous Gianni even if it only involved ordering Roka salads and goat feta. They didn't want to interrupt and hoped that Sharon would order more things on the menu, or even off the menu. On his part, Gianni was glad that Sharon was doing the ordering because he was always afraid of what Robin might say; sometimes she would confuse him on purpose. Besides, it was so much more pleasant to look at Sharon's face and lips and eyes as she ordered.

"And some crispy Greek village bread," added Kitty, her smile revealing a perfect set of gorgeous well attended teeth compliments of Phil Lambert.

"Yes, Mrs. Albiona. And will you have the usual *Chateau Perron Blanc* with your lunch?" asked Gianni to no one particular.

"No, we'll have that same robust, red Bordeaux, that seems to have lost its way here from France, apparently, Johnny, my man," hissed Robin to bug Gianni.

There it was again; the mock unfriendliness that would confuse Gianni.

She loved teasing handsome Gianni who really was Italian. She would purposely Anglicize his name in pretended pleasantness, and smile. But she was always in her rich form, and handsome as Gianni was, well, he was just a waiter.

"Probably Argentine," she had one day defiantly demoted Gianni to her friends least they think she hungered after his handsome body. In her fantasies she thought him most handsome but low class. She would have loved to shack up with him a few times, but he was just an alien waiter. Besides, what if he had responded in kind to her fantasies? What if he showed no respect, pushing her disrespectfully, or made fun of her, or her name?

"Ti amo, my little bird, my lovely Robin!" she fantasized him mocking her.

"Excuse me, Mrs. Calder, but I thought since you're having the greens salad, may I recommend the…"

"Bring the bloody red, Johnny dear," Robin unkindly interrupted him, barely managing to keep her civility under control. Professional waiter Gianni's fawning attentiveness had always made Robin uneasy; even with her bluest eyes, she just couldn't see that he was simply playing the attendant waiter.

"Yes Mrs. Calder," said Gianni with a smile, and off he went to get the wine.

"Well?" she turned to her friends who were accustomed to her sometimes inclement frostiness. "It pisses me off how all these damn waiters, and him especially, presume to know the right wine for you, as if you're an idiot. It's always white wine with fish, and chicken, and salads, and pinot noire with red meats, and yellow piss-tea with Chinese, as if any fucking order ever makes any fucking sense or difference, ever! Never happened in the Peace Corps! It was always *injera and wat.*"

"And … what?" asked Kitty.

"They're just trying to justify their tip, Robin," said Sharon coming to Gianni's defence.

"Never happened in the Peace Corps," repeated Robin.

To all returned PCVs, as much as they might have denied it, the Peace Corps experience always did have a mystical reference bundled in a transcendent reality of hugely personal secret spirituality though of undetermined amount, and not apparent to the rest of the world. By far, like Robin, most Volunteers were convinced of the separate Peace Corps Paradise that awaited them after this insignificant post-PCV life. For Peace Corps Volunteers, Paradise would be spend with President Jack lecturing on the merits of democracy for the poor. It was the magic stuff that held the Corps together during their imperious assignments abroad. Lovely stuff that kept you conceited for a whole lifetime.

Kitty hated the Peace Corps. She too had applied to join but had been turned down. What a waste of name, she thought. She was glad she hadn't spent two years of her life pretending she had made a difference.

"Well, they're not doing anywhere near enough for the goddamn huge tips that they've become accustomed, thanks to soft touches like you two," said spirited Robin, who at the same time gave a pretty good pinch to Kitty's soft left arm.

"Both of you cut out this touchy-feely stuff," cried Kitty.

There had been a time when the girls were unconscious of their close physical touches and cuddly embraces of friendly adolescent familiarity. They had been hugging, pinching, and squeezing each other since junior high school days. But now, at their age, these familiar caresses had become awkward; grown women just don't touch each other. Even cheek kisses demanded a practised distance.

With the passing of years, the friends had become more privately body-centric, more sensitive to bodily contacts, so when they now touched each other, it reminded them of immature high school goosing.

"Well, Kitty, let's start with you. What's new with you since we last saw you," chimed in Sharon, well recovered now from her out-of-this-world spiritual jaunt. She thought Robin's criticizing of Gianni as impolite and racist and wanted a new topic. Like they couldn't afford a fifty-dollar tip? Anyway, there were more important issues to be covered than Gianni's tip.

"As if there's anything to know about food and wine," Robin continued harping in a pissed mood still agitated for reasons even she didn't know. "Some son-of-a bitch will next boil cabbage and add cilantro and oregano to it and it'll become the next must try for every middle aged fatty-frightened woman in town. Frigging boiled cabbage and cilantro at ninety bucks a throw. And God forbid that Mick Jagger gets a hold of the recipe because he'll make a fortune jarring it for his next several super lean long legged twisting in the air marionette groupie wives…"

"Jamming with cilantro," said Sharon.

"You're right, Robin," Kitty said. "Really all you need to know in life is how to eat the food and drink the wine. Duh, hello, you know, like we're not born with the skill?"

"Well, you should have some notion of what you're eating or drinking," said Sharon. "For example, during communion…"

"Shut up, Sharon."

"And the biggest rip off of all is that pretentious wine list shit. No wine on earth is worth more than ten dollars a bottle. The only reason people drink wine is that it's good for the digestion especially after a lot of dark fatty meats."

"You drink it for pleasure; bad wine makes you fart," said Kitty.

"Not if you have faith in Jesus," said Sharon.

"Let me put it this way to you Sharon: it makes you burp and fart. Right now we're not talking religion but the wine list. There is no bad wine and there is no such thing as luxurious wines to be dearly paid for. Any bottle more than ten dollars is a rip off. All wines are either vinegary, or sugary sweet alcohol, or somewhere in between."

"It's those in between wines that we all love," smiled Kitty.

"A lot of people think that wine is sacred."

"They all come from the same grapes and every year is the same year. Best wine I ever had was a cheap red with some black pepper in it. If you want relief, try a couple of spoonful of good apple cider vinegar," said a feeling good Robin.

"If it was good for Jesus, it's good enough for me," said Kitty.

"Thou shall not blaspheme, Kitty," Sharon couldn't help it.

"Sorry, Sharon. I didn't mean to bring up the religious issue again," smiled Kitty.

"For shame, on both of you," hushed Sharon, and sensed her brain rushing again.

"What a rip off!" fumed Robin.

"All right, Robin, calm down. Here comes Gianni with the Bordeaux. Now, what were you going to say, Kitty?" said Sharon.

"If that son-of-a-bitch asks me to taste before he pours once again, I'll spit it out all over his prick-n-span white frock and cocktails," Robin continued to bristle.

"It's coat tails, Robin. And it's spic and span. All waiters should wear red," said Sharon.

"Well, I think I have some good news about Mick and me," said Kitty.

"Mick?" Sharon and Robin crested their eyebrows.

"Just kidding, you guys. I meant Claudio and me."

"Just open the bottle and leave it with us, Gianni," said Sharon.

"Yes, Mrs. Merker."

"So, Kitty, you were about to share some good news about you and Claudio."

"Well, Sharon and Robin, you two are the first to know. As it should be between friends! My husband Claudio and I have been thinking of getting out of the rat race of recycling grease; we're thinking of buying a farm. Especially Claudio who says that a man needs to have a small piece of land if for no other reason than to periodically piss on it," and the girls laughed at the image.

"I thought you were going to say that you're pregnant," sighed Sharon. "Like Justine."

"We want to get out of this boring world of the crazy maze big city life. He can't get Sicily out of his mind so he wants to buy a farm. Get a farm and celebrate the seasons again, he says. We now have more money than we'll ever need, and, he says, that the only thing we're short on is time."

"You wanna make a bet?" wickedly laughed Robin.

"That's unfair, Robin," said an angry Sharon. "I know you didn't mean that. So, be a good girl and apologize to Kitty."

"About what?"

"We all know that Claudio is much brighter than he appears," said Sharon momentarily coming to the defence of a man she knew only Biblically, while his wife was sitting next to her.

It took Kitty a second or two to catch on to where Sharon was coming from. Anyway, like any housewife knows whenever her husband strays, Kitty had guessed about her husband and Sharon from the several suggestions that Claudio had made.

"Did you know he's an author?" continued Sharon almost spilling the beans.

"Is that what he told you?" laughed an unflustered Kitty.

Robin was unmoved from her frustrations about waiters and cheap wines. She was a bit puzzled though, because she didn't know where Sharon was coming from with this suddenly found kindness for Claudio, and her insistence that she apologize to Kitty for implying he was short of brains. True friends shouldn't have to apologize no matter whose prim and proper etiquette Sharon was sucking on, including Old and New Testaments.

"Did you know, Sharon, that palm trees are symbols of fertility," said Robin. "I thought you might have run across that in your Biblical studies. Maybe you should straddle on top of a palm tree and sooth what's itching you."

"Oh Robin, sometimes you're the grossest …"

"Oh, that's ok, Sharon. I know Botox Robin meant no bad insult. And if she thinks she's got more brains than I do, well, the weight shows on the crick of her wrinkled neck. Right, smart-ass Robin?" said Kitty, and she waited with a broad grin.

"Here's one for you, and to your farm, wrinkle free Kitty," and Robin gave Kitty the finger. And then she began to laugh, hiding her big mouth with her palm.

"Palms are symbols of peace, Robin, peace as in Palm Sunday, and not the phallic symbols you're always thinking about," said Sharon.

"I can picture Claudio humming 'home on the range' while planting palm trees in the sunset to let you know that you're his only love," said Robin.

"Home, home on the range," Kitty recited the words without the melody.

"Where the deer and the antelope play," Sharon continued the words.

"Where seldom is heard, a discouraging word, and the skies are not cloudy all day," Kitty was thoughtfully continuing the great outdoors when suddenly, not to be outdone, Robin burst forth with her own improvised country poem for her best friend Kitty:

> *City babe,*
> *I'm gonna take you*
> *down to my doggie farm home,*
> *where you belong, baby,*
> *I'm gonna make you love me*
> *ghee-tshu down to do some dirty laundry*
> *to do some dirty laundry*
> *down by the creek*
> *where I'll pinch your fat cheek…*

And she did teasingly pinched Kitty's cheek.

"Cut it out," said Kitty, all the time loving it.

Ad-libbing the little poem was Robin's way of apologizing to Kitty for implying that she and Claudio were running short on oil.

It was, after all, Robin's quick mind, which all the friends, now and forever, gave her great credit and made them want to be her friends. And Robin knew and never outgrew that, though at times, she could be unkind. One time Robin had described Kitty to Myrna as not being "one of the sharpest tools in the shed."

There was an awkward moment of silence, and the yawns began to slowly descend upon the day as noon gave way to afternoon nap time. Afternoons are of those moments when all people, including true friends, feel alone, lazy, and the brain is not firing on all pistons. It was an uncomfortable pause, consumed without words, each friend waiting for the other to say something. The moment felt like yesterday, and all the yesterdays piled up into the memory of skinny and not so skinny girls who grew up and married and all the time pretended that nothing had changed in all the years they had been leaning on each other. In the tranquillity of the pacific Beverly Hills, there was nothing to suggest that their collapsing long time unfulfilled love affair, while outward calm, was jangling on an ocean of many years' of soft accumulated feelings now maturing to a squish ripening, and rupture splattering in an inevitable ending that comes to all things. As the separation slowly invades the skin, circuitous shit, like literary prizes, begins to convolutedly flow out of pretty mouths, and you hope it leaves no stink behind to soil the indomitable friendship. For it is said that friendship, like virginity, once lost is irrecoverable. But then, again, there's a lot of grey in both friendship and virginity, both vital to a woman's mental wellness.

"It's not such an unheard of thing to want to get way from this daily hassle and slow time a bit, Robin. After all, aren't we all tired of this absurd life we all lead? We greedily rush and get fat on one bubble market after another and all too soon we get old, and no time left," Kitty threw her hands up in the air.

Robin yawned.

"That's exactly how I feel. Wow, time does fly," excitedly responded Sharon. "Time is such a precious commodity, yet most of us waste it, like Kitty just said. Time is a spiritual concept requiring ..." both Kitty and Robin were staring at the tablecloth so Sharon shut up.

"Claudio and I have been thinking, like a lot of other couples think these days. We're pretty sure we want to slow things down by just getting way from the city; getting away from all this neurotic LA madness. Get out and do a little contemplation on what's it all about, and how did we get here so fast. You know what I mean?"

More yawns.

"Like, I'm beginning to suddenly feel old," continued Kitty.

They knew what Kitty meant: that contemplation is the pastime of the old as they get closer and closer to death. And in spite of Sharon's fleeting sermons on the go, none of the friends wished to take that disquieting route to join Christ yet. You reflect too much and before you know it you're dead.

"Let me tell you Kitty, contemplation is the quickest path to death. Anyway, you didn't have to go on a farm to reflect," suggested Robin.

There was more unnerving silence because nobody wanted to admit they wanted to devote the rest of their lives to prayer and penance on some stupid farm, like Myrna's husband was now doing. It cannot be that 'that's all there is' they all prayed.

"Go buy a little farm near Santa Barbara, he says, and wake up to a bright new day, every day. Have coffee on our huge deck with the birds and the bees buzzing around a myriad of wild flowers in the great outdoors where there's lots of sunshine, away from this here pollution, and have the sun splash light and heat on us all day long," Kitty's teeth shone brighter than her pastoral images as she gesticulated her husband's bedazzling dream.

"Right out of Wordsworth; butterflies, mosquitoes, and all," said Robin.

"Claudio does write poetry, Robin," poor Sharon was confused again.

"Of course you'll both be invited to visit because you're my best friends," said Kitty.

"Did you know that the California palm tree is a symbol of peace," said Sharon. "Palm trees as in Palm Sunday ..."

"You've said that already," said Robin as she bottomed up another French red, at the same time wishing it was a more muscular vodka, or even a, ugh, muscular bourbon; anything to drown the spastic murmuring of her friends, now registering flat in her soaked brain.

"Claudio says he'd buy me a horse, and when you guys visit, I'd let you pet it."

"Another phallic symbol, Kitty, as if you didn't know," said Robin.

There were too many bees and too much yellow sunshine in Kitty's farm and Sharon had been stung. She was having difficulty accepting all the highlights of country living; all that light and sun had totally blindsided her and were a contradiction to her lovable, intimate moments for lovely, cool, shade, and preferable darkness. How could there be contemplation in bright disturbing sunlight?

"You were doing alright there, until you got to the part of lots of sunshine stuff, Kitty. What, you want to get away from the pollution and crime just so that you could get blinded by lots of sunshine? And I mean blinded. Haven't you heard or read that sunshine is evil; that it blinds; that it'll give you cancer? Worse, too much sunshine will blow your mind, you know, with, like excess sensual overload and no time to think? Are you trying to tell us that you want to forget how to think or never use your brain again? Just like all them farmer boys?"

"Sharon, you don't come to the farm; Claudio wouldn't like you there," said Kitty.

"Right you are, Sharon. Sunshine! Shit! Give me the deep purple dusk of vespers and the darkness of the long night of old times," said Robin and tapped into another glass which by now was becoming worthless to spike you on a spin.

"Anyway, I think Claudio is joshing you," said Sharon.

"Also, Sharon, a Roman symbol of fertility," said Robin.

"Sharon, why else do you move to a farm if not for the birds and flowers, the glow of dawn, and the serenity of an evening's sunset? Isn't the hush of dusk, with its thousands of starlings flying in formation to find a safe place to roost, away from the deafening insanity of big city noises the reason people seek out the farm? The green, and yellow, and soft browns and reds of autumn rolling hills and pastures full of the bright sunshine to warm the tired soul even on a wintry day?" redirected Kitty.

"Starlets, in Southern California?" said Robin.

"Robin, what do you mean symbol of fertility? Do you mean the palm trees, or Claudio," said Sharon, away from Kitty's hills and pastures canvas.

"Well, duh, coconuts, Sharon, big cojones; coconut trees are tall palm trees, and some have huge cojones hanging, like in ancient Roman statues …"

"Robin, you're crazy," said Sharon.

"Well, when you think about it Sharon, I suppose people could just as easily be put out to pasture in the city as in farms," Kitty splashed an autumn smile.

Another dead end. Still, there was no reason to think that Kitty and her Claudio had not done a lot of soul searching in reaching out to the promise of the farm. It was their dream and no one had the right to deny their wish.

"I wanna go home … where I belong…down by the buoys of my soul…"

Robin beamed another shaft of delight toward Sharon and Kitty trying to bring the friends back to Beverly Hills again.

"Here's your Grecian peasant's bread, ladies."

It was Gianni. Just in the nick of time, again, the trademark of a good waiter.

"Your salads are coming right up."

"Thank you, Gianni," said Kitty in a very sweet voice, and Gianni smiled back to match the splendour of her teeth.

Sharon had reached for her Louis Vuitton purse and was fumbling through it not exactly knowing what she was searching for. She thought she wanted to put on her Dior sunglasses to blunt Kitty's sunshine and then realized that she had them smartly on her head. Somewhat embarrassed at her fumbling, she took them off her head, shoved them back into her purse, and nervously put it on the floor. The sudden intrusion of farm light was too much for her unprotected eyes. She felt fidgety, uncomfortable, and thought she wanted to tell Gianni to pull the restaurant curtains shut, but the sun was already setting behind the restaurant, away from the window openings to the east, and their table was already in the shade.

"Robin, you're the weirdest, man," said Kitty, knowing that Robin could take it better than fragile Sharon.

Somebody had to say something.

"No, I think Sharon's the weirdest. She's off to la-la-land again. I think she needs to get laid; big hunk Hank must not be putting out, is he Sharon?" said Robin.

"I don't think she's listening to what you're saying," said a concerned Kitty.

"Maybe you could lend her your Claudio stallion for a few nights," said Robin.

"Claudio is always approached by women," said an embarrassed Kitty. "You should try him sometime, Robin," and she tried to hide in silence.

Once again Sharon was lost between the sound of her friends' voices and the storming of her mind. She was being inundated by an immense emotional rural rush full of happy yellow sunshine scenes and huge palm tree cojones which she could not comprehend. Here she was, in the company of long-time friends, so why this anguish? She thought she would have liked to say something to her friends, to find relief in speech, but was too afraid to open up to them because of the damn light; afraid that if she did, her words might have been full of the unpredictable lapses of … fuck it; that sob was the biggest mistake of my life, she thought of Hank.

Her head had begun to ache, a built-up that was going to explode. She wished she had a pill, any kind of a pill, even an aspirin, as she sat there in agony between her friends. The best she could do was to give a little warm smile to her friend Kitty who always seemed to be politely understanding of her best friend.

"Or maybe you could loan her your David, Robin," said a recovered Kitty.

Robin also was embarrassed by her words to Kitty.

"So, you think that Sharon's the weirdest? Well, if she's the weirdest, what are you?"

"Well, Kitty, what kind of a woman do you think I am?"

Robin felt the unanticipated stupidity of that one, but sensed the need to continue the cover up of Claudio's assault on Sharon.

Kitty was good at juvenile banter, so she took up Robin's challenge, hoping to bring Sharon out of her new down-in-the-dumps dive.

"You're the kind of a woman who would derive great pleasure screwing your friend's husband," said Kitty with an indulgence that might have been viewed as contempt, because she knew that Robin knew, but wouldn't tell her, because the three were the best of friends.

"You know I would never fuck Claudio," said Robin.

"Is everything alright here, ladies," asked Gianni.

"Fuck off, Johnny," said Robin.

"He asked me, Robin," said Kitty.

They were just best friends kidding with each other with the help of a great Bordeaux and trying to keep a slippery afternoon moving along.

"Who so ever believeth in me shall be saved."

And every-so-often, Sharon would proclaim the now tired words, in the calmest of voices, far removed from the puerile language of her friends.

"What the hell does that mean, Sharon?" Kitty had beaten Robin to the punch. "For God's sake say what you want to say, but stay away from this Biblical shit."

"It means that if you believe in Jesus, you will find eternal salvation. And right now, you should believe in my words, Kitty. And maybe you too will find salvation even in this life. Even without a farm. That goes for you too Robin."

"Sharon honey, you're sailing into the wild blue yonder again. You know I wouldn't ever want to live on a farm," said Robin with a little forehead frown. She wished she weren't there; this is the last time, she thought.

"Pour some more wine, Robin," said a pissed off Kitty. "She's getting on my nerves too with all this sermonizing shit."

"You mean pour some holy blood, don't you?" said nasty Robin.

Independently of the others, Sharon took three good swigs of her life sustaining red, whispered some holy words to herself and exhaled to her friends,

"For I am the Light of the world sayeth the Lord, Jesus."

"And here, Jesus doesn't mean the physical light of the sun," continued disoriented Sharon, "but the inner light, the enlightenment of truth, that leads to cognition …" and here she hesitated for a moment because she wasn't sure of that word, "…for we may have the light of the eyes and still be blind if we lack the light of the inner spirit, who is Jesus."

"Yes, the inner spirit, like this good red Bordeaux, which I must admit is delicious," said Kitty in full resignation to Sharon's smashed mind.

It was no use. There were no fun anecdotes to be had this day. It was going to be one of those jagged afternoons difficult to lighten up. Kitty took one look at Sharon, felt her pain and decided she was going to be supportive of her friend in need from that moment on. Even if she has to go to confession, and communion, she would do it for her friend.

She smiled, looked at Sharon, and said, "They say that Vince did not become a great painter of light until he gave up all his worldly possessions and retired to the countryside."

"Who the fuck is Vince?" said Robin in a very low, deliberate voice.

"Vincent Van Gogh," calmly replied Kitty. "That's why he died poor."

Robin lowered her head at Kitty's twisted mind.

"I direct my prayer towards our salvation, oh Lord, my Destiny,"

"Cut it out, both of you. You're gonna drive me crazy," Robin had had enough. What should have been an easy happy lunch was turning schizophrenic.

"What the hell is going on here? Who are you people? You're both turning psycho-schitzo … psychoshtso … crazy …" for the first time Robin was searching for words.

"I'm doing this all for you, Robin," calmly responded Sharon with all the serenity and assurance of a woman in complete inner peace. "It's my way of showing my love for you."

"Bet you can't say that again, Sharon," said Kitty tipping her glass.

"A little less love and a little more wine, please," sneered Robin as she set full sail ahead riding on a barrel of red Bordeaux. "And pass the pissy Greek peasant's bread this way."

Sharon grabbed the basket of bread away from the others and brought it in front of her. Disarmed, the other two looked at her in total bafflement.

"That's not funny Sharon," said Kitty who tried to take the basket away from her.

It was no use. There was a despotic stare in Sharon's eyes that was now piercing right out of the Seven Seas and deep into distant Galilea. She took one bun, did the sign of the cross over it three times with her knife, and murmured something like, hhhhmmmh-hhh, hhhhmmmhhhh, and enunciated,

"Grant this o Lord,"

She then carefully cut the bun into three pieces. She gave one piece to Kitty, and one to Robin, and absorbed in her very own magic began the mass:

"Take, eat; this is my Body, which is broken for you for the remis-sion of sins."

"Screw it Kitty. Let's just watch the show," quietly laughed Robin.

"Don't laugh, Robin; this is serious, she's totally flipped out; we've got to help her."

"Drink of this always this is my blood…"

"Don't worry Kitty. It's just the wine."

They waited for a second for the prayer to ascend to Heaven.

"Never have I felt, so happy, as now, Kitty and Robin, my best of friends. I now know that life is a mystery, and you know, you never know that this too might be our last supper," smiled Sharon, and she did politely take and kiss her best friends' hands to their polite social horror. Too late, they withdrew their hands; everyone in the restaurant had witnessed the act.

And a miraculous communion did then occur. The words that had come from Sharon's holy lips did invade the friends' souls and were immediately purifying; the words had been subliminally transmitted in the diffused wisdom emanating from Sharon's lips directly into their souls. It filled them with love, and they felt the need to cross themselves, and to return to their childhood of pretty angels, and believe in Jesus again.

Which was strange because Kitty was Lutheran and Robin was at best agnostic.

"Amen," said Robin, very subdued.

Sharon continued under the gravity of her own mind's liturgy:

"Kyrie Eleyson, Kyrie Eleyson, Kyrie Eleyson,"

"Here are your Roka leaf salads with boiled squid and champagne dressing, and your goat cheese, ladies, excuse me," said Gianni, the angelic messenger.

"That's it! I'm out of here. Between the two of you and the Latino waiter, it's Looney-toon times at the Seven Seas," said Robin and she got up as if to leave.

"Sit down, Robin," said Sharon in the sternest of voices. For that one resolute moment, Robin sat meekly in her chair.

"For the wisdom and gifts that we are about to enjoy, let us be thankful," continued Sharon now very poised and self-assured.

"And let there be peace and tranquillity all over this land; no, all over this world, always to all, and to all times, forever and ever," chimed in Kitty with a broad smile.

"And in our souls let there be peace," whispered Robin, her head against her will bowed in submission to the power of the words.

Beyond doubt, there was communion now among the three friends.

"What the fuck am I saying," suddenly whispered Robin in disbelief as she stuck her fingers in her mouth to remove a piece of Roka leaf stranded between her molars. "Now you got me doing it."

Sharon took Robin's left hand and softly said to her, "It's ok Robin. You are shedding your sins. Don't be afraid. Life without sin is not possible, for to be alive is also to sin."

"We were born into sin," exclaimed Kitty happy to be part of it.

"It wasn't until Eve sinned that time and life began. Before that first sin, all eternity was perhaps one week old. Sin is what gives life the sweetness and the abandon to piss on the forbidden. And the price of sin is forgiveness," spoke Sharon.

"It's a cheap price," said Robin unsteady with Sharon's bullshit.

"Not when you consider an eternity in hell, Robin," smiled Kitty.

The Roka cellulose was still stuck between Robin's teeth and she was desperately trying to dislodge it. At that moment, the only thing that she could think of was going home to floss and brush her teeth. The horribly smelly Roka leaves made her feel like her mouth was full of farts, gagging her throat and making it difficult for her to speak. She took another swig of her wine trying to wash her mouth of the foul fart smelling Roka leaves and like a blast from hell she had a vision of her grandmother who had died of Alzheimer's and who had hardly ever spoken the several years before she died. Dead grandma's breath smelled like the Roka salad. Guilt, abruptly fizzed from unknown depths foul flooding Robin's Roka landscape both physically and mentally. Grandmother first, and then mother, both joined her in a parade of odors totally uninviting. Her mother had long been troubled after her mother had died and had long bouts of manic depression. It was incurable, the psychiatrist had said; probably genetic. There they were, both her mother and grandmother now sitting next to a youthful, blond bearded Jesus, and for forgiveness Robin gulped her full glass of bloody red Bordeaux.

"God bless and forgive my Grandmother's soul," Robin surprised herself, and without warning ghastly fumes burped out of her mouth, making her eyes almost tear.

"Robin, you're crying," said Kitty. "May your grandmother rest in peace."

"Can you imagine humanity without sin, Robin?"

Oh my loving Lord, thought Kitty.

"The only way that life could be without sin is if the sun burns out; when there is no light to feed the senses. In darkness not even imagination can cross into sin."

"You ought to know, Sharon; darkness does provide a nice cover," said Robin.

"You're right, Sharon. God bless Sharon's and our souls, as well," said Kitty who thought this might do it.

"Kitty, you're always in the dark," said a frustrated Robin.

Kitty looked at Robin who was carefully wiping away something from her eye so as to not smudge her mascara. Though till now completely foreign to her way of thinking, she imagined that, conceivably, thoughts about dead people could, probably, bring tears to someone's eyes. She herself had never deliberated about dead people, let alone dead relatives, so she never had to cry for them. She had long before accepted the finality of death and thought it lame to cry for dead people who undoubtedly were beyond any need to be remembered. To cry for the living has some meaning, but to cry for the dead smacks of perversity.

She didn't want to look at Sharon because in Kitty's eyes it was pretty obvious that Sharon had transcended into a realm of convoluted obsessions possibly with the dead. For sure, she was full of dead memories. The trouble with Sharon was that in her dizzy spells she travelled backward to live in a children's Samarian world, which, on second thought, is pretty much what old people do: as old age dementia sets in, their mind shops in the past. Trouble was,

Sharon wasn't that old, though lately, she definitely seemed to be preparing to meet her maker.

She's not getting any, the thought merrily jangled before Kitty. Maybe I should ask Claudio to volunteer for some extra duty. What the hell, he's nice enough to happily do it. Anyway, she's such a tight ass, she probably wouldn't enjoy it. Maybe we could do a little husband swapping: if she wants Claudio, I want a little of Hank.

"You know, I'm beginning to think that maybe Sharon, in some absurd fashion, might be making sense," said Robin.

"I'm happy to see that you now understand that only in darkness is sin, as is time, totally obliterated," said Sharon. "There is no sin in darkness!"

On the other hand, maybe we should have ordered some brains, thought Robin.

Damn dysfunctional receptors, thought Kitty.

She remembered her first husband having talked about dysfunctional receptors with respect to their young son, one time.

It has to be the wine; Kitty didn't want to pursue the dysfunctional receptors. It has to be the wine feeding Sharon's brain, and it has to be the wine tranquilizing Robin and me to listen to her pathetic theology.

"Lord save us and bless us all," said Sharon who tenaciously held on to her freeze.

"*Kyrie eleyson*," said Kitty, smiling sarcastically.

"Well," thoughtfully echoed Robin, somewhat recovered from her brief melancholic moment of tears, in memory of her beloved grandmother, and now more sympathetic to the persistent Sharon, "it's an intensely scrutinized and well researched phenomenon these days that moral issues, sin to be exact, often, but not always, precede disturbances and other anomalies in the healthy functioning of the human brain. But human beings simply are neither able to anticipate what particular sins will affect the body, nor the degree to which the body will be affected. You yourself, Sharon, had just said a moment ago that sin is so ever present around us that one is rarely able to monitor the guilt, which probably brings about the psychosomatic illnesses so prevalent in our society. The dissolution of the soul is an event of a thousand little sins. Don't you agree, Sharon?"

Oops, thought Kitty. It had nothing to do with Robin; her bladder was full.

"That's why we must hasten our souls to the will of Jesus," smiled Sharon, humbly, and without raising her eyes, which like an evangelistic nun's, were now focused on her and her friend's salvation.

More moments of involuntary silence filled with friendly smiles.

"Hastening our will to Jesus is simply a socializing aspect to a healthy life," joined in Kitty, feeling the need not to be left out. It was a way of controlling her bladder by being occupied by other thoughts. "It may appear that many events are chance happenings, but, let's face it, we all have our little sins, our little secrets. It is in the sharing of our little sins and of our little secrets that we will all find comfort and ultimately, salvation."

"Yes," agreed Robin, "it is a well-known, recorded phenomenon that hopelessly terminally ill people experience miraculous recoveries, which are attributed to the healing powers of the belief in the atonement of little sins."

"Sorry girls; I've got to go to the bathroom. I'll be right back. Don't say anything more until I get back," said Kitty.

Sharon continued.

"Undoubtedly the goodness of forgiveness is but one of the many gifts from God. We must all ask the Lord's forgiveness, and love each other, and all our fellow human beings, even those that have done us great harm. And if Jesus can forgive us of our sins, who are we not to forgive the sins of others? We must forgive even our worst enemies and give ourselves to the Lord. In that, wellness lies. Don't you agree Robin?"

"When you wish to be healthy, you can," smiled Robin. "You have only to get out of your bed and get a job."

This religious shit really dries you out, she thought.

"Where's Kitty?" said Sharon.

"She got tired of listening to your shit so she went to the bathroom. Come to think of it, that's pretty funny: from shit to shit," and Robin laughed.

"But the valley of darkness is not to be feared as long as the Lord is with you … oh shit, shit, shit," said Sharon realizing she was preaching to an empty room. She felt exhausted, unable to continue. What more could she do for her friends? If they weren't able to see what she was trying to show them, then it would not be her fault.

She wanted to cry and scream but no sounds came out of her dry throat because her worldly love for her friends was interfering with her spiritual attestations. She took another drink of her red wine, but it was no use, she felt betrayed by her human limitations. Surges of melancholia poured forth and choked her and made her sad at her frailty. Only two soft perfectly rounded goblets of tears timidly dropped out of the tear glands of her bluest eyes which she carefully dabbed away as not to smear her perfectly applied eye makeup. Strange how even on these occasions of great emotion and even greater flight, her thoughts travelled to her youth and particularly on that spring day field trip bus.

"I wonder what's taking Kitty so long," said Robin.

She felt sorry for Sharon because she now understood how lonely she must be. She reached and took Sharon's hand and with tears rolling out of her eyes she said, "I'm so terribly sorry for you …"

"Oh Robin, what has he done to you?" cried Sharon and she got up and went and hugged Robin who, in sudden fear, thought that Sharon surely knew her secrets.

"Sharon, sit down," said Kitty back from the bathroom.

"Thank God you're done," said Robin.

"You all know of course that one of the best places for contemplation is while sitting on a toilet," said Kitty. "It's funny, but every time I sit on the toilet, I think of Hank."

"Oh, shut up, Kitty," said Robin who strangely had been overwhelmed with empathy for the living and the dead in her life, and was now crying huge drops of tears, all her defences finally having caved in.

"Is everything all right here?" It was Gianni. "Is there something else I can get for you?"

Sharon meekly sat down in her chair and most properly crossed her legs under the table. Crossing her legs did bring her back to reality for her. "Yes, Gianni, you may bring us another bottle of this excellent Bordeaux," she said.

They still hadn't finished the previous bottle so Gianni poured it for them and off he went to get another bottle of the red Bordeaux to everybody's great satisfaction.

It was time to re-establish the devotional connection to the true Bordeaux that had nothing to do with Jesus' blood. Back to rich normal, they drank and ate the bread, and happily skipping on church pieties; they smiled and forked the salad and feta cheese and drank, and they poured more of the Bordeaux, empty as they drank that too, while waiting for the next fine bottle of robust red Bordeaux.

"He has another wife," out of nowhere blurted out Robin, no longer able to contain her bitterness. "My husband, fucked up David, the first who had me, the bastard bank president, thanks to my kindness, to whom thousands of people are entrusting their savings and futures, has ruined my life. The ungrateful bastard has another wife and a fourteen year old son by her."

There, it was out; amazing histories that only the rich can so easily write.

"Vice Presidents of Human Resources, dear," reminded Kitty.

"You get no pity from me," said Sharon.

Not the real truth about hated husband Dave, nor the truth that might have included her own indiscretions as a bad girl while with husband David, and others, not so long ago, and not to the many other inappropriate debaucheries whose vivid recollection had almost burst her psyche during all the talk of Jesus. The cuckolded wife was a good substitute story, but quite remote from her pretended unselfishness, concocted in the nick of time to protect the private memory of her vigorous love affair, for a skinny Ethiopian, from spurting out under the pressure of the wine. It was a lie she told about her David, aimed at the soul of her now defunct husband.

Ingenuously she had sought applause for her forbearance with an unkind man, and kindly asking sympathy from her friends, or from anyone who could empathize with her wounded, never to be healed, broken heart. The tears were leniency intended to relieve the awful pain in her soul that betrayed all that she ever loved, all for her daddy's duteous approval. Once again she had caught herself, saved herself, just in time, from the painful truth of having betrayed her once happily anticipated Ethiopian future for a honky-tonk jerk like David Calder. She knew that one day, but not now, she would have to honestly confess to a priest or psychiatrist the haunting feelings of her sorry heart, or else go mad.

During moments of warm bouts of the sweet wine of sisterhood, the mind's unconscious gates stream open to flush out the painful little libidinous secrets that perversely prevent us enjoying our life. Infinite firings rush in sublimated confessions of love, or sadness, or desire. Words become insufficient to catch the meaning of the flow, and the ear gives way to feelings. The storm unfolds cataracts of meaningless chatter, but nothing matters because we rarely feel the emotion behind the words. It's then that the miracle of the little white lies occurs. At first they're little rivulets of white lies, but wanting to win our friends with our love, the little lies expand into bigger and bigger lies and all the time we invent more lies to feed our friends: it's all out of love. But then, unconsciously, guilt muddles our subliminal thoughts on our desires and we rationalize that in the heavens of infancy, all lies, like all truths, dissolve into nothingness, and this thought then becomes the feed of our corporeal brains. It is possible that all human beings live on lies, during a whole lifetime. They tread on bullshit from morning till night and never smell the stench they talk and walk on. Human beings, then, love their lies which they conveniently call shooting the bull. It's not a lie, then, for even such faultless human beings as Sharon, and Robin, and Kitty, so close to beauty, as is the rose, as is the truth, to dwell on such wicked little white lies whose marvellous purpose is to mask the monotonous realm of not always knowing if that's all there is. Repressing the truth with obsessive little white, spicy lies keeps one from madness.

Robin quietly hid the Ethiopian ghosts residing beyond the reach of her friends with lies about her bastard. Not an easy thing to make, a false confession about your husband, while your most persistent secret remained buried in your soul. But without confession, there can be no communion and without communion no salvation. Before all this gooey stuff a little white lie is nothing.

"Robin, are you doing a Sharon?" said Kitty feeling left out.

"Robin, I'm so sorry," said Sharon.

More white lies.

"He said it was time that I knew and that we should also tell our Justine and Meredith, since they were getting into an age when they, unaware of the relationship, might unknowingly have sexual intercourse with their half-brother Lyndon, who's David's bastard son," she teared.

"You've had too much wine, Robin. Justine and Meredith are Myrna's daughters, not yours and David's," said Kitty. "What you're afraid is that David and not some imaginary Lyndon is going to have sex with Justine and Meredith."

"David is fucking Justine?" said an astounded Sharon.

"Not yet, dear," said Kitty.

"Well, for your information little Kitty Kat, you little pussy, David and I are going to adopt the girls, and Myrna's ok with that," lied Robin coming out of her funky mood.

"I don't know what to say," said Sharon.

Kitty was calm; after her dump, the wine wasn't messing with her brain. She knew that Robin even when stewed could make up stories. But Sharon was speechless for a change. Robin's confession was a heavier load than she had bargained. You think you know somebody, somebody who's your best friend, and after one quick revelation, they become strangers. Though she loved Robin very much, she honestly had never been party to such debilitating outpouring like today. Normally, in the past, during silly torrents of soul-baring sessions, one girl would try to outdo the other's true confession by telling stories more outrageous than the previous ones. But each knew that these were in fact simple little lies, intended to titillate the fantasies since they usually revolved around remote sexual misadventures, more like dirty jokes. They were innocent little jibes that shielded their fanciful lives and diverted them away from the depressing reality of their nowhere, boring, opulent existence.

"What a miserable son of a bitch," said Sharon.

"Oh, how I hate that miserable son-of-a-bitch who has made my life so painful. Ever since Peace Corps I've hated that son-of-a-bitch so much I could easily bludgeon him with a hammer. And my poor little step-daughters, how can I tell them that their loving step-father is a vicious adulterer, a monster who all these years has hugged and kissed them, after fornicating in sin with some hag or other? Forgive me my little girls, forgive me."

More uncontrollable not so little white lies spewed into her pink linen handkerchief.

"Well, Robin, at least you know that your Justine and Meredith are adopted children and no incest can occur with Lyndon, unless they too are David's," said Kitty, feeding the bullshit with more Bordeaux. Unlike vodka, which too much knocks you out mindless cold, the think about wine is that it keeps you alive even when your mind is gone.

"This is all bullshit, Robin. I don't believe a word of it," said Sharon with great relief. "Anyway, even if true, it's not all that tragic. It's in the nature of men to be fuckers. But I still can't see David with Justine."

"How long have you known, Robin?" asked Kitty, more to cut off Sharon than to get to the facts of the story, which she knew to be absurd, and did not believe one word of it.

"Oh, fuck you Kitty," said Robin.

She lifted her newly filled glass of red Bordeaux and finished it in one luxurious gulp. Screw the lasting friendship. She really didn't care what Kitty and Sharon had to say or what they might have been thinking of her. She especially didn't give a shit about Sharon who had dingle berries for brains, anyway.

There was renewed silence. The silence was intellectually welcomed, for after all, it isn't every day that one hears these kinds of disjointed true confessions, even among best friends. Maybe Myrna, or a psychiatrist, or a priest could have dealt with Robin's sad and pathetic marriage, but Sharon, too lame, and Kitty, rarely gave a shit, were brand new to this kind of buried in your basement excess baggage rot.

"You must forgive him, Robin, rot or otherwise," rushed in Sharon thinking of her own transparent marriage. "He doesn't know what he's doing. You must forgive him and help him with all your love. Help him and show him the way to find the Lord."

"Sharon, that last remark shows that you've lost it girl, that you are crazy?" calmly said Kitty. "Don't listen to her, Robin. She's been spending too much time with the Lord and not enough with Hank."

There was another awkward moment of silence.

"You go straight to the police, Robin," said a devious Kitty, now having fun. "Put that bastard away where he belongs. Bigamy is punishable by death in California. Take the son-of-a-bitch for all he's worth, and then blow him and that other bitch of his away."

Robin laughed because Kitty was right on.

Sharon felt nervous at Kitty's words. For her killing Hank was not on her agenda.

"You gotta draw the line somewhere, nice Sharon! Would you forgive Hank if you found out that he's been humping some bitch?" asked an unyielding Kitty.

"Or you Kitty, if you knew that Claudio was being unfaithful?" said Robin.

"Kitty, it's her money and not his for her to take him for all he's worth. Whatever he's worth is all hers, anyway," said an uneasy Sharon trying to seek some way easy out. Anyway, she didn't care who Hank was humping because he'd been doing it since high school, and everybody knew about it.

Robin had another glass of the robust Bordeaux. As she drank it, she thought Sharon correct in ordering the red that day. The headache had already begun but she didn't care. It would be a familiar, long hangover, but she would not pass out.

"Listen to me, Robin. My husband, idiot Hank, has been screwing bimbo waitresses for as long as I've been married to him.

Screwing everyone but me. He's also told me, but I don't believe him, that he's also screwing our friend Myrna."

Aghast, aghast! More heavy stuff! In truth there's wine!

They all knew it was true.

"Sharon, honey, screw Hank," said Robin who felt the luncheon turning vicious.

"But not in the way you'd like," giggled Kitty, to Sharon.

"All men are stupid," said Robin, as if to wash away all evil.

"But, do you see me angry? No. It's true I don't love him anymore, never had, but I have long ago forgiven him. So, what's the big deal? So he screws other bimbos, including Myrna. You think that's going to upset me? You think that's going to make me sick? Not in this life! That bastard will never touch my ass again. So, here, let's have another glass. We're running late here. It's after three already. Tomorrow's another day. For your and Justine's sake, forgive the bastard, let bygones be bygones, and maybe then Dave will realize the immensity of his sins," said Sharon who was babbling again. Kitty and Robin thought Sharon goofy stupid for believing all that stuff about David and Justine.

Sharon was scared goofy because she was running on empty. The brain was sliding, and wasn't firing the way she would have liked. Everything had been excessive.

"It's all right for you to say that, Sharon. The good thing is your husband is screwing bimbos for the fuck of it and not to get heirs. Just thank your lucky stars that you don't have any sons to count the many bimbos in their future," mumbled Robin, tired of being nice.

"He has an heir?" said Sharon almost inaudibly.

"It's not because I don't want to have children, Sharon. God knows I do. And although my husband screws me in more ways than yours does you, emotionally at least, I have been left a stinking virgin whore. I hate myself and I hate him and I must confess I could kill him, God forgive me, just as easily as you could kill your husband."

The atmosphere was becoming absurdly circuitous with magic and deception; above all murderous, thanks to the wine and the long litanies of guilt, regret, and vengeance. Another red was called for, but somebody said "no more."

A watery glaze now neatly dampened all their eyes. In spite of the wine, all the funny little lies had left them feeling cold. The luncheon was turning out to be a miserable snivelling affair full of heart-felt distortions, even with Jesus present.

"There was this boy, long ago, his name was …," Sharon's voice and face happily traipsed of in the memory of her boy-love. She wanted to tell the world how much she has regretted that that boy didn't fuck her that day when she was first in love. Wistfully, she gently pushed her breasts up as if to catch a grape and continued in reminiscence of her childhood love affair. "How sad … I cannot for the life of me remember his name. Maybe I never really knew his name … Anyway, I dream about him all the time. Isn't that silly! I want to have babies by him, as weird as that might sound, and the only way I can have babies with him is if I kill Hank. When I dream of my secret love, my breasts become hot, and God forgive me, as hot as they are now."

She was aglow, smiling pensively, and bringing sunshine to the table.

It was the clue that Kitty had been waiting for. It was back to true confessions time. Easy to cope with shared secrets meant to pleasure the soul, and make a girl giggle that eternally practiced laughter that all girls are born with.

"For a moment there, I thought we'd never get to enlarged breasts and hung penises," heartily laughed Kitty now on familiar, chatty solid pleasurable ground.

"Well you happy virgins, I guess we're all out of our minds," Robin was now beginning to slur her in vinous words. "We are the bearers of the seed, and the offspring of our wombs are the universe of every season, and time immemorial, for all time to come, for all ages and all ages, right Sharon?"

"Just you and me Robin," said Sharon.

Robin and Sharon shared a good laugh making Kitty feel left out as she looked down at her shoes.

"That's right, Kitty," said Sharon, smartly. "Don't tell me you and Claudio, the gigolo, hot Dago, don't fuck around when you take your separate long vacations?"

"It's the only time Claudio and Kitty aren't apart. At least it's the only time that virgin Kitty gets corked," roared Robin as she poured more wine.

"Well, ok, it's my turn," admitted good-natured Kitty. "Here it is: Claudio is impotent. I didn't know it when I met him, but he had syphilis. He didn't know it either. It wasn't till a few years after he came to the States and after we got married that he was diagnosed with syphilis. One day his dick was dripping puss; guess who else got the syphilis? Thank God it wasn't AIDS. Anyway, that left a bad taste in my mouth … don't laugh … and we haven't made love in years. We're like strangers in our own house … and I have a son who would rather stick his arms up cows' vaginas, instead of women's. What of it? It happens to many people but for sure I'm not going to leave my husband. He goes his way and enjoys his Southern Comfort and I go my way and enjoy my variety of comforts. As for my son, I love him in spite of his bestial preferences and I'm sure one of these years he will find his way back to human vaginas."

They were the best of friends and what the hell, they could say anything to each other; knowing they could keep a secret. And they did: Robin confessing she was worried about her husband's illusory bastard son erroneously screwing her fantasy adopted daughters, and Sharon sharing that Hank was screwing one of her best friends, Myrna, and having had a son with some bimbo. And now syphilis.

"Trust me, Kitty, Claudio is not impotent," said Sharon. "I hope he's syphilis free."

"Sharon, don't say another word," said Kitty.

"I'd say the boy's in trouble if he don't know the difference between a woman and a cow," Robin tried to cover the stinking shit that Sharon might step in.

"Kitty, you didn't have to admit your private affairs to us," giggled Sharon, and once again she drained into her glass the last drop of the excellent bottle of expensive Bordeaux.

"Well, you guys confessed harsher things than I did," said Kitty.

"No we didn't," retracted Robin. "All that stuff that I said about my husband, David, was made up, to liven up a boring lunch of stinking Roka leaves. My Dave blows a trumpet straight and thick, if you know what I mean."

"I'll drink to that," said Sharon. "And my Hank is the finest man around, and I hold him in high veneration, even though he can't…"

"Stop it, Sharon," said Robin. "I can't take this shit anymore. We're beginning to sound like Myrna just before her collapse."

"Is it true, Robin, that there's no fountain of youth?" asked Sharon.

"We're all inanimate objects, Sharon, like the Bible says, made out of mud, and for one second, like a tiny glowing ember, we beautifully glow among the spent ashes and we think we own the universe," said Robin to her friend, not knowing whether she said it out of meanness or out of love.

"Is it just that, Robin? Just one moment's sparkle?"

"Yes! Just one moment's sparkle, never to repeat again; just like the ember glows for a second and then dies, returns to ashes, to mud, never the sparkle to return again," said Robin.

"But sometimes there is a second flare, a spark, a delayed glitter," said Kitty.

"But the wind blows all the ashes into scattered dust throughout the universe never to return again, never to re-kindle the ashes. It's the absurdity of life that the one second sparkle is followed by one second eternal dark nothingness," said Robin.

"Well, then, my Big Claudio is not impotent either," said Kitty. "And I'm still a virgin at heart and soul no matter how many lovers I take."

"Robin, you break my heart," said Sharon.

"The world is too much with us," said Robin, quoting the famous poet. She coughed out a huge glob of phlegm and neatly spat it out into the fine linen napkin of the Seven Seas Restaurant. "My head is killing me."

"Gianni, the check, please," said Sharon. "And please call us three separate cabs. I've had enough of these two for the week."

She reached in her purse and took out her Dior sunglasses to duck the vicious afternoon sun which is especially harsh on smashed brains.

"It sure is damn hard to take the Lord's word seriously now days," Kitty smiled. "What with Christmas sales so early …what was all that mumbo-jumbo about, Sharon?"

"I was trying to put a little character into our neat striped suits …" Sharon betrayed Jesus and lied.

Robin felt her throat clogging up again. She coughed to clear her throat but this time swallowed her spittle. Deep in her soul she had the depressing thought that indeed in wine there is truth. She wanted to get home and have some more wine.

Lovely, lovely wine, she thought; our Lord's blood, to make you think clearly.

"As usual, it was fun," said Kitty. "See you guys next Wednesday. Give me a call Sharon; you too, Robin."

They all laughed and emptied that last swig of the fine Bordeaux.

They parted company as quietly and as lonely as they had arrived; but for their friendship, their treasured memories would blunt the dullness of their everyday existence into a cutting edge of bouncy insouciance 'till next time. There had been a little bit of gossip, a little bit of posturing, a little bit of acrimony; it was all to be expected from a normal rich girls' exaggerated vanity.

They parted full of irony, detached from any dishonest friendship. The honest thing about drinking is that it removes from debts. You owe nothing to the world, nothing to anyone, friend or otherwise. You're sailing clean and light. It's when you're sober that doubts begin.

There is no better friendship than booze.

They went their own ways feeling good which was always the reason for their get-togethers. Only best friends get together to feel good.

Chapter Fifteen

My Dearest Myrna,

Before I met you I thought I was in love with another woman. She was the daughter of a visiting German physics professor at UCLA. She was a true Teutonic unassuming beauty and definitely an insatiable nympho which was ok with me because I too was a young man at my peak and I couldn't get enough either. We were both graduate students and had all the time in the world to make love every day. Other students ran around the UCLA campus trying to cool their sexual needs but we just met and "focked" as she always said. The more we made love the more we wanted. Every afternoon we met she would say things like "you've been gone so long" and "I've missed you so much". And then with her Germanic full lips she would say, "You want to fock me now, it's ok with me," and gladly I would.

After several months of this fucking around I began to have guilt feelings thinking that I was taking advantage of a naïve, beautiful young woman alone in a foreign country. I became convinced that what we were doing was nice but probably immoral and sought to dampen our humping afternoons with a talk to her father hoping to get some sort of approval, or his wrath and thus to discontinue what I was doing to his daughter and erase my guilt feelings.

He was a serious man, in his early fifties with a big bald spot on the crown of his head.

"Vell," he said with a Germanic chiselled thick accent, "I understand what you are saying. But you must also understand that Ursula is my dear daughter and if that's what's making her happy that's what I want for her too."

I then suggested to Ursula that before we could carry on with our dirty little affair we should at least get another opinion. She being a Catholic from Bavaria proposed that we should go for counselling, or perhaps to confession, at a local Catholic priest.

The priest, a kindly old celibate, agreed to listen to our common sin.

"Do you love this woman," he asked me?

It was the first time that I was confronted with that question. To me it was an obsolete inquiry right out of the Middle Ages. The question of love is relevant only in instances of intended marriage.

"Well, to tell you the truth, Father, I've never … well … I'm not sure," I answered humbly truthfully.

"Do you love this man," he asked Ursula.

"What the fock does that have to do with this, our confession?" she asked in true Teutonic fury.

"You are standing in the Holy Garden of the Blessed Virgin," said the priest. "Get the fuck out of here the both of you. You are the worst of sinners, damned for Hell."

Ursula never wanted to see me after that. More importantly, the old priest made me realize the enormity of my sins and I was so very glad when I met you who was so very different from nympho Ursula. If you recall, we went days without even kissing which made me love you even more.

'How shall I tell thee how much I love you' when I behold your beautiful face come alive before the wide screen memory of my mind? Your hair, your eyes, your smile, they're all forever captured inside my brain. Most of all I miss your intestinal fortitude. I confess, I love and miss you very, very much and even though I'm not with you, don't think of my absence as an abandonment of you or my daughters. My leaving you is my way of telling you that, like nature's way of signalling that life's seasons and their blossoms must come to an end, so, it's all over for us too in spite of our past perfect romance.

You and I are sinners, my wife. I look up to Heaven and I ask myself, do I love her? Really love her? And the answer is 'I'm not sure.'

Which I suppose makes us sinners. There's no going back; I believe in the future.

You might think my departure as sudden, that I lack proper judgement, but if you search your heart you'll find relief that I'm gone from our once exaggerated muddled life; you'll wonder why it hadn't happened earlier. Like the trees that consume their discarded leaves beneath them, so we too had begun to consume each other, and worse, our little girls. I left you because I didn't want to be a cannibal. As I grew older I began to sense a downhill slide; that my being was drowning in pathetic despair. I began to forget what loving you was like, and though we dutifully made love every so often, I could no longer smell you beneath me, didn't care to touch your body as I used to; and you too had lost your appetite and impatiently huffed and puffed beneath me desperately trying to fool the passions. It was no use; we had crossed into old age. The habit was all in the mind and the yawn was irreversible. There was no chance for replay.

I saw Justine and Meredith growing up and I realized that I didn't want to stand in their way. If I had stayed with you I would not have been able to bear watching our daughters go their natural way, growing up, no longer my little girls but someone else's brash and wanton young women. Jealously, I would have stymied them, curiously wanting to spy on them and relive my pointless life through their most natural, lively, self-indulgent enthusiasm. It would have been dishonest for us to interfere in the pleasures of their youth; and surely, I'm ashamed to admit, I would have, if I had stayed around.

In some aimless way, I felt that I was standing in your way as well. I realized that we had completed what nature had intended for us and that the angst we were beginning to sense in each other was nature's way of telling us that we had come full circle, that it was all over for us. Unlike our daughters, our leaves and colors have turned yellow, and though yellow is beautiful to behold, few want to bend over us, to touch and smell us. We are in the late July of our years with our petals drooping, thirsty, with no sweet flowing nectar to offer. Like the myth of Persephone, we too must now find our way through the darkness of our winter lives sans love, sans friends, alone until our daughters give birth to new seasons, and I don't want to be there.

I turned away from the life we knew, like nature has intended me to do. I want to encourage you to do the same. I'm only sorry I can't love you anymore. So slide to your end without me, with all the pleasing ways you know, and never think of sin, a most unnatural invention. Enjoy what life still has to offer you and never look back for I might surprise you and be there, and I don't want to. Think of the magnificent afterlife that awaits us all.

You are no longer my destiny. My destiny has always been to try and save my soul.

And thus we are alone; even in the arms of another we are alone. Imagine, I prefer being alone to being with you. In all honesty, I don't know how long this will last. Other monks here have similar doubts. The head monk says it's only natural to have doubts, and that God understands. You might say that a lot of guys have thought about what I'm now saying to you but few have become hermits. Anyway, sometimes I think I should come back to you but then there's all the other baggage that you carry; like your beautiful daughters who, together with you, were driving me crazy.

I could say forgive me, as I forgive you, but in an irony that I've finally understood in, of all places, a holy monastery, where I had hoped to find humility and forgiveness, I realized after much prayer and contemplation, that forgiveness is God's cruellest joke. I can imagine the Lord and his saints in continuous hilarity every time someone prays for forgiveness. For what is there for me to forgive in you, or you in me? Forgive that we were born? That we grew up driven by nature's relentless instinct to find happiness and to reproduce like all other life forms on earth? That we loved the sweet taste of life and found wonderful feelings of pleasure at the sight of beauty? There is no sin in me nor any sin in you that we need to ask each other for forgiveness. No, there's nothing to forgive. Remember, pleasure and death are the only true passions in life; that pleasure, happiness, love, and so much more are synonyms for life, while death has no meaning, no synonyms; it is alone and unforgiving, a final act of nothingness. So, have no guilt in what you do and ask not for forgiveness for there's nothing to forgive.

And so also with Justine and Meredith: leave them alone; let them preen to their fullest colors. Give them room to find their own way and never admonish them. They need to have their own space, unbridled by the unnatural morality of aging parents who've conveniently forgotten their own natural desires. Let them have their way, Myrna; let them taste of all that comes their way, for all is life. Don't stand in their way. They can do no wrong in your life. Do not love them too much.

And what of your friends?

Fuck them. They're just trying to save their own ass from assured defoliation. They will invariably betray you because betrayal is in the nature of friendship.

You are a beautiful woman, very clever, have no regrets.

I free you, I love you, fare thee well.

*

What a fucking dolt, thought Myrna as she continued to read the constipated letter. For years you live with the son-of-a-bitch and you think you know him and then he sends you a schizoid letter like this. She was glad he was out of her life.

Chapter Sixteen

It was a most beautiful moment. Hundreds of young stunning naked vestals danced among the wild flowers swaying to the breezes within the printed wallpaper all around her bedroom. Such alluring alabaster young girls' bodies with full firm hips on long slender legs, and voluptuous pink breasts with ripening red nipples dancing in tandem with long arms freely whirling through the sensuous fields of paintings and pleasure. Unkindly the adolescent girls of the wall reminded her of her aging, and of her softening breasts now fully matured with no bounce in them and no longer adolescent, and the unstoppable swiftness of time and the inevitability of death. The dancing was too furious all around, the room too hot, and the damn light as always too bright. Her nude body was sweltering hot and she turned on the house sprinkler system and instantaneously the bedroom became the great outdoors of spring. Sharon too now danced amidst the vestals, the fine mist of the spring afternoon denuding her of all sin on top of her immense garden bed.

She popped another treasured pill to feel a more poignant high, and another swig of lovely vodka, and the lysergic acid unfolded even more powerfully in her mind as did the multi-hued petals of the wall-paper luscious roses whose every unfolding of one virgin petal after another let surface in her mind unending rows of more impetuous petals of her own, each row more pink, more vibrant, and more blushing than the one before. She was in a dancing universe, in a starry sky of infinite sparkling lights, in a presence beyond death. She touched herself and felt as if she were a red, red rose in the sparkling dew-filled early morning of Eden. With soft gentle fingers she opened herself with touches from the running rivers of the seas within and without her. Alone, she was alone; she wanted to be alone forever, deep in her mind's endless pleasure. No one, she wanted no one, she cared for none; not Kitty, not Robin, not Myrna, not her husband, not even God. If only she could be left alone to sail the mesmerizing roars of the immense silence of her wildest seas and oceans between her ears, forever and ever, amen. She twirled and pirouetted, her long yellow hair splashing far from her nebular eyes, hands spinning above her head, reaching high to touch the heavens, she spread her legs to straddle her revolving universe, and fearing the fall, sucked in a huge gulp of dizzying air. A rush of hot air circled her naked body making her twist and shout in tune to the ancient flute sounds reverberating from the walls all around and with eyes wide open she saw spheres of perfect water droplets running down her bouncing breasts. She found the tit droplets insufficient as a sea to sail on, and popped another sugar cube, the whirling trip to be the ultimate one. Her heart and arteries pulsated more powerfully than ever before and all the neurons of her brain and body went into warp speed, a thousand times faster than the speed of unholy light. Powerful neuron pulses older than the old rainbow white stuff floating throughout her universe, older than time itself, the same old endless stuff emanating from its intensely dark source, brightly exploding from the engulfing darkness of her unconsciousness that the thoughtless mind accepts like seamless reality, all the time new-born baby signals pulsating in her devastated mind. She filled her empty glass again and drank it all in one long swallow and heard the oceans roar the dull thud of the profoundly hollow depth between her ears. Sound changed to light and became one. Everything changed to light and became one with Sharon. She was crawling through light which through the magic of her soul had been slowed to a trickle by the voyages of LSD to an everlasting eternity within her brain where everything outside it was standing stone still, durably dead and unable to keep up with the celestial pulses of her neurons. More water droplets from the sprinkler high in the sky floated forever in space too slow to keep up with the already finished splashing wondrous display within her brain. A single drop splashed on her open hand and exploded into a billion droplets baptizing Sharon in awesome rapture. She tried to catch the drops but her mind was way ahead of her senses. In full ecstasy she shut her eyes and totally withdrew inside her loving soul. Outside was sluggish ugliness, and all the beauty was inside. Shut your eyes and close the dumb world out. That boy on the bus! Where is that boy on the long ago bus to kiss my mouth with his hot, rash red lips? She lay back down on her wet bed and in the iniquity of her pleasure awaited for the righteous boy-man to anoint her lips with his. His appearance enclosed the few faint breaths around her lips and her brain sailed deeper into ecstasy. Lost in the sensational rhapsody of her pleasures, the notes of measured stereo music flowing through her space were derailed, they were too slow in their arrival for her over-pulsating mind to heed. Patiently she rubbed and touched herself, his image carried by the infinite photons of light years away, frozen in tantalizing slow motion; and in rapid succession, her ceiling was a fireworks display full of the spectacular. He was there, the smiling, tit teasing boy, her lifelong hallucination, chemically energized her brain barely this side of consciousness, her lovely silken yellow hair exhaustingly dangling from her head on the side of her bed.

There, where you've always been, deep in my heart and mind! Kiss me little boy, fuck me little boy, there are no excuses in sin. Oh fuck you little boy; you're such a numbing baby; you haven't changed in all these years.

In one pointless cry, Sharon screamed her adolescent disappointment of unrequited love of a dumb boy: all those years clinging to an illusion that was baby soft. High in her one-sided high, alone in her feelings only, she longed for someone to walk towards her, to cross the lovely desert that her lonely soul was now sailing towards her second birth.

She thought she heard her husband's voice and like a balloon it completely exploded her minimal, frail retarded reality, and hissing air further emptied her mind. And with every outside sensation there was less and less recognition until everything disappeared within the whirlwind of her vacuous eyes. In the unbounded hallucination full of the infinite light, she witnessed one last thread to a disjointed reality: more sugar cubes to feed her dreams.

She dropped two more sugar cubes and finished her last resort vodka. Spinning around an unending vortex, she wanted to hymn along with the monks in her brain. She found her young monk gazing excitedly all about her, from head to toe, all around her ass, and staring rudely in adoration, just like that boy on the bus, just like all the boys throughout her life, at her outstanding forever beautiful breasts and… it was no use; she could not sustain the shattered thoughts…she swooned as he put his arms around her shoulders and let them slide down to her fabulous ass and then delicately press his sentient hand up and down her silken back, and round and round, between her thighs and she openly endured his lovely lips upon her wet nipples and her mind dizzying spun into a vertiginous fantasy; and for a long time he made exposed love to her in front of Jesus and all the other saints, before the altar of the Holy Church of the Sepulchre. She tightened her lysergic eyes to better feel the touch against her skin that covered her whole body. Lovely angelic voices sang all around their love. They started soft and deep and the melody was a prolonged 'alleluia', 'alleluia', 'alleluia', softly fading into the distance, caressing her soul for ages to come. In Heaven's sweetness all external sensation blended with the 'alleluia', making her acid trip forever lasting. In her mind's celestial pleasure, she found happiness and became one with her universe and in the dazzling light of creation she saw the vastness and timelessness of love. Bless me, bless me now and forever for I am yours as I've always been.

She saw God and Jesus and the Holy Spirit as she approached Heaven.

"Lord, I am crying," she said. "Listen to my prayer, don't listen to my lips for they have sinned. You are my hope, take my soul, I have no strength left."

When her lips had fainted within her, she saw the path that the Lord had set for her.

Rising high on sheer spiritual spirals of new dawns, she transcended her dead corpse and in deafening silence she reached beyond the touch of light and time. Nothing really mattered. She never wanted to have anything to do with the outside world again. Her mind was quietly floating in God's presence and that's where she wanted to remain forever and ever, amen.

Sharon floated off her fabulous bed landing on her mahogany floor stone dead.

Chapter Seventeen

Alone, one morning, and bored, as usual, Kitty decided to go and spend some hours at the Fashion Island Mall in Newport Beach. Though a serious drive from Brentwood, it was one of her favorite places where she could hang out when feeling down. Ever since Sharon's overdose senseless suicide (Why did she do such a stupid thing? they all thought at her funeral), Kitty had found it difficult to fill her lonesome days. She woke up to a rich, cavernous house that seemed to echo strange sounds when she was alone in it, which was most of the time, since Claudio left for the office before she woke up. She was sure they were sounds from her past which nonetheless didn't make them any less deafening. Real or imagined, the short circuited chatter in her brain was welcomed more than the dumbness of an empty house. From the moment she woke up, to the shower, to the coffee, to the vodka, for hours, her unconscious strangely reverberated that stupid song her daddy used to sing, 'another day older and deeper in death …'

Other people sing Elvis in the shower but Kitty sang daddy.

Was it 'death' or 'debt'?

She couldn't remember as she dusted herself in ground aromatic powder.

It must have been death because daddy was never in debt. Daddy had been a renowned ophthalmologist in a private practice in Santa Monica charging four hundred dollars a visit while also selling his own brand of vitamins especially designed for eye health. Her daddy was an American visionary, a proud Lutheran who never had an ambivalent feeling about money. It was evil, but definitely nice.

That's why she didn't want to stay alone in that house full of riches. All day long, between subliminal visits with daddy, she walked the unforgettable fields of her high school days. She happily would recall those days of inflated feelings of affectionate friendships, now disguised as grown up affectations, and impatiently she would charge her mind to more of the innocent same, if only she could go back. Mixed-up days of vodka effusive feelings of lovely emotions bolstered by the presence of best friends, Sharon, Robin, and Myrna, the best friends forever, if only they would last forever, which after Sharon's suicide, she knew was an impossible wish. It's easy to wish that nice things would last forever, but Kitty knew that they don't. God damn days rushed like bridges under the water, or something like that, she didn't want to think about the passing of time and the gratuitous accumulation of money thanks to daddy's various trusts and Claudio's grease.

A year after Sharon's suicide, fear had paralysed the best friends. They had tried to recover, to continue their friendship but found themselves numb to each other's touch. The open chasm created by Sharon's absence had been filled with unexplainable feelings of guilt as if they had been responsible for her death. They tried to console each other during less and less get-togethers but strangely enough they didn't feel the need for consolation; so the gestures fell by the wayside, as each looked the other way. And as the dark side of their obscured emotions continued to overtake their once youthful, sunny outlook, more emptiness invaded their hearts and no amount of booze could bring back the merriment that was once their foursome friendship. Their bonding, like all friendships, had been surreal, based on the seductive nuances of love and of everlasting youthful exuberance. One thing had become pretty obvious to Kitty: people, even the best of friends, at all times, do hide things from each other.

"Even best friends have secrets," she mumbled to herself just so that she could equalize in her mind the stuff of reality.

Deep in her unpleasant thoughts, she was almost crushed by a trailer truck as she tried to exit to MacArthur Boulevard off the Interstate 405. She neither saw nor heard the massive truck brake hard when she changed lanes in her Mercedes 500. On automatic, she found her way to Fashion Island and parked in the one of the many familiar parking lots that she knew by heart: outside Nordstrom's.

She walked the wide pedestrian areas of Fashion Island without aim. She needed nothing; she just wanted to be with people. Absentmindedly she gazed into the chic store displays for a while and then lethargically sat on one of the many benches strategically placed along the ways of the fantastic mall to catch the sun and ocean breezes of Newport Beach, alone in her dreamlike thoughts. Disconcerted by her thoughtless nothingness and oblivious to her fantastic surroundings, a gentleman approached her bench and sat next to her. He looked at her, took her hand and without much ado proposed to her that they try to retrace their lives back to their youth, "…let's say to age six," he said.

"Oh, much too early," she replied.

He was very handsome and from the penetration of his eyes, his deep, dark sparkling blue eyes, he was obviously very intelligent. You don't have blue eyes and not be highly intelligent. Unlike her uneducated husband Claudio, who also had blue eyes and blond hair but being Italian should've had dark hair and dark eyes, the man beside her had all the evidences of erudition and cosmopolitan sophistication. Instinctively she knew that he belonged to the hierarchy of the many centuries refined Northern European successful.

She shook her head trying to reject the illusion but the man would not go away. She thought the scene absurd, and feared that people might be watching, but found herself reaching out to him, for his arm, and she did intertwine hers with his. Surprised at how easily she had welcomed the cheery thought, she decided to find another more comfortable bench so that she could regain her sense of reality in the midst of the fantasy of Fashion Island but the illusion became even more delusional in the brightness of the Newport Beach sun as he began to talk to her and she to him.

"I didn't mean that we should marry at the age of six," he said, delicately holding her hand and exchanging child-like smiles with her.

"Maybe you mean that we should have had a torrid love affair at the age of six," she said with a smile of reasonableness about her.

"It has been known that children sometimes do fall in love at a very early age and with the passing of years eventually marry and spend a lifetime together."

If only it were so, she thought.

She had heard of such instances on television but it was difficult for her to believe such nonsense. Fall in love at six, make love at seven, marry at eight, she continued? Why not? Definitely intriguing. Who am I kidding?

"In any case," he continued holding her attention, "right now I just want to impress on you that I am real, not some fancy of your imagination, and that as sure as the swallows return to Capistrano, sometime in the future I will find you, and I will marry you."

This is the way it should always be, she thought, and caught herself not wanting to appear like a lonesome nobody.

"And I suppose until that day I'm supposed to remain a virgin, pristine from any other touch, faithful like a Holy Crusader's long distance wife, until you claim me," she smiled.

"Yes," he squeezed her hand and smiled back.

"You're crazy," she said most emphatically.

Haughtily, he stood up to walk away.

"No don't go," she regretfully called out, not to the unsuspecting type walking by, but to her six year old lover manifestation.

"I beg your pardon," said the unsuspecting, and he quickly moved away.

"Was he talking to me?" she said to herself.

She looked at one of the apathetic trees that are often planted in shopping malls. It was near her, alone, pretending to be part of a forest, and again he appeared and sat next to her as real as any tree. She touched her hair and smoothed out her skirt and her world was fine. It had been a very long time since she had felt so wonderfully happy; not since even before than when she had first met Sharon in seventh grade.

She made her way to Bloomingdales holding her secret affair hard within her hidden smile. The entrance opened to a huge erotic vestibule filled with a myriad of competing exotic perfumes diffusing from the many counters and glamorous salesladies everywhere, a familiar aromatic scene that never failed to make even Kitty drunk with pleasure. She was indulging in pubescent sensuality as she proceeded from counter to counter to fine spray her frail neck, and freshly dyed blond hair, and give relief to her stressed out armpits with the free samplers. She often bought expensive perfumes which she later didn't recall she had done so, let alone why she had bought so much, thanks to daddy, and Claudio who also had made a lot of money recycling used, stinking, burned-out, killing, overly used, saturated restaurant oil fats and greases.

She felt refreshed and was aware that all the sales ladies and even other well to do customers were looking at her, wishing they had her money. It was like walking through a flowering park in May, and after trying out the finest of essences, she felt revitalized, like Hera bathing in her pristine, magic springs of yore. She was once again young, touched for the very first time by all the perfumes of Paris. She wickedly smiled and wished she didn't have to leave Bloomingdales, but there were other surprises, so many more sweet surprises in Newport Beach's Fashion Island than just perfume stores. So, out she went happy as a lark, a bird whose melody she had never heard, but knew that it sings longing songs in distant exotic lands, somewhere beyond the sea.

"The two worst things about getting old are age and poverty. You can't avoid age, but damn it, you must do everything to avoid poverty. Even fuck your way out of it," she recalled Claudio's resolve against poverty, which was something that Kitty always admired about her immigrant husband. And on this shopping day, Kitty was determined to do her best against both age and poverty. And aren't all malls intended to make you feel juvenile?

Next door was Neiman Marcus and every time Kitty went through its heavy doors she felt deep humility. For Kitty, shopping at Neiman's was like praying in a cathedral: she walked the aisles slowly with respect; it was a necessary ritual to warm up to the celestial prices.

She bought some heavenly chocolates as a starter and sauntered to the ladies floor.

A classy-chic saleslady floated out of nowhere and offered to serve, and Kitty felt flattered. The lady was gym-tall, and thin, immaculately dressed, her complexion without blemish. It was hard to tell how old she was because she was a living mannequin.

"Can I help you, Madam? Are you looking for something special?"

"Do you have any suggestions?" said Kitty, well versed in the ritual.

"We do have some new pretty dresses that just arrived today …" she said.

Kitty did buy three dresses on this Neiman Marcus occasion: an evening gown for $1690.00, a leaf-print zip dress for $675.00, and a fancy dress for $3950.00. Kitty knew that even for her this was a lot of money, and that Claudio would never stand for it, as much as he loved her, but it made her feel good to make the trade knowing that within days she could return the dresses and get her money back without any questions from an establishment that above all prized its clientele. It's only middleclass people who are afraid to make the deal, and Neiman doesn't deal with middle class.

She felt exhausted and hungry as she proudly walked the smart ways of Fashion Island showing off her Neiman Marcus shopping bag. She took a booth at La Table and ordered a cup of bisque, and modestly, a diet coke. The bisque was always creamy lovely pink at La Table but this day it tasted like shit. It must be the coke, she thought and left unsatisfied, and looking for a hard drink. She settled for La Viande restaurant where one could always depend on a great Angus burger and an excellent Grey Goose martini. She requested an outdoor table, and the martinis were lovely, one preceding the juicy burger, and the second during it. Lovely luscious vodka to take away the pain from aching feet.

While sucking on her quarter pounder medium rare overly juicy burger packed with slices of tomatoes, onions, lettuce, and pickles, and not intending to stare, her eyes, unaccustomed as it were, travelled to a nearby table where sat a gorgeous thirtyish-something blonde lady eating by herself. There was something familiar about the scene. It wasn't just the blond hair.

They're all blondes in Fashion Island now days, thought Kitty; blondes with Spanish dark eyes, and modern-living blondes aimlessly floating among the TV waves of rich towns.

Kitty quickly re-focussed her eyes back on the gorgeous lady. She busted her brains trying to make the connection without being accused of staring. Finally, it was the beautiful actress Susan Kelly breezing the air all around her. Kitty decided right there and then that she loved Suzie, as all her fans knew her, because even while sitting, Suzie had statuesque class in her expensive clothes and blond hair. It was strange, though, that Susan Kelly was sitting alone, famous as she was. You'd think that there would be at least a couple of young beaux escorting her. Then she had this unkind thought about Suzie: rumour had it that she is like a London police station, dicks going in and out all the time, Kitty looked past herself.

She felt unkind. Even she knew that it was an old silly sixth-graders joke. She should have been more generous because today's everyday shopping day had become a bit more glamorous special, thanks to Suzie's presence.

What the fuck? Being cheeky is part of the business, Kitty keenly tried to show off her familiarity to the many Hollywood myths about the business. After all, living next door to Hollywood, she felt an affinity to the Susan Kellys of the business.

They serve the best martinis in Fashion Island, she make-believed.

Back on the 405, she figured she would make it back to Brentwood by three pm, just in time to catch the Tom Hanks movie on HBO. She couldn't recall the name of the movie but it didn't matter because all of Tom Hank's movies had the same title. She justified the long drive to Newport Beach because the shopping there was worth it and she loved the name, Newport Beach. It had all the right stuff: new and port, and beach, she thought, as she recklessly weaved in and out of the car pool lane on her way home. Besides, it was a nice way to kill time of which she had plenty of, and she half-heartedly yawned.

When she got home she felt the boredom still there. Nothing had changed since she had exited the house hours earlier in an attempt to escape it.

"Too much money and nothing to do," she said to the house.

And always, the thought of being alone scared the shit out of her.

After a quick shower, she made her way to the TV room that also included a wet bar and turned on the humongous TV that Claudio had bought for them and their friends. She thought that Claudio had said that it was nine hundred inches, or maybe that it cost nine thousand dollars. She found Tom Hanks on HBO and she tried watching the movie but on this day, just like the bisque, the movie sucked too. It was too unbearable, cute as Tom was.

She searched the waves for a more titillating movie affair and she was in luck. The affair involved a beautiful young American woman, twenty three, Kitty figured, travelling by her lonesome self in Paris, of all places. The place was kind of mute though because she and her French lover, a man old enough to be her father, hardly ever left the bedroom. But the dashing actor, probably gay, thought Kitty, was barely believable as a likely lover only because the young woman was hot and he never promised her anything more than a few fucks a week. After a few scenes of he on top, she on top, with interruptions of maximal stares and minimal conversation, and lots of the same spoon yogurt licking, Kitty decided that the movie was one of those French comedies that pretend to be kind of porno but they never are because French male actors are not manly enough to keep a real woman interested, and invariably she fell asleep watching the boring slop.

*

"No let's not go out to eat," said Claudio.

He had found Kitty sleeping on the huge leather sofa in the TV room.

"But we never go out," said Kitty.

"You're out every day and you were out today too," said Claudio who lovingly cupped Kitty's breasts and then petted her on the head.

"But only for shopping," she said and she happily accepted Claudio's sloppy kisses. Kitty loved being made love to while half asleep. So they made love and forgot about dinner though there were all sorts of foreign cheeses and wines in the house that they munched on while watching TV together.

"You'll never guess who I saw today," lovingly said Kitty to her husband.

"It's whom," said Claudio.

"It was Susan Kelly! She was gorgeous and she was sitting two tables over …"

"Oh yeah? Was she blond or redhead today?"

"What do you mean?"

"Her real name is Georgia Laughman, you know," said her husband.

Kitty stopped and thought for a moment.

"I suppose you've fucked her too," she sighed in shallow despair. She had long ago thrown in the towel resigning herself to her husband's escapades of fucking Hollywood starlets.

It was the favourite pastime of moneyed types to shack up with beautiful young girls who weren't making it otherwise in Hollywood. If you had the money, you could get laid as often as your penis erected in the business. Kitty knew that Claudio, Hank, tight ass David, and Phil, before he went monkey, would often get invited to parties where many young women would be available. With the exception of Phil, the others, Claudio, Hank and David were easy millionaires who were making many more millions than they were investing in showbiz. Now days, it was Claudio and Hank who would hang out together. They took pride in partaking in Hollywood social events such as the various Oscars and Grammys dressed in their tuxedoes. There was nothing that Kitty could do every time she saw Claudio in his tuxedo: he was out to pillage in search of more spoils. On several occasions Claudio had confessed to Kitty of semi-serious affairs with well-known starlets but she knew that he was never in the mood for prolonged serious love affairs. He was simply incapable of deeply loving any woman.

"You know who's fucking your friend Myrna, don't you?"

"Claudio, I would never forgive you …"

"No, no. It's not me. It's Hank. He fucks her all the time. She goes to him. Even when poor Phil was still married to her, she would sneak around to his restaurant."

"That doesn't mean that she was fucking him," said Kitty.

"Get serious, Kitty. It's no big deal. Phil probably couldn't fuck as often as Myrna wanted it," summed up Claudio.

"I wonder if Sharon knew about it?" said Kitty.

"Now there was a piece of ass I wouldn't have minded to dip into."

That was what Kitty best loved about her husband: his raw artlessness. He never withheld anything from her, was always up front, and shared all his fantasies with her.

She followed her husband into their bedroom and had more sex with him. It was a lazy act and he immediately fell asleep. She was wide awake and bothered by incessant thoughts that spun around the world. Incoherent thoughts that gave way to apprehensive uneasiness whose source she couldn't identify. She looked at Claudio and he was sleeping like a baby.

You would think that with his background as an orphan in Sicily he would be loaded with neurotic disorders, she thought. He was sleeping deaf to the world. In a strange way she felt pity for him. Pity for the dolt, but he was an honest man. And then she thought: can an ignorant man be an honest man? She thought of her first husband who was not a dolt and who tried to be honest with his feelings but wound up a schizophrenic.

Her mind shifted from pity for Claudio to fear for Milton her once despondent, crazy, now pretty much forgotten, first husband. She thought she had put Milt out of her mind but every so often like a zombie he would suddenly arise from the not so happy days of the past and haunt her as if she were to blame for his going nuts. They had met in San Jose State College and it took her three years before she realized that Milt was an emotional blood sucking leech. Not in the sense of taking her for her money but for slowly sucking her happiness out of her, and for sadistically distorting her once happy view of the world.

She looked at her husband Claudio snoring by her side. Totally opposites, she thought.

"He made my every sense of love and friendship foreign to me," she cried to herself.

Well into their college warped relationship, she learned that Milton was the bastard son of fornicating cousins who had put him up for adoption even before he was born. She tossed and turned in incredible frustration trying to squeeze the thought like a pimple out of her memory, this Milt, who had crept into her life when she was so silly innocent. What a hysterical little girl I must've been to have been attracted to a juvenile dwarf like Milt, her mind revved up in disgusting thoughts about her first husband whom she now felt nothing but loathing.

She kicked the sheets but no reaction from Claudio who was used to her kicking.

Her mind swirled full of frustration because it was too late to now regret let alone erase that midget's improbable presence in her mind.

He was a mulatto, she swallowed the thought that surfaced as a revelation. He had dark curly hair and green eyes suggesting of miscegenation and not of fucking blond cousins who probably conveniently made the sacrifice to take the blame and save the family from dissolute embarrassment.

In reality, he was an effeminate little fellow who had thought he had found a cheap cure for all his anxieties in Kitty's arms. One day, two months before their graduation, he was getting a degree in sociology, she in psychology, young Milton got into a clothes drier in the dorm's laundry room and had a bro put in a quarter to spin him around. Fortunately, the dorm bro wasn't as dumb as Milt and after a couple of hot spins he stopped the drier and took Milt out, nose bleeding, broken arm, and face all scratched up. It was then that it became apparent to Kitty that she deserved someone bigger than

Milt. She felt sad for him and sorry for herself but it was too late, she was pregnant with his baby. She married him anyway and soon after had Albert, her one and only son. At the time her best friends never said a word to Kitty about the whole scandalous affair though they all had doubts about Milton being the sufficient man for their Kitty.

They tried counselling and all the various herbal medicines on the market but nothing seemed to put out the fire in Milton's brain. One day Milton simply dropped out of sight and no one was the worse for it. The friends were all the glad for it; they didn't have to ostracize Kitty from their group.

Years later, Albert found Milton somewhere in Oregon. Apparently Oregon's overcast climate jibbed well with Milton's cloudy personality. He told his son that he was a contented man and had no intention of ever returning to that "cunt that is your mother."

It was never clear to the friends whether Kitty and Milton had ever divorced, but then, who the hell ever cared about the details?

Chapter Eighteen

⸺ ∽⟡⟡⟡∼ ⸺

Robert Sargent woke up uneasy one morning, looked out of his bedroom window, past his high privacy wall covered with morning glory, and caught sight of the enormity of the universe. His eyes carried him high to the few thin streaks of grey clouds whose underbellies were glowing to a variety of crimson red hues under the flood of sunlight from the fast breaking dawn. His mind gladdened at the morning colors of the fast rising sun still hidden from him beneath his view's horizon. He saw the morning's orange rays powerfully reflecting off the fast thinning night's clouds and he was glad that he was alive. In an act played out in endless repetition, dawn's soft lights swelled and moved across the heavens giving life to the early day and he wished the moment would never end. Mesmerized by all the morning's spectacular performance spreading out before his eyes as night gave way to day, he sank into sadness that his seventy years he foolishly had been too much in a hurry to get to his secluded office that shut out the beauty of the universe now awakening before his eyes. He stood paralyzed before the unfolding scene and realized how recklessly he had spent his few mortal days never stopping to enjoy the beauty that nature freely offered. His eyes stayed fixed on the morning's glowing scene until the streaking clouds began to melt away and disperse under the piercing rays of the sun. The crimson red gave way to orange and orange gave way to thinning white clouds, the same color as his hair, and it was all happening too fast. Yet it was all so sweet for nature to generously display such wondrous scenes to Robert and to all of God's creatures, if only they stopped to look. And in that morning's heart-breaking dawn, the white clouds quickly gave way to an azure blue dome above Robert's head, a spectacular renewal of a promising world that makes young people feel the excitement of bold adventures to come and older people angry that their time is running out.

"It's going be a beautiful day," he said loudly to his still asleep wife, recalling an old country saying that you can tell the day from its morning.

What a beautiful sight, he continued, quietly admonishing himself for his pathetic little life that had consumed his years in useless pursuit of money without ever stopping to look up and see the universe rising before his eyes at every dawn. And that heart breaking little slice of the universe that he was now witnessing, almost too late in his aged life, was totally removed from his worthless millions. He fell into an unexpected sadness which gave way to melancholic depression, angry that he had mortgaged his life chasing the paper trails of Pioneer Bank. He wondered if he had time left, that there was so little time, and he sighed and took a deep breath but there was no relief.

"What time is it, dear," said his still sleepy wife lying next to him.

"It's so absurd," he said to his half-awakening wife, "that this amazingly beautiful dawn, this beauty that repeats forever each morning is ours free and we never took the time to say thank you Lord."

"Give me five more minutes will you dear. I love you," said his wife.

"I suppose dusk is just as beautiful," he said to himself more than to his wife.

It was then that Robert Sargent, majority stockholder and CEO of Pioneer Bank, decided to retire from the drudgery that had been his preoccupied moneyed life and to breathe his last few years tuning into the universe that was his, beautiful and free.

At breakfast that morning he was unusually thoughtful. Gone was that determined angry look that would take control of his mind and face, early every morning, and fortify him to do daily battles with his finance competitors across the senseless universe of computer apps and Bloomberg charts. Today his face showed anaemic, down in the dumps; it said, 'I just don't care about that shit anymore'.

"Are you alright, dear," asked his wife. "You don't seem the same as other mornings."

"I'm alright, Helen," said Robert.

"You look tired, and aren't you late for work this morning? You're usually at the office by five. What's going on this morning?" she said.

He looked at his sweet wife whom he loved very much and sweetly smiled back at her.

It was no use. He could no longer muster any sense of ambition to strengthen his determination to charge ahead and catch up on vapid stock market news on CNBC and CNN.

"Did you see the dawn this morning," he quietly asked his wife.

Helen Rodgers looked hard at her husband and saw that he was a different man. The only thought that came to her mind was about the chauffeur waiting in the car.

"What do you mean?" she said in her usual reticent manner.

"It was so beautiful; it made me think of our mortality. We have such a brief life in this world, and how sad that, too late, we realize how pathetically we've wasted our precious time."

"That's been said before, Robert, and it hasn't been such a waste of time as you might now think. After all, you've managed Pioneer Bank into a major international institution that provides work for thousands of people worldwide. You should be proud of that. And not to sound too dumpy, or too greedy, we aren't hurting for money either. And don't forget our beautiful daughter Robin who has brought us so much happiness and pleasure in our lives. We have a lot to be thankful, thank God," said sweet Helen with a smile.

Robert wasn't listening to the blessings his wife was listing; they really had nothing to do with the thoughts he was celebrating that morning.

"The ugliest thing in my view was our privacy wall. Why do people put up such ugly privacy walls?" he said to his wife who was barely dressed in a revealing negligee.

"Why don't you take the day off, Robert? Maybe we could take a walk along the beach - in Corona del Mar, if you like. They say it's beautiful this time of the year. We could watch the pelicans fly above us. You know those pelicans have been around for millions of years, descendants of dinosaurs, they say."

It had been the rule in the Sargent household that the master of the house should be addressed with his full given name as opposed to Bob, or God forbid, Bobby. It just wasn't kosher for a CEO of a major Corporation to be called Bobby. Too late, he now regretted that all these years his lovely wife had referred to him as Robert.

"I haven't thought things through yet, Helen, but I promise you there will be some changes made very soon to our selfish lives."

"You're exaggerating again Robert. I don't think of my life as having been selfish."

"How would you like to go on a cruise, Helen? Go on a month long cruise on one of those luxurious cruise ships?"

"That would be nice, dear," said Helen matter-of-factly.

"Yes, I think I'd like that," said Robert who then set off for his office.

*

He took his son-in-law, David Calder, Vice President of Human Resources at Pioneer Bank to lunch in a seaside restaurant that specialized in broiled fillet of Chilean bass. David was surprised at his father-in-law's invitation, a very rare occurrence. More surprising than the invitation to lunch was Mr Sargent's casual look that day: polo shirt and jeans. Robert was not Apple hi-tech to ditch the suit and tie, so David sensed something new was in the air. Other than the few get-togethers at their home on special occasions, the Sargents pretty much kept to themselves and everybody else out. Partying wasn't their thing. Because of his French background Robert never felt excited about being fully part of the American social scene though he appeared relaxed and friendly with his fellow corporate Americans. He believed that a banker should be a man of few words, a prerequisite to earning respect from his subordinates. This foreign demeanor on Sargent's part was all too familiar to his all-American son-in-law who had recognized it as a replica of his wife's likewise dismissive attitude. It didn't bother David that his in-laws kept him more as an acquaintance than as a close member of the family. He knew that one way or another great fortune awaited him regardless of the Sargents' lame people skills. As long as he was captain of Robin's ship, firmly sailing the waves of her mind's wilderness, David knew that he would be the last to go down.

Robert Sargent ordered a Grey Goose martini, clean with a twist, and it reminded David of Robin's tastes. He wanted to smile at the thought but he didn't. In deference to his father-in-law, and his work supervisor, David ordered a diet coke. Robert approved, looked at his son-in-law, and for the first time saw that he was a handsome man, and that his daughter was lucky to be married to such a good-looking guy. Like the earlier morning's revelations it dawned on him that he had been socially unkind to David. He had always blamed David for Robin's inability to get pregnant. He knew of his daughter's wild and crazy night life, but again, the fault was never with his daughter but with insufficient David. Too late, on this day he saw a different son-in-law and he recalled that David had been in the Peace Corps, a very worthy accomplishment that surely highlighted laudable qualities.

"David, I wish we had done this more often, but it's too late for regrets now."

David Calder's summation of his father-in-law of more than twenty years was that Sargent, at best, was a difficult man to like. His inability to be happy generous with people around him kept him always guarded in the way he spoke, and even walked. The man was awkward and had no sense of humor. After a couple of years of being a member of the family, though always at an arm's length, David began to feel sorry for his father-in-law. Initially he had thought that in time he would have developed some sympathy for Robert except that in Robert's face he saw reflections of daughter Robin and he badly disliked his wife. David Calder was a delicate and elusive man, shrewd in his calculations of people, qualities that Robert's and Robin's inattentive brains never wished to see.

"Why, Robert? Are you going to commit suicide soon?" said David with a straight face.

He looked into his father-in-law's face which had turned ashen and realized that poor Robert didn't deserve that comment meant as a joke.

"Sorry, Robert, I was just kidding."

"Well, I'm not," said Mr Sargent, regaining his color. "Things are about to change, David. For years now I've known that you and Robin have had a fucked-up marriage. I've known that she goes out almost every night and fucks men of different skin colors and you don't do anything about it."

David hadn't seen that one coming. Nonetheless he knew that he had a straight flush in his hands and knew that Sargent would lose whatever hand he was playing. What a dumb-shit, he thought. Why is he telling me all this crap, after all these years, during a business lunch?

"Did you know that she had had a bungled abortion right after you got married?" said a formidable Robert. "And she never got pregnant again?"

David looked at his father-in-law in disgust.

"Yes I did," he said most calmly. "You probably thought that it was because I wasn't fucking her."

"You're disgusting," said Robert.

"Anything more?" said a lucid David.

"Had you known that the fetus was a black, probably an Ethiopian?"

"I suspected it, but unlike you, Robert, I didn't want to know the details."

"Why did you put up with it?"

"What would you have had me do? Blow her brains out? Besides, in truth, I liked being a Vice President in your bank. I liked the way you generously took good care of me; fed me rich and well, and I had no complaints."

They looked at each in an empty gesture of manly sizing up. The gig was up; the truth was out: the only thing that bound them was crazy Robin who found sanity in booze and two leftover high school friends.

"I have decided to retire from the Bank. Normally I should make you, my one and only son-in-law, married to my one and only daughter, the new CEO of Pioneer Bank. But I don't like you, David, and I want to separate you from the Bank altogether."

There was a long delay while David digested the news of being at last dumped from the organization chart that had been the Sargent family. He had long before concluded that inevitably a divorce would have been forthcoming. Given what he had just heard he remained very calm. It was simply another good reason not to like the Sargents.

"Well, Robert, I'm not surprised. More importantly, I don't care. I'll gladly shake your generous hand and say 'good by' to you too."

"There's more to come, David. I expect you to also divorce Robin for whom I've arranged to be my sole heir and so the largest stockholder in the company. It would have been weird to dump you from your position in the Bank while you'd still be humping the CEO of Pioneer Bank, don't you think," smiled Robert most restrained.

"Believe me, Robert, I totally understand. I would do exactly what you're doing if I were in your position," said David.

They looked at each other and each wondered on his own whether, as men, they ever had anything in common. It had always been a mystery to David what Robin had seen in him in the first place and why she had decided to marry him. Looking at Robin's father damned the mystery only more. Robert Sargent was displaying a stiff, sub-zero stare that also made his old hands tremble with hostility. The man was quivering in an icy film of old age arterial plaque. At that moment, nothing could've warmed up Robert to a little sense of decency.

"I will be kind to you, David. In the face of no nuptial agreement, I will still give you a handsome ten million dollars for you to divorce Robin with no questions asked."

There was silence as David loudly sucked through his straw the last ounce of diet coke. He looked hard at the old man and he felt sorry for him. Sorry because Sargent was a wimp before his eyes, hardly the adversary that he was positioning himself against.

"I think that I'm being very generous, don't you agree?"

More calculating silence from David.

"You could do a lot of things with ten million dollars ..."

"Geeewhheezy, Robert," said David with a mean and ugly chuckle. "It's times like these that I wish I were a red bull kind of a guy, all strung out on caffeine, so that I could pound the shit out of you, you ungrateful old geezer. But lucky for you I'm not going to pound the shit out of you today. So listen carefully to what I am going say to you, father of my whorish wife. I don't understand how it happened, but first your daughter and then you somehow screwed me into a marriage for many years which was full of guilt on my part, and now you think you can dump me over a diet coke. It'll cost you one hundred million, not ten, you old blood sucking pioneer of circle the wagons ruthlessness. One hundred million buckaroos to dump me."

Poor Robert, mega CEO of Pioneer Bank, went black for a few seconds, probably a mild stroke; he recovered, and then he tried to comprehend if he could suffer a one hundred million dollar loss. He hesitated, not for the money, but to see whether his brain still functioned. For the very first time in his life he was very uncomfortable and very afraid.

"You must be worth at least six, seven billion, Robert, so what's a measly one hundred million for you. Imagine you and your pretty little daughter alone, together again, as it used to be, and me out of your way for a shitty one hundred million dollars. You'll both be so happy after I'm gone. A brand new life for you, Robert!"

The thought of once again being alone with his little girl brought gushes of warmth into Robert Sargent's arteries and blood flowed back into his brains. He saw Robin as the little girl he knew; as his happy bop, bop, bopping Robin days and he was happy. A one hundred million dollar deal was simply one of many that he had concluded and this one was no brainer. It was a good deal to get rid of that minimal son-in-law of his.

"You drive a hard bargain, David, but I agree; it's a deal," he said to his ex-son-in-law and he extended his cold wrinkled hand to him.

David stood up, gently pushed Robert's martini glass spilling it all over the table.

"Peace Corps volunteers can be ruthless too, Robert," he said.

He then walked out of the Sargents' life. Within a year he moved to Sardinia where he bought a huge villa with a small vineyard to keep him occupied. A year later Justine and Meredith visited him as they were touring through Europe. Justine had an unlikely sexual escapade with David and decided to stay on with him in Sardinia. Nineteen years old Meredith also fucked David but decided to continue on with her European trip. Two years later Meredith, for good, also joined forty seven year old David and her sister in a *ménage a trois*. For years they lived happy, long lives together, and the girls easily adapted to the ways of Italian culture. Rarely if ever did any of them think of Robin, or Myrna, even though Myrna had visited the girls one summer. Throughout the visit she felt very alone.

Chapter Nineteen

I t had been a shocker.
It had all started out as a promised one month luxury cruise in the Mediterranean and now Robert and Helen Sargent were dead. Suicides, the cruise company had said. And they weren't lying because there had been witnesses to the event of first Helen, with the help of her husband, jumping overboard, and then Robert himself doing the same, both without lifejackets. The whole ghastly affair had been extensively videoed by some Chinese tourists to background laughter. Unfortunately for the Sargents, the whole thing took place at night, and although there was a full moon, they went into the choppy waters yellow, somewhere off the island of Cyprus, and they never surfaced above the frothy white caps of the famed sea. The warm Mediterranean waters on calm summer nights can be invitingly deadly. A dinghy was lowered and they searched for a while until all hope, along with the Sargents, disappeared into the ancient waters of Aphrodite in the Eastern Mediterranean as the cruise ship was heading for the Holy Lands of Israel.

After their bloom, the next thing the Sargents knew was that they were holding hands while traversing through an aura of subtle non-sensory stimulating, yet enchanting music. Aside from the spiritual harmony enveloping them, everywhere there was peace; and definitely there was no salty water anywhere to drown their sorrows, because they no longer felt unhappy. It was as if they were effortlessly floating through a space filled with fluffy pristine creamy white puffs of clouds not unlike what Robert had witnessed some weeks earlier one dawn from his bedroom window.

"What a surprise," said Robert to his wife.

"Not for me," came a glowing response. "I've been expecting you."

"I know you," said Helen. "You're Robin's best friend Sharon, aren't you? Robert, you remember Sharon; she's the one who committed suicide … oops …"

"That's ok Helen. We're all in the same boat now," said Sharon and they all laughed.

"Is this Heaven or Hell," asked a curious Robert.

"It's whatever you want it to be Robert," said Sharon who continued to straighten out a tablecloth over a round table similar to the one that had been in the Seven Seas Restaurant. The cloth seemed to be one of those intensely blazing red and blue hues depictions of Paradise from Adam and Eve's time. "In Heaven, each of us has his or her own Paradise."

"You're so real," said Helen.

"I'm anything but real," said Sharon. "I exist only in your spiritual minds. But I am as real as you wish to make me. For example, if Robert wanted to fuck me right now, he could by simply wishing it, which I can now sense that he wants to, even though I exist only as a spirit in his mind. Mind you, he'd be fucking his own fantasy and thus he could do whatever he would want with me. This after all is true Paradise, as everyone would wish it, don't you think?"

It was a little embarrassing for Robert to have angelic Sharon read his mind so obviously. True, when alive, lustful thoughts did invade his heart when in young Sharon's presence, but he wasn't an animal and he was able to contain himself though it wasn't easy; maybe if she wasn't Robin's friend …

"There are no fears and no secrets in Heaven, Robert," said Sharon. "Here we act out all our feelings at no offense, for what is Heaven for? It wasn't until Adam and Eve hid their love-making from the Lord that they were kicked out of Heaven."

"Go ahead, Robert, fuck her; you have my permission, for what's Heaven for," laughed Helen somewhere in Robert's spiritual Heavenly mind.

"Yes, but I want the real Sharon, as I knew her when alive …"

"You're an idiot, Robert. Here we are in Heaven and all you can think about is fucking Sharon. There must be something more pleasant to think about than fucking Sharon?" suddenly said a noticeably aggravated Helen, this being her first time in Heaven also.

"Like what," said an unabashed Robert?

More Heavenly music suggesting that Robert was right.

"To the point Sharon: is there a real corporal Sharon, not just spiritual, floating around on her own, and out of my mind in this here Heaven?" said Robert who was having a hard time adjusting to spiritual Heavenly existence.

"Does it matter?" said Sharon. "Don't worry, you'll soon adjust to being in Paradise. You must, you know, for you'll be here for an eternity, and that's a very long, long time."

"Yes it matters," said the bean-counting banker, "for what's the thrill in fucking a spirit. We've all done that millions of times and it's just not like the real thing."

"You're an idiot, Robert," repeated Helen. "You could wish for Cleopatra or Liz Taylor, for example, but no, you wish for your daughter's best friend," said Helen.

"Happens all the time," said Sharon.

"OK, smarty-pants, with whom do you wish to make out in Heaven?" asked Robert.

"Hercules," said Helen.

Robert and Helen then settled down in each other's minds. You had to be there, but settling in each other's minds for an eternity was difficult to comprehend, as was difficult to know how long they could stand to be in each other's minds, or whether the dead-beat drowsy music settlement now luxuriously sedating their souls, was in any way going to be as pleasant as the brief corporeal earthly life. The thought did occur to them that perhaps they had gone overboard with their suicides. At best it was irksome to have someone continuously in your mind and you be in someone else's mind without a corporeal existence of your own. Did she really know what he was thinking or doing? And did he really know what she was thinking or doing? All the time?

Unfair! Unjust! Un-Heavenly, thought Robert. And yet even in Heaven companionship was necessary for no one could exist alone even in one's own Paradise, and he thought of Adam. Jesus, it was almost like being married again. 'Till death do us part,' he thought. Well, here they were dead: where the hell was the 'part' part? Then he thought that a little wickedness must be especially necessary in Heaven, or else he would go out of his mind.

Robert Sargent, while now in spirit, decided to erase his beloved wife, once and for all time, to get her out of his mind for all eternity. Instantaneously, Helen was gone and in so far as Robert was concerned, that was the way the kitty bounced. He thought of Adam and hoped to meet him sometime. Free at last, free at last, he thought in the spirit of at last being relieved from the one corporeal bind most suffocating: marriage. He was surprised that the Good Lord was not offended with the ease in which he had done away Helen. Whoever came up with the saying 'a marriage made in Heaven' didn't know what the hell he was talking about. He caught himself swearing again, but once in Paradise, he thought, you can probably do anything without offending the Lord. After all, you're there at his invitation, so, what the hell, anything goes. God does not go back on His Word; not really.

He was feeling good, alone in his Paradise that was his Heaven. He found himself ghostly swooshing through a religious fervor of ecstatic delight. Here now was true Paradise where anything went. No more Helen, just pure pleasure; pure pleasure that for a change was not sinful. There must be pleasures in Paradise; for if there are no pleasures, there must only be pain in Paradise, or even worse, nothing, and that would be absurd. It would amount to an abrogation of God's promise, surely an absurdity. He wanted to find Sharon again, and this time, not just in his own mind, but on her own naked corporal self. But until then he did fantasy fuck her several times. It was like masturbating, ok, but he would have preferred the real thing.

While searching for more Heavenly pleasure, and corporeal Sharon, as he remembered her in the Paradise of his mind, he thought about food and drink! Again, the thought was absurd, for what spirit needs food or drink?

He felt remorseful when he remembered the lines, so true,

'Come let us drink while we have breath
For there's no drinking after death'

Well, so much for spirits in Heaven, the ultimate paradox, he laughed to himself.

But there must be some form of pleasure that even a spirit in Heaven could appreciate, and Robert was never a sports fan. And what could be duller than the absence of pleasure …

And, there it was: sex, the supreme pleasure for the greatest happiness! Here was the perfect fantasy in Heaven as it is on earth. Pure and dirty sex equally available to all with no moral strings attached; no hang-ups; no hard feelings; just pure pleasure. For isn't it true that sex is the most Heavenly reigning chock full of sensual pleasures? It made perfect sense, and suddenly Robert began to sing in Heavenly ecstasy looking for Sharon.

"Take my hand, I'm a stranger in Paradise,
All lost in a wonderland, a stranger in Paradise.

The lyrics were pure delight, better than *'you are my destiny'* and Robert was certain that he had connected with Sharon's spirit which must've been floating somewhere nearby.

"I must say, Bobby, you're definitely the husband I never had. I've never been the recipient of so much fucking."

It was Sharon! A ghost of her former self but still as ravishing as ever. She was real, naked breasts and ass as real as he had always fantasized on Earth.

And lo and behold Paradise was exactly as the song exclaimed. Such a wonderland full of ass and tits. How could it be otherwise? As a former CEO Robert understood that the good Lord would have wanted it that way. Also birds and other animals among plush vegetation.

*

"Go ahead, Robert, you could be twenty five again, and just tell me how old you want me to be, and it'll be so." It was Sharon, now gloriously in the buff. "And everything goes in Paradise, which is of course why it's called Paradise."

"Can you read my mind?"

"I don't have to read it, I see it," said Sharon. "I can see all you are thinking, and just like in down-to-earth imagination, I can make you coarse corporeal and so can you make me coarse corporeal. I make you, you make me, there are no secrets in Heaven, but no need to go into this stuff now, or ever, because it is common nonsense as you will understand soon enough," said Sharon. "By the way, where's Helen?"

"I got rid of her. Ever since we got married I wanted to get rid of her. She was such a pain, and there mustn't be any pain in Paradise," said Robert laughing. "Anyway, I never did like that name, Helen, as in Helen Sargent. Suzy, Suzy Sargent! Now there's a name I can dance to. I suppose I could call her back and call her Suzy ..."

"You have a lot to learn, Bobby (I say Bobby, you hear Robert, that's part of Heaven too). Listen, Bobby, as long as there's a mortal somewhere that recalls the memory of Helen, you cannot get rid of her. That's why we have tombstones and memorials, and other forms of rituals on earth: so that we may remember those gone before us and thus we too may become immortal in the memory of our descendants after we die," explained Sharon to the newly arrival, who should have intuitively known all this anyway, but instead found huge lustful pleasure sucking Sharon's fabulous lips. They were Heavenly luscious as he shamelessly gulped away and he wanted more of her everything, all naked in the plush gardens of a Paradise full of corporeal sensuality.

"I have no idea where Helen is roaming around, Sharon, and I don't care," said Robert with a silly little boy's grin on his angelic face. He wasn't breathless because there's no need to breath in Heaven; what, you're going to die if you don't breath in Heaven?

"You would think that I'd be surprised at your thoughts and desires," said Sharon, "but ever since I was a young girl all men have been looking for me. I love it, because it keeps me immortal. It's such a pleasure being with you, Bobby."

"But you are in Heaven, so you're already immortal," said Robert somewhat unnerved at the ease with which Sharon was accepting his lecherous mix.

"Hello, Robert, I see you've found Sharon again," it was Helen. "Have you fucked her already? Go ahead, Robert, she's your daughter's friend, not your daughter."

Every time the topic of pleasure came up for people new in Heaven some interruption intervened away from the insatiable desire.

"What have you been up to, Helen?" said Robert.

"You know what, Robert? I've discovered that there's no libido in Heaven," said Helen.

"How would you have known what it was," said Robert, recalling his days on earth.

Ever since Eve blew it with Adam, the Lord had decreed that men should not be able to read women's minds. It made for peace in Heaven.

"As we were saying Helen and Robert, we spirits exist as immortals as long as mortals remember us."

"Make's sense," said Helen.

"The moment that not a single memory fails to register any of us in any mortal mind, we as spirits in Heaven cease to exist; hence the existence of rituals on the part of those we leave behind," said Robert who was beginning to understand the continuity between God's Heaven and His Earth.

"Doesn't sound right to me," said Helen.

"It's ironic but those who hate us the most conjure up our memory the most and extend our immortality," smiled Sharon. "Can you imagine, in Heaven our enemies become our best friends, forever, I might add."

"Those that we've offended the most will remember us the most, while those we've loved the most, too soon forget us," said Robert.

"Yes, look at the Nazis," said Helen.

"That's right, Helen," said Robert. "Good for Robin; she hated the Nazis so she'll be an immortal the longest."

"No, Robert, it works the other way around. You know, for an ex-banker, I bet you're the only spirit that makes mistakes in Heaven," said Sharon and they all laughed.

"I get it," said Helen, who wasn't very good in math but could be very intuitive when she wanted. "That's why Plato, and Shakespeare, and Beethoven and all those guys are called immortal: because mortals always think about them!"

"And don't forget Jesus – truly the immortal," said Sharon. "Those who believe in Jesus will definitely be immortalized in His Spirit far beyond the regular extension."

"Oh the poor, common people who'll never know the world of Plato, or Shakespeare, what chance do they have at becoming immortal?" and Robert wanted to cry except he didn't have any eyes since he was pure spirit.

"You're right, Robert. Common people pretty much cease to exist soon after they die. That's why they're cremated now days. It's burn them up and good riddance, none of this memorial after death rituals for the poor; straight into the flames and dust them out over the sea - oops! Sorry guys," said Sharon.

"But burial in a cemetery with a tombstone is different," said Helen, "for every time some mortal – anybody – walks by your tombstone and reads your name, presto, once again our spirits rise and we exist for at least one faint moment again."

"What's a moment in an eternity? I wonder if it works with fish," said Robert.

"Oh look! It's Robin at your burial site and she's thinking about us all. Aren't you glad you had best friends who think about you, Sharon?" said Helen.

"I never had children to think of me; only my best friends ..." said Sharon and she suddenly realized where from, all those enigmatic thoughts about Jesus, and Leonardo da Vinci and the Last Supper, and destiny, and red wine, and, and, and …had come from: they were a scream for immortality; a beg not to be forgotten. They were the cry from one common person to another to "please always think of me."

And then Sharon thought of her parents. Too late now to think of them, she wished she hadn't been aloof, removed from them. She longed for them and thought if she longed hard enough for them they might find their way to her in Heaven and be with her forever and ever. Her poor father more than her mother had always been alone and he deserved so much more of human love than her ambitious mother who had, after all, written a book, a cruddy little book, but a book nonetheless that as long as it existed somewhere, her memory, faint as it might burn, would also continue to exist. But her father? She wished she could hug him; not in some flimsy spiritual way but in an earthly warm bodily hug full of the squeeze.

"Don't be sad, Sharon," said Helen. "After all, we are in Heaven; it could be worse."

"I would give all eternity and Heaven for one more earthly hug from my parents," Sharon was not being careful in what she was wishing.

"Hey, that's an idea! I tell you what," said Robert. "Why don't we take a little spin down to earth again and see what our loved ones are doing? Even as spirits, it should be fun."

Chapter Twenty

I t had been more than two years since Sharon's untimely death, and age, as well as life's unforeseen twists, had begun to gnaw away into the good times of the remaining still living friends. Within months after her parents' suicide in the Eastern Mediterranean, Robin had secured uncontested ownership of the Pioneer Bank, a loving in memoriam gift willed to her by her father. In spite of the tightly detailed will document, legally unchallengeable, which clearly left everything to Robin Calder, nee Robin Sargent, daughter of Robert Sargent, the document was contested by the Pioneer Bank Board on the basis that Robin was professionally unqualified to lead a large company like Pioneer Bank. The Board's crushing argument had been that her character had been tainted by abortions and a ruthless divorce from a previous officer of the Bank. It was also brought forth in court that Robin had whored for years and that she was most likely an alcoholic. During the difficult days of the trial Myrna and Kitty daily stood by their best friend as best they knew how, though some observers thought their presence in the courtroom worked against Robin. It was with tremendous relief that the three friends would get together, most days, after court, and enjoy each other's company, as they once used to; and in their moment of need and uncertainty they always wished that Sharon had been with them. Not a day went by when they did not think of beautiful Sharon. The loss of their gorgeous friend was much greater than the loss of any bank, a thought full of great relief to unload their grief.

"Screw it, Robin, let them have their shitty bank. You'd still be the major stockholder anyway," Kitty would say during times of haggling frustration.

But Robin was determined to make Daddy proud, wherever he might have been. The Pioneer Bank was to stay under the control of the Sargent DNA, and eventually Robert Sargent's will prevailed in the courts.

During these many months of courtroom battles the friend who solidly held Robin's hand throughout the ordeal was Hank Merker. Beautiful Hank from the days of Magnolia High School, he of the best friends' longings forever and ever, who had never left Robin's deep aching postponed heart-felt memories of the man she always wanted. He stood strong by her side, like a Corinthian column, and Robin found solid comfort to lean on him. And every weekend they would get away from it all and drive up to Santa Barbara, and Robin would rediscover the feelings she had always had for handsome Hank, star high school quarterback, ex-husband of her now dead best friend Sharon. Dormant all the years since high school, the carnal desire exploded into days of teen-aged feelings of rampant sex with lovely long legs stranded high in the air. Mature now in their rambling desire, it was like travelling back into their dream, wonderful unadulterated memories of being young again.

"She's dead," they would remind each other.

"I hope she's in Heaven fucking some angel," smiled Robin.

"A woman's life should be full of action, full of sexual adventure mixed with lots of adultery, if it's to be a happy life," Hank would try to reassure Robin. "For a man these things are given."

Sentiments like these coming from the mouth of Hank would surprise Robin who still remembered him as a high school jock. And she would surrender into his arms and make love to him over and over again.

"I love you Hank. I've always loved you," Robin would feel at home on such moments of high emotional surrender.

He's quite the man, Robin would be pleased, and she finally understood that it wasn't Hank's quarterback agilities that had attracted all the high school girls but the huge amounts of testosterone that the man exuded even then. He was a man, a true alpha male, an unending stream of hot spermatozoa. For the life of her, Robin could not understand what Hank had seen in anal Sharon, nor why hysterical Sharon could not appreciate husband Hank. Some marriages simply don't work out as well as they might.

Then she would think of David and the Ethiopian guy.

It was during one of their robust love making bouts that Hank suddenly stopped his vigorous thrusts and looked up in the air as if checking for mosquitoes.

"What's the matter," asked Robin?

"I don't know. It was like somebody was here watching over us," he said.

"It's all in your mind, dear," said Robin, and she strangely thought of her father.

It was during one of their Santa Barbara weekends that Hank and Robin decided to marry. It was a surprise wedding call, especially for Myrna and Kitty, and appropriately enough, when it did take place, after the court battles were over, it was a small wedding, just for the friends; Claudio and Mark were there too. Hank remembered his feeble wedding to Sharon and convinced Robin that in memory of Sharon they should have a wedding without fanfare. It was thus a simple affair with Myrna crying during the ceremony, and throughout the reception, until Hank convinced her that nothing would change between them, and that he was sure Robin would understand. Kitty danced a lot with Mark and it was obvious Claudio didn't care, his mind swooshing through the sea shores and balmy afternoons somewhere in Sicily. It seemed to Claudio, that with Sharon gone, he simply no longer belonged with the best friends' crowd who ultimately had no concept of the world outside sunny Southern California. During the small ceremony, nobody talked to him so he nibbled on the catered food from one of Hank's restaurants and toasted the many wines catered by some black guy from an expensive cave. He thought of dancing with Myrna but Mark beat him to it and he was relieved. Out of politeness he did dance a slow one with bride Robin but he kept his hand well above her waist.

While Claudio was quietly pining away for his childhood memories of Sicily, he hadn't noticed that his wife had changed partners and was now doing a slow two step with Hank.

They make a lovely couple he thought to himself; they will burn in hell for fornicating on the dance floor of their friends' wedding, he smiled. He vaguely remembered that Hank had told him he was going to do his Kitty but Claudio didn't care. His marriage had been a slick, makeshift affair, its inevitability charted by a well-heeled, tight ass, little Kitty. Really, not much there but money. He used to think that he was lucky but now realized that Kitty had been the driver the whole time. Better yet, send her to Purgatory, alone for an eternity, he smiled a vengeful smile and looked away from Hank and Kitty dancing.

"Do you remember fucking me in the school gym one night," she inaudibly whispered in his ear? She was breathing hard remembering the event.

"How could I forget," he held her tightly against him. She was so tiny in his arms.

"We all know that you're fucking Myrna," she said. "So now you've fucked all of us. You've fucked the four best of friends."

"I had fucked all four of you while we were still in Magnolia High, if you remember Kitty," he whispered back and maneuvered her slightly in such a way as to cup a breast feel so that only Claudio could see. Claudio did notice, Hank gave Claudio a wink, and Claudio smiled back, keeping his word.

"You were such a tight fit …" he started to say.

"You bastard," said Kitty, "and all these years we all thought that Sharon was the only one you wanted."

Hank gave a loud manly laugh but nobody paid too much attention because after all this was his wedding day and everyone knew that women just floated his way.

"All of you wanted me, Kitty. You, and Sharon, and Robin, and Myrna, and just about all the other girls in Magnolia High. Don't you know, Kitty, that all girls, young and not so young, always want the quarterback? It's that bounce we have that makes all girls judge our character as supremely excellent; all girls want to score with quarterbacks."

"Well, your supreme excellence, it's never too late and I want my fair share," said Kitty.

"Only Sharon couldn't see my excellence," said Hank regretfully. "But for you, Kitty, I have it from Claudio that I can fuck you anytime you want. Maybe the three of us could all get together honestly some time."

"And I thought my husband was the jealous type," said Kitty in slight disappointment.

"Well, Kitty, the Lord works in many strange ways," and he made her jump with a good goose up her ass, in view of all, who thought it funny.

Later that evening when he was making love to his new bride, there again occurred coitus interruptus when Hank thought he heard a hushed 'shhhhhh' sound, and again several 'shhhhh' sounds breaking into the sound barrier above their bed.

From below, his surprised wife said, "What is it, dear?"

"I thought I heard ... like a 'shhhhh' sound," he said.

"Hush! It's all in your mind," she said.

*

Immediately after their wedding, Robin made Hank the CEO of Pioneer Bank to the consternation of some of the Board who resigned in protest. Hank once again found his old quarterback agility and he exercised it ruthlessly. Leadership comes natural to a star quarterback who like a maestro coordinates a team of eleven champions. For Hank, assuming the CEO position was like lobbing easy sixty yard touchdown passes. With supreme confidence he appointed his wide receiver Mark Freeman on the Board as well as President of Pioneer Bank. In a similar manner he also appointed Robin, Myrna, and Kitty on the Board. They all received lucrative bonuses in addition to fat salaries. And in a most heartfelt exhibition of loyalty, he appointed many of his former football teammates from the Magnolia High School championship squads to positions throughout the company; mostly innocuous staff positions, for he knew his men. It was a generous gesture, full of humility, of a forever friendship that had bound the team since their teenage beer drinking days. In his heart Hank knew that any one of his buddies would have done the same for him if they were in his place. To his still bafflement, this resolute friendship was something that his now dead wife Sharon had never understood.

He ruled Pioneer Bank like any champion quarterback, on any Sunday afternoon, showing no mercy to any incompetence. From his high school days Hank had learned from his coaches that as a leader he should love his teammates but show no pity in his demands of loyalty and in the execution of play. His work philosophy was straightforward: those who dropped the ball, who did not carry their fair share of the burden had to go because they made it difficult for those that were out there giving their best. He would spend long hours in the office, including weekends, but in spite of Hank's valiant efforts the Bank's shares were plummeting on Wall Street. Articles were written in Forbes, Fortune, and the WSJ, about how to turn the Pioneer Bank's fortunes around, and there was criticisms about the Bank's management style on TV by pundits galore, who were also merciless in their condemnation of the CEO's cronyism. He tried, but it was difficult for Hank to understand that just because you can throw a football doesn't mean you can run a bank.

In defiance to the media short-sightedness, and the office politics buzzing around poor Hank, Robin unconditionally supported her husband. She had no doubts that he was the right man for the job, being the man she had loved from their high school days, all her life. She knew her man well, and she strongly believed that a woman without a man was a lost soul.

Unfortunately, like in the past, Hank had no time for Robin, nor for Myrna, nor for Kitty, for that matter. He was an expert, and it was never difficult for Hank to stop in the middle of a game to fuck a cheerleader as she high-kicked her pretty legs. Like cheerleaders, there were plenty of pretty young management trainees, just out of college, who, like groupies everywhere, were all too perky and thrilled to fuck the boss. Cocky and self-assured, they would wait till after work hours to be taken to the CEO's Executive Suite to be quickly undressed and fucked. He had his favorites, though he would confuse their names, but they didn't care, for they all knew that he had also been a high school quarterback. Lovely young things, they were all beautiful adornments to his many other trophies.

Aside from the trainees, the one woman that he would invite to his office, especially on weekends, was Roberta, his former waitress now the manager of his favorite restaurant. She would bring their son Adam, whom Hank loved very much, to the office and they would spend much of the weekends playing touch football. And whenever Adam might tire and fall asleep in the office, Hank and Roberta would make love. Hank thought that he loved Roberta as much as he loved Adam but the thought was too complex to process to a happy conclusion. When such thoughts crept into his mind, he went muddy and found relief by dreamingly travelling back to throwing his football through the old tire in the back yard. He was appreciative that Roberta had never questioned him, or forced the issue.

One late evening while Hank was hard corking one of his pretty young management trainees, insatiable perks they were, he had a massive heart attack and he died on the top of his huge desk, cushioned by his shrieking trainee under him.

"He was gurgling and foaming at the mouth, heavy on top of me, and I didn't know what to do," she explained to the police shortly before she quit her management trainee job. People just don't expect star athletes to keel over, so young, so easily.

Robin was crushed at the news of Hank's death. So were Kitty and Myrna. They consoled each other with true confessions about their feelings for poor dead Hank. Who would've thought? It seemed like an era had come to a dead end.

"We belong to the sisterhood of beautiful women," was the way Kitty put it. "We are adored as any piece of art and all men blindly desire us. They worship us and give themselves wholly to us. We are goddesses."

"As any piece of ass," said Myrna.

"Yes," agreed Kitty. "We never fall in love with any man and yet, we enjoy all the pleasures that men can offer!"

As always, during sad times, for Robin, it was so nice to have Kitty and Myrna around. They had a way with words. They made the obvious sparkle with truth.

Six weeks after Hank's heart attack episode, Robin married best man Mark Freeman. It was the clear think to do; none were getting younger, and "loneliness is a bitch", as Myrna would often repeat. It was a magnificent wedding with lots of strangers among the invitees.

"Marriage is a delusion; nobody should ever marry," said Myrna on that occasion.

"As Sharon use to say, nobody belongs to anybody; we are all independent as the Lord meant us to be," was the way Kitty put it.

*

"Poor Mark, he'll never understand that beautiful women like Robin will always seek a dull husband rather than one who's brilliant, or privileged, or educated, because beautiful women sleep easy with dullards. And by beautiful, we mean physically beautiful."

It was Sharon explaining events taking place on earth to ex-husband Hank who had predictably surfaced next to Sharon, in Heaven, immediately after his heart attack. Predictably, because, Sharon, one of the privileged angels in her Paradise section of Heaven, had petitioned to have Hank join her when he became available.

"I could've been someone important, if you had loved me Sharon."

It was the first thing he had said to Sharon when first seeing her in Heaven.

"Like what, Hank? What would you have liked to have been?"

"Well, I could have been a Senator, or maybe the mayor of Los Angeles."

"But you were the star quarterback of Magnolia High; why would you have wanted to lower your goals, my love," wickedly said Sharon.

"Fuck the star quarterback shit," said a regretful Hank. "Boy that was a lot of horseshit they fed us in high school," and he cried dry tears because he was a pure spirit in Heaven and there are no tears in Paradise. But apparently there is regret in Heaven.

"But think, Hank, you are an angel in Paradise now! Surely that's more than being the mayor of Los Angeles?"

"Have you seen God," he asked his ex-wife Sharon who seemed to know a lot about their predicament. When they were alive, his wife knew a lot about these things.

"You're my god," said Sharon and she immediately realized that once again she had lied to poor Hank because at that very moment she had been thinking of Claudio who in her present state of Paradise had become a continuous luminous erotic presence. Her mind was always with Claudio behind the bar, and she repeated that night throughout her Heavenly stay. She regretted not having fucked Claudio many, many times, while in life

Funny thing, Hank was thinking of Claudio too. He could see Claudio in Sharon's mind, but he didn't care, he once again realized that she was truly heavenly. But like old times, when he libidinously knocked on her door, she again, as always, was absent.

Then they made love. It was the first time that Sharon and Hank had made spiritual love and she had to admit that it was overly exaggerated because there was no mystery to it. Hank was Hank and there wasn't much spirituality to him

"Whadyuo wanna do now?" said Hank.

Chapter Twenty One

Like his weddings, there had been no loud soundings of the trumpets during Hank Merker's cremation. His parents and a younger sister briefly wiped dry tears away at the sight of his corpse lying cold in his casket in the funeral parlor, but, since they had shied away from making any requests about the funeral, they left the details of the cremation to Robin. Hank's parents had never recovered from the disappointment of their son not making it as a star quarterback in the NFL. To them, he had died long before, when he was denied football scholarships and, then again, when he married Sharon against their wishes. It wasn't that they had anything against Sharon, they hardly knew her, but they thought their son not ready for marriage, just out of high school. Nonetheless, Mr. Merker did loan Hank his first two thousand dollars for his hot dog stand, a decision he regretted all his days. Old man Merker secretly had wished that Hank not make it. In a final memorial to his son, Mr. Merker shook his head in disapproval of a wasted life, rather than in pain of his loss. He remembered teaching his son how to throw a melon; and after the heavy melon, the football was a snap.

The arrangements for the cremation were left to the funeral home that Robin had paid upfront before the event. No details were provided for Hank's remains and the crematorium dumped his ashes in a back alley garbage can. From a very early age it had been apparent that Hank was not made of the right stuff and rightfully he had paid for his unrealistic expectations of NFL Hall of Fame immortality. To put it simply, life for Hank had been a trap.

Chapter Twenty Two

"How's Mark?" asked Myrna.

The three friends were enjoying each other's company, as they always had, their table facing a blazing sunset that was fast fading over the tranquil Pacific. They took their shades off to gorge their hearts with the warmth of the light magenta Santa Monica sky before the sun would disappear into the huge Pacific. The setting sun was gentle and sweet as were the three friends, and the effect was ethereal. They were sitting at the Le Bistro Café on PCH, richly dressed as always. They had been driven there by Kitty whose idea it was to get together for they hadn't seen each other since Robin's wedding to Mark. It felt good being together again, but watching the disappearing sun was heart breaking to the magic spell of their beauty. Like the day coming to the end, they too felt a bit lethargic.

"You know … he's fine. You know how it is with men. Hank was his best friend and he keeps repeating that once you die, people forget you, and your life ends," said Robin.

"Duh, there's a twist; once you die, your life ends," said Kitty. "Jesus, you sure pick them, Robin."

"He keeps saying that he will never forget Hank … and then he sometimes cries," said Robin her voice weakening.

"He sounds queer to me," said Kitty, and she gave a wink towards Myrna. "I mean, he's not a Hank, is he?"

"Well, he keeps telling me he especially wants to fuck you, Kitty," said Robin.

There was a moment of silence. Kitty felt disgusted at the gratuitous comment. She took a nice big swig of her martini and said, "Are you pulling my leg, Robin?"

"You don't have one, Kitty," laughed Myrna.

And then, as in the days past, together, they all laughed.

They were back and they were hot; three beautiful women, pathological victims of their own good looks; sexually powerful women who since adolescence were intertwined in a fateful friendship expected to last forever. Their charm was full of attraction; but they could also be cold bitches, for all beauty is stone cold and immortal in its indifference. Again they were in form: predatory women born into rich unhappy homes who enjoy crushing male weaknesses. They were the best friends, for forever, and they wished that Sharon was there with them.

"I wonder if God forgives narcissism," said Robin. "If not, poor Sharon is swimming in Hell."

They all giggled a nervous little sound that aimed at being laughter.

"Claudio said that he wants to go back to Sicily," laughed Kitty. And then they all laughed aloud together with her.

They were in tune to each other; it was like holding hands back in high school again.

"He said he misses the Mediterranean sun and beaches, except he says 'bitches'", said Kitty with huge hilarity.

"It must be the olive oil," said Robin.

"What an idiot," said Myrna, "as if any of us cares."

"Especially Kitty," said Robin.

"Wouldn't it be great if Heaven were like this," said Myrna as she stared deeply into the now almost purple Pacific.

The martinis were getting as melancholic as the friends under the stare of the fast setting sun, and the soft splashing of the nearby tides were compelling as they beached on the shore. Whatever thoughts the girls had or spoke seemed insufficient to the fading day.

"Forget it Myrna," said Kitty. "Let's get the fuck out of here."

"And go where?" said Myrna.

"I don't care! Somewhere where there's more action than this deadbeat barn pretending to be a 'bistro'" said Kitty and they all laughed. "Bistros are for old winos."

"What about Claudio? Won't he miss you when you're late?" said Robin.

"Fuck him," said Kitty.

"What about your Mark," asked Myrna?

"Fuck him too," said Robin.

"OK, let's go do them both tonight; scare the shit out of both of them," laughed Myrna.

They decided to go have martinis in the new international terminal of LAX. Driving in the car pool lane in the mellowness of the twilight and the Le Bistro martinis, for three seconds Kitty's brain suffered a syncopated event and went into darkness. Her Mercedes, on its own, swerved out of the car pool lane and was immediately crushed by a semitrailer truck barrelling on the 405 at 75 mph. The three friends died instantly, forever.

Chapter Twenty Three

All Heaven was before their eyes' and they were all ecstatically happy being together again, and this time, truly best friends forever. Their Heaven was a Paradise full of pleasures, a magnificent Garden of Magnolia High Eden. Sharon, Robin, Myrna, and Kitty were all alive in a Paradise of eternal fantasy more beautiful than any vivid imagination. They walked in friendship, holding hands, feeling breathless in the forest of their Garden. Trees of plums, and pears, and red pomegranates, twin and triplet cherries, burgundy figs, wild strawberries and blueberries, purple and yellow-green grapes, and three hundred types of peaches; pink flowering almond trees competing with the claret blossoms of the pomegranates, and the silver leaves of the sweet olive. Does with their fawns, curly white haired lambs, and kids nipping the endless variety of leaves and flowers; larks, and nightingales, the song of the blackbird, and white doves all in a row; every kind of luscious temptation to satisfy the pleasures of the spirit. And all the while, there were many rainbows across the Heavens to break the dullness of the bluest of skies that fluttered full of the many colored butterflies.

In time, besides the four best friends, with them were Hank, and Mark, and Rick, and Todd, and in brief, all the Magnolia High School friends and buddies that played on the team, too many to count by name but very welcomed additions. In effect, Sharon's Paradise was the reunion of their high school crowd.

"Sharon, do you remember when we were in high school and you told us how sometimes your breasts felt like grapes? Well, that's how mine feel right now, with all these naked guys around us," said Myrna.

"What a lovely thought," said Robin. "Imagine, grapes for breasts, with wine coming out of them for anybody suckling them."

"Wine, so much better than mother's milk," said Kitty.

"Did you have anyone in mind, Kitty" said Sharon.

"We all know that we're all gonna be fucking Hank all day long, for a long time."

"You just have to have a vivid imagination. Hey, let's all fuck him at the same time," smiled Sharon.

"I believe it can be said that Heaven is the original virtual reality," said Robin.

"Remember, Kitty, first in and not last out," said Myrna and they all laughed.

And so it was. He was still the desired squeeze of all the girls. He was the trophy of being high school Mr. Popular, an accolade that obligates you to display even beyond life. The earthy sinful desire kept secret when alive, now made pure in Heaven, for all the friends to fuck Hank as often as they wished, without the jealousy of who is whose, for there's no mine or yours, and everybody is everybody's to be happily shared eternally. The friends, ethereal spirits now, shared and enjoyed the carnal love of Hank, and Phil, and Mark, and the rest of the team, and at times, even Albert and crazy Milton, who refused to abandon his schizophrenia and always threatened to join the Heaven of the Holy Prophets instead of Sharon's.

"There's no serious commitment, no monogamy, in Paradise," said Sharon who somehow knew of these things even when she was still on earth. "Think of it as a new experience, undemanding, with no obligations; a new way of enjoying the pleasures of beauty especially made for the common man. Our Paradise in Heaven is full of pleasures and everything in our Garden, including us, is to be enjoyed by each of us without being tainted."

"Sharon, have you seen Him?" asked Robin.

"Well, I think so. What I saw was mostly light. But it was light emanating from 'jasper' and 'carnelian', and there were 'emeralds' all around as if a rainbow of jewels; and in front and all around there was a 'crystal sea' above where chanted thousands of angels with bright shiny faces, and right in the middle there was a white dove …"

"Bless you, Sharon, that's quite a revelation," said Kitty.

"Ask her if she ever saw the four horsemen of the Apocalypse," asked Phil.

"Not while I've been dead, but when I was alive, I had a dream, once, that I saw the white horse and its horseman – you know they stand for conquest - hovering over me in the desert and I was afraid until I understood that I too was a conqueror …"

"Conquerors are terrible people, Sharon," cursed a Biblical Phil.

"You're an asshole, Phil," said Myrna.

"There are no rectums in Heaven, Myrna," said Phil.

Naturally, all present thought about that one; they all took a peek at each other's asses and it was true. There was no reason why spirits should have rectums. They looked at each other and in unison their spirits realized: where's the fun in no shit to sling at each other? No rectums, no sweet smelling shit in Heaven. Melancholia set in, a strange phenomenon in non-repressed Heaven.

Instead relief was found in the dear heart throbbing school song

"Go Magnolia, go Magnolia … " and here all the friends led by Kitty, and the whole team in Paradise, reverberated the dear nostalgic song *"… best school in the land, we're behind you, cheering for you, can't you hear the band? Rah, rah, rah … Gooooh Tigers!"*

For the first three million years they sang their Alma mater song in Heaven before getting tired of it.

*

Claudio and David, even after death, were never there to sing the school song because they were never part of Magnolia High and so they were never part of the 'in crowd'. One day, after they both had settled in the Med, he in Sicily, David in Sardinia, quite by chance, they met over martinis in the Carlton Hotel in Cannes. Justine and Meredith were with them and they all looked spectacularly stunning in their summer tans. The girls wore light, cotton, miniskirts and nothing underneath. Claudio guessed and David knew. They renewed their old acquaintance into a warm friendship and together over their first summer together, they bought a small villa on Santorini where they spent many a summer day and summer month over the next several years. It was a cosmopolitan sharing affair with Justine and Meredith at the center, shamelessly hot aboard one or the other of their yachts from which they all went skinny dipping off their boats, morning, noon, and evening, throughout the long Aegean hot summer seasons. The girls couldn't help it; they were always hot; they got used to the good life that a lot of money buys, and the warm sun felt so good over their glistening bodies. In their summer love games, Meredith became the favorite of Claudio who reminded David of an old Sicilian saying that the "greener the wood, the fiercer the fire."

The endless Aegean sailings were summers full of pleasures allotted only to the rich. Their luxurious easy access made for a long life for David and Claudio, and for Justine and Meredith, whose unblemished skin beauty became the main organ of their golden bodies, a sun drenched treasure awkward lacking in spiritual Heaven. And the in-crowd that often looked down from their Heavenly perch painfully resented the awareness of the desire that can only be felt in the touch of the human skin.

"Give us this day our daily pleasure as it is on earth, so let it be the same in Heaven," prayed Kitty from her Heavenly paradise one envious afternoon as she looked down on Claudio and Meredith. "After all, we're going to be here an eternity," she sighed.

It was during one of those great, happy summers, when at the age of twenty three, Justine wrote a best seller on friendship, published and promoted in Paris. It was a leviathan tome contenting that love was overrated; that the world did not need more love but more friendship. She insisted that long term love was like term insurance – in the end you got nothing. But true friendship was the sounder investment delivering safety, happiness, and long term goodwill. Watching from Heaven, Myrna was proud.

"It's only friendship that lasts forever without the mental and emotional hang-ups of periodic betrayals and pains of love," she had said during one interview on French TV.

She and the book became instant international best sellers.

David was very proud of Justine, and her book, and the public attention it got, and he took her many times to Paris and fucked her a lot during that period without the baggage of making love to her. He knew that few men understood the desires of beautiful women, and of those that do, they seek to experience it in more than one. He also knew that loving a beautiful woman could destroy a man, but he believed that it was worth it.

"But even in Heaven pleasure becomes all too familiar, less and less exciting, and in time we become tired of it," in a moment of clarity explained Sharon to the gang as they watched David and Claudio, carouse with Justine and Meredith while they were sailing the endless summers of hot entangled bodies from one Greek island Paradise after another.

"It was the Devil's coveting of Eve, as he watched her with Adam, that banished him from Heaven," said a troubled Robin now watching David entangled with beautiful Justine.

"Yes," said Sharon. "But the Devil asked the Lord's forgiveness, and true to his Word, the Lord did forgive, and now all of Satan's little devils have become angels again. So let us all forgive Justine, and Meredith, and David, and Claudio."

"What is there to forgive?" said Phil.

*

Included in Heaven, but not part of the Magnolia High team, were the Sargents, Robert and Helen, who were soon joined by Judy and Anton Langdon, Sharon's parents, Alice and Bob Lawson, Myrna's parents, and Barb and Michael Irvine, Kitty's parents. Also, somewhere lost in their own Heaven were Kitty's first schizophrenic husband Milton, and son Albert.

After their long bubbly filled days of luscious fruit and cold white wines had come to an end in the Med, excluded from the group were Claudio who had been invited by Sharon to join the group, but he kindly refused in favour of the Catholic Paradise somewhere in the depths of Heaven. David too was excluded by Robin who refused him entry. Together with Justine and Meredith, David had converted to the pagan gods of Olympus and had doubled their pleasures in the blissful fields of Elysium.

Daddy Sargent approved of Robin's veto of David, though neither of them could remember why they were unforgiving of David.

For similar reasons of once deeply felt rejection, Myrna nixed her beautiful daughters' presence in her Paradise to the chagrin of all the team's men whose vivid imagination wasn't going to be enough.

Roberta Denise and son Adam in time also made it into Heaven but not on the Magnolia High team, by choice. She had found the original Adam, the Daddy of us all (he was barely over seven thousand years old at the time), and introduced her son Adam whom the older Adam introduced to his stepbrothers, Cain and Abel.

All these good people who may have or may not have done harm to anyone in their earthly life became contented creatures without desiring vivid imaginations eternally grazing on the tradition of their particular Paradise. They were merciful, pure, gentle people with no pretence to wisdom; the patient, meek and mild children who had inherited the universe after asking for forgiveness, just in time, and who were especially loved by the Lord.

*

For thirty three million years Sharon's version of Magnolia High School daily luxuriated in the scented air of her presence in her Heavenly Paradise. She had arisen from the dead as the Daughter of the Lord and her friends from Magnolia High saw her as the beautiful flower of their once lewd longing. Daily all the alumni gathered around to worship her Saintly Beatitude and listen to her words which the four winds of Heaven draped throughout the four corners of their Paradise. Her angelic presence was full of grace generating the love that kept all of them secure within a firewall of unadulterated holiness. Above all, her loveliness still held an air of royal friendship that was sweeter than any other thought. When they were in school, Sharon reminded them, they were the in-crowd.

"What boy or girl did not want to be our friend?" said Sharon.

"And at the heart of all of us was you, Sharon," said Hank. "Shy and beautiful Sharon."

"What a composition of wealth it is to be shy and beautiful," said Robin.

"We were all that: shy and beautiful from the very beginning, easily taken advantage because of our generosity," said Myrna.

"Our faces lit up the world with our smiles and we didn't know it," said Kitty.

"It never occurred to us that our smiles were anything special," said Mark.

"We were lovers to the world that had fallen in love with our youth and beauty; we were friends, warm and binding friends, in love forever, the best of friends, forever," loudly cried out Beautiful Sharon, she of the fabulous breasts.

Immediately they stood up and with tears in their eyes they sang:

> *Go Magnolia, Go Magnolia*
> *Best school in the land*
> *We're behind you cheering for you*
> *Can't you hear that band*
> *Rah, rah, rah … Goooh Tigers!*

*

After three hundred million years in Paradise the four friends had blended into a blurred One and all the spiritual pleasures had become an ambiguous sterilized illusion. No amount of vivid imagination could overcome the geometric multiplication of Heavenly boredom, a bacteria that inevitably eats away all souls. Well before eternity ends, boredom overwhelms all pleasures and loneliness becomes a long distance runner, with fabulous Paradise a short sprint. All illusions disappear along with time and light, and all things slowly fade into nothingness.